Centennial Swan

by

Sally Garrett

A Trumpeter Book
from
Unconventional Press

Copyright © May 1996 by Sally Garrett Dingley
First Edition

Cover art © 1996 Kathleen Tayne
Cover design: Michael Dougherty

All rights reserved under International and Pan-American Copyright Conventions.

Except for use of review, the reproduction or utilization of this work in whole or in part in any form, including electronic, now known or hereafter invented, is forbidden without the permission of Unconventional Press or the author.

This is a work of fiction. Other than names in the acknowledgement presented at the back of this book, these characters, incidents and dialogues are from the author's imagination and are not to be construed as real. Any resemblance to actual events or persons, living or dead, is entirely coincidental.

Published in the United States by Unconventional Press. Trumpeter Books and Unconventional Press are registered names with the Montana Secretary of State.

ISBN 1-885916-21-3

Trumpeter Books are available through Unconventional Press. For brochure and price list of titles available call (406) 683-4539 or write to:
   P. O. Box 414
   Dillon MT 59725-0414

Dedication

To my Grandchildren,
with Love over the Miles

Daniel Bible-Olson
Amanda Bible-Thompson
Jessica Bible-Olson
Christopher Bible 2nd
and
Annessa Bible

Books by Sally Garrett

Fiction

CENTENNIAL SWAN	1996	0-885916-21-3
BACHELOR FROM BANNACK	1993	0-373-70557-3
STRING OF MIRACLES	1992	0-373-70524-7
CHILDREN OF THE HEART	1991	0-373-70464-x
DESERT STAR	1989	0-373-70344-9
PROMISES TO KEEP	1988	0-373-70309-0
VISIONS	1987	0-373-70275-2
WEAVER OF DREAMS	1987	0-373-70243-4
UNTIL NOW	1986	0-373-70225-6
TWIN BRIDGES	1986	0-373-70201-9
NORTHERN FIRES	1985	0-373-70173-x
MOUNTAIN SKIES	1984	0-373-70139-x
UNTIL FOREVER	1983	0-373-70090-3

Non-fiction

MONTANA COWBOY   1995 1-885916-01-9
   with Edward R. Rebich

ROARING THROUGH THE TWENTIES
in Beaverhead County   1994 1-885916-00-0
   with Edith Hansen Palmer

Coming

LISA: LOST AND FOUND   1996 1-885916-22-x
   (fiction formerly titled River of Time)

DINGLEY-HUFF AND ALLIED FAMILIES:
Their Lives and Times   1-885916-02-x

Centennial
Swan

Book 2
Centennial Valley Series

"I am, I suppose, 82 years old today.
I do not feel any older than when in my teens.
I had so much trouble off and on.....
but.....I have had a very eventful life."

--from unpublished journal entry 21 August 1932
by Lillian E. Hackett Hanson Culver
(1850-1936)
Centennial Valley pioneer settler

"Most of the critical things in life,
which become the starting points of human destiny,
are little things."

--Robert P. Smith
(1818-95)
English clergy

Chapter One

Wilcox, Nodaway County, Missouri
(Early May, 1886)

"YOU TAKE THIS, BETHEA. Don't ever lose it," Polly Mayfield said, holding out a package wrapped in brown butcher paper and tied with twine.

"Yes, Mama," the young woman said.

"It's a Bible, a family Bible like your pa and me have," Polly explained. "Every family needs a Bible to record their begets and you certainly have enough to fill the first page." She smiled fondly. "I never thought my little Bethea would be a mother of all those pretty little children and still look like a child herself."

"Thank you, Mama," Bethea Kingston replied, adjusting the black ribbon of her gray bonnet. "Our train leaves from St. Jo at ten tomorrow morning." She tucked a wayward strand of brown hair beneath the brim of her bonnet. "Daddy and Jonah want to be back home tomorrow before dark. We really must go," she added as she retied the bow before turning and scanning the yard.

Adam, Benjamin. Where is David? She spotted her eight year old son perched on top of the farm wagon, sitting proudly on one of the trunks she and her mother had carefully packed.

Esther and Faith, her only daughters, were playing with three mongrel pups beneath the shade of an old oak tree in Bethea's parents' yard. Her youngest son was nowhere in sight.

"Gabriel Kingston, where are you?" she called. When his tow head popped up from between two of the trunks on the wagon and he waved, Bethea breathed a sigh, pursing her lips. *Clifford should be here,* she thought. Her husband had promised to accompany them on the trip but she had received a letter a week before their scheduled departure date informing her that he had been detained in a place called Butte City, Montana Territory.

She sighed. He was her husband and she would have to accept him for the type of man he'd turned out to be. She hoped her parents did not know of the strain his habits had put on the bonds of matrimony. He had sent her funds for the trip plus one hundred dollars that she was not to spend unless a dire emergency arose. They would need it once they arrived at the place he'd acquired.

In the letter, Clifford had written a confusing explanation about a man who had trouble holding his liquor and played a poor game of faro. The man had had a falling out with his brother because the brother had married a squaw and disgraced the family name. Bethea had been thoroughly confused by the time she'd finished the letter, not knowing for sure if they would be living on the land belonging to the man or his squaw man brother.

Clifford had said their new land had a spring, a grove of aspen trees and a house, and was within walking distance of a lake where the view would take her breath away. She should count her blessings that they would be warm and cozy in a nice house during the winters.

She had read that the land of the northwest consisted of one giant mountain range covered with virgin timber, filled with all kinds of wild game, and occupied by savage Indians who rode around wearing leather breech cloths and refusing to live on reservations the government had been kind enough to provide for them. She had never seen a real live Indian in her life and hoped she'd never be confronted by one.

"Bethea, come back inside," Polly called.

"Mama, there's no time," Bethea said, not wanting to be impolite.

"If you've time to daydream, you've time to come inside," her mother scolded, taking the sleeve of her white shirt waist. "I do wish one of your brothers had been able to go with you. A young woman your age should not be traveling alone. It's not proper. Your papa knows it, too, but he can't go, what with the spring planting and all. Oh, Bethea, whatever will happen to you and these precious little ones?"

"Mama, we'll be fine. Sooner or later a family has to strike out on its own, to find the right place to grow and prosper. Clifford says Montana Territory is that kind of place. He says there's gold for the taking even without a pick and shovel and pan, and if that doesn't work out, Clifford says we'll grow wheat and raise sheep and a dairy herd and maybe have chickens, too. We'll sell the milk and butter and eggs. Don't you see? We'll make lots of money. Within five years we'll have a grand house and when you step off the train, you ask where the Kingston farm is and everyone will know all about us."

Polly frowned. "It's much easier to dream about fame and fortune than to earn them. That man has never stuck to anything for long, especially hard work."

"Oh, Mama, don't talk like that," Bethea replied. She didn't want to leave on an unpleasant note. "You said yourself the good land is all taken up here."

"That husband of yours never struck me as a farmer," her mother murmured. "He don't stick to nothing for long."

Bethea forced a smile. "Don't you worry, we'll be fine." Bethea glanced across the yard at her offspring. "Children, time to pay a last visit to the necessary," she called, motioning discretely to the outhouse behind her parent's modest white frame house. "Let the girls go first. Adam, you watch out for Gabriel and see that he doesn't just pretend. Once we start, your grandpa will not, I repeat, *will not* stop until it's time to rest the team. Hurry now."

Bethea waited until she saw a grimacing eleven-year-old Adam drag his little brother down the dirt path and out of sight behind the house, then she followed her mother back inside. Perspiration trickled down between her breasts and she pressed her camisole against her skin. The temperature was unusually warm and muggy for early May.

When Clifford had first written her about the land he'd acquired, the crops in Missouri had been harvested and winter had been just around the corner. He had written that he was working in an underground mine in Butte City to save money for them. He'd said that Butte City's air was so filled with mining dust a person could hardly see the sun at midday and he certainly didn't want to bring them there to live. He had described the clear air and bright blue skies of the Centennial Valley, insisting it was like nowhere in the world.

She thought back a few months when out of nowhere, Clifford had shown up at their door in the middle of a March blizzard, only to leave again ten days later. She didn't want to think about the disappointment she had felt when she'd realized the consequences of his brief visit.

Polly pursed her lips. "I just don't see why that man of yours has to take my little darlings thousands of miles away into some uncivilized wilderness."

"Mama, don't be upset," Bethea said. "I'll write you a letter when I get there and tell you all about our new home. And someday you and Daddy can come west and see for yourselves."

"But only the good Lord knows when." Her mother's voice became a woeful moan. "I don't see why anyone would want to live out there."

Bethea smiled. "Clifford and I want to raise our family there, and if we don't like that place, we can file on a different piece. Mama, how are we ever gonna save money if we stay here?"

"Then take this," Polly said, shoving a thin roll of green backs into her daughter's hand.

"Mama, Clifford gave me money," Bethea protested.

"Knowing him, it's not enough," her mother said. "Put these coins in your shoes, down in your stockings."

"Mama!"

"Now listen, daughter, no woman ever lost her stockings unless she did it on purpose. You put them in the bottom of your stockings, three under each foot. That way every time you take a step, you'll know you have some extra money in case that husband of yours forgets some of his promises."

Bethea stared down at the six gold coins in the palm of her hand. "Mama, I won't be able to walk with double eagles in my shoes. I'd be crippled by the time we got to Omaha."

"Then put them down inside your camisole," Polly insisted. Before Bethea could resist, her mother took the coins and slid them one at a time inside the high buttoned collar of her white shirt waist and against her skin, tugging on the cotton camisole in order to hide the coins. Her mother stepped back and surveyed Bethea's appearance. "That's looks fine. No one would ever know. Sweetheart, I think you've put on some flesh these past few weeks. Your cheeks have a rosiness to them that's quite becoming." She gave Bethea a tight squeeze. "Now you get out there with your little ones."

"Aren't you coming outside?" Bethea asked.

Polly shook her head and wiped a tear from her cheek. "I couldn't bear it, darlin.' You go to that man of yours, but remember, if you need us we're always here. Write to me when you can, and tell Clifford to see that your letters get mailed. Surely they have mail service out there. If they got trains, they must have mail runs." She whirled away and ran to the kitchen in the back of the house.

Bethea's father's shout came from the wagon. Feigning courage she didn't possess, Bethea Kingston adjusted the ribbon on her bonnet. Other women had traveled to the western territories. Why couldn't she? She wasn't a child. She was twenty-six years old. Wasn't she brave, courageous, strong willed? She walked to the wagon and accepted her father's hand and a boost onto the wagon.

"Let's go, Mama," David called from the rear of the wagon.

"'Fore we miss the train," Benjamin added.

"It don't leave until tomorrow, stupid," Adam retorted.

"But St. Jo is a long long way from Wilcox, isn't it, Mama?" Faith asked, tugging on a blond braid.

"Yes, dear, it is," Bethea replied, nodding and smiling to each child. "Now you all sit still. I don't want anyone falling off and getting hurt." Six fair haired children grinned back at her.

She turned toward the team and settled on the seat between her father and her brother. Her brother, Jonah, slapped the reins against the rumps of the two Belgium geldings and they started their ambling journey toward St. Jo.

Thirty minutes later, four year and a half year old Gabriel jumped to his feet. "Are we almost there?" he asked, clutching the front of his trousers with his small fist. "I gotta pee."

Sally Garrett

CHAPTER TWO

Monida, Madison County, Montana Territory
(late May 1886)

CON ADLER'S HAIR was dark brown. The women in the county discussed his physical attributes in the privacy of their parlors and argued among themselves that perhaps it was black. His skin was deeply tanned from working cattle in the high altitude of the Northern Rockies, but some insisted he'd inherited it from his mother's people.

He had his father's blue eyes and that made his skin appear copper, but any man who had faced him in a dispute knew his gaze could pierce an opponent as surely as a bullet from the Smith and Wesson Scofield revolver resting in the fine leather holster he wore on his hip. He was considered an outsider by many of the influential men of the county, yet he had more right to be there than any of them.

He took a seat at one of the tables in the dining room of the only hotel in town. The other men in the room looked away. They might be thinking the words, but it had been years since anyone had called him "half-breed" to his face.

A pleasant faced woman with streaks of gray in her curly red hair came to the table. "Hello, Con," she said, smiling as she set a cup of coffee in front of him. "We thought you boys had all pulled out when the train rolled south this morning."

Con leaned back in his chair and looked up at the woman. "I couldn't leave without one more of your meals, Mrs. Burns."

"So it's only my cookin' that keeps bringing you back?" She gave his shoulder a gentle punch. "And I thought it was me that brought you Alice cowboys into this fine establishment," she said with a wink.

His mouth softening into a smile.

Mrs. Burns patted his shoulder. "Maybe I should call you Mr. Adler from now on. When a man does what you did this morning, he deserves the honor. The others just stood around 'till you took charge."

Centennial Swan

Con's mouth tightened. "Mrs. Burns, if you have a steak, cook me one nice and pink, and fry some spuds if you have them."

"Sure thing, Con," Mrs. Burns replied. "I'll put it on the Alice account. You Adlers are the best paying customers in this hotel's ledger." Another man slid into the empty chair at the table. "George, do you want a steak, too?" she asked.

Con glanced at his uncle. "George, order up. My father will settle the bill."

The older man grunted.

"I reckon that means 'yes'," Mrs. Burns remarked, then sauntered toward the huge hotel range that was her pride and joy. Con watched as she stroked the raised silver lettering, *Great Western Stove Co.* She glanced over her shoulder. "Want a beer or whiskey?"

"None for me, thanks," Con said.

"Whiskey," George Adler called, then returned his attention to the window in the front of the dining room that looked out toward the Utah Northern narrow gauge railroad track with its small depot and water tower several dozen yards away. "Train's late," he mumbled.

"Maybe they're working on the track again," Con said. "I hear they plan to complete the switch over to standard gauge next year." He scanned the dim interior of the log building. "This is the first meal I've had today. I hope I get to eat before it comes." He looked out the window past the empty railroad cattle car to the snow covered mountains beyond. "Too bad about old Charlie. He was a good man. Wish I could have saved him."

"He always was a careless old coot," George said.

Their steaks arrived and the two men began to eat. Con rubbed a hand over his eyes, trying to forget about the man who had bled to death in his arms. "God, I'm glad to see those three cars on their way to Omaha. We should have sold them last fall. When Father comes back, I want to talk to him about the herds going into the valley next month."

George concentrated on his steak, making Con wonder if he had been listening. It didn't matter. George had always been a man hard to get next to. He'd walked into their lives when Con was ten, wearing the coat and trousers of his Confederate unit. Now gray haired and about to have his fiftieth birthday, he continued to fight

13

the war back in the states, unable to accept the reality that his Confederacy had lost.

Con had always wondered why the men in his family continued to be fascinated with a war that had killed half a million young men and left wounds still raw after two decades. It wasn't as if the area where they lived had been directly involved, but that had always been at the heart of the arguments.

His father's family had sold its large tobacco auction business in Paducah, Kentucky, and moved to Boston when the winds of civil strife seemed unavoidable, at least everyone but his uncle George. His own father had lived outside of the states since 1849, yet his uncle continually implied that he should have returned to fight for Kentucky's rights.

Con knew his father had supported the Union viewpoint, as did his other two uncles.

"I'm going to visit my uncle Tendoi before we move the herds," Con said.

"Why do you want to keep going over the hill?" George asked between bites of meat. "They ain't really your people anymore. Living in all that filth and poverty? If I was you, I'd be thankful I didn't have to be one of them."

Con didn't expect his English uncle to understand, but his own thoughts drifted to the trip he'd planned for months. His uncle, Unten-doip, was the chief of a small band of Shoshonis who lived over the border in Idaho Territory at a place called Lemhi Agency. His uncle's name had been mispronounced as Tendoi by the white men who had first met him and the English pronunciation had come into accepted usage in the area.

Thoughts of his uncle made Con nostalgic. He hadn't seen his uncle since the previous fall, when he had joined part of the band on a hunting trek to the geyser basins of what the easterners had dubbed Yellowstone Park. He always enjoyed returning to the Lemhi Valley and visiting his uncle. Tendoi's intelligence, wisdom and integrity were superior to many of the white men in the area.

"Straight as an arrow, and of fine physique," Con's father had said once in describing the chief.

Centennial Swan

With Chief Tendoi's three wives and at least ten living children with families of their own, Con Adler could count on numerous relatives to spend time with.

George punched his arm, disturbing his reverie and Con glanced up. "What's wrong?" he asked

"Train's coming," George said. "I can hear the whistle. Let's go outside and watch heap big iron horse roll by."

Con ignored his uncle's innuendoes toward the Indian population. They merely reflected the opinions of many men living in the area. A man couldn't justify riding rough shod over a culture if he treated its people like equals.

"It won't stop unless someone's getting on or off and who would want to get off in this god forsaken place?" George added. "They'll ride on to Spring Hill or Dillon if they have good sense. I bet you plumb forgot to let 'em know you wanted a ride."

"I spoke to the station master," Con replied. He tossed a coin on the table, motioning to Mrs. Burns. "That's for you, not the hotel's ledger," Con said. "The steak was cooked the way I like it." He shoved his felt hat down over his forehead and reached for his heavy worsted coat. He glanced at his uncle. "Do you want to ride along with us?"

"I figured I'd ride over to Spring Hill. The Crystal has a new girl upstairs. I hear she's wild. See you back at Alice."

The train rolled into the station, steam pouring from the engine's undercarriage as its brakes screeched to a stop. The conductor jumped to the ground and dropped a heavy metal step into the mud and slush that lingered from a snow storm a week past.

"Gawd damn, do you think someone's really gonna get off the train?" George asked.

Con shrugged. He didn't have time to waste welcoming guests to this miserable little town with no more than thirty full time residents. He strode to the conductor to confirm a ride for his stallion. The conductor glanced toward the man standing in the doorway of the depot who nodded, then pointed past the two passenger cars and a baggage car to three stock cars. "Plenty of room for your horse in the last car," he said. "You're welcome in this car. We'll have plenty of empty seats in a few minutes. I'll punch your ticket after we pull out. Now excuse me while I help this little lady."

The dark haired conductor reached up and took the gloved hand of a woman. The woman's face was hidden beneath the deep brim of a gray bonnet that had seen much wear. Con stepped back to give them room. The toe of the woman's black boot touched the ground, landing directly in a mud puddle.

"Oh," she exclaimed, trying to salvage the hem of her gray traveling skirt. The edges quickly absorbed an inch of brown moisture.

From the height of her bonnet she wasn't nearly as tall as his sisters. Perhaps she was some stock investor's daughter, traveling from the east to visit. He doubted that she would come to his shoulder.

She turned to face the train again. "Come, children, and be careful where you step." She hiked her skirts a few inches, revealing frayed lace on a petticoat, and just as quickly dropped them. "It's muddy out here," she cautioned, stepping backward directly into Con's path. When his hands touched her shoulders, she flinched.

"Sorry, ma'am," he said as she turned to face him. He found himself gazing into the greenest eyes he'd ever seen on a woman, and she was a woman rather than a young girl as he'd first thought. Her cheek bones were high, accenting the rosy hollow below. His gaze lingered on her slightly upturned nose before shifting to her mouth, now opened in surprise.

"Your trunks are being taken into the hotel, Mrs. Kingston," the conductor said. "Let me help your children."

Con turned, along with the pretty Mrs. Kingston, and watched as a boy, another boy, then a third and fourth child jumped to the ground. The youngest landed directly into a nearby puddle of melting snow. *Four sons; quite a fine family,* he thought.

He glanced back at the car again and saw two blond girls clinging to each other and balancing daintily on the step. The conductor lifted them one by one across the mud to the wooden platform in front of the hotel.

The boys joined their sisters on the wooden planks. Mrs. Kingston remained rooted to where she stood, staring at the facade of the hotel. The rosy blush on her cheeks had disappeared. Con felt as if he could read her thoughts. "Ma'am, is someone meeting you?" he asked.

Centennial Swan

She continued to stare at the hotel, then shifted her gaze to the mercantile store, the blacksmith shop and livery stable next to it, and the Utah and Northern office that was usually closed. She frowned at the buildings. "This can't be the city of Monida." She studied a piece of paper she clutched in her hand. "Mr. Kingston said...I thought...I expected..." She glanced to Con, then back at the buildings. "It's not much of a town, is it?"

Con followed her troubled gaze. "No, but you should see it in the fall when we ship the beef stock from the valley. You'd swear it was the busiest siding west of Omaha."

She turned to him, looking directly into his eyes and he could sense her concern change to curiosity. She continued to study his features and he wasn't sure he wanted to know what was going on in her mind.

"Who are you?" she asked. "Are you a...?"

"Conrad Adler, ma'am, at your service," Con said, touching the brim of his felt hat and bowing slightly. "My family calls me simply Con. We have a little place called Alice Livestock Company northwest of here. And your name, ma'am?"

She continued to stare at his face and he wondered if he had food on his chin. Unconsciously, he rubbed it, then felt sheepish.

"I'm Bethea Kingston, I mean Mrs. Clifford Kingston," she replied, her voice as lovely as her face.

What a shame, he thought. She should be a carefree maiden still, not a married woman with six rambunctious children and a husband who had obviously forgotten to meet them. "My apologies, ma'am, but I don't know the gentleman."

"Mr. Kingston was supposed to be here," she murmured, glancing at the buildings once more. "Is that really a hotel?" she asked. "It's not...quite like the hotels we have in Missouri."

He followed her gaze and saw the two-story log structure in a different light. "It's small, but they have rooms upstairs and Mrs. Burns is a great cook. If your husband has been detained, let me escort you inside and Mrs. Burns will make you comfortable. If you need lodging, she'll put you up. Her rates are quite reasonable." He mentally calculated the cost of food and lodging for seven people. "If funds are a problem, I could be of assistance."

Her gaze flew back to his face. "No, of course not," she said, touching the front of her buttoned gray jacket.

He grew curious when she touched the fabric again as if confirming some secret part of her was intact. Could she be wearing a money belt? Not likely, he thought. She was far too slender and womanly to be hiding a bulky pouch around her middle. Such contraptions were used by wealthy male travelers with greenbacks or gold to hide.

She frowned again. "We've been traveling for three weeks. The children are tired."

"And you must be exhausted, yourself." He offered her his arm. "Come with me, Mrs. Kingston and I'll introduce you to Mrs. Burns. She'll make you welcome, I'm sure."

The whistle blew and Mrs. Kingston flinched, her hand clutching his coat for an instant. He glanced down in time to see her look up at him once again.

"All aboard," the conductor called.

The stallion whinnied.

"Last call for passengers going north" the conductor called out. "It's now or wait 'till morning."

The home ranch beckoned, but the image of a forlorn Mrs. Kingston and her six little ones took its place and he waved to the conductor. "Tomorrow will be soon enough," he called.

The conductor grabbed the step and boarded the car.

Mrs. Kingston turned, still clinging to his arm, and watched as the caboose of the six car train grew smaller in the distance. She looked up at him again, down at her hand, and quickly withdrew it from his sleeve. Her mouth tightened. "I'm sorry, Mr. Adler, I didn't mean to keep you from your journey."

Her gaze took in the road consisting of wagon ruts filled with mud. When she lifted her gaze to the rolling hills with only hints of new spring grasses, he felt as if he could read her mind again. He'd always considered this country beautiful. Now the patches of discolored snow and last year's yellowed grasses lying flattened from months of snow cover looked ugly, barren and desolate.

He offered her his arm again. "Give it a month and this will all be green and lush," he said, keeping his voice steady as he motioned across the horizon.

Centennial Swan

"I have no reason to doubt your word, Mr. Adler," she murmured, accepting his arm and assistance around the puddles to the boardwalk. "Children, stay together," she called.

The six youngsters lined up in age order and stood immobile. Perhaps they were more disciplined than Con had first thought, but what did he know about children? The sun slipped behind the snow capped peaks in the distance, bringing a dusk that would be short lived. He escorted her into the combination lobby, dining room and saloon of the hotel and motioned to Mrs. Burns.

Mrs. Burns adjusted the wick and replaced the chimney of the lamp mounted to the wall near the black and silver stove, then came forward. When Con explained the family's predicament, Mrs. Burns opened her arms wide. "Then you'll be my guests until Mr. Kingston arrives. I don't have the pleasure of knowing the gentleman, but I'm sure something's delayed him. How could he not be worried about this fine family?"

She surveyed the children who were standing quietly in a row. The youngest boy's gaze drifted toward the plate on the counter piled high with donuts. Mrs. Burns laughed. "I made those donuts this very afternoon. I must have known you boys were coming."

She looked at Mrs. Kingston. "I reckon these little ones are starving to death. Why don't you sit down at that big table over there and I'll serve you up some grub. Got some stew left, made with venison the mister brought in just a few days ago. If you clean your bowls, I'll let you each have one of my donuts, two if you're good boys and girls." She winked at Mrs. Kingston. "Donuts are on me, ma'am. Don't you worry."

"We..." Mrs. Kingston looked at Con, then back at Mrs. Burns. "May I speak to you privately?" she asked Mrs. Burns.

"Sure can," the robust woman replied, taking the younger woman aside where they had a whispered conversation. Mrs. Burns chuckled. "Out back," she said, pointing.

Mrs. Kingston whispered to her boys and they scampered out the back door, returning several minutes later.

"Boys, sit down and Mrs. Burns will give you some venison stew. Girls," she said, motioning them to follow her. Ignoring an amused Con, she disappeared through the same door.

Con drifted over to the short bar where two cowboys nursed whiskey glasses and a bottle. After a few minutes, the girls returned and joined their brothers. Con visited with the cowboys but kept glancing toward the back door.

He looked around the room, curious about Mrs. Kingston's failure to return. Mrs. Burns had seated herself at the table and was chatting with the children.

"See you around, boys," Con said to the cowboys, then slipped out the back door and closed it quietly behind him. Halfway between the hotel and the outhouse, he saw two figures. The silhouette of Mrs. Kingston's long skirt was easy to spot as it swayed in the night breezes. The air had grown chilly and she wore only the light jacket of her traveling suit.

Con heard a man's voice slurred from drink. The man stepped closer and grabbed her. "A woman alone in thiz place can only be one kind," the man mumbled, reaching for her again.

Bethea Kingston stepped backward quickly, stumbling on a sagebrush root near the edge of the path. Her arms flailed the air, then she regained her balance.

The man chuckled. "I heard you got that room out back of the store. It's been a long time since I've been with a white woman." He reached into his pants pocket and withdrew a coin, tossing it at her. "Here's your pay, going rate."

Mrs. Kingston knocked the coin away. "I don't..."

Con stepped from the shadows of the building. "Need some help, Mrs. Kingston?" he asked from behind her.

"Yes," she said breathlessly, her hand reaching out behind her.

"She's mine," the drunk snarled.

She bumped against Con and he shoved her behind him, as his right hand dropped to the butt of his revolver.

The drunk stumbled and straightened.

"Leave this woman alone," Con said. "She's with me." His hand eased the revolver from its holster to let the other man see that he was armed.

Cursing, the man turned away and disappeared into the darkness. Con fought down the outrage he'd felt against the stranger. He turned and looked down at her bonneted head and slowly became aware of the thudding of his own heart.

Centennial Swan

She was a total stranger, yet he would have killed for her. She looked up at him and for a fleeting second he wanted to put his arms around her. His fingers touched the cool metal of the cylinder, bringing him to his senses, and he dropped the gun back into its holster. Had he gone crazy? She was a married woman with a family.

He touched her shoulders. "Are you all right?" he asked softly. She leaned against his chest and pressed her face against him. If not for his shirt, her lips would be touching his skin. They would be soft and warm. Before his thoughts could gain momentum, she looked up at him again.

"I'm sorry," she whispered, her voice quivering. "That man terrified me. I...I thought I might faint, then what would he...? Oh, praise the Lord, you came in time. Thank you."

He felt her tremble and ignoring a deep warning in the back of his mind, he pulled her close again. Her shoulders shook, and he suspected she might be crying. Better here than in front of Mrs. Burns and the children, he decided. This brief moment under cover of darkness would be the only time they would ever be close. The thought saddened him.

She pulled a handkerchief from somewhere within her clothing and dabbed at her eyes and nose.

"You'll be fine," he murmured.

She looked up at him. The ribbons on her bonnet had loosened, and the bonnet fell to the ground. In the darkness, he could make out a thick coil of brown hair. *If only I had an excuse to touch it...silky...long...* He chided himself. If he kept this up, he'd be as despicable as the drunk he'd chased away.

"Thank you for...scaring him away," she said, her voice steadier now. "I...I shouldn't have lingered behind the girls. I wanted to see the hills again. I had no idea anyone else would be out here." She looked up at him again. "Why are you outside?"

He smiled. "I went looking for a missing mother before her children noticed her absence." He removed his coat and draped it around her shoulders, burying her in its bulk. "The nights are cold here all year round."

He stooped to retrieve her bonnet, slapping it against his thigh. Carefully he placed it back on her head. Still surprised at the liberties she allowed him, he took the ribbons and tied a neat bow beneath her chin. His fingers touched her skin, confirming his expectation that it was as smooth as silk. He cleared his throat and stepped back. "Better to search for one missing woman than six children."

She smiled back at him. "I believe you're right, Mr. Adler. And how did you learn to tie a woman's bonnet?"

"I have three sisters and a step-mother," he replied. "Enough said?"

"Yes. Oh, good gracious, I'd best rescue that nice woman from my own children. Sometimes they can become...overly lively. Whatever will Mrs. Burns think of my dalliance?"

He offered her his arm again. "She'll welcome an excuse to watch over for them for a while. You must be hungry yourself. Shall we go inside so you can have supper?"

Smiling, she accepted his arm and walked with him along the narrow path toward the glowing light coming from the window in the back door. "You must be hungry yourself, and it's hours past supper time. Will you be our guest?"

He thought about the steak and potatoes he'd eaten just before her arrival. "It would be a pleasure," he replied.

CHAPTER THREE

BETHEA KINGSTON CREPT from the narrow cot she'd been given for the night, clutching the sides of her flannel gown in her fists. Her sons were bedded down on the floor, two to a mat, their heads at opposite ends. The girls were snuggled together in a double bed a few feet from her own.

She could have slept with her daughters, but when Mrs. Burns had offered her the luxury of sleeping alone, free of small knees and poking elbows, she had graciously accepted.

Carefully, she opened the lid of the trunk Mr. Adler and Mr. Burns had carried upstairs. She had thanked Mr. Adler again and again until the Burns couple had grown curious.

"For his helpfulness," she had explained, hoping that he'd respect her wishes to not speak about the altercation outside. He'd eaten a bowl of venison stew, then two donuts and she had been pleased to see the hungry man enjoy his meal so heartily yet with good table manners. She'd observed that the further west they had traveled the more careless many of the men had become in regards to the social amenities of mixed company.

Mr. Adler's image surged forward in her mind. When he'd removed his coat from her shoulders as they reentered the hotel, she'd felt a loss. She had tried to avoid staring when he hung the coat on a hook inside the main entrance and came to their table. Now, in the privacy of the darkness, she smiled. Mr. Adler was indeed a fine specimen of young manhood.

Bethea had wanted to inquire into his background. Mrs. Burns seemed to know him well. But she had no right to even be curious, not when she was waiting for her own husband to show up. Feeling beneath several camisoles in the trunk, she removed a small brown leather book tied with a red ribbon, a writing pen, and a bottle of black ink, items she'd stored in leather drawstring pouches. She'd been careful to make entries in the book each day of the trip, but now they were behind schedule after a three day layover in Salt Lake City to visit her mother's elderly aunt.

The trip had taken just over three weeks, allowing for a derailment of another train, stock cows being on the tracks, a prairie fire, and other unscheduled layovers. The most exciting event for everyone on board had been a herd of mixed breed cattle being trailed from Texas to the plains of eastern Montana. The train had encountered the herd in western Nebraska. The conductor had estimated the size to be in the thousands. The animals had covered the land from horizon to horizon and it had taken the better part of a day before the train could resume its journey.

Thankfully, the days of Indians and buffalo being the causes of delay had long past. Still she felt as if they were experiencing something her children would enjoy reading about years later. Young children would soon forget the day-to-day events of the trip.

Now three days behind in her entries, she was anxious to catch up. Tiptoeing back to the cot, she tugged it close to the small window to take advantage of the full moon now shining. She pulled a chair next to the cot and used it as a desk for the ink bottle and pen, then adjusted her pillows and pulled the quilts up to her breasts. Using her knees to rest the book against, she began to make her entry.

"I..." She scratched out the letter and began again. "We met the most fascinating man today. He is about my age, I think, although of course I didn't ask. At first I wondered if he was an Indian, but he has blue eyes so I think not, but who can I ask? I know little of the truth about the Indian race." She thought of the kind Mrs. Burns.

No, she thought, *the woman would wonder about my curiosity.*

She returned to her writing. "His hands are rough yet gentle." Surprised at what she had written, she leaned her head against the chinked logs behind her and closed her eyes.

Clifford's hands were rough. Any laboring man's hands were rough. Clifford wasn't seldom gentle with his hands. Her eyes flew open. She tried to scratch out the sentence but the ink on her pen had dried. She dipped the tip in the bottle and returned to her journal. "I know because we shook hands," she wrote.

Pleased with the adjustment, she continued, describing his appearance and how he had helped them upon their arrival. She thought about her first impression of the town. "Monida is disappointing," she wrote. "I think Clifford exaggerated, but I'm sure when we reach our new house in the grove of aspens overlooking the lake, all will be fine."

She reread what she had written, then continued her entry. *"Mr. Adler has very handsome features and when his eyes looked into mine..."* She smiled, then glanced guiltily toward her sleeping children. *"Are eyes the windows to the soul?"* she wrote. *"If so, then this man's soul is good, for I cannot imagine him doing an ill deed to any man. We were strangers in need and he helped us."*

She smiled as the pen flew across the page. *"He saved my life tonight,"* she wrote, adding a brief description of what had happened. *"Well, at least my virtue,"* she concluded.

Frowning, she stopped writing and began to flip back several pages, reading what she had written over the past week. She had completely forgotten to bring the journal up to date and instead had leaped into describing the mysterious Conrad Adler. She touched his name on the page, saddened to find the strokes absorbed into the paper and as flat as the page that held them.

Deciding she'd written quite enough about her reaction to meeting Mr. Adler, she described the hotel and the Burns couple. *"All these happenings has made this a memorable day."*

She capped the ink bottle, wiped the pen clean with a scrap of muslin she kept in the pouch, and put the writing utensils safely away. She had two blank books, one extra bottle of ink, and a replacement point for the pen, and would have to make inquiries into writing supplies once she became settled.

She closed the journal and tied its red ribbon, aware that the entries had become progressively more personal over the weeks since leaving Missouri, far more than she had originally intended. Perhaps the book was no longer suitable for her grandchildren to read. What would they think of their white haired granny writing about handsome dark strangers who had swept her off her feet? She vowed to give Clifford equal lines in the journal during the weeks to come.

The air in the upper room had cooled considerably. Now past midnight, she could see her own breath as she lay quietly, mulling over the events of the day. She slid beneath the covers, the journal book pressed against the ruffles of her flannel gown covering her breasts. As sleep claimed her, she smiled, secure in the knowledge that Conrad Adler's character had been safely recorded in the book before his presence could fade.

The next morning, she found fresh clothes for the children. "Your father will be here today," she said. "We must be clean and tidy for him." She tucked Gabriel's shirt tails inside his pants, buttoned the front and adjusted his suspenders over his thin shoulders, then gave him a quick kiss on his round cheek.

The children were eager to meet the day. "Wait until I've dressed," she cautioned, slipping a fresh day dress made of blue muslin over a clean camisole and petticoat. She had removed her corset the first evening on board the train out of St. Joseph, Missouri after a miserable day of being unable to breathe, vowing to put the contraption on again only if she were going to a social gathering of mixed company.

If the good Lord had wanted women to have hourglass figures, why hadn't He made their bodies that shape? Hers wasn't, and with a new life beginning to grow inside her, it was doubly true. Some of her fellow travellers would be shocked at her impropriety if they knew, but at least she could breath.

Looking at the pile of soiled clothing on the floor, she knew what she would be doing within days of settling in at her new home. But concerns about laundry could wait. Their new place would surely have a washing shed and a pole and line to hang the clothes to dry.

Buttoning the last of the tiny pearl buttons on the front of her dress and patting the collar down, she unpinned her hair and tried to smooth it with her brush, twisted it again and coiled it back into place. Without a mirror, she had to guess with her fingers as to its neatness.

Esther came to her aid by sticking a few hairpins where wisps had escaped her efforts. "Mama, I'm sorry I lost your pretty hand mirror," the girl murmured. "I didn't mean to leave it at Aunt Lucia's."

"Well, Salt Lake City is too far away to go get it," Bethea said. "Maybe someday we can buy another one."

The boys grew restless as she began the laborious task of combing her daughters' long hair. "Boys, find the necessary and don't dawdle or go exploring. We'll do that later." She shooed them out the door and finished the girls' hair, tying fresh blue ribbons to keep their blond curls away from their faces.

"Well, girls, are we pretty enough to meet the public?"

The girls nodded and smiled.

Bethea retrieved a white and blue striped sun bonnet from the trunk. "We wouldn't want anyone to think Missourians have no sense of proper dress, would we?"

She had never been vain about her appearance before. Married at fifteen and a half and delivered of her first child days before her sixteenth birthday, she had experienced little attention from admiring young men. If she had stood firm and resisted Clifford's advances that Sunday afternoon years ago, she would never have had to enter matrimony so young herself. "Fiddle faddle," she murmured. That was a part of her life she couldn't undo. "Let's go, girls. Time to go down and have breakfast and wait for your daddy."

Downstairs, she followed her daughters out the back door and took her own advice about not dawdling. After breakfast, she settled her bill with Mrs. Burns. "Is there someone who can help me with the trunk?" she asked.

"Sure, honey, but why not leave it upstairs, just in case Mr. Kingston is detained another day." Mrs. Burns patted her hand and hurried to another table where three bewhiskered men were eating.

After breakfast the children grew restless and Bethea gathered them around her. "We'll go for a walk about town." She tied her bonnet sashes into a prim bow beneath her chin and hurried to catch up with her impatient children. A few minutes later, they reached the last building and she turned around to look at the town from a new direction. Out west, the citizens were more generous with their definition of the word 'town' than people were in Missouri.

"Mama, can I go with Adam and Ben?" David asked, pointing to his two older brothers who had turned into tiny dots of movement half way up the sloping hill behind the hotel.

"Oh, my goodness," Bethea exclaimed, frightened for her sons' safety. There were no mountains such as these near their farm in Missouri, just rolling hills and an occasional gully. Even the streams seemed in a hurry out West. Perhaps they, too, were anxious to return to the states. "Ben, Adam, be careful," she called.

The boys stopped and turned to wave to her. They cupped their hands around their mouths and shouted, "Come on up. It's an easy climb. You too, Mama. Follow the path."

"Can we, can we?" Faith and Esther pleaded.

27

"Me, too?" Gabriel asked, tugging on Bethea's skirt.

Bethea glanced overhead. The sun was a ball of white fire in the brilliant blue sky. She had no idea of the hour. She had left her lapel watch in the string purse she had entrusted to Mrs. Burns for safekeeping.

"Why not?" she murmured, noticing for the first time the indentation in the grass.

"Good," David said and waved frantically to his older brothers. "We're coming, wait for us," he shouted.

The climb proved more strenuous than she'd thought. Halfway up the hill, she had to stop to catch her breath. No matter how deeply she breathed, her chest felt tight and her heart pounded. A wave of nausea swept through her and she had to sit down on a large boulder for several minutes before she was able to continue the climb.

She removed her bonnet and unbuttoned the top several buttons of her dress. The temperature had warmed dramatically since she'd begun the climb. Lifting her skirts almost to her knees, she resumed the climb. Surely she wasn't too old to climb a simple hill. An hour later, she joined her children on the crest but her knees were wobbly and she again sought a boulder.

Adam raced to her and proudly displayed an obsidian arrowhead. "I bet it was made by a real Injun," he boasted.

"Where did you find it?" David asked, impressed by his brother's success.

"Down there," Adam replied, pointing to a spot about fifty feet down the backside of the hill. "They're all over. Can we go find some more?" he asked.

Bethea nodded, unable to discourage their exploration when she felt so poorly herself. Thirty minutes later, her lap was filled with arrowheads and pieces of broken black glass. The children continued their exploration. Her stomach settled and the breezes blowing across the narrow valley from the snow capped mountains to the west cooled her flushed cheeks.

She glanced around her in search of a more suitable perch and spotted a large boulder flat enough to make a seat. Once she had found a comfortable position, she lifted her skirts and petticoats and waved them in the air, savoring the cool air that found its way beneath her garments.

Centennial Swan

Beneath her cotton stockings, her skin was damp from perspiration and she didn't like the sensations. She wished she could remove them, but certainly not out here in the open. She had expected the temperature to be much cooler. Pulling her skirts up to her knees, she leaned back on her hands and studied the countryside.

To the south was the pass the train had taken. Some travelers had called it Pleasant Valley Pass but the conductor had reminded them it had been renamed Monida Pass when the rails had been laid. To the north, the mountains widened and the bottom land formed a flat valley that gradually widened into a long narrow trough of land for as far as she could see.

"Mrs. Kingston," a man called and she looked down the hillside toward the town, shoving her petticoat and skirt back down over her knees. Her heart lurched at the sight of Mr. Adler, mounted on his magnificent bay horse, approaching them. She hadn't seen him at breakfast and had assumed he'd caught the early morning freight train north.

He let the animal pick its way through the sage brush until they reached the winding path, then began to work their way up the hillside to where she sat. When he reached them and dismounted, dropping the animal's reins to the ground, he seemed taller than he had the evening before.

His gaze sought hers and for a moment she forgot her children were present. She rose from the boulder, sending a shower of arrowheads to the ground at her feet. The sashes of her bonnet slipped through her fingers and the bonnet joined the treasures on the ground. The children swarmed around their feet retrieving the arrowheads from the grass and sage brush. One of her sons reached for her bonnet and began to fill it with the arrowheads, but Bethea paid no mind.

"Good morning, Mrs. Kingston," Con said, glancing down at the children at his feet. He removed his felt hat and wiped his brow with a red kerchief.

"Good morning, Mr. Adler," she replied, using her hand to shield her eyes from the blazing sun. "I thought you...might have returned to your ranch."

His mouth moved as if he wanted to smile but decided against it. "I'll be on tonight's northbound."

29

"Oh, then we...won't see you again."

"My family...," he replied. "We summer our beef stock in the Centennial Valley and Alaska Basin."

She smiled. "I'm not sure where our home is." She recalled Clifford had purchased land from a man whose name she couldn't recall. "Perhaps it's near this Centennial Valley you mention."

"Then perhaps we'll meet again," he murmured. He smiled and she returned it with one of her own.

I hope so, she thought. The idea of wanting to see him again startled her. Had she lost control of her thoughts?

They gazed at each other, and she wondered if he, too, would regret never seeing her again.

David shrieked and jumped to his feet, bumping into Con. The man steadied the boy. Adam swung a fist but Con deflected the blow.

Ben kicked at Gabriel. "He's got more arrowheads than anyone. That's not fair. Adam and I found them first."

Gabriel reached for a rock not much larger than a good size pebble. Before he could let fly with the missile, Con grabbed him by his waist and swung him up onto the horse's back, uncoiled his fist, and tossed the rock several yards away.

The children, intent on their treasures until now, stopped their quarreling and stared at Con.

"You can't have him," Esther said, her fists on her hips.

"He's a terrible little brother, but you can't take him away," Faith added.

"Mama, don't let him take Gabriel," Esther pleaded.

Bethea pursed her lips to keep from smiling. "Well..."

Con winked at her and turned to David. "Want a boost up?"

David stepped away. "Do you wanna take me, too?"

"Most boys like riding a horse," Con said. "Don't you?"

"Sure, but where are we going?" David asked, chancing a step forward again.

"Back to the hotel," Con said, his voice low.

"Oh," David said.

Con frowned down at the boy, touching his wavy blond hair. "Where did you think we would be going?"

Ben grinned at his younger brother. "He thought you were gonna take him captive, like my friend Joey's papa said."

Con frowned. "Why would I do that?"

Shyness took Ben's tongue for a moment. "Adam, he's my big brother. He said a man at the hotel said you was an Injun."

Con's gaze flicked to Bethea, then returned to the boy. "My mother was. My father is an Englishman, born in Kentucky and lived in Boston before he headed west."

Adam's eyes filled with curiosity. "When did your pa come out here?"

"He lived with my mother's people in '56 and married my mother a year later."

Ben elbowed Adam. "Did he have to get all gussied up and do it in a church?"

Con shook his head. "No, the Shoshoni don't do it that way." He offered nothing more.

Six sets of blue eyes gazed at the man. "You got blue eyes just like us," Ben murmured.

"So does my father," Con explained.

The boys continued to study Con. Adam was the first to grow bold enough to press the query. "Where's your ma now?"

Con glanced at Bethea again. "She died giving birth to my younger brother."

She turned to her sons. "Boys, it's impolite to ask such intimate questions when we hardly know Mr. Adler." She looked at Con. "I'm sorry for my children's ill manners, Mr. Adler. Please forgive them, and me for not correcting them."

"Better to clear the air," he said. "It isn't the first time I've been asked. Blue eyed half-breeds are the exception to the rule when a white man takes up with an Indian woman. My mother was Lemhi Shoshoni and very pretty. My father gave me a tintype of her taken in Corinne, Utah, years ago. She was a half-sister to the chief. Some will argue he is Bannock and Sheepeater, but those are sub tribes within the Shoshoni. The names come from where they live or what they eat."

Adam stepped closer. "You mean sheep eaters eat sheep? Where do they keep their flocks?"

"They hunt the wild mountain sheep," Con said.

31

Adam's eyes widened. "You mean the sheep are wild around here? Like the deer? We have deer in Missouri but the sheep are pretty tame."

Con chuckled. "Our wild sheep don't look much like the woollies you're talking about. Some of the ranchers have sheep, thousands of them in fact." He looked at the hills around them. "This is good land for sheep, beef too." He kicked at the ground. "We didn't have much snow this winter and the grass is slow to turn green." His gaze skipped to Bethea before returning to the boys. "I reckon that's enough Indian lore and stock growing advice for one day to give to newcomers to the territory."

Bethea couldn't think of anything to say.

To break the silence, Con turned to Esther and Faith. "Would you girls like a ride back to the hotel? Mrs. Burns is serving dinner."

When they nodded, he shifted Gabriel forward and lifted Faith, then Esther into the saddle.

"I reckon if you're not gonna take us captive, I'd like a ride, too," David said, sticking the toe of his shoe into the stirrup. He lost his balance and Con caught him, giving him a boost up behind his sisters.

Con looked at the four children on his stallion, then smiled at Bethea again. "Maybe I should have brought another horse."

"I don't need to ride," Adam said. "Beat you to dinner," he shouted to Ben and the two older boys raced down the hill.

Con offered his hand to Bethea and she laid hers in his, not questioning the gesture. He held her bare hand lightly, giving her opportunity to pull free if she chose to, but withdrawing was the last thing she wanted to do.

Bethea glanced toward the hotel. What if someone was watching them? She eased her hand from his and started down the pathway, clutching the sun bonnet full of arrowheads against her stomach. She turned to find him several paces behind her, leading his horse down the trail and watching her.

Her children had warmed to this stranger's kindness and had begun to chat with him. Perhaps she had responded to him for the same reasons. But as they worked their way back down, she knew she was deceiving herself. It was more than kindness that had drawn her to him, but she couldn't approve or accept the emotions he brought forth. Aware of his lingering gaze, she felt the flesh across her shoulders and torso grow warm and prickly, as if he were the sun and her body was the earth.

The path widened and she dropped back beside him. "You needn't have come all this way for us," she said, refusing to look at him.

"Mrs. Burns has a message for you," he replied. "The conductor on the south bound train from Dillon passed it on. She was busy cooking, so I offered to bring it to you."

Bethea stopped walking as a heavy weight pressed against her lungs. "Who was it from?" She lifted her gaze to his.

He looked past her head to the snow capped mountains peaks in the distance. "Mr. Kingston." His gaze dropped to her face again. "He said he'll be here tomorrow on the morning train."

CHAPTER FOUR

YOU'RE A FOOL TWICE OVER, Adler thought, reining in his stallion. The horse's sides heaved from the miles of galloping and lathered foam began to run down its neck.

Con had ridden as if the devil himself had been after him once he'd escorted the Kingston family back into the hands of the Burns couple. He'd settled his account with Mrs. Burns himself, since the reasons for his lingering had had little to do with the beef stock business.

"Won't you be taking dinner with Mrs. Kingston?" she asked.

"It's best if I get on home," he'd replied.

"But the train won't be here for hours."

"Hellion needs the exercise," he'd said. He'd glanced once more over at the family enjoying Mrs. Burns's pot roast. "Keep an eye on them?" he'd asked, slipping an extra few coins into her palm.

"Then you take this," she had said, wrapping a chunk of meat in oiled brown paper along with half a loaf of fresh baked bread. She had squeezed his hand as if she understood the many unspoken reasons for his leaving. "I'll look after her," she had said softly. "She's a pretty little thing, and so young to have all those younguns.' Wonder what Mr. Kingston is like."

I don't want to be here to find out, Con thought but kept the opinions he'd already formed to himself. If she had been his wife, neither hell nor high water would have kept him from meeting that train. She had said they had land near the valley. Or had she said in the valley? *Hell*, he thought. What did it matter? They wouldn't be the first family from the east to come and think they could tame the land and make a fresh start.

He had been unable to resist one last glance at Bethea. To his dismay, she was looking directly at him. He was the first to break the bond. "When they've suffered through a few cold spells, they'll leave." With that, he had ridden away.

His stomach growled as the stallion lifted his head and nickered. The river that drained the twin lakes deep in the Centennial Valley flowed out of that high country and into this valley, winding its way northward, joined occasionally by creeks that flowed from the mountains on either side of the valley. All he had to do was follow it until the trail forked.

To the left, the trail crossed the old Bannack road coming from Corinne, Utah, to Bannack, then continued west over the territorial boundary into Idaho and to old Fort Lemhi, near where many of his mother's relatives still lived. No Indian agent or government official had yet convinced his uncle to move the band down to the Fort Hall Reservation miles to the south. He had always admired his uncle's steadfastness.

Several miles up the left fork, he would pass Alice, a stage stop, post office, and mercantile store his father had established and named after Con's step-mother, Victoria Alice Adler. The Alice Ranch was a half mile up the Medicine Lodge trail. His father had taken up the original homestead in 1867 and had added to it over the years.

He glanced overhead, estimating the hour. His horse began to reach for small patches of green along the trail that followed the river. When Con's stomach growled again, he knew it was time for both horse and rider to take nourishment. After removing the saddle and felted horse hair blanket, he slipped the bridle from Hellion's head and replaced it with an Indian lead.

Hellion was usually dependable, but Con had no desire to go chasing after a risky virile stallion through the meadows just in case, so he shoved a spike into the ground with his boot heel and tied the lead securely to the picket. He grabbed several handsful of dried grass and gave the stallion a quick rubdown until all traces of lather had been groomed away.

Beneath a cottonwood tree just beginning to leaf out, Con pulled Mrs. Burns's package from his saddle bag and opened it. The bread had soaked up some of the juices and gravy of the meat, and he ate it with relish, wasting none but the crumbs. As the stallion grazed near the stream, Con stretched out on the ground. He'd been unable to sleep more than a few hours the previous night. He tried to avoid thinking about the woman who had kept him awake. Adjusting his hat to shade his face, he closed his eyes.

A noise came from behind him and he smiled, knowing Bethea had come to him in spite of all his misgivings. She wore a pink gingham day dress, its full skirt sashaying as she strolled toward him. A pink sun bonnet fell to the ground near his shoulder and he grabbed it.

35

"Give me back my bonnet," she insisted, dropping to her knees. She lay down beside him, leaning over him to gaze upon his face. A finger stroked his cheek, then touched his mouth. He nipped it and she laughed, her voice as melodious as the birds singing in the trees or the waters cascading over the rocks in the river.

He rolled onto his side and began unbuttoning the front of her dress, exposing a few inches of creamy skin below her throat. His tongue tasted her flesh and she moaned. Luxurious brown hair flowed around her shoulders and when he ran his fingers through it, he found it warm from the sun.

Clutching a fistful of hair, he drew her closer, closer. Her hand slid beneath his shirt and around his body, her warm fingers caressing his skin and turning him inside out. She moaned again as his mouth covered hers.

Icy water splashed against his chin and he sat up with a start, his hand dropping to his holster. When he spotted four bay legs within touching distance, he looked up. Hellion's wet muzzle touched his cheek again.

Con shoved the horse's head aside and got to his feet, angry at Hellion's intrusion but angrier at himself and at Bethea Kingston and outraged at her damned husband.

He paced the bank of the river. What the hell was wrong with him? If he needed a woman, there were plenty available in Dillon or Spring Hill, and if those didn't appeal to him, Butte City was a wide open mining town with whore houses to meet any man's fancy.

If ever there was a woman out of his reach, the pretty Mrs. Kingston was that woman. He didn't want her anyway. Surrounded with proof of her child bearing capabilities, such an encounter would probably result in another child, its copper skin marking all three of them with sin.

If only a man and a woman could come together, letting love and passion be the justification, and not worry about the consequences. His pious Aunt Sophie, who lived in a fine house in Dillon, had voiced her opinion more than once that the only reason for marriage was to produce children to carry on the family name and reputation.

In all his twenty-seven years, he'd never wanted a child of his own, nor a woman of his own, come to think of it.

Women like Mrs. Kingston didn't commit improprieties with half-breed sons of wealthy ranchers. For the first time in his life, he resented his heritage.

BY THE TIME THE SUN EDGED closer to the western horizon, Con had regained his usual stoical composure. He reached the Utah Northern depot at Red Rock, stopping for a few moments to visit with the station master. Turning left, he followed the wagon trail. Hellion nickered as if he, too, knew they were almost home. He rode past the Alice stage station and store without stopping.

In the distance he could see the new house his father was having built for his stepmother. Con had stayed out of the design of the house, but after the foundation had been laid and they had paced off the rooms on the first floor, even he had been impressed. As the house came into full view, he could make out the second story and the high pitched roof that would give them a third floor. When he'd asked about its use, his father has simply shrugged.

His birth mother would have been able to take down poles, pack up skins, and be ready to move in a few hours.

His stepmother would be chained to this house for the rest of her life. But he knew she was excited about its completion and his father was proud that his financial success over the years had made such a gesture possible.

He stopped for a moment, sitting loose in the saddle, to study the construction. The roofing crew had started work before he'd headed south, and now he could see they were almost finished. The house, a long rectangular box design, sat on the hill like a queen who had put her fancy hat on and forgotten her dress. He smiled. Women seemed to be on his mind lately. The exterior walls were almost completed, made from shingles from the timber in the valley he'd left a few days ago.

His father and mother had experienced some private bonding there, in an isolated cabin, but Con had never talked to them about it, even though he had been present. He had been a child of four, malnourished and cold and small for his age, terrified by the quietness of the cabin when his father and future step-mother had found him. Only later had he come to realize that the silence had been due to the two dead bodies that he had huddled against.

While the house was under construction, his parents still lived in the five room cabin nearby. His two younger brothers had left home to work in the mines in Butte City and Hecla. His three sisters had married and were now scattered on ranches in Horse Prairie and Beaverhead Valley. Con, the oldest and only one still living at the home place, tried to leave his parents alone as much as possible, feeling they needed the privacy.

Love radiated between his parents. Perhaps that was one reason he'd never married. They had set a standard that he doubted he could equal.

Maybe that was why he had been drawn to the unobtainable Mrs. Kingston. Admiring her safely from a distance? But he had been unable to keep that distance, touching her at every opportunity. Had she realized his weakness? He doubted it, knowing a decent woman's thoughts were loyal to her husband. But Bethea Kingston had allowed him to hold her hand. Why the hell had he done that? And why had she seemed to want it?

The front door of the cabin opened and his step-mother came out onto the porch, wiping her hands on a flour sack dish towel. He dismounted, flipping the reins over the rail near the porch, and took the steps two at a time.

VICTORIA ALICE ADLER threw her arms around Con and hugged him tightly. Although she had not given birth to him, she had nurtured him, watched his emaciated arms and legs flesh out and begin to grow over the years. Many times she had lent an ear when he'd come home in tears from the school house at Red Rock when some schoolmate would call him a heathen or Injun or worse.

After a few months of seeing what the taunts were doing to him, she had talked Matthias into letting her educate all their children at home. This special son had grown up to be a fine Christian man who practiced his faith without the hypocrisy of many of their peers.

She loved the five children she and her husband had brought into the world, but they had been born with a light skin, the gift of acceptance into the white man's society now dominating the area.

She knew Matthias was riding to Omaha with the carloads of beef stock, but Con should have come home days ago. When she had seen the lone rider approach and recognized the tall bay stallion trotting along the trail, her heart had lurched with relief.

She smoothed the patch of gray hair at her temple and smiled as she stepped back and looked at him. "No blood, no bruises." She studied him from head to toe, then wiped a trace of moisture from her cheek. "I was worried about you. I felt you had a problem that might be more than you could handle."

He bussed her cheek. "Do I look like I couldn't handle anything that came my way?" Before she could respond, he scraped his boots and went inside. She followed him, still uneasy.

"Your uncle George rode in early this morning," she said. "Coffee?" He nodded, and she poured him a fresh cupful. "He said you'd left Monida yesterday."

Con took a long sip and said nothing.

She sat down beside him. "Con, I don't mean to pry, but are you in trouble?"

He glanced at her. "With the law?"

"Yes. Are you?"

He shook his head, but as she watched his profile, she sensed his thoughts drifting away. Such a handsome, strong profile, she thought. This son, with a foot firmly implanted in two cultures, was his own man in every way. He was a loner yet enjoyed the company of others. To the best of her knowledge, Con had never courted a local woman openly. "Could it be?" she thought aloud.

He turned to her. "Could what be?"

"You've met someone."

He looked away again. "I meet lots of people. You can't go to a railroad town without meeting people."

She had no right to pry, but his happiness was of primary concern to both her and Matthias. She refilled her cup and took a seat across from him, where he could not evade her questions. "I think you've met a woman," she hinted.

"I've met lots of women."

If only she could convince him to open up. "Tell me about her." She smiled. "Nothing would make me happier than to see you head over heels in love with a woman who could bring you happiness and children. You need your own home. Have you met the right woman at long last?"

He looked at her, his gaze stormy and dark. "The right woman? Not quite. She has a houseful of children already."

Victoria's eyes blinked several times. "Then she's a widow. That's all right, Con, but do be cautious. Widows can have ulterior motives for attracting a man."

"Don't worry, Mother, this woman isn't a widow. Her family is complete with a husband." He stood up, frowning at her. "I found myself attracted to her. I don't know why the hell it happened, it just did. Now she's back in the care of her husband, so forget I said a word. I don't know how you manage to get me to talk, but you've always been able to interrogate me."

"Interrogate you?" Had she been guilty of that? She rose from the table and went to the stove, checking the hen boiling in the pot on the back plate. "I'm sorry if I ask too many questions." She waited for his reply, but none came. She wanted to grab his shoulders and give him a loving shake, but when she turned again, the room was empty.

Later, when the men gathered around the table for supper, she dipped out the pieces of chicken into a large serving bowl, ladled in the thickened broth, and topped the dish with dumplings. "I found some greens growing on the hillside," she said. "First ones this spring." She looked at her brother-in-law. "George, would you bless the meal?"

His words were mumbled and unintelligible, but Victoria let the matter pass. No reason to make a fuss when Matthias was away. Everyone seemed to be in a foul mood today, including herself. For her, it was knowing that Matthias would be gone for weeks. The trips to Omaha had always been lonely times for her, even when the children were young and at home. Now, she missed her husband more than ever.

As for why the men were also moody, she couldn't begin to guess. Her exchange with Con had been upsetting enough. She had never liked George Adler and wished he'd stayed in the south where he belonged. She'd grown tired of his bemoaning the Confederacy's loss, but did her best to keep her mouth shut.

Mexican Pete was a hired hand who had worked for them since the early 1870s. That might be because as his joints gave out, he was wary about being shunted aside. She chided herself for giving in to so many negative thoughts. This was not a country for any man or woman to be without a home and hearth, especially in winter.

The men served themselves while she went to the sideboard board and cut several thick slices of bread and put them on a platter, then set a jar of huckleberry jam, fresh churned butter, and a peach pie baked earlier in the afternoon on the table.

"How was the roundup?" she asked, seating herself next to Matthias's empty captain's chair. "Matthias had hoped to fill four cars."

"We stopped at three," Con said between bites. "Old Charlie got hurt. He died."

"Charlie? Charlie Forman from Spring Hill?" she asked. "He used to work for us back in the seventies. What happened?"

Con shrugged.

"Charlie fell under the stock car and it rolled," Mexican Pete said. "Poor damned Charlie never did have much good in his bucket of luck."

Victoria glanced at Con. He'd stopped eating. When he looked at her, all he said was, "I pulled him out."

"Were his...legs cut off?" she asked, hating to hear of one more fatality brought about by what should be an asset to the territory.

Mexican Pete shook his head. "Cut him almost in two pieces, right across here," and he sawed an imaginary line across his belly.

"That's enough, Pete," Con said, shoving his plate back a few inches. "He's dead and we buried him there. I never heard him talk about family, so who would want to know about his passing?"

Everyone concentrated on his meal for several minutes. Victoria had lost her appetite as had Con from the looks of his scowling features.

"How did the valley look?" she asked, wanting to lighten the atmosphere in the room.

"Pretty as ever, Mrs. Adler," Mexican Pete said. He smiled, brushing his blond hair from his forehead. He'd gotten his nickname because he'd once worked for Charles Goodnight rounding up mavericks along the Texas Mexican border decades earlier. He'd been born in Sweden and spoke English laced with Swedish and

Spanish, but had lingered at the Alice Ranch, claiming that Mrs. Adler was the best cook in the west.

"Has the valley turned green yet?" she asked.

"Not quite," Mexican Pete replied, "but any day now. The springs are gushing and the ice is plum gone from the lakes. We seen a few swans setting down and those Canadian geese are already back. The place is crawling with birds."

"That Latimer family, the one that took up a claim on the north side of the lakes...are they still there?" she asked.

Con shook his head. "They changed their minds as soon as the snows got deep. Mrs. Burns said they came out with what they could carry on one wagon as soon as the lake froze over and they could drive the team across it."

"That's a shame," she murmured, saddened to learn of any family giving up on its dreams.

Con glanced up and when she looked at him, he smiled. Someone who didn't know him would deny he had even moved his lips, but she knew he had and she smiled back and nodded. He was asking her forgiveness in his own unique way, not that there had been anything to forgive. They had both been on edge, perhaps about matters that were similar in nature.

"The Smith families are still there, all three of them," Con said. "Mrs. McGyver is hanging on to her claim near the upper springs. She's suspicious as hell about anyone who drops by, but her son seems to like it there. They're inseparable." He leaned back against the slats of his chair. "Thank God the south side is still unclaimed except for our holdings."

Victoria nodded. "Someday we're going to have to deal with an invasion when the rest of the territory is taken up and the land locators and promoters find us." Victoria refilled the serving bowl with chicken and dumplings and Con took a small second helping.

"We've managed to get several sections tied down," he said, "but the open grasses won't be ours for long. If Father wants to keep the farmers away, he'd better find some more relatives to file."

Mexican Pete looked at the older man at the table, then to Victoria. "I hear tell a new family is moving into the valley."

"Really?" Victoria asked. "Where?"

"On the south side of the upper lake, hear tell they have the place with that pretty little cabin you always like to stay at, ma'am."

"Our cabin?" She frowned. "But that belongs to George. How could that be? George, it sounds like someone is squatting on your land. You'd better chase them off before all their relatives join them and we get a taste of our own medicine."

"Can't do that, Victoria," George said, his voice muffled as he chewed a mouthful of meat.

"Why ever not? Send Con." She turned to Con. "Would you go see what's going on, dear? It's difficult enough knowing the free grazing won't be available much longer, but if we hold title to the land, no one has a right to claim it."

"I sold it." George reached for the peach pie tin.

"You what?" Victoria cried. "My springs? My cabin?"

"What the hell are you talking about, Uncle George?" Con asked, rising a few inches from his chair.

George shrugged. "I'm going back to Kentucky. I needed some traveling money."

"But Matthias would have paid you a fair price," Victoria insisted. "Surely, you're teasing us. We could never let that piece of land leave the family. It means too much to us."

George stood up and wiped his mouth with the back of his hand. "It's my land. I can do with it what I damned well want."

"Who did you sell it to?" Victoria asked, desperate for a way to get her special piece of land back. "Give us his name and we'll buy him out. Tell him we'll pay double whatever he paid you. Maybe he hasn't had a chance to get to Virginia City yet to record the transfer."

Mexican Pete helped himself to another slice of pie. "I hear tell he went directly to Virginia City before the ink was dry on the piece of paper George here signed. Two men at the Mint in Spring Hill swear they went with him as witnesses, said he paid them for taking time off."

Pete studied the ceiling as he chewed. "They said he was some dude from the East who planned to bring his family out and wanted to get everything legal like before he sent for them. Said he'd won heavy in Butte City playing faro."

Victoria fought down her tears. If only Matthias were here. He'd know what to do to stop this terrible mistake. "Please George, who is this man?"

George edged closer to the door. "Some cocky little bastard I met in Butte City. He can't hold his liquor, but Lady Luck sure the hell was sitting on his knee that night."

She stood up quickly, knocking her chair over. Con retrieved it, then rested his hand on her arm. "Take it easy, Mother. I'll look into it."

"Thank you, dear," Victoria replied, sweeping her hand over her temple. "I couldn't bear to lose that place. George, what can you tell us about this man? What's his name?"

"Kingston," George said. "Some know-it-all son-of-a-bitch from Missouri named Clifford Kingston."

CHAPTER FIVE

"THE HELL YOU SAY." Con grabbed his uncle's shirt front, lifting the man's heels off the floor.

"Kingston. I said his name is Kingston," George said between gasping breaths. "That was his woman and his brats getting off the train at Monida. Hell, you saw them, more kids than livestock I imagine. That woman of his must be some piece."

Con's complexion flushed beneath his tan. "Shut your damned mouth. She said near the valley, not in it."

"Then she lied," George said, trying to pull free from Con's clutches.

"She wouldn't lie," Con insisted.

"She'll be about as deep in the valley as a body can get," George retorted. "She must have known. Didn't you tell her who you were? Kingston sure's hell knows my name. Maybe she tricked you. What'd she do? Talk you into spending money on her and the brats?"

"Don't judge a person when you don't know her," Con said, easing his hold on his uncle.

George snorted and jerked free. "And you do? Is that why I beat you home, nephew? Did those flouncing skirts get your heathen blood all riled up? Wawl, I can see why. She was quite a little looker from what I could tell. Maybe you saw more of her than I did." The snarl that curled his mouth tightened. "Don't mess with her would be my advice. If you bedded her, the kid would have your mark for sure and you'd have a hard time denying it."

Con's doubled fist caught his uncle on the chin and sending him spinning across the room. Only his mother's scream brought him out of his fury.

Across the room, Mexican Pete helped a dazed George Adler to his feet. He retrieved his hat and shook Pete's assistance aside. "I'll be gone first thing tomorrow morning. I've been looking for an excuse to clear out," he said, not looking at Victoria. "I'll be in touch with Matthias. I'm staying in Butte City until I make plans to head to Kentucky."

Mexican Pete excused himself and headed to the bunkhouse. Victoria busied herself clearing the table. Con had chores to do and they'd be easier if he completed them before darkness fell. He worked his fingers, rubbing his fist with his uninjured hand as he glanced out the window. If he hustled, he could do them without the aid of a lantern. His stepmother needed time to herself to settle down. Then he'd attempt to an explanation.

Under the cover of darkness, Con lingered outside. Taking a thin piece of paper from the package in his shirt pocket, he pulled out a pouch of tobacco and rolled himself a neat cigarette. He inhaled deeply, savoring the surge of pleasure he received from the tobacco. He never smoked while working and never in the cabin, but when pressures were closing in on him, he'd discovered two ways to cope. Either he would ride to Lemhi valley and become a member of his uncle's tribe or he could have a smoke. Tonight, the smoke would suffice.

When the cigarette grew short, he tossed the butt into the dirt and ground it with his boot heel. Maybe he'd stalled enough and his mother would have gone to bed.

Inside, a lantern still glowed on the table where the quarrel had begun. The rest of the room was dark and quiet. He saw a movement near the stove and stepped away from the door.

"May I have one, too?" he asked, keeping his voice low and easy. Victoria didn't flinch, and he knew she had been aware of his entrance. "It's sage tea," she said without turning.

"Sounds good."

She filled a second cup and brought them both to the table, then added a matching cream and sugar set made of bone China, one of her finest possessions. She had asked little for herself in the way of material goods over the years, yet he knew his father and the Alice Livestock Company had the financial resources to provide her with the trappings of success if she asked.

Not until they had shared a few silent moments together, did he speak. "Please try to understand why I can't go check on George's land," he said, turning his cup in a tight circle.

She looked up at him, her hazel eyes shimmering.

Centennial Swan

Ironic, he thought, she had the eyes more suited to his coloring and he had hers, but fate wasn't always considerate. That he'd learned over the years. "Her name is...Bethea."

"A pretty name," Victoria said. "Is she? Pretty, I mean?"

He continued turning his cup. "It wasn't her looks that attracted me. She was hardly waiting for me to sweep her off her feet. She's a little thing and a man could do that very easily."

Victoria smiled. "So she's pretty and petite. What else?"

"I never said that," Con insisted. "I swear I didn't know she was going to our old place."

"I raised all my children to know what's right and what's wrong," she said. "You're my child, just as the others are. You know that, but...you have an extra cross to bear. I know that, too. Unthinking people can be cruel and heartless when they don't know you. Does she know...about your mother?"

"I told her," he replied. "It didn't seem to frighten her."

She sighed deeply. "When I first arrived in Bannack, I was ignorant about the Indian tribes who lived here long before we did, but Matthias and Tendoi and the others were patient with me and I changed. I think the Lord made all of us equal. It's the white man who changed the rules and set himself up as ruler."

"To the victor goes the spoils," he murmured.

She squeezed his hand. "When I was younger and had a houseful of children, I envied you being able to ride off with your uncle and spend the summer at his camp. I knew there were times when Matthias wanted to go with you."

He squeezed her hand in return. "He rode over to check on me several times each summer. You came with him occasionally, even after Rhoda and Sarah were born."

"And I loved those times," she replied. "But now it saddens me to see what's happened to your mother's people. The government has broken its promises again and again. It's not a popular view to take, so I don't express myself when I go to the county seat."

"Opinions can have repercussions," he said.

"These are not easy times," he said. "My mother's people will never be treated justly. The supplies and meat you and Father send in the winter help. There are other ranchers who send supplies, too, and they ask for nothing in return. Why can't the men in the east

47

keep their word? The Shoshoni gave up their lands and now the government refuses due compensation. Why? Is honor unknown to Washington officials?"

The silence deepened until she looked across the table at Con. "But that's not why we're here, is it?"

He twisted his cup again. "I can't go to the valley."

"Tell me about this woman, this Bethea Kingston," she murmured.

He left the table and brought back the porcelain tea pot from the pipe shelf of the stove. When their cups were filled again, he rubbed the back of his neck and tried to compose his thoughts.

"I don't know why I found myself drawn to her. Before we'd even said a word to each other, I knew this was a woman I wanted to be with." He shook his head. "I don't mean to bed her..." He glanced across the table and couldn't suppress a grin. "Since then, the possibility has occurred to me, but not at first."

"Thoughts are safe, unless you try to carry them through," she cautioned.

"I know that. Mother, how did you know that my father was the man you wanted to spend your life with?"

Victoria smiled. "I admired him from afar, as we ladies would say in polite society. He was a squaw man and I was a school teacher. He came to Bannack City when Tendoi's band traveled through the area.

"Your father would come to my brother's printing shop and read the newspapers from the East. He was especially interested in the Boston Herald. He'd bring you in with him. You were a darling. Not many local children came to school at first, so I closed it and worked the counter to help my brother."

She looked across the room. "That was twenty-six years ago, Con. He brought you into the office several times when the women were traveling with the band. You were about two when I first saw you. I never knew then that someday we'd be sitting here discussing all that."

"Then there was no immediate attraction?" he asked.

Her eyes took on a faraway expression. "I thought he was the handsomest man I'd ever seen. He was the talk of the town and I'd heard all the stories, but whenever he spoke to me, little shivers would shoot down my spine. When he touched my hand, I'd feel light headed and I'm not a fainting female." She gave an exaggerated sigh. "When he gazed into my eyes, the word swoon took on new meaning."

"You? Swoon?" He chuckled "Does he still make you feel that way?"

"Yes."

His thoughts drifted to Bethea Kingston. "If I see her again...or worse yet run into her husband, I don't know what I'd do. I want to kill him, and I've never met the man. I wouldn't know him if he walked in that door."

"Let's not talk about him," Victoria said. "Tell me about her."

Before he realized what he'd done, he'd described Bethea and her six children in details he'd been unaware he'd noticed. "But I haven't done justice to her."

She raised her brows. "I think the pretty Mrs. Kingston would be impressed to hear your words."

"How could she? She's a married woman."

"Married women appreciate compliments."

"But not from men other than their husbands," he countered.

"Some women are trapped in a marriage not of their choosing," she said. "She must have married quite young. There's usually only one reason for that."

He frowned at her, unable to imagine Bethea Kingston in a sexual liaison. "She'd never do that...unless that bastard forced her."

"Passion and desire can be powerful motivators, dear," she relied. "Aren't you finding that out?"

He studied his hands for a few minutes. "If George leaves tomorrow, I'll stay until Father returns. I'll hire the crew for the summer in the Valley. I'll have everything arranged by the time he gets back, but then I'm going to Lemhi for a few months."

"But we need you here," she insisted. "Your father plans to go to the Valley as soon as he returns. He'll be very upset over this George business. You know how headstrong he can be. Con, you've met this woman. You can see both sides of the picture. Please, stay and go with him, at least to talk to the Kingstons. We can't let that land out of our hands."

"It's too late for that, thanks to George," Con said, feeling himself drawn into a web of intrigue with the Kingstons.

"Perhaps seeing her again would clear the air," Victoria said. "Maybe this is all in your mind."

He chuckled cynically. "Bethea Kingston is very much a reality for me, Mother." He peered at the pieces of sage leaves in the bottom of his cup. "But maybe you're right. Seeing her with her damned husband and all those children should bring me to my senses. She'll be so busy, she won't look at me twice."

"Your father will be very grateful for your help in this matter, Con. He's had too many worries. He doesn't need this, too. I don't understand how he and George could have come from the same parents. George is so...and Matthias is all..." She blushed an attractive shade of pink and looked away. "With last year's drought and the threat of falling beef prices, sometimes I wonder if we've made a mistake building the new house."

"But it's been your dream for years," Con said.

"More Matthias's than my own," she replied.

"Someday the house will be full of children," he assured her. "You'll see. Rhoda has her son already and I'm sure you'll be hearing from Sarah and Angeline any day now."

Victoria smiled. "I did just last week. We'll have two more babies by Christmas time, and someday you'll be a father, too. You're so patient with little ones."

"With my brothers and sisters and growing up with my cousins at Lemhi, what else would I be? Children's spirits should never be broken. I see no reason to beat a child."

She laughed. "That's easy to say when you have none of your own, but you're right." She covered a yawn. "All I'm asking for is that you make one trip to the valley."

He nodded. "But then I'm going to Lemhi," he insisted. "It's either make a fool of myself by hanging around the valley all summer or get the hell out of the territory."

"We'll miss you," she said.

"Don't say anything to my father about Bethea...as a woman."

"I won't."

"Then it's settled," he said, rising from his chair. He went around the table and kissed her cheek and left her alone with her thoughts.

Centennial Swan

BETHEA KINGSTON fought a battle with her emotions and found no solution. Perhaps writing in her journal would bring the peace that would allow her to find sleep.

But when she opened the book and reread the passages from the previous night, her heart grew heavy. Had it been only one day? She felt as if she'd known the mysterious Mr. Adler for ages. When Mrs. Burns had come to their table and expressed his regrets, she had hidden her disappointment but his absence had put a somber shadow on her mood that lingered throughout the endless afternoon and evening. She'd even snapped at the children several times.

She looked at the blank page before her and picked up the pen. *"Mr. Adler left without saying good-by."* Feeling as if her hand had written the entry without guidance, she closed the book for a few minutes, then opened it again. *"We've..."* She crossed out the word and decided to be brutally honest in her entries.

"I" and she underlined the letter, *"enjoyed his company immensely. I wonder what his life is like, who his friends are, if there is a special woman? Could he be married?"* She looked across the room. *"No,"* she wrote, *"I don't think so. He is a man of character, of essence...and I could gaze upon him..."* She scratched out the word *forever* and wrote *easily*. *"Have I committed an act of unfaithfulness right here on the page? Is this adultery in my mind?"*

She stared at the entry. Surely her own hand hadn't written the words. The journal had become something very different from the diary of a trip to the wilderness. Now it would have to be hidden away where no outsider's eyes could ever read it. The thought of Clifford's arrival brought a lump to her throat. She should be anxious to see him. They had been separated for months, yet here she was, pining for a stranger she hardly knew.

Stories had been circulated about women going insane in the west. Was this the first sign of her own oncoming madness? Her hand shook as she closed the book, tied the ribbon, and put it away. How could a person write when the lines on the page waved and shimmered?

She pulled the covers up past her shoulders, but when her chin began to quiver, she yanked the covers over her head and buried her face in the pillow. She didn't want to live with Clifford. He was an

51

insufferable braggart and twisted the truth to suit his purposes. She'd known that for years now, but she had pretended all was well.

But what could she do? She had met only one woman who had obtained a divorce, and that woman had been shunned by the other women in Wilcox. No, divorce was unthinkable. How would she care for her children? She had no money of her own other than what her mother had given her. She owned no property, had no trade at which to work. Cooking and sewing were the extent of her skills.

She was trapped in a loveless marriage for the rest of her life, for worse. Other than her children, there had never been a "better."

Con Adler coming into her life had been an accident, perhaps temptation that the devil himself had placed in her path. Hadn't the great preaching orator, Dr. DeWitt Talmadge, expounded on that very subject two summers ago when he had brought his traveling tent program to Maryville, the county seat not far from her home town?

She rolled onto her side. Con Adler was a stranger but she couldn't imagine him being the devil's tool. Mrs. Burns seemed genuinely fond of him, but the woman was a stranger. Maybe that was the cause of her despondency. She and her children were alone in a land of strangers. Mr. Adler had been kind to them, and she had overreacted to that kindness. No man and woman could be drawn together the way they had been without a reason. For her it had been the fear of being stranded in an unfamiliar land.

But what had been his reasons? *Conrad Adler.* She repeated his name over and over in her mind, enjoying the pleasure of its sound. She slid her hand between her cheek and the feather pillow, and gave in to deep despair as she remembered the moments that first night when he'd rescued her and embraced her, the time he'd held her hand on the hillside before slipping out of her life without a word. If only they had been blessed with time.

Tears dampened the pillow until she had no more to shed. *"Lord,"* she prayed against the wet pillow, *"bring me peace and strength...and bless Mr. Adler and keep him from harm's way."*

BETHEA STRIPPED THE COT and wrapped her tear stained pillow case inside the sheet. She felt renewed this morning, ready to

Centennial Swan

face the day. The night's outburst was safely tucked away, along with the journal she now must keep hidden from all prying eyes.

The children dressed and went down for their morning trip out back while she put the trunk in order and locked it. Clifford would arrive in a few hours and they would begin the wagon trip to their new home.

Now she had a second change to learn to be a dutiful wife. She would be more patient, more enduring. She would devote her energies to keeping house, caring for her family, and preparing for the long hard winter that Mrs. Burns had warned her about. Most importantly, she would try to find the happiness that had eluded her most of her married life.

When the train pulled into the station at Monida a few hours later, Clifford Kingston was the first passenger to hop off, brushing aside the assistance of the conductor. In a cloud of steam, he stepped away from the car and scanned the area.

"Wait here, children," Bethea cautioned, keeping them safely on the porch of the hotel. Mrs. Burns had described the horrible accident that had involved Con Adler the day of her own arrival. She closed her eyes. This was not the time to let Mr. Adler's presence intrude.

She reopened her eyes and this time she kept her gaze on her husband, following his steps through the graveled surface near the track and around the mud puddles. He seemed shorter than she remembered. Perhaps that was because...no! Had she lost her mind completely? She raised her hand and waved discretely to her husband.

His smile brought out traces of the handsomeness that had first drawn her to him, when as an impressionable fifteen year old, she had found him a debonair and worldly man ten years her senior. In recent years, his hair had begun to recede at the temples. The loss was more noticeable when he removed his Derby hat and waved again. He was wearing a finely tailored traveling suit and she strived to focus on only his best qualities.

When he stepped onto the porch, he ignored the children. "Good morning, Mrs. Kingston," he said, his voice low and suggestive as he kissed her lightly on the cheek.

53

She forced herself to stand immobile until his lips left her skin. "Good morning, Mr. Kingston. The children are excited about your return."

He looked down and for a moment she wondered if he'd forgotten his offspring, but when he dropped to one knee and hugged the girls and squeezed the two younger boys, she knew she was just being silly. He shook the older two boys' hands, then seemed to dismiss them again. "Where the devil are those goods I bought in Dillon?" he asked of no one in particular. He waved to a man near one of the freight cars and the man came to them.

"The second and third cars, boy, can you get them unloaded right away?" Clifford put his arm around Bethea's shoulders and squeezed her. "My misses and the children are anxious to get on the road. We want to get to our new place before dark."

The Utah Northern employee scratched his head. "Where you folks moving to?"

"To the Centennial Valley, my boy," Clifford boasted. "I've acquired a little place from Mr. George Adler."

Bethea's heart dropped into the pit of her stomach at the mention of Con's surname.

The railroad employee scratched his head again. "One of the Adlers from Alice? I reckoned they were hell bent on getting control of the entire south side of the valley. Are you sure? Just where is it?"

"A house and acreage on the south side of the upper lake," Clifford replied, beaming a smile at Bethea. "It overlooks the lake and give a view deserving of a fine artist's brush."

"You mean that little..."

Clifford cut off the man's remark and motioned to the railroad car. Several men had begun to unload the contents, first a spring wagon, then sacks of staples, crates of assorted sizes and several barrels. Last to be unloaded was a crate marked, "Great Western Stove Co., Leavenworth, Omaha and Denver." He smiled at her again. "Bought you a little house warming gift in Butte City, Mrs. Kingston."

Bethea ignored his remark as she walked around the sacks and barrels, trying to inventory what he'd purchased. Potatoes, flour, salt, coffee, rice, even a barrel of salted beef. She looked at him from across the merchandise. "We must talk, Mr. Kingston."

Centennial Swan

As the children began to climb onto the sacks of potatoes, Clifford grabbed her elbow and led her out of earshot of the workers. "What's wrong now?" he asked. "I know that look you get when you're pissed off."

"Clifford, please." She tried to pull free but he squeezed harder, sending a shooting pain up her arm.

When she cried aloud and one of the men looked their way, Clifford dropped her arm. "What's wrong?"

"Is our new house furnished?" she asked. "Is it furnished? How many bedrooms will we have. Do we have beds to sleep on? Chairs to sit on? I brought linens and pillows and enough feather ticks, and cooking utensils, too. What about other meats? Hams and side pork? And greens, we need fresh vegetables and fruit, and of course a milk cow. Did you think...I mean did you remember those things?"

He groaned, as if he were tolerating an imbecilic child's questions. "The place is furnished, and if it's not enough, we can build more. Hell, woman, the place is surrounded by timber. We'll get sacks of turnips and parsnips and carrots from the store here or in Spring Hill, and I bought you some seeds. You can plant a garden and grow your own greens."

A wave of nausea turned her stomach sour. "I don't know if I can dig up a garden...in time."

He shook his head and sighed again. "I bought a plow and the livery here has a team ready for us and a saddle horse for me. We'll hitch up one of the draft horses and work the ground." He spoke louder. "Did you think I'd let my wife plow up her own vegetable garden? Not on your life." His voice dropped again. "Now quit your complaining."

She turned her attention to the spring wagon. "It isn't large enough to haul all this and the trunks, too."

"Then I'll hire another team and driver to help us." He strode over to the livery stable and spoke to a man who had been lounging against one of the door jambs watching the unloading activity. When the man nodded, Clifford looked over his shoulder and grinned at Bethea. "It's all arranged."

Within the hour, the wagons were loaded, and they had purchased a sack of carrots and a half sack of apples. Bethea had found the

55

apples in the root cellar while selecting the carrots and an extra sack of potatoes. The merchant had refused to sell them, stating he'd been feeding them to his stock because they'd become shriveled from storage. When two of the boys had bitten into them and juice had run down their chins, she asked again if he'd part with them. The merchant had carried the sack to the wagon but refused payment.

Inside the hotel, Bethea introduced her husband to Mrs. Burns. When the woman offered to provide them a meal in spite of the early hour, Clifford declined.

A brown wrapped package was shoved into Bethea's hands seconds after she gained her seat on the wagon beside Clifford. When she looked down into Mrs. Burns's tear filled eyes, her throat tightened and she bit her lip. "Thank you."

"We don't take charity," Clifford said.

Mrs. Burns ignored him. "You'll be stopping to feed the children somewhere along the trail. You take it. It's meat and cold potatoes left from yesterday and some cheese. Consider it a welcoming gift from the Burns family. And here are three loaves of bread and some sugar cookies for the little ones."

"Thank you, Mrs. Burns, you're so kind," Bethea said, her voice quivering. "We're little more than strangers and you've been so very generous."

Mrs. Burns shushed her with a squeeze of her wide hand. "You won't want to bake until you get settled in, and you'll have no time to churn so here's a crock of butter. And the children need milk to drink with their meal, so here's a jar fresh this morning from the cow. You can return the crook the next time you come to town. Keep the jar. The peddler gives them away when he passes through here."

"We got to go," Clifford said, ignoring Mrs. Burns completely.

She reached up and squeezed Bethea's hand once more. "We'll be thinking about you, honey. If you have troubles, come to us."

Clifford slapped the reins against the horses' rumps, and the team jumped in their traces. Mrs. Burns stepped away from the wagon with inches to spare. Bethea and the children turned and waved until Mr. and Mrs. Burns grew smaller, then disappeared when the wagon dropped down over the first hill.

"Will we ever see them again?" Esther asked.

"I'm sure we will," Bethea murmured.

"Christ, you're all acting like they're damned relatives," Clifford said. "They're just making sure you'll stay there and pay them again. I'll bet they charged you an arm and a leg for staying there as it was."

Bethea ignored his remarks. "She was very nice, so was her husband. In fact, everyone we met was kind to us."

Faith crawled between Clifford and Bethea on the wagon seat. "Especially Mr. Adler, heah?" She turned to Bethea. "Will we ever see Mr. Adler again?"

Clifford stared at Bethea. "You met Mr. Adler?"

Bethea pulled Faith onto her lap. "Yes, he helped us when you didn't show up, but his name wasn't George."

"What did he look like?" Clifford asked. "Gray haired? Tall? That would be Matthias, one of the most powerful men in the county."

"I believe one of them had touches of gray but he wasn't very tall," she replied, staring at the winding trail ahead. "There were two of them, but the older man left right away."

"And the one who stayed? What did he look like?" Clifford asked.

"He was part Injun, Pa," Adam shouted, "but he had blue eyes just like us."

"We thought he was gonna take Gabriel captive, but Mama talked him out of it," Ben added. "They laughed about it like it was some kind of joke."

"I liked him," David said. "He knew all about Injun stuff like hunting and wild sheep and everything!"

"Yeah, Pa, I found this black glass." Adam pulled the piece from his pocket and showed it to his father. "This Injun Mr. Adler knew it was a hide scraper, and Mama put the arrowheads we found in her blue trunk. Are all Injuns like this one, Pa?"

"That's enough, Adam," Clifford shouted, grabbing the obsidian and tossing it between the traces.

"But Pa!"

"No kid of mine is going to associate with Injuns. They're closer to being wild animals than humans." He scowled past Esther, who had joined her parents and sister on the seat. "You kept company with one of those damned degenerate savages? What kind of woman are you, Bethea?"

Bethea tightened her arms around Faith. "The man could hardly be described a savage. He was very civilized, more than many white men I've met." She met Clifford's furious gaze and refused to back down. "He helped us when we needed help. I stood close to him and he didn't smell, so he obviously bathes."

Clifford's face turned crimson.

"His teeth were white and straight and well cared for." If she had good sense, she'd stop now, but some inner force loosened her tongue. "He was clean shaven."

"Damned heathens aren't men enough to grow a beard," Clifford said. "Don't you know a thing?"

If Clifford wanted a quarrel, he had selected the right subject. Bethea adjusted the folds in her skirt, then slid her arms around her five year old daughter again. "Mr. Adler's trousers had the usual dirt on them and a few other stains because he and his cowboys had been loading carloads of beef stock before we arrived. You might be interested to know that he wasn't wearing beaded moccasins."

She looked down at his footwear. "In fact, his boots were newer than yours and expensively made. I believe he might be considered wealthy. He had a pocket full of gold coins."

"More than likely, he stole them," Clifford said. "You can't trust them damned heathens. They walk into your house as if they have a right. They beg for food."

Her chin lifted. "Mr. Adler paid for his own meals at the hotel except for one." She glanced at Clifford's tight mouth and couldn't suppress a smile. "I invited him to join us for the evening meal. His table manners were impeccable and we enjoyed his company. Immensely!"

CHAPTER SIX

CLIFFORD'S GAZE DARTED from the team to Bethea. The horses lost their footing on a steep downgrade and he concentrated on the driving for several minutes. She knew the discussion hadn't ended. As soon as they reached a flat curve around another side hill, he glared at her again.

"You had no right to associate with riffraff, Bethea, you know how dangerous that can be. When a woman alone gets too friendly even with a white man, he can get the wrong idea. God only knows what goes through a red skin's mind when he talks to a white woman."

"Wrong idea?" She met Clifford's angry gaze, keeping her eyes wide and innocent. "You mean he may want to buy me as his wife?"

"Or worse."

"Oh, then if we meet again, he'll try to steal me? Perhaps carry me away on his magnificent stallion?"

"Injuns don't ride magnificent stallions," he retorted. "They ride scrub pinto ponies."

"Perhaps he'll want to make me his slave and ravage me at his leisure," she hinted.

"Mama, what does ravage mean?" Esther asked, her blue eyes filled with curiosity.

"Now see what you've done, Bethea? Talking that way in front of the children," Clifford said, urging the team up another hill. "Has he corrupted you already?"

Bethea knew she'd pay for her impertinence later. "The man is quite handsome and much taller than you. He was definitely not a degenerate. If you insist he be called a savage, I would say that he is truly a noble one."

Clifford's complexion darkened several shades but at least she had shut him up. What had possessed her to speak so insolently to her husband, and in front of the children as well? Such a poor example she had proven to be, yet in spite of the possible consequences, she was pleased with her defense of Con Adler's reputation. Meeting him had been a significant experience for her and the children. Better to have the children share in the discussion than for her to keep Mr.

Adler a secret. She had enough secrets to hide from Clifford already.

The sun was high in the southern horizon when they stopped near a grove of scrub cedar and ate the lunch Mrs. Burns had provided. The driver of the second wagon ate with them and Bethea was thankful for his presence. Clifford said little until the driver began talking about the valley.

"You aren't going to stay the winters, are you?" the man asked.

"We plan to live there year round," Bethea said. "Didn't you say that, Mr. Kingston?"

Clifford grunted an acknowledgment.

"Then pack in provisions and gather lots of fire wood," the driver suggested. "The winters ain't for the sick, puny or faint hearted."

"We're used to cold weather," Clifford said. "Missouri has its share of snow storms."

"With below-zero weather for weeks on end?" the man asked. "When you have to chip ice off the water bucket behind the kitchen stove in the mornings after you've kept a fire going all night? That's cold." He got to his feet and stretched. "If you folks hope to make it to your place before nightfall, we'd better get a move on."

The children became cranky when the temperature turned warm and the sacks of food grew lumpy. Bethea coaxed them to find a spot on the sacks and try to nap. Bitter silence settled between Clifford and Bethea for miles. They crested another hill that wound around a small stand of pine. Off in the distance, shimmering blue water filled the eastern horizon for miles.

Bethea pointed. "Is that the lake?" Excitement swept some of her anger away and she touched Clifford's shirt sleeve. "It's beautiful."

"That's the first one," he said, glancing down at her hand. "The bigger one is still out of sight. Our place is right on the edge of the upper lake. Trust me this time, Bethea. This is the place for us. This valley is just beginning to open up to homesteaders. Most of the land has been preempted by the big stockmen, but now it's time for the common man to have his turn."

He flicked the reins and the horses broke into a trot as the road changed into a gentle down grade toward the water.

"How much land do we own?" she asked.

"A quarter section; one hundred sixty acres more or less and it's free and clear." He patted his vest pocket. "I got the deed right here, recorded at the courthouse in Virginia City with all the proper seals."

"How much did you pay for it?"

He tossed his blond head and laughed. "I won it fair and square in a faro game in Butte City."

For several miles, Bethea mulled over what he'd said. They left the first lake behind and the river that had bridged the twin lakes seemed to break into hundreds of small ponds for a few miles. Ahead another glistening sea of blue appeared.

As they approached the second lake, she turned to him again. "What if the Adler family decides you cheated this man George?"

He shook his head. "Deal is a deal, but I made him put a price into the bill of sale just to make sure. I gave him a five dollar gold piece, so he couldn't say I stole it."

In the distance, aspen trees came into view. "Are we getting close?" she asked. She reached back and shook Ben's shoulder. "Wake your brothers and sisters. I want you to be watching when we get to our new home."

It was another hour before they reached a thick stand of aspen trees, the barks white with black patches, the limbs still barren of leaves from their winter dormancy. Through the stand of tree trunks she spotted a cabin, small and alone, as if the world had abandoned it to the elements.

The wagon rolled to a stop, then Clifford guided the team onto a side trail at the edge of the aspens, down a slope to a flat bench on which the cabin set.

Bethea grew uneasy. The cabin could be no larger than fourteen by sixteen feet. Some of the chinking had fallen out. Weeds kept company with the dead grass on the dirt roof. Two golden dandelion blossoms at one corner of the roof bobbed gently in the breeze, offering the only greeting to the new arrivals.

There were no other buildings. Past the cabin, a foot path led down a slope to the lake. Huge white swans gathered several yards from the shore, paying little attention to the intruders.

She laid her hand on Clifford's arm again. "Where is our house? You said we'd have a house."

He jumped from the wagon and offered his arms to her but she brushed his hand away and continued to stare at the cabin from the vantage point of the wagon seat. The children climbed down and began to explore the area.

Bethea swallowed the lump in her throat and clutched her clammy hands. She closed her eyes and pleaded for God to change everything. When she looked at the cabin again, it was still the same gray weathered log shack. If it had changed at all, it appeared smaller in the last rays of the sun shining through the skeletons of the grove.

"Come on down, Mrs. Kingston, and I'll show you around." Clifford grabbed her hand and hauled her off the wagon seat. "This is it," he said. "You're home."

EVERYONE HELPED with the unloading of the wagons. Even four-year-old Gabriel made himself useful by finding pine cones and twigs for the campfire to be built later in the evening.

As the men and older boys worked, Bethea tried to keep the food sacks separated from the household items. "Mr. Kingston, we'll need to dig a root cellar."

"We will. There's a spring between here and the lake," he called back. "We'll build a spring house, too, so don't you worry none." He halted in mid stride. "We've got all summer."

"Summers are short up here," the man from Monida said.

A breeze blew down from the forest on the mountain south of them and Bethea shivered.

As the man passed her, he paused. "This ain't the lowlands of Missouri, ma'am. You plan ahead for the worst. It's the only way if you're determined to stay. If you was my family, I'd haul you into town before the snows come."

Clifford, Adam and Ben spread a large tarpaulin over the crates and trunks and pounded stakes into the corners. Clifford came to peek into the cabin where they'd put the sacks of food. "You should have cleaned this out before you loaded it up." He glanced around the shadowy interior. "Where the hell do you expect me to sleep?"

Bethea knelt at an open sack of potatoes and dropped several into her apron. "The girls and I can sleep in here. You and the boys can bed down outside." She forced a smile. "I promised the boys they could sleep out under the stars the first night here. They need their father with them."

Clifford glanced over his shoulder at the man removing the last crate from the extra wagon. "We'll see."

Bethea watched him leave. Would he try to make amends by coming to her during the night? She grimaced. Love making had never been his way of apologizing, she thought. If anything, he used their conjugal unions as punishment, as if he had to prove he was her master. But that was his delusion. No man would ever be her true master, especially not Clifford.

"Make the best of where you find yourself," her mother had admonished more than once. Drawing from an inner well of strength that had begun to go dry, she went to the pile of household goods and retrieved a galvanized bucket.

"Where did you say the spring was located?" she called to Clifford. He pointed in the general direction of the lake. She already knew that much.

The older boys were still helping the man from town. David had joined Gabriel in bringing in pine cones. The girls were clearing the ground of twigs and stopping continually to talk to the rag dolls they carried in their arms.

She found a narrow foot trail leading toward the lake. Had human feet made it? When she spotted fresh deer droppings, she knew she was following a game trail. She stepped around a pile of larger droppings but couldn't identify them. Elk? Moose? *Do the local Indians use this trail? Mr. Adler's people?* No, she decided, he might be of mixed blood, but he had been raised in the ways of his English father. To her he was a man, not a half-breed as he had called himself, or the Injun term her own husband enjoyed using.

Twenty feet from the lake shore, she found the spring nestled in an outcropping of stones and springtime growth. She put her fingers into the flow. The temperature was tepid, not icy as she had expected. After filling the bucket, she straightened, pressing her hand against the small of her back. Weariness could easily get the best of her, but there was no time to give into it now. She had hours of work to do before she could retire.

Out on the lake, several huge white swans flapped their wings, squabbling among themselves. Bethea had never seen such large fowl. Their beaks were dark, and their wing span several feet from tip to tip. She set the bucket down and began to creep toward the shore. Not wanting to startle the swans, she eased down onto a large boulder and watched.

Oblivious to her presence, they went about their routine. Were they courting? Did swans court? She had read in one of her father's magazines that many species of birds practiced an unexplainable trait of mating for life, and if they lost their mate, they spent the rest of their lives alone.

Did that mean that birds could love the same way a man and woman could love? She sighed. How many men or women really loved the person they found themselves bound to? She had dealt with that reality, and still hadn't found a solution other than endurance. But wouldn't the Lord want more for his people? If He had made men and women with the power to love, why hadn't he given them the wisdom to select the right partner?

She pulled the woven shawl tighter around her shoulders. The sun dropped behind the mountains and the temperature cooled rapidly.

To the east, a glow began to fill the sky. She sat perfectly still as a full moon made its appearance above the darkening horizon. Had the Lord heard her prayers and sent this light? Was it a beacon to her, a promise of a new life here in this wilderness? Cynicism dimmed her joy. She should be thankful that they would not have to spend their first night in total darkness.

The swans, startled by movement behind her, took flight and were gone, dark objects against the golden orb of the moon. She stood up and turned. Clifford was standing at the spring, the full water bucket in his hand.

"This is no place for dawdling, Bethea. We're hungry. Get to cooking."

He headed toward the cabin, leaving her to find her own way up the path, but the glow of the moon comforted her. At least, he had had the decency to carry the bucket.

Another hour passed before she had supper ready. She looked at the boiled potatoes and carrots and knew it was not enough to satisfy the men. Inside the cabin, she felt her way to the smooth cloth of the flour sack and slid her hand upward in search of the fabric opening. Filling a tin cup, she hurried back to the fire.

She fried several thick slices of salt pork and used the drippings to parch a double handful of flour. Adding water from the bucket, she made a pan of brown gravy. When she tasted it, it was flat. She'd forgotten where she'd put the sacks of salt, she crumbled the fried salt pork into the gravy and hoped it would add enough flavor to satisfy everyone.

Mrs. Burns had given her three loaves of bread and she sliced two of them, then called everyone to supper.

"Tomorrow I'll be better organized," she said.

"Tastes fine to me, ma'am," the driver from town said. "Much obliged. This here is a feast compared to my beans and hard biscuits I'd have at my cabin in Monida." He helped himself to a second serving to show his appreciation.

Once the tin plates and flatware had been washed in a pan of water she'd heated on the stones around the camp fire, she opened the trunk with the bedding and the boys selected their spots around the fire. The girls complained they couldn't see in the cabin. To Bethea's surprise, Clifford carried the feather ticks inside. He returned to take the bedding from her arms and disappeared into the dark building again, reappearing several minutes later with two smiling daughters trailing behind him.

Bethea thought of her journal. There would be no entry made tonight. What could she write other than her disappointment over discovering her "house" had not lived up to her expectations?

She found the girls' and her night wear and took them into the cabin. From the glow of the campfire, she could see the bed rolls. Hers was near the sacks of staples while the girls had been placed against the opposite wall several feet away. She didn't much care. All she wanted to do was go to sleep.

After a trip to the willows with the girls, they bid the others good night. Esther and Faith were asleep within seconds of being tucked in, Bethea a few minutes later.

From a deep sleep, she heard a whisper and opened her eyes. Disoriented for a moment, she stared up at the man's silhouette looming over her. "Clifford?"

65

"Expecting someone else?" he asked, crawling onto her feather tick and adjusting the blankets. "I waited until everyone was asleep." His arms slid around her and his mouth sought hers.

Lying stiffly in his arms, she waited for the kiss to end. His tongue forced its way into her mouth and for a moment she thought she might gag. "We can't," she whispered when he lifted his head.

"We can if you stay quiet," he replied, his beard scratching her cheek as he nuzzled her ear.

"Clifford, please."

His hand slid beneath the covers, stroking her breast before sliding downward. He was fully dressed. In the darkness, she heard the soft clicking of metal as he unbuckled his belt and loosened his trousers. His breathing grew heavy.

"Lord, I've waited a long time for this," he said, pulling her gown up past her waist and stroking her naked abdomen. Without another word, he rolled on top of her, yanking her legs up on either side of his body and sliding into her.

She groaned from his weight and he took it to be pleasure.

"About time you showed a little passion toward you husband," he said, his hot breath scorching her neck. His mouth ground into hers as his thrusts pounded her against the ground.

He shuddered and lay heavily against her.

She shifted beneath him. "I can't breathe," she whispered.

He rolled off and settled onto the tick, his hand continuing to stroke her breast. To her disgust, her nipple hardened under his fingers.

He chuckled. "Why don't you let go and enjoy yourself?" he whispered. "Some women do, you know, like those gals in Butte City."

She bit her tongue to keep from asking how he knew. Had he been with other women while away from home? She'd never given it any thought before. He was a virile man. When at home, he'd taken her many nights in a row until her monthly flow gave her an excuse or a child had been conceived. He never touched her once she was carrying a baby again.

Through the flannel material, he took her nipple between his teeth. She tensed, knowing what would come next. When pain shot through her breast and he released her, she fought the tears that filled her eyes. How did he expect her to respond to him when he always ended their time together by inflicting pain?

She reached down and pushed her gown over her hips, ignoring the wetness between her legs. Her hand touched the warm flesh of his bare hip and his rumpled trousers and she jerked it away.

"Afraid you'll get me riled up again?" he whispered. Within minutes he had mounted her again.

When he got up from her tick and fastened his trousers, tears streamed down her cheeks and into the covering of the tick, but she sobbed without a sound. At least she couldn't conceive this time. That had been taken care of months earlier in Wilcox.

The next morning, she vowed to put the previous night behind her. She dressed quickly and quietly. The men would expect breakfast early. If she left her daughters asleep, she could work more efficiently.

Outside, the ground was covered with a white layer of frost. Her heart sank. How could she garden in this valley? The tender young plants could never survive to produce vegetables here. Over breakfast, she broached Clifford and the man from Monida about her concerns.

"You have to be careful what you plant," the man said. "Potatoes, carrots, peas. Root crops do the best but cabbages make heads sometime." He peered across the early morning campfire at her and shook his head. "Livestock does better here than vegetables."

"But what do they eat?," Bethea asked, recalling the miles of dry yellow ground cover on their way into the valley.

The man chuckled. "Why, ma'am, the grass grows lush in the meadows around the lakes and you can cut and cure it for winter feeding. Alice Livestock brings in mowers and teams and hauls it out by the wagon load. They move most of their stock back to Alice for the winter, but they've left the older steers here for the last few years. Seems they do okay if they have water and a few hay stacks to work on."

Clifford ignored the man's comments. "We'll mark off a garden plot tomorrow," he promised.

"I'd wait until next month," the man suggested.

"Tomorrow."

The man shrugged.

"And the cabin," Bethea said. "Eight people can't live in that one room, not if we have to stay inside for months at a time." She looked at the cabin again. Every time she stepped inside, it shrank. "Could you build another room, even just a lean-to?"

Clifford grinned at everyone. "George Adler had planned just that. He sold me a load of logs. They're seasoned and ready to use. They're up on the side hill." He pointed to the forest to the south.

The man from Monida scratched his head. "George Adler never cut a log or built a room his entire life."

Clifford sent him a warning glance. "The boys and I will start on it as soon as we get your garden plowed. There's enough for a spring house, too, so don't you fret your pretty little head about a thing, Mrs. Kingston. I'll make the decisions. You work on making this cabin a home and we'll get along fine."

"We need an necessary."

"Woman, don't nag."

"Away from the spring," she insisted. "People get sick when the outhouse is close to their drinking water. Papa told me."

"Your pa thinks he knows everything," Clifford said. "I know where to put an outhouse, for Christ's sake."

"I wouldn't want my family to get sick." She looked over at her sons and daughters who had grown quiet as the discussion between the grown-ups had escalated. "I don't even know where the nearest doctor lives."

"Eagle Rock or Dillon," the man from Monida said. "But I hear tell that one might be coming to Spring Hill before snowfall. He's a railroad doctor. The last one left because no one paid him."

"We're a healthy family," Clifford.

"Are there midwives around?" Bethea asked, knowing the question was inappropriate for mixed company.

"Mrs. Burns helps out and I hear tell the woman at the upper springs knows about herbs and healing, but if you want a doctor or nurse with training and education, you've come to the wrong place, ma'am."

Bethea sighed. She had six months to find a woman to come and help out. She had always had easy births and she had helped with a neighbor woman's birth of twins once.

Clifford leaned forward. "Any more concerns?"

She looked away, preferring to gaze at the lovely swans on the lake rather than the arrogant face of her husband. She doubted Clifford would be of much use during childbirth. He had always left such matters to the women in the family, scoffing at their preference to have a physician or midwife on hand.

"Why waste the money?" he had asked when she had gone into labor for the first time and had been terrified. He had sent for his mother.

"Don't forget firewood," the man from Monida said. "It takes a heap of fuel to survive the winter. You won't find coal around here, and the cow chips will be buried under three feet of snow by November."

Clifford scowled at the man. "I got a two-man saw and two strong boys," he said, pointing to his eleven and ten year old sons. "Boys, the wood pile is your job. You see that your mother has all she needs. You hear now?"

The boys looked at Bethea, then back at Clifford. "We never used a two-man saw before, Pa."

"What is this?" Clifford shouted. "A family of weaklings? You're almost grown men. You can handle it. I'll show you how. Nothing like a little sawing to build muscles."

LATE IN THE AFTERNOON of the third day, Bethea hurried to the spring to refill the two buckets with fresh water. She had nine people to cook for now. Clifford had hired the man from Monida for a week to speed up some of the construction of out buildings. The man's name was Chester Smith and he had become the peacemaker in their lives. A drifter in his younger days, he had settled in to work for a stockman who owned even more livestock than the Adlers.

When he'd been injured and could no longer cowboy, the rancher had given him clear title to the cabin and an acre of land at Monida. Now he earned a modest living hiring out to the Burns couple and the trickle of immigrants who occasionally got off the train in Monida and Spring Hill.

He never tired of answering the children's questions and at meal times Bethea would direct most of her remarks to him rather than her husband, for he was a pleasant natured man who enjoyed sharing his knowledge of the land and telling wild stories about the history of the county.

She set the heavy buckets of water down on the flat stones and ran light footed to the lake. She had time to enjoy the view for a few minutes. A pair of swans were several yards from her, three newly hatched gray cygnets paddling between the adults. Bethea smiled and watched in silence.

"Bethea?"

The shout startled the swans and they took flight for a few awkward seconds before settling back onto the water and swimming away with their cygnets.

Bethea turned around. Clifford stood behind her, an axe in one hand. His shirt was dark with sweat and even from where she stood, she could smell his strong odor.

She adjusted her sun bonnet and looked at him. "Did you want me?"

He smiled, but it held no affection. "I'll control myself. I've left you alone for two nights now. You're my wife and you owe it to me, company or no company. We wouldn't want Smith to think we weren't getting alone." He reached out and his grimy fingers stroked her cheek, leaving a streak on her skin.

She forced herself to stand still. "You...may want to change your mind," she said, swallowing hard.

"Why?" he asked, sliding his fingers to her breast.

"I'm...expecting...a baby again."

His eyes narrowed. "How could you know after three days?"

She took a deep breath and exhaled. "It happened in March, when you came to Wilcox." She dropped her gaze to the pebbles in the sandy beach. "I'm sorry. I didn't want this to happen." When she looked up again, the expression in his eyes confirmed her hope that now he would leave her alone.

CHAPTER SEVEN

"I'M TAKING the team and wagon to Red Rock Station," Con said as he emptied his coffee cup.

Victoria leaned against the counter. "I do hope Matthias gets home today. It's been almost a month now. If he caught a through train to Salt Lake, could he?"

"I'll wait around for the train," Con murmured. "If he's not on it, I'll leave a message with the station master about the team in the livery. Don't fret, Mother, he's fine."

Two hours later, Con reclined in a chair on the porch of the station reading the weekly newspaper from the county seat. It wasn't a bad newspaper, if the reader was satisfied with prewritten articles about world and states events, serialized novels, lots of advertisements, and a page and a half of local gossip. Sometimes he wondered why the editor didn't write more news of substance about the county. He scanned the gossip columns again and a paragraph jumped from the page.

"Bannock bucks and squaws have been numerous around town lately. The new crop of papooses compares favorably with last year's crop."

Damned insensitive bastard, Con thought. The next paragraph reported, "The ladies of Beaverhead Valley are attending the Saturday afternoon rink reunions and joining in the pleasurable pastime of roller skating." *One group of women skates without a care in the world while the other spends its time collecting seeds and berries so their children won't starve.* Con looked across the dusty road that lead northward to the county seat. *Where's the justice of it all?*

Caught in between the two groups were women like Bethea Kingston. She had been on his mind daily and now that his father was due to return, the time had come for the inspection trip to the upper Centennial Valley and its neighboring Alaska Basin where they summered their stock. That meant a stop at the Kingston cabin to try to convince them to sell their land back to the Alice Livestock Company. The livestock had already spent a month near the lower end, but the dry weather had stunted the grasses and soon it would be time to move them to the basin above the upper lake.

The train came and left without Matthias Adler. Con rode home on Hellion, keeping the stallion at an easy lope.

"He wasn't there," he said to his disappointed step-mother.

Two days later, as they sat down to the evening meal, the front door opened and two men stepped inside.

Victoria leaped from her chair. "Matthias!" Her smile said more than words could have, but when she looked at the other man, her eyes filled with tears. "Lee, oh, Lee, you've come home." Her attention shifted back to the taller, older man whose only acknowledgment was a subtle arch of a dark brown brow. "How did you two...why are you...? Oh, who cares, you're here."

She ran across the room and threw her arms around Matthias's neck and claimed his mouth. When their lips finally parted, Matthias took Victoria's face in his hands and gazed at her for several seconds, then kissed her again. Gradually becoming aware of their audience, they separated and she turned to the other man. An inch or two shorter than Matthias and still displaying the slenderness of youth, the young man shifted from foot to foot as Victoria gave him her full attention.

She wiped her cheeks. "Leander Taylor Adler, if you aren't a blessed sight to your mother's eyes." She reached out and touched his cheek, then laughed. "And you're shaving now. Oh, what have I missed? You're not a boy anymore."

His face showed the promise of the handsomeness of his father, but now he looked every bit a sixteen year old boy. "Hello, Mama," he said, holding his arms out to her.

She hugged her youngest son until Matthias touched her shoulder. "Don't squeeze the life out of him, Mother."

She laughed, then took their hands and led them to the table. "You must be starved. We're just sitting down. I promise to withhold all questions until you've eaten, so hurry."

Con watched his parents and his youngest brother approach the table and stood up. "Welcome home, Lee." He started to extend his hand but instead embraced his brother. He'd been touched by the reunion of loved ones, yet he felt strangely detached from it. Lee was their blood son. He shook the feeling aside.

Moodiness was seldom a problem for him, but now with the return of his father, the trip to the valley loomed, and with it the chance to see Bethea Kingston again. He reached for the bowl of mashed potatoes, took a generous serving, and passed the bowl to his brother.

"Con, we haven't had the blessing yet," Victoria said.

He looked up to find everyone staring at him. "Sorry," he mumbled and waited while Matthias blessed the meal. When he stared down at the roast beef and gravy, the potatoes, a big helping of greens, all he could see was the image of Bethea Kingston's face as they had shared their first meal at the hotel in Monida, her animated features as she discussed their train trip west, her loving gazes at her children, and the way she had looked into his eyes when their hands had touched as she passed him a platter of sliced bread.

"Now, tell me why you two are together?" Victoria asked after she cleared the table of the main course and put a berry pie on the table and began to serve generous slices to everyone.

Matthias withdrew a piece of paper from his shirt pocket and handed it to her. "We did well in Omaha, better than I'd expected. The buyer liked the condition of the steers and said to contact him this fall when we have more to ship."

Victoria studied the bank draft, then handed it to Con. He whistled softly and gave it back to his father.

Matthias touched his youngest son's shoulder. "I rode back on the Northern Pacific." He looked at his wife. "I've been thinking about Lee and wanted to see him...so I got off in Butte City. It took me three days to track him down. That's one bustling mining camp, isn't it, son?" He grinned at his son.

Lee's face flushed. "It's okay if you like everything dark. Sometimes they have to light the gaslights at noon because there's so much stuff in the air. I couldn't breath."

Matthias nodded his agreement. "The lights were on this morning when we caught the train. When I found Lee and saw where he was living, I convinced him that we needed an extra hand in the valley this summer."

"So you hired your own son?" Victoria asked.

Matthias chuckled. "He told me he grew up on a cattle ranch about this size. I told him I wasn't always easy to work for, and he said his own father was bull headed, too, and we went to dinner and talked about fathers and sons. I told him I had a son about his age but he ran away from home when he was fourteen to work in the mines without ever telling me why."

"I told him the reasons didn't matter, but that the kid must have been stupid," Lee added.

Matthias shook his head. "I said everyone has to find his own way. We made a pact. If we have a good year, he can take his bonus pay in shares of Alice Livestock." He looked at Victoria again. "Did I do the right thing, Mother?"

She paused in the pouring of coffee from a large granite pot, set it down on the table, and came to them. She kissed her husband's cheek, then her son's. "I sincerely hope so." She looked across the table to Con, who nodded subtly and smiled. "Maybe Lee can go with you and Con to the valley to see if it's ready for the stock."

"Being in the saddle is what I've missed most," Lee said. "I told Dad I'd work wherever he needed me." Lee looked over at Con. "God damn, I hated those mine tunnels. No one should have to go underground to earn a living." He shuddered.

As Con watched his father, he sensed a change in the strong willed man who had always had a problem with his two younger sons. At times Con wondered if the fact that he had relatives at Lemhi had been a reminder to his father that Con had an alternative life to adopt if he wanted it.

For his two white sons, that option didn't exist, yet they had found their own solutions when Matthias's heavy handed manner had gotten the best of them. Quentin had been working at the Glendale smelter for two years and now at eighteen had been promoted to assistant timber foreman on a logging crew that worked above the mines to get timber for the charcoal kilns.

Lee, as strong willed as his father, had hopped a freight to Butte City after a violent argument with Matthias about Matthias's refusal to listen to Lee's reasons for disobeying the foreman. Con couldn't even remember the details of the blow up, except that a week later his father had fired the foreman for pilfering.

Matthias would be having his sixtieth birthday soon. Maybe he had begun to mellow. For everyone's sake Con hoped so. Families were too precious to tarnish with conflict.

He concentrated on his pie. How was the Kingston family doing? Settled in? Was Clifford Kingston the devoted husband Bethea deserved? He stared at the purple filling of the pie. Were they good lovers? Did she respond to him, enjoy his touch, give him thrust for thrust? He choked down the groan that surged up his throat at the thought of them in bed. He hated the man sight unseen. His body began to respond to the visual images of his unruly mind. Thank God no one at the table could see the heavy beats of his heart or the way his blood had begun to boil.

"Don't you agree, Con?" Victoria asked.

His head jerked up. "What?"

Victoria studied him for several seconds, then patted his hand. "I was telling your father that the sooner he makes the trip to the valley, the sooner we...*resolve*...any problems he may find there." She looked at the men around the table.

Mexican Pete took his plate and utensils to the sink. "I reckon this is a family matter," he said, excusing himself. "I hear the bunkhouse calling."

Matthias ran his hand through his graying hair as he watched Mexican Pete leave the house. "What did he mean by that?"

Victoria glanced at Lee, then Con, but avoided direct eye contact with her husband. "Con, you know more about this than I do. All my knowledge is second hand from you and George."

Matthias scowled at his wife. "Where is my brother?"

"Gone," Victoria said, her voice so soft that Matthias had to lean toward her to hear.

"Gone where?" Lee asked.

Victoria squared her shoulders. "To Butte City and then Kentucky."

Lee slapped the table edge. "See, Dad, I told you I saw Uncle George down on Mercury Street." He glanced at his mother. "I saw him in one of those places."

"I know what's on Mercury, young man" Victoria said. "And what were you doing in that part of town?"

"Mom, all the men go there after a shift underground," Lee replied, but his youthful face didn't strengthen his argument in Victoria's eyes.

"That city is the Sodom of Montana Territory," she said.

Matthias chuckled. "Then Dillon is the Gomorrah."

"I thought that honor went to Spring Hill," Con said.

"The guys in the mines say Last Chance Gulch is better," Lee offered.

Matthias laid a large hand on his youngest son's shoulder. "I don't think we're talking about degrees of goodness here, and before we upset your mother, let's get back to the problems of Centennial Valley and your missing uncle." He leaned toward Victoria. "Why did George leave?"

"There was this...difference of opinion," she murmured.

Con stretched his legs under the table and slouched in his chair. "I slugged him."

Matthias's gaze shifted between his wife and son. When neither offered an elaboration, he leaned back in his captain's chair and pressed his palms against the table. "Why did you slug your uncle, Chugan?"

Con flinched at the use of his Indian name. "He insulted a woman."

"Why?"

"Because he didn't know her."

"And you did? Where did you meet her? Spring Hill? Dillon? You probably both wasted your energies. I know the kind of women George messes with, but I'm surprised at you. You're not a drinking man, so what were you doing with George in a whore house?"

Con straightened. "She got off the train at Monida," he said. "George knew who she was but I didn't. George left but I stayed to help her and the children. Her husband didn't meet her so I...oh, hell, I stayed an extra day. She was a stranger and she was very..."

"Pretty?"

Con's gaze met his father's as the two men tried to read behind the masks of their equally strong features. "I don't remember."

"Oh? You laid over an extra day to help a married woman in distress but you don't remember what she looks like?" Matthias continued to stare across the table at Con.

"She might have been...noticeably attractive, but she and the children were stranded." Con kept his face immobile. "I came home as soon as I knew her husband was coming."

"How does this involve my brother and why did it lead to blows?" Matthias asked.

"Uncle George sold this woman's husband one of his quarter sections of land in the Valley, the piece with the cabin on it, the one where my mother is buried." Con tried to recall that period in his childhood but no memories surfaced. "I'm wrong. He didn't sell it. He lost it at a gaming table in Butte City."

Matthias's complexion turned gray beneath his tan. "I told him I'd buy it from him anytime he wanted to pull up stakes and return to the states."

"He was losing at faro and if I know my uncle he had been drinking all night," Con said. "Now the Kingstons have come to the valley to live. It's his fault the woman is there, but he had no right to insult her." He stared down the length of the table before returning his gaze to his father. "I lost my temper and knocked him on his backside. He left the next day on the train. We haven't heard from him since."

Matthias looked at his wife. "Then we'll leave first thing tomorrow morning. I want to see what kind of woman could bring my own family to blows."

"Please, can't you stay a few days to rest up?" she pleaded. "Lee needs to settle into being home. Con can tell you about the family and you'll be better prepared when you meet them."

"Con can tell me about her while we're on the trail," Matthias said, rising from the head of the table. "I'll help you clean up here so we can...I brought you something special from Omaha."

Con stifled his chuckle but his younger brother was less successful. He couldn't remember the last time his father had helped in the kitchen. Maybe he was anxious to get his wife alone in their bedroom for a more intimate reunion. The thought of a married couple alone brought his thoughts rudely to the Kingstons again.

"Damn it," he hissed, standing up.

"What did you say, dear?" Victoria asked, standing next to Matthias with her arm around his waist.

Con frowned at them. "Did I say something?"

"I believe so."

He tightened his mouth and left the cabin. Searching out a shadowy corner of the porch, he pulled the makings from his pocket. In minutes, he was smoking a clumsily rolled cigarette. Tonight his hands couldn't manage the paper and tobacco any better than his mind could stay away from Bethea Kingston.

MATTHIAS ADLER AND HIS TWO SONS rode away early the next morning, caught the train at Red Rock and rode it to Monida, and headed to the hotel.

Emiline Burns greeted them with her usual gusto. "Hi, good looking," she said to Matthias, bussing his cheek.

He grinned like a young boy.

"And you, Leander, you've grown a foot and filled out," she said after giving him a generous hug. "Give you a few more years and the girls in these parts will be a'panting at your heels."

Lee blushed beet red.

"But you'll always be my favorite Adler man," she said to Con, who accepted her embrace. She peered into his eyes and patted his cheek. "You okay?" she asked softly so the others wouldn't hear.

"Fine," Con replied, knowing full well who she was referring to. "If you still have a fire in that stove of yours, how about cooking up three of your fabulous steaks, with fried potatoes and whatever else you can find."

"I'll get 'em started right away," she said, hurrying to the stove. Her husband came in and visited with the Adlers.

"What brings you three to Monida?" Bill Burns asked, as Emiline Burns served their steak dinners.

"Seems we have squatters on our land at the upper lake," Matthias said.

"They're not squatters," Con said. He looked up and caught Mrs. Burns's gaze. "Have you heard from them?" he asked.

"No, but Chester Smith has been working for them off and on this entire month," she replied.

Con shifted uncomfortably. "How are they?"

"The misses, I hear, is fine," Emiline said. "Chester says she works too hard, but a woman on a place like that can't expect much else."

"And the children?"

"Normal," she said, smiling. "One minute they're under foot and fighting and the next, they're helping like little beavers."

Con took a bite of his steak and tried to enjoy it.

"Don't you want to know about the mister?" Emiline asked.

"Not particularly," Con admitted.

"I hear tell he's a real son-of-a-bitch," Bill Burns offered.

"You could tell that the minute he stepped off the train that first morning," Emiline added.

Con's eyes narrowed. "He arrived on schedule?"

"Pompous ass," Emiline said, then scurried to another table. When she had taken their orders and started the cooking, she returned to the Adlers. "I listened, maybe I eavesdropped. He belittled her every time she asked a question. She's as intelligent as she is pretty, and he treats her like an idiot."

"Why does she put up with it?" Lee asked, glancing at Con.

"Count all those younguns for one thing," Emiline volunteered. "She's trapped, that's what she is, and all because she chose a bastard for a husband."

Bill Burns laid his hand on his wife's arm. "Emi, you don't know it's as bad as all that."

"I'll wager it is."

Bill didn't answer, so she huffed and went to check the food cooking on the stove.

"What's Chester Smith doing for them?" Matthias asked.

"Building a root cellar and adding a room," Bill Burns relied. "He comes in for supplies every week or so. He brought the oldest boy with him once. He says he'd quit if it wasn't for the woman and kids. Says Kingston takes trips to Virginia City and leaves them alone, but Chester says he gets more work done with him away." He shrugged. "I try to stay out of another fellow's business. Hope this fellow isn't as bad as everyone's speculating. She's a determined lady, and if he leaves her alone, she'll make it."

"Not if I have my way," Matthias said.

Bill scowled. "Are you going to drive her off?"

"Hell, no. I'm going to buy her out, then I'll drive her off," Matthias replied. "Well, boys, we might as well get this over with. I'll meet you at the livery in a half hour. I want to speak to the station master first."

"I want to look around the store," Lee said. He followed Bill Burns out the door.

"I'll hang around here," Con said. After several minutes the room was empty and Emiline Burns joined him with two cups of fresh coffee.

"How is she really?" he asked without looking up.

"She's coping."

He mulled over her remark. "She deserves better."

"I know." Emiline took a sip. "I send her little things whenever Chester comes to town. She hasn't come in once. Bill and I talked it over and decided we'd send her and the kids old Bossy, but it's hard to sneak a milk cow onto the place without Kingston noticing it. Chester says Kingston rules his roost with a heavy fist."

"Damn him."

She touched his hand. "You fell for her pretty hard, didn't you, honey? But with all those kids, maybe it was just as well that her husband showed up. What if he hadn't? What would you have done then?"

He shook his head slowly from side to side. How could he explain the emotions that churned inside him whenever he thought of Bethea Kingston?

"She was disappointed when you ran out on her," Emiline said. "When I went to get the bedding I couldn't help noticing the pillow case she'd used on that little cot you moved into their room. She either cried herself to sleep the night you left, or she spilled something salty on it."

"You can't be sure," he murmured. "Why would she come all the way out here to be with her husband if she didn't love him?"

She arched a brow. "Sometimes things happen, people meet, maybe even fall in love, when everything about it is wrong, but sometimes the problems flip over and everything works out right."

"We've only spent a few hours together," he murmured. "We never had time to talk. I know little about her and she knows next to nothing about me."

"Maybe that's the reason you liked each other," she countered. "The two of you had no distractions."

"Have you forgotten about her husband, the six kids, and my mixed blood?" He stared across the room. "I wanted to stay the rest of the day, but what would it have proved?"

She nodded. "And if you'd stayed, there could have been trouble."

Matthias stuck his head in the door and called to Con.

"See you round," Con mumbled, retrieving his hat from the peg near the door as he left the building. Emiline Burns had been right. There would have been trouble, and trouble was probably waiting for them if Kingston was home.

The ride into the valley was silent except for the steady gait of their horses' hooves. Con's thoughts were on Bethea. He was sure his father's were centered on getting the deed back into Adler hands, and his little brother Lee? Who knew what was going on Lee's mind? He'd surprised the entire family by his disappearance at such a young age, and had written to his mother only twice, yet he had returned with the very person who had driven him away.

Con glanced over at his brother. The older Lee got, the more he looked and acted like his father. At least Con had never had the added burden in growing up of being a carbon copy of Matthias Adler, a man who had become a legend in his own time. Con was his own man, and came and went at his own pace. The mother he couldn't remember had left a legacy beyond the shade of his skin, for she had given him options.

Several hours later the cabin loomed in the distance.

Lee pointed. "Look, they've added a new room. Hey, Dad, why didn't you ever add on to it for us? Remember how the girls and Mom stayed inside and we slept out under the stars."

Matthias shrugged. "I'm a good stockman, and a damned good trapper and tracker, but a carpenter I'm not. Why do you think I hired McCune from Dillon to do the new house?"

"If I stay on, do I get my own room?" Lee asked. He was beginning to sound more like a sixteen year old, Con thought, and the idea of him living on his own for two years in a mining boom town, with all its worldly temptations, seemed inconceivable.

Matthias frowned. "If that's what it'll take to keep you around for a few years, sure, you can have one. It has eight bedrooms. Take your pick, except for the large one on the north end of the second floor. That one belongs to your parents."

"Eight bedrooms?" Lee looked at Con and grinned. "Is one of my sisters expecting triples?"

"You're behind on the news, Lee," Con said. "Rhoda made you an uncle, and the other two are expected around Christmas."

"Whoopee," Lee exclaimed. "Why didn't someone tell me?"

In the distance, two little boys came running down the trail, waving their straw hats wildly.

Matthias reined in his mount. "How many children do they have?" he asked.

"Six."

Matthias's head whipped around. "Six?"

Con stood up in his stirrups, took off his felt hat and waved it at the boys. "Yeah, six. Good kids, too."

The boys raced down the trail, their bare feet kicking up puffs of dust behind them. The three horsemen stopped and waited for the boys to reach them.

"Hi, Mr. Adler, did you come to see our ma?" the taller boy asked.

Matthias looked curiously at Con, but Con ignored him. "Want a ride to the cabin?" he asked the boys.

The boys jumped up and down excitedly.

"Father, do you have room?"

Matthias's frown deepened.

Con turned to Lee. "How about you? Got room for the little one? He's Gabriel."

Lee reached down and grabbed the boy's hand and hoisted him up behind him. "David, you can ride with me," Con said, swinging the other boy up behind him. David's thin arms slid around Con's waist. In spite of what might lay ahead for them all, he was glad to see the children. They had become constant companions along with their mother in his thoughts.

"Is your pa home?" he asked David.

"Nah, he and Mama had a fight and he rode off yesterday, that way!" David's finger pointed to the east. "But Mama's here. She'll be glad to see you!" He bounced on Hellion's rump. "Can you make Hellion go faster?"

Con kicked the stallion's flanks and the horse broke into a gallop. "Hang on," Con said, but to be sure the boy was safe, he pressed the boy's hands hard against his stomach. They reached the yard in a cloud of dust, and the other children gathered around them. Con swung David to the ground and dismounted.

"We galloped all the way," David bragged. "As fast as the wind, didn't we, Uncle Con?"

The title brought a lump to Con's throat. "Sure, David. Father and Lee, come meet the rest of the family."

Matthias was still scowling when he approached the children. "Ragamuffins, the whole lot," he grumbled under his breath.

The children were all barefoot. The boys' trousers reached half way up to their knees. The girls wore faded calico dresses that had seen many scrubbings on the wash board.

"Children, this is my father, Mr. Adler, and my little brother Lee."

Faith smiled up at Lee. "He's not so little," she said.

Con chuckled. "Maybe you're right," he said, brushing a strand of blond hair from her eyes. "This is Adam, Ben, David, Esther, Faith and Gabriel." Con found the youngest child's grin irresistible and tickling the boy's tummy, he swung him up into the crook of his elbow. "Say hello, everyone."

Matthias Adler extended his hand to each of the children, nodding and repeating their names in order, but when he straightened again, his frown had deepened.

Con touched his father's sleeve. "Mr. Kingston isn't here. He's gone to Virginia City." He looked at the children again. "Where's your mother?"

"The water buckets were empty and she couldn't do dishes, so she went to the spring," Esther said. "I'll show you."

"Father, will you and Lee stay here with the rest of the children? Esther and I will find Bethea, I mean Mrs. Kingston, and let her know she has company. Maybe she has coffee and we can all sit down and discuss this like reasonable grownups.

"Doubtful," Matthias grumbled, but when Gabriel held up his small cupped hand, the older man knelt on one knee to inspect some treasure the boy had pulled from his pocket.

Esther took Con's hand and led him down the narrow foot path to the spring, but the only evidence that Bethea Kingston had been there were the two empty water buckets perched on the flat stones nearby. He looked down at Esther. "Where could she be?"

"Sometimes she walks along the lake," the girl said. "We like to watch the swans and their little babies, but you gotta be very very quiet. Mama says so."

As they approached the shoreline, the ground changed to a pale sandy beach for several yards before disappearing into the shallow lake bed. Movement caught his attention and he looked toward the west. His heart twisted when he saw her. Her back was toward them and the bright sun to the west had cast her outline into a dark silhouette.

A gray shawl covered her shoulders and beneath it the dark green fabric of her full skirt billowed in the breeze. Her head was bare and several strands had slipped from the knot on the back of her head to coil down her back. The sun turned her hair into a copper halo.

Con cautioned Esther to silence. Together they walked toward the solitary woman.

"Bethea?"

She stiffened, then slowly turned around.

"Mama, don't you remember Uncle Con?" Esther asked, tugging Con closer. "He brought his daddy and his little brother with him, too." She giggled. "Only he's not so little. He's almost as tall as Uncle Con."

Bethea pressed her fist to her bosom and her mouth opened and shut. For a moment he couldn't tell if she was glad to see him or not, but when her mouth changed to a trembling smile and her eyes turned as shiny as the lake water behind her, the vice around his chest began to loosen.

"Well, aren't you gonna shake hands?" Esther asked.

Bethea released one side of her shawl and slowly extended her right hand. He'd forgotten how small her hand was until he felt it slide against his palm. After an endless month of missing her beyond belief, he had to be content with this simple gesture. She tugged the shawl around her and tossed one fringed end over her shoulder, then offered her other hand.

Clasping both of her hands in his, he squeezed them. "I've been thinking about you," he murmured.

"And I've thought about you, so many times," she murmured.

"How are you?"

"Busy."

"Feeling fine?" He didn't understand the flash of concern that passed over her features.

"I'm fine," she said, tightening her grip. "I didn't expect you."

"I didn't think to send my calling card ahead," he said, unable to suppress his joy. "But there's no mail service, is there? Want to apply for a post office?"

"Would you write me a letter?" She smiled and her eyes sparkled.

"As long as only your eyes would see it."

"That could prove difficult," she murmured. "But we did get a letter from my mother one time. The driver of the stage going to the geysers brought it."

"Someday I'll take you there," he said and as he spoke the promise, he wondered why he had made it.

Her face turned pale, and she eased her hands from his. She tied the ends of her shawl into knots and shielded her eyes with her hand. "Why did you really come?"

She fiddled with the fringe on her shawl until he took her hand again, forcing her to met his gaze. "Bethea, he came to buy this place back."

CHAPTER EIGHT

BETHEA STARED at Con, still startled to see him again, and here at the lake of all places. Yet, as she gazed across the few feet that separated them, she felt herself edging closer to breaking he vows of marriage, in her thoughts if not in deed.

"Our land is not for sale. If we sold out, we'd have to leave." She turned away to stare across the expanse of the lake. Happiness for her loomed as out of reach as the distant shore. If she moved back to Missouri, she would have to give up the smallest hope of ever seeing him again. He should mean nothing to her, but as the entries in the journal had progressed, she had created a fantasy world in which she had found happiness.

She had written Clifford out of the journal and replaced him with a warm and loving Con Adler. Their days were filled with working together to make a good life for themselves and the children. Their nights were filled with passion and whispered words of longing followed by fulfillment, caresses that made her pulse surge as she wrote the words. It mattered not that they were living in sin in the eyes of man, for God in heaven had blessed their union.

No one must ever read her journal. Clifford would be outraged. Con would be shocked. Her parents would deny their daughter could ever have written such scandalous thoughts, and her children? She refused to imagine what her children would think, much less the grandchildren whom she had in mind when she'd started keeping the journals. Yet she knew she could never stop writing until the story was completed.

She hugged herself, trying to ignore her thickening waistline. Thank goodness, she had wrapped the shawl around her. Entering her fifth month, her condition would be obvious to another woman but not to most men. She had felt movement for the first time a week earlier. In order to cope, she had separated her hatred for Clifford from her love for this unborn child. At times she wondered if she was slowly losing her mind.

Con's hands touched her shoulders, and she turned. His face swam before her eyes. "Hold me," she whispered, and without a word, he drew against him.

Her arms slid around him and in her mind's eye she saw the flexing of his muscles as he held her. He was taller than any man in her family, yet his size seemed to fit hers, her head nestled against his shoulder, her breasts cushioned against his shirt front. By shifting her hand a few inches she would be able to rest them against his hips. Such fine hips, she thought, not too narrow but in perfect proportion to his trim body and broad shoulders. And fine shoulders, well shaped from years of work, masculine. Would he be tanned or pale?

If only I could see for myself, in private, touch his bare skin, caress him, tell him... Her cheeks flamed from the heat of her own wanton thoughts.

She felt a tug on her skirt. Con eased his embrace and they looked down at Esther.

"Are you gonna kiss him now?"

Bethea's breath caught in her lungs and she dared to look again into Con's eyes. Dark blue and stormy, they revealed his desires, and she hoped his will power was stronger than her own, for she had little. His mouth moved and her gaze slid to his lips. How would they feel against hers? Soft? Rough? Eager to take hers?

"I think you should," Esther said, giggling. "I won't tell Daddy."

The child's words brought reality crashing in and they stepped apart. "The buckets," Bethea murmured. "I came for water. The cabin is a mess with dirty dishes." She tucked a coil of hair back into the bun. "But I have a pie left and I could make fresh coffee. The pie is from canned fruit. The berries aren't ripe yet. The cabin is crowded but..."

He put his finger against her lips. "I know," he said, his voice deep and mellow. "My parents used to bring us here during the summers when I was young. Maybe that's why my father wants the place back. He has memories."

She stepped away. Only by staying away from him could she think rationally. "Someday it will have memories for us, too. It's not for sale, but you're still welcome to pie and coffee."

His handsome mouth softened into a slight grin. "If those are your terms, I accept. My father will have to speak for himself. He can be a strong willed man."

"I'm stronger than I look," she said.

His smile widened. "I'm sure you are."

At the spring, she filled the buckets, but when she started to grab the handles, he stopped her.

"I'll do that," he said.

When they reached the cabin, Con took the buckets inside but Bethea turned to her visitors. The older man removed his hat, revealing a full head of chestnut brown hair liberally salted with gray. He and Con shared a strong family resemblance and were almost the same height, yet the two men were different. Not so with the teenaged boy sitting on a stump talking to Adam and Ben. He was a carbon copy of his father.

She approached the older man. "I'm Mrs. Kingston." She extended her hand. He hesitated for a second then took it.

"I'm Matthias Adler," the man said, "and that's my youngest son Lee." He glanced up as Con joined them. "You and my oldest son seem to know each other."

She pulled her hand free and rubbed it against her skirt. "Yes, we met in Monida."

Matthias shook something in his fist. "Your youngest son showed me this coin. Maybe you didn't know he had it. He insists he found it."

He dropped a gold coin into her palm. Startled, she turned to Gabriel. "Where did you get this?"

"The morning Papa came on the train," Gabriel exclaimed. "I found it in the dirt on my way to the necessary. Ben says only a crazy man or a drunk would throw money away and he tried to take it from me, but it's mine. Finders keepers, heah?"

Images of the encounter behind the hotel the first night of her arrival came rushing back and she looked at Con and was doubly shaken when he came to her side and laid his hand on her shoulder.

"Right, Gabriel, finders keeper," he said, his hand tightening before dropping to his side. "Maybe you should give it to your mother for safe keeping."

"No, I don't want it," Bethea said. "I mean...Gabriel is a careful boy. He won't lose it." She turned her attention to Matthias again. "Con told me why you've come. The land is not for sale, but you're welcome to come inside and have something to eat before you ride on." She turned to the children. "You can all go play."

"Can we hike to the second hill?" Adam asked, pointing to the east.

"Yes, but stay within shouting distance," she warned.

"I'll go with them," Lee offered.

She waited until they disappeared over the first hill before going inside, motioning for the two men to follow her. After putting on a pan of water to heat for the dishes, she prepared the coffee and served the pie.

Con represented the dark side of passion and desire for her, while Matthias was the epitome of power and authority. She studied the two men. In another woman's eyes the descriptions of the two men might well be reversed.

When the coffee had been served, she sat down across from them. "This place is not for sale," she said, pulling the deed from her apron pocket and spreading it on the table. "My husband bought it for a valid sum, so you have no right to challenge the faro game or anything else, only the wisdom of the former owner for letting it go for five dollars." She took a deep breath and waited, her hands clutched in her lap out of sight. They were shaking and she wasn't sure she could retrieve the paper.

"You're right, Mrs. Kingston, my brother was a fool to put up this property," Matthias said. "I'm prepared to pay you a thousand dollars for it, and pay your expenses for moving. Where are you from?"

"Wilcox, Missouri, but we're not going back there," she said, glancing toward Con.

"Then anywhere you want to relocate."

She shook her head.

Matthias's brow furrowed, and she clinched her teeth until her jaw began to ache.

"Two thousand, that's my top offer."

"Fine," she replied.

"You accept it?" Matthias asked.

"No, I wouldn't sell for ten times two thousand," she insisted. "This is going to be our home ranch someday."

Matthias burst out laughing. "Your husband must be a dreamer."

Her shoulders stiffened. "It's not his dream, it's mine." Her eyes narrowed. "Come back in ten years and you'll see."

89

"Woman, you have no common sense, not an ounce of it!"

"I have as much as you do," she shouted back. "Did you start with your giant Alice Livestock land and cattle? You must have had a dream, or you wouldn't be so successful. You fought for what you wanted. I will, too."

Con laid his hands on each of theirs. "Father, she's right. Why don't you admit you've met your match?" Con looked across the table at Bethea and smiled again. Matthias glanced at his son, then at her. "If I didn't know better..." He frowned again. "For hell's sake, Con, she's a married woman."

"I know that," Con replied. "She's also a determined business woman. Give her credit for that."

"For Christ's sake, whose side are you on?"

Bethea rose to get the coffee pot again.

"You have no right to deny me my land," Matthias said.

She turned to him again. "If it was your land, the deed should have been in your name." She lifted her chin. "It belongs to the Kingstons now. Accept it."

"Stubborn woman," Matthias said.

"Bull headed man," she retorted.

They glared at each other, and Con stepped free of the table, ready to protect Bethea if necessary.

"Forget it," Matthias said scornfully. "This is a damned waste of time." He stalked to the stove and glared down at Bethea. "I don't know what's between you and my son, but I raised him to know the difference between right and wrong, and this god-awful thing between you two smells to high heaven. You're a fool to turn down my money and you'll live to regret it. If you think you can survive a winter in this valley, you're crazy. It's a killer. No one stays."

She stepped away from him, feeling her confidence beginning to crumble. "That's your opinion, Mr. Adler. I'm entitled to mine. Con and I are simply friends, so you needn't worry about your family and its sterling reputation, if that's what's bothering you. So leave me be!"

Matthias stomped back to the crude slab table and grabbed his hat. At the door he turned. "We'll be moving livestock through here next month. Keep out of our way."

"Are you threatening me?" she asked, chasing after him. "I can't move the land or the cabin, but you can move your damned cows, and if you try to run over us, I'll...I'll shoot you and the cows, too. I have a gun." They didn't have to know that Clifford always took the guns with him when he went on his mysterious trips.

He stared down at her and laughed. "You wouldn't have a chance at either, young woman. Con, we're wasting our time here. Say good-by to her if you must. I'll go get Lee. Mark my words, Mrs. Kingston. You'll live to regret this decision to stay here, and my son will live to regret ever meeting you." He turned away, his broad shoulders hunched as he slammed the door behind him.

Con lingered inside the door, his face immobile.

Bethea retrieved the deed and folded it carefully before slipping it into her pocket again. "I'm sorry."

"I'm sorry, too," he said as he cupped her cheek in the palm of his large hand.

She wanted to turn her head and kiss it, but she suppressed the urge. "You should go," she murmured.

"When my father cools down, he'll admit he's wrong," he said. "The Adlers don't have a sterling reputation but we've never run our stock over another person's property just to destroy it. You're safe here as long as I'm around." His hand slid to the underside of her chin, stroking the soft skin a few times. "If you need me, send a message to Emiline Burns."

"I'll be fine," she replied, wanting him to pull her into his arms again and hold her, but he didn't. She followed him outside and watched as he rode over the hill and out of sight.

THE GOOD LORD had been watching over the Kingston family for sure, Bethea thought, as she stooped to pull a handful of radishes from her garden. The weather had turn quite hot during the middle of July and now in August, the days were scorching, but the nights still cooled to the forties and fifties, giving a person a comfortable sleep beneath a blanket.

Under better circumstances, she could fall in love with the valley. It was a place of mixed blessings. Clifford had kept some of his promises. Before she had unpacked the trunks, she had a garden plot to plant.

He had listened to her suggestion that they hire Chester Smith, the man from Monida, who had proven to be a competent jack of all trades and who could turn the most sobering moment into laughter. It had taken six weeks but the second room was now finished and the children slept in it.

After a month of using the bushes for their personal needs, Chester had built a two-hole outhouse. To christen the structure, Bethea had furnished it with a picture of President Washington and two outdated mail-order catalogs.

Persistent nudging and reminders had brought a small spring house where she could keep butter and milk cold. Clifford had gone to Monida for building materials and had returned with a ham, two pieces of side pork and a hind quarter of beef he'd bought off Mr. and Mrs. Burns, bragging all the while that he'd practically stolen the meat considering the price Mrs. Burns has asked for it.

Clifford's manner was forgotten when she spotted an old milk cow tied behind the wagon. She threw her arms around Clifford's neck and kissed his cheek. "How wonderful. Where did you get her?"

"That damned fool woman Mrs. Burns pawned her off on me, but you've been complaining that you wanted one, so here she is. Don't expect me to milk her. She's all yours." With that, he had ridden away, returning two days later.

Mrs. Burns's generosity seemed to know no bounds. The animal's udder was as broken down as her spine, but the milk was rich and consistent.

Once she'd determined Clifford's mood upon his return, she convinced him to help her salt down the beef to keep it from spoiling. They managed to keep from quarreling until the beef was safely preserved.

The long hot days were miserable, bringing out mosquitoes and biting bugs of all description, but in the coolness of a new morning, Bethea insisted she could hear the vegetables grow.

They had already had fresh shelled peas and the kale had been surpassed only by the orach leaves she had grown from the seeds Mrs. Burns had sent to her. The orach plants had been the first to shoot from the ground and now were more than three feet high and still showing no sign of bolting to seed. She would have to be sure and catch seeds for the following season.

Frost came many times during June but July had remained warm and dry, sweeping Bethea's concerns aside. Her garden was safe now and they would enjoy its bountiful harvest. She crossed her fingers that the cabbages would be in the root cellar before the October snows came.

The children had thrived in the clear mountain climate. Adam and Ben's trousers were half way to their knees. They could be passed down to David and Gabriel, but for the older boys, she'd have to make a trip to Dillon or Virginia City for a bolt of fabric. She had never thought to bring fabric with her from Missouri. Whatever had she been thinking?

She had two worn jumpers she planned to make into dresses for the girls. Clifford had left four days earlier for Virginia City, Madison County's seat of government. He'd not informed her of the reasons, but had said he'd be gone for several weeks. She welcomed his absence.

For months now, she and the children had watched the swans mate and hatch their young, the gray cygnets swimming between the parents on the lake and ponds. They had counted fourteen pairs of nesting swans near their cabin alone. The lake abounded with the noble birds.

The meadows and marshlands around the lakes and ponds turned green with lush grasses and a few cat tails. Each month brought a dozen new varieties of wild flowers to grace the table. Chester had built it for her one day after Clifford had pounded the original one with his fist and broken the thin slab into three pieces. The Lord himself must have sent Chester into their lives.

In mid July, he gave his notice, saying he had promised the county superintendent of schools to make repairs to many of the outlying schools in the sprawling county.

"But I have time to do a few things before I leave, ma'am," he said, giving her one of his smiles that showed three missing teeth on his right side. "From a little disagreement in Spring Hill," he explained when David had asked about them.

"We must do something about all the beds in the new room" she said. Together they had studied the room and its wall to wall arrangement of narrow beds he had made out of lodge pole tree trunks. "Could we stack them?" she asked.

He scratched his head. "Let me fool with it." By the end of the day, he had redesigned the beds two to a wall, one above the other, which left room on the slab floor to play and work. "If I had time, I'd put in a floor in this old room, too," he said, pointing to the dirt of the front room.

"You've already done more than I've been able to pay you for," she said, nodding her satisfaction with the brilliant arrangement.

"Your mister paid me what we agreed on," Chester said.

"But he didn't expect you to be such a good worker," she replied. "Excuse me." She went to the trunk in the corner of the second room and withdraw a twenty dollar gold piece, recalling the day her mother had given it to her.

"Thank you, Mama," she whispered, and hurried to the main room. "This is your bonus." He tried to refuse but she insisted. The next morning he bid them all good-by.

Adam and Ben had learned to use the two-man saw after many bouts of tears and whippings from Clifford. The wood pile grew slowly and Bethea agonized for her sons, knowing they had been given responsibilities many men couldn't handle.

The new stove Clifford had bought burned the wood almost as fast as the boys could cut it, and she had begun to wonder if they would have any left for winter.

A week after the unexpected visit by the Adlers, Clifford had returned with a feather mattress and the disassembled pieces of a shiny brass bedstead tied to the bed of the wagon. He bragged he'd bought it in Virginia City to show everyone in Madison County that they were making progress toward establishing a fine home in Centennial Valley.

The bed now took up one side of the original cabin, bringing Bethea embarrassment each time Clifford brought some man into the cabin for coffee or to share a meal. He seemed to have become well known to men who drifted through the valley. More often than not, he would leave with them and be gone for weeks on end.

The most exciting arrivals were the stage coaches that ran from the depot in Monida to the entrance of the land of the geysers a hundred miles away. Filled with passengers wealthy enough to pay for the trip, the stage company had been formed without much thought. Recently the owners had announced plans to build stations along the valley's south side road, some to change teams, but other facilities to give the tourists places to rest, eat and sleep overnight.

She stopped her hoeing and recalled Con Adler's promise to take her there. The thought was sweet but the reality far fetched. Someday she would take the children to see the geysers, but those days were far in the future. Until then, she planned to talk to Clifford about the possibility of having the stage stop at the Kingston place for a meal. The stage line paid handsomely for the service.

Once a coach had broken an axle near their cabin and she had invited four women and two gentlemen in to take tea while the repairs were made. On their return trip, the six tourists had stopped for tea again and had entertained Bethea and her children with tales of what they'd seen.

"Surely, those things can't exist," Bethea had said, finding the enthusiasm of her guests infectious. "Please, tell us again, especially about the boiling pots of mud and the steam geysers and the animals, too. Oh, the wild animals must be plentiful."

She had taken the visitors down to the shore and pointed out the long necked swans and cygnets gliding on the lake. "Are there swans, too?"

One man studied the black-billed white swans. "Yes, we saw some and I believe they're the same type, but maybe not."

When the tourists had left, one of the men slipped Bethea two gold coins and insisted she keep them. She had secreted the coins away with the ones her mother had given her, deep into the trunk and beneath the journal books.

When half the garden had been hoed, she wiped her forehead with her apron, put the tools away and washed her hands at the wash stand outside the door. Inside she checked on the bread loaves she had in the oven. Still pale crusted, they needed more time to turn golden. The noon meal was bubbling on the back of the stove. Taking advantage of the children's outdoor work and play, she retrieved her journal and writing equipment and brought the book up to date.

Since Con's visit, her sense of hopelessness had been replaced with joy and expectation, but when July came and went and the Adler livestock had not passed by on the trail, she began to face the reality that they may have taken another route to the late summer pasture land. Now her entries were terse comments on the weather, the garden, and her children's health.

She put the journal away and peeked in the oven. "Perfect," she murmured, removing six loaves of bread from the cast iron oven, then pushed the pot of beef stew to the back warming plates of the stove. Dinner was ready to eat any time, but the children were still outside and she didn't want to spoil the serenity of the cabin.

She propped open the heavy front door to let the breeze cool the interior of the cabin, then poured boiling water from the tea pot into her china cup on top of a few tea leaves. She knew Clifford had his own stomach in mind when he had bought the stove, but in spite of that, she had grown quite fond of it, much more so than the offensive but comfortable bed. It was by far the most attractive piece of furniture they owned.

Shouts came from outside. She set her cup down and hurried to the door.

"Mama, Mama, look," David shouted, pointing to the west.

"Cows, Mama, lots of 'em," Gabriel added.

"Hundreds of 'em," Adam said, racing to stand beside his brother.

"Thousands of 'em," Ben insisted, joining the other boys.

"Millions of 'em," David insisted. Bethea joined the boys, laying her hand on David's shoulder. He looked up at her. "Well, lots of 'em, anyway."

A chuck wagon rolled past the cabin and the driver waved to the children. Bethea glanced at it, then turned her attention to the approaching herd, its breadth spanning from the timber line to the lake. Dust obscured its depth but she didn't question the size of the herd or the number of cowboys with it. Her gaze centered on the tall rangy bay stallion in the lead.

Her hand fell to her swollen abdomen, hidden beneath the loose folds of a pink and white prairie style dress she'd worn during three previous pregnancies. The sight of the approaching rider brought a sharp spear of longing that tightened her womb, causing the infant inside to kick violently.

Inhaling deeply, she tried to slow her pulse. She had no right to feel this way. He was nothing to her. She meant nothing to him. A hay cutting crew had stopped at the Kingston cabin and partaken of a meal. They were from Alice Livestock and would be working around the lakes for a few weeks.

Gradually, she had begun to inquire about Con and had learned that he had gone to the Lemhi valley and spent time with an Indian chief named Tendoi. Later she learned of Matthias Adler's accident that had laid him up for several weeks. No one called Con Injun or savage or half-breed and she sensed the deep respect in their manner when they spoke of him.

The horse and rider rode closer, following the deep ruts of the wagon trail. They complemented each other to perfection. The rider applied a flick of the reins and the stallion broke into an easy cantor, its black mane lifting and falling with each stride.

The rider wore a pale blue shirt beneath a dark leather vest. His pants were dark, too, possibly leather, and as he drew closer she recognized the leather chaps most cowboys wore while riding through sage brush. A red kerchief, tied loosely around his throat fluttered in the breeze. His eyes were hidden beneath the wide brim of his black felt hat, but she knew his cheeks would be clean shaven and deeply tan, his chin firmly set.

Without a doubt, the stallion's name would be Hellion. Her heart raced. At long last her wish had come true. Con Adler had come back to the valley.

CHAPTER NINE

CON REINED his mount in to a walk again as the woman in the distance ran from the cabin door and joined her children at the edge of the road.

She wore pink. He squinted, trying to see her face, but he was still too far away to know her reaction to the herd bearing down on them. The Alice chuck wagon was scheduled to set up camp a mile up the trail. He'd asked the cook to stop and tell the Kingstons they'd be trailing the herd up to the Alaska Basin where they would stay until they brought them down in early October to winter at Alice.

She had come out to see them pass. That was all. She had left no messages with Mrs. Burns, so everything must be well with her and the children. Maybe Kingston had begun to stay home. He looked toward the cabin, hoping and praying her husband wasn't there.

The sight of her and the children pleased him, not in the physical way he'd feared but with a warmth that rivaled the sun overhead. She shielded her eyes with her hand, just as she had that morning on the hill in back of the hotel.

The cowboys would be taking their noon meal beyond the Kingston place, letting the stock rest for a few hours before pressing on. The calves had begun to falter and that unsettled the cows. The only prudent action would be a layover. They had spent a month and a half on the Alice patented lands about fifteen miles west of the Kingston quarter section.

He would have paid a visit weeks ago if not for his father's accident and subsequent infection. His father's health had been on everyone's minds for weeks and only now had he felt relieved enough to leave his parents and tend to the work in the valley. He tore his gaze from the people near the cabin to scan the horizon. Turning in the saddle, he motioned to the cowboys to draw the herd out.

"Keep them above the trail," he shouted, standing in his stirrups and motioning toward the pines. The Kingston place wasn't fenced and the herd would trample everything. After the threats his father had made, he couldn't allow anything to happen. When the herd began to drift across the trail and climb into the tree line, he breathed easier.

He continued to act as sentinel until the bawling cows and calves began to pass the cabin with a few hundred yards clearance. He spotted the chuck wagon less than a quarter of a mile ahead. Why had it stopped so close? The cattle couldn't stop until it was safely past this place.

He kicked the flanks of the stallion. The children waved as the stallion trotted by. Their smiles pleased him immensely. When he chanced a glance at Bethea, her mouth was tight, but it wasn't the grimness of her face that made him rein the stallion around.

Hellion balanced on his haunches, then came to a stop breathing heavily. Slowly, as if in a dream, Con dismounted.

The children ran to him, all chattering at once. He tried to listen but his eyes saw only Bethea Kingston in the pink dress. Rather than checkered as he'd imagined, the gingham had a narrow white stripe every inch with tiny white and yellow flowers forming a trellis on alternating stripes. Little green leaves and stems completed the pattern running down the material, from the yoke to its ankle length hem.

The shape of her body beneath the fullness of the dress made its own statement. Hadn't his step-mother worn similar garments during the months leading up to her own confinements? His heart rejected what his mind already knew.

A sickening denial cramped his stomach. She had only been in the valley for three months. She must have been pregnant long before coming to Monida. She'd deceived him, betrayed him, acting as if...as if what? She was a married woman and there was no reason to expect her husband to avoid her. Weren't the children proof enough that he didn't?

Where the hell was Clifford Kingston? he wondered, as he dismounted, then pulled off his leather gloves and stuck them in the nearest saddle bag.

Gabriel held up his arms and without thinking, Con swung the child up into the crook of his arm. Faith, the younger girl, claimed his free hand.

Gabriel patted his cheek, trying to gain his attention. "What, Gabriel?" he asked, dragging his gaze from Bethea to the child's flushed face.

Gabriel's eyes were wild with excitement. "Didja see all the cows?" the boy asked.

The children giggled. Con gave Gabriel his full attention and smiled. "Yes, son, I saw the cows. They were hard to miss, weren't they?"

"Yeah," Gabriel murmured. Suddenly taken with shyness, the boy began to wriggle. "Lemme down now."

Con eased him to the ground. "Don't go too close. Cows with calves can get a little crazy sometimes." He looked up to find Bethea staring at him.

"Where's your father?" he asked, seeking out one of the older boys. "Are you Ben or Adam?"

"Adam," the boy replied. "Pa went to Virginia City. He's going to buy some stock and a saddle horse for me."

"When did he leave?"

"Last week."

"When will he be back?"

The boy shrugged. "I don't know. Maybe next week."

Esther frowned. "When he goes away, he stays a long time."

"But he comes back with lots of money," Ben chimed in.

Bethea turned toward the cabin. "Children, the meal is ready. Wash up and come inside. Mr. Adler must tend to his cows and get his own dinner."

Stung by her coolness, Con grabbed the reins and started to remount.

"Mr. Adler, you're welcome to join us if you'd like," Bethea added, then disappeared inside the cabin.

"Will you stay?" Ben asked.

"How could I turn down a warm invitation like that?" Con replied. He walked with Ben to the wash bench outside the door and waited his turn to use the pan and bar of lye soap.

He followed the children inside. For several seconds all he saw was the garish brass bed, covered with a well worn patchwork quilt, taking up much of the room. It hadn't been there when he and his father had come to see her. He became aware of the toys scattered across it, turning it into a play area for the younger children with rag dolls and doll clothes, a small wooden wagon with several short twigs, two beginning McGuffie readers and a red ball. He exhaled. At least Mr. and Mrs. Kingston hadn't used the bed for the past week and wouldn't for some time.

"You may sit there," Bethea said, pointing to a vacant place on the side bench. She met his gaze as he sat down. "This cabin is like the hotel in Monida, not quite what I expected. But we're doing the best we can under the circumstances."

"Hey, Mama, Mr. Adler says you give warm invitations," Gabriel declared with a broad smile.

She didn't answer and refused to look at either the child or Con as she ladled the beef stew into tin bowls and gave each child a thick slice of bread.

"You may serve yourself, Mr. Adler," she said, still not looking at him. "We have plenty," she added, looking at the children. "Clean your bowls and you can have seconds."

"Me, too?" Con asked, but she still refused to meet his gaze.

The children pounded him with questions during the meal. Their curiosity about the herd was boundless and he tried his best to answer them all, but Bethea's silence remained foremost in his thoughts. At first he'd been angry, then hurt. Now he was worried. Something was wrong at the Kingston place and before the herd moved on, he intended to find out what.

The children finished eating and carried their bowls and spoons to the primitively made dry sink along one wall. Now was his chance.

"Bethea? What's wrong here?" he asked, getting to his feet.

Before she could reply, a knock sounded against the open door jamb. His foreman, Jacob Dingley, cleared his throat and doffed his hat. "Sorry to bother you, boss, but Stub has a problem. Could you come sort it out?"

"Can't it wait?" Con asked, irritated at the intrusion.

"You know how short-fused Stub can be when anyone tampers with his domain. He and that new cowboy almost came to blows over a missing pie," Jacob explained. "He accused the boy of stealing it and hiding it out for later. Some harsh words were traded, boss, and Stub is threatening to shoot the next varmint who touches the chuck wagon, no questions asked."

101

"I'll go settle it," Con said. He looked at Bethea. "But I'll be back." He stacked his bowl with the others. "How's the stock?" he asked his foreman.

"Fine, the little ones have filled their bellies and the mamas are laying down chewing their cuds like a bunch of dairy cows in a Georgia meadow." The man grinned and spoke to the children, then excused himself.

Con followed him outside but left Hellion tied to the aspen sapling near the corner of the cabin and walked alongside Jacob.

"It's good to stretch the legs, heah, boss?" Jacob said.

Con nodded.

"You know that family?"

Con nodded again.

"Ain't that the place George lost in the faro game?" When Con didn't answer, Jacob glanced over his shoulder as if to confirm the existence of the cabin. "I was just curious, boss, that's all. Seems like a nice family to me, but the woman don't look none too happy." He looked over his shoulder again as they reached the cow camp. "Boss, we got us some company."

Con turned around and found the Kingston children following them to the cow camp like ducklings in a row. He scowled. "I thought I told you to stay away from here, that you could get hurt."

Gabriel grinned up at him. "But we're with you."

"Does your mother know you've followed me here?"

"Mama told us to go play," Esther said. "She..."

Adam elbowed her ribs. "Mama goes for walks down by the lake," he said. "Sometimes she's gone a long time, but Ben and Esther and me, we look after the little ones."

"We wanted to see a real chuck wagon up close," Ben explained. "We don't have chuck wagons in Missouri." He looked down at his dusty shoe and tried to pull his big toe back through the hole in the thin leather. "If you're mad, we'll go back."

"No, stay here," Con said. "I'll go find your mother. Jacob, watch the children. Stub?" he said to the cook, "Put that revolver back in its holster. We need all the hands we can get on this drive. The grass is turning already, and if we don't get rain, we'll have to bring them down next month, so for God's sake maintain law and order. Do you hear me?"

Stub's face turned liver red beneath his bushy beard and waxed mustache, but he stopped waving the gun around in the air.

"Stub, put that gun away before you hurt someone," Con ordered.

"I just want these wranglers to know this wagon is off limits if they expect me to do my job," Stub insisted. "I ain't never had a sneak thief to contend with before. If that pie don't find its way back into that there pie box by the time we move out..." He took time to point out the location with the barrel of his gun. "...there won't be no supper tonight." He glared at the young cowboys milling around. "Try bedding down with empty bellies and you'll have a change of heart by morning, believe you me." He eased the gun back into its holster.

Con nodded his support on behalf of the cook. "Boys, you've heard Stub. Maybe you can organize a search party of your own and find that pie tin before that den of red foxes we saw up on the hillside get into it." He dismissed the cowboys. "Stub, see if you can find some sweets for the kids, and you, Jake, keep an eye on them while I find their mother."

Jacob frowned at the children. "Boss, I ain't no baby tender. I only know about herding beef stock."

"Then it's time you learned," Con said. He looked up toward the western horizon. "Looks like a thunderstorm might be brewing. If it starts to rain, put the kids under the tent," he said, motioning toward the tarpaulin the cook and his helper had tied to several saplings. He looked skyward again. "If the drums start to roll, keep an eye on the herd."

Before the two men could protest, Con strode back to the Kingston cabin. It was empty. The children had said she'd fallen into the habit of taking long walks by the lake. That was where he had found her the last time. He followed the narrow path leading toward the springs, recalling the pleasant memories the place held.

He stopped halfway down the path and scanned the area below him. The Kingstons had built a narrow log shack to take advantage of the coolness of the smaller second spring, located a few feet from the warm spring. This one flowed year round as well but its waters were icy cold, proving its source very different from the warmer one.

Good choice, Con thought, conceding that maybe the husband wasn't as bad as he had heard. Rumors had lingered in the wake of

Clifford Kingston wherever he traveled and the rumors weren't complimentary.

He scanned the shore of the lake but found only the swans and some noisy ducks on the waters. He spotted pink fabric billowing in the wind at the side of the spring house, then disappear. Stepping carefully through the lush undergrowth, he made his way to the building and into the small clearing.

Bethea Kingston stood pressed against the wall that faced the lake, her eyes closed, tears streaming down her cheeks. Her teeth bit into her lower lip, holding it immobile, and a fine trickle of blood ran down her chin. Only the shaking of her shoulders spoke of her misery.

"Mrs. Kingston?" he called softly.

She flinched.

"Bethea?" He stepped directly in front of her and touched her shoulders. She opened her eyes and gazed up at him, and his heart exploded into a thousand pieces.

"Con?" she whispered. She closed her eyes again and swiped at the tears but they continued to flow. "Con, what am I going to do?" She began to hiccup as she looked into his eyes again.

Afraid she might shatter, he pulled her into his arms. She fell against him, her body trembling. He forgot her condition and began to stroke her back through the loose folds of her dress. Her legs collapsed, and he caught her, easing her to sit on the ground. When he joined her, he leaned against the logs of the spring house and pulled her onto his lap.

Her arms went around his torso and she clung to him as if he were her lifeline to sanity. Her loose dress had become shifted, exposing the slender shape of her legs and the hole in one of her cotton stockings just below her knee. He tugged it down to her ankles again, then tightened his arms around her.

"Be still, Bethea," he crooned.

"I was afraid you'd never come back," she sobbed.

"But I did," he murmured, kissing the top of her head.

"I know it's wrong, but I needed to see you again."

The pins that held her bun began to slip free and he pulled out the rest and let them fall to the ground. "That's why I'm here," he replied, nuzzling the thick mass of curls that cascaded around her shoulders. "God knows how I tried my best to stay away. I asked the boys on the hay crew to keep an eye on you."

She shifted on his lap and looked up at him. "You did? I thought they were just being neighborly."

"I pumped them every time they came back."

"I was afraid that after your father was here, you would never come back. He was so furious."

"He got over it, well almost, and the hay crew rotated every two weeks, so I kept tabs on your coming and going."

"Now I know you're jesting," she whispered. "I've never left the place since I got here. Only Clifford comes and goes, and he goes more than he comes."

"I know that, too." His mouth softened into a half smile. "The boys were under threat of firing or worse if they mentioned my name." He took his thumb and wiped the trickle of blood from her chin, then smoothed the curls away from her temples.

"They only talked directly of you when I asked about you by name," she said. "But always in a general way," she insisted.

His smile widened. If he had a brush, he would turn her around and brush her hair until it shone with the brilliance he knew would come. It would fall to her waist, and if her shoulders were bare, he'd part her hair and arrange it over each breast, but only after tasting their nectar, and that would happen after he'd become satisfied with kissing her mouth and her throat and the tiny lobe of her ear. His heart tightened to a painful knot in his chest.

If he could take her away to some secret place where they could talk without fear of discovery, he would tell her all the things he longed to share, deep feelings he'd never expressed to any woman. As he gazed down at her, he knew such actions could prove dangerous. His arms tightened around her, pulling her snugly against his body. The price they would pay for the slightest indiscretion could prove deadly.

Many of the men in the area, especially in the county seat to the north, were double-mouthed. They proclaimed righteous indignation if they encountered an Indian or, God forbid, a man with black skin, in town, expecting them to step off the newly installed boardwalks of the business street.

They boasted of their progressiveness, yet the sight of a mixed-blood man seemed to incite them to riot and occasionally murder. There had been more than one unauthorized execution in the county, with a lifeless body found hanging from a limb of a cottonwood, and always along a trail where travelers would pass and read the message.

He'd been the target of their tirades more than once as a young man. He trusted no man fully. He knew many of them carried hatred and bigotry beneath their friendly smiles.

He looked down at Bethea in his arms. The good citizens would be outraged at the sight, but he had found her hurting in a manner no woman deserved. They had been provided a secluded spot and given a change to be together, if only for a few moments. He savored the pleasure of holding her at last.

Her head dropped back against his arm. "You are a very handsome man when you smile," she whispered.

When he looked down, her eyes had closed and her lips were parted as if some secret thought pleased her greatly.

"Bethea, look at me."

Her eyes opened and the turmoil of their depths matched the churning of the lake against the early winds of the approaching storm.

"Yes." Her voice quivered as her hand touched his cheek. Suddenly she sat up and faced him, kneeling between his legs. "I'm expecting another child."

"That's obvious...and it doesn't matter."

"I'm married to another man."

"I know." He took her chin in one hand and brushed her damp curls away from her temple with the other. "You are a beautiful woman. But you must see that each time you look in your mirror."

She looked away for a moment. "I have no mirror. I haven't seen my own face in months."

Touched by her honesty, he admired her as she knelt before him, her dress billowing about them and trailing over one of his legs. He caressed her forehead, tracing her hairline down past her temple to her ear and around to her jaw. His fingers were shaky when he stroked her cheek until she pressed his palm against her skin and wouldn't let him move it away.

"Oh, God, Bethea, what are we going to do?"

She leaned forward and brushed his mouth with hers. He pulled her roughly against him. Her lips opened as he claimed them, eager to discover this forbidden fruit.

Her breathing was as ragged as his own when he raised his mouth from hers. Shifting her onto his lap again, they held each other, aching with longing.

"Are we committing adultery?" she asked, her cheek pressed against his chest.

He leaned his head back against the logs. "Not yet."

She lay quietly in his arms for several minutes. "And we won't." She looked up at his face again. "But I'm glad you kissed me. Now I have something to remember when I feel so alone, so isolated here."

He gazed down at her. "Does your husband go away and leave you and the children alone often?"

"Yes."

"The bastard," he cursed.

"And it frightens me," she said, touching his bare skin at the base of his throat.

He fought to douse the fire her fingers ignited.

"What would I do if one of the children had an accident or got sick and I couldn't cure them?" she asked. "Once the stage coaches to the geysers stop running and your men move the cattle out, we'll be alone, completely alone."

"There are a few others in the valley," he said. "Have you met them?"

She shook her head. "Clifford says neighbors get to be busy bodies. We stay home when he's here. When he leaves, he takes the team and wagon and his saddle horse. We have to walk wherever we go. Gabriel gets tired but I can't carry him."

"I could leave a couple of saddle horses here for you," he said, desperate to ease her existence.

She laughed scornfully. "However would I explain your generosity to my husband? Thank you, but we'll manage. It's just that I get so weary. If I could only sleep, but I wake up in the middle of the night and worry about the garden, if we can survive the winter, about the children wandering off. Sometimes I come down here and watch the swans. A swan family is protective and loyal to its members. Why can't human families be that way?"

"The Adler family tries to be," he replied.

"Then you're fortunate," she said. "If I hear a sound that scares me, I go back to bed."

"With your husband in that god awful brass bed?" Con took his hat off and slammed it onto the ground. "Damn, I have no right to ask you that."

"It's hideous, isn't it?" She shifted on his lap and smiled sadly. "No, I sleep alone. Clifford puts pregnant women right along with leprosy victims and babies in soiled diapers. We haven't been...together for months now. I can't stand for him to touch me. He's mean when he...he likes to make me cry out. He hurts me...then he laughs." She glanced away. "I should not have said these things."

His index finger traced the outer curve of her lips. "When a man and a woman come together, they should share passion." He held her tightly in his arms again, wanting to protect her, to keep her safe from all harm, especially harm from her own husband. "Someday we'll be together, Bethea, and I'll show you how it can be. Until then, beloved, take care. I'd go insane if harm came to you. Don't let the children go too far, either. Do you have a gun?"

She shook her head. "Clifford takes all his guns with him. Are we in danger from the Indians?"

He chuckled. "No, the Lemhi and Bannock bands and other Shoshonis are too busy surviving themselves to bother whites, unless it's to beg for food and that's because they're on the verge of starvation. If an Indian comes to your door, think of me. If you have food to share, be generous. They'll return the favor when they can. No, the dangers you have here are the elements and the wild animals."

She nodded. "We saw a black bear once, and we hear howling. I think they're wolves. Clifford said I was silly, that it was only a pack of coyotes. We don't walk far and we keep the cabin in sight. We might not get back before dark."

He stroked her temple and kissed her lightly again. "There are many dangers here, but not if you stay alert, know the landmarks, learn the plants that are safe to eat. The garden looks fine, and the older children must be a big help to you. If I had the time, I'd take you all in one of the Alice wagons to meet Mrs. McGyver over at the upper springs, across the lake."

"Another woman in the valley?" She smiled. "I didn't know. Where does she live?"

He pointed to the northeast. "We'd have a picnic and you could visit. Women need each other's company. She has a young son. She keeps her reasons for being in the valley to herself, but that's her right." He sighed. "Unfortunately, that may have to wait until next summer." He explained his father's injury.

"Then if not for that, you wouldn't be here?"

He gazed down at her again. "If not for that, I would have come sooner, but it might be wisest for both of us if I stayed away."

Her arms tightened around him. "Please don't stay away. I need to see you, to talk to you. I have no one, only the children and they don't understand. Please don't avoid me."

He pointed to the swans floating on the lake, and she shifted in his arms. "Most of them will leave when the lakes begin to freeze over. Perhaps the Kingstons should take a lesson from the swans and winter elsewhere."

Cradled in his arms, she studied the swans and their cygnets. "Clifford insists we can live here year round, only he's gone most of the time. What if he leaves and can't get back because of the snows. We'd be trapped in here. It's like paradise now, but Mrs. Burns warned me about the winters. I couldn't bear to see my children starving...or freezing. Adam and Ben do their best to keep the woodpile supplied, but the stove is insatiable. I tried to help the boys with the sawing, but my arms seem to be weaker than when I was young."

He chuckled. "You're far from being an old woman, Bethea. How old are you?"

"Twenty-six," she whispered. "Twenty-seven the first day of December. And you?"

"Twenty-seven. You see, other than a few obstacles, we're perfectly matched, as my uncle would say."

"Your uncle George?"

"No, my mother's half brother and chief of his tribe."

She turned in his arms. "Does that make you a prince?"

He chuckled. "Hardly. I'm nothing."

She traced the curve of his lips. "You're everything...to me." Her arms slid around his neck and she drew his face down to hers. Her mouth opened and shyly her tongue reached out to his. The heat of their dancing tongues made them unaware of the increased winds whipping the willows nearby. She pulled away and buried her face against his shirt again.

Thunder rolled across the sky and a flash of lightning jabbed at the shoreline across the lake. She flinched in his arms. Rain drops splattered on the ground around them. He retrieved his felt hat, put it on his head, and continued to hold her. Thunder rolled again.

He looked skyward. "It's been a dry summer. We need the rain, otherwise the cattle will go hungry this winter."

The sprinkles changed to a downpour and he hunched over, trying to protect her, but in minutes they were drenched. Content to be together, they waited out the storm's fury. When the brief deluge stopped several minutes later, he helped her to her feet and they left the meager protection of the spring house roof's overhang.

He twirled her around and the fresh washed breezes lifted her dress and whipped it about her body. "Madam, I believe we chose the wrong side of the spring house."

She grinned. "We could have gone inside."

"That might have been more dangerous than staying out here."

She chewed her cut lip, deep in thought.

"You're soaked to the skin," he said, looking down at the material clinging to her rounded belly. All the words he wanted to say were buried beneath his anguish for her. Somehow he'd find a way to make her life easier, whether she had a husband or not. If they lived in the ways of his mother's people, she would leave her husband and he could claim her as his woman and that would settle the matter. In the white man's society, dissolutions were not so easily made. He held out his arms and she came into them and strained upward to receive his kiss. "We should go back," he whispered between kisses.

"In a moment," she replied, and he held her once more.

A twig snapped underfoot and Con looked up, shielding her protectively against him. His foreman, Jacob, and Bethea's middle son, David, stood several feet away at the other spring.

Jacob cleared his throat. "We was just looking for you, boss. When the shower passed and you didn't come back, we was worried." He laid his hand on the boy's shoulder and turned him toward the cabin, keeping his own lanky body between the child and the embracing couple.

Refusing to explain their actions, Con took Bethea's hand and escorted her back to the cabin. Squeezing her hand, he motioned her inside, then returned to the cow camp and the other children.

"We found her," David said, looking at Con.

"She's changing," Con said. "We got caught in the shower."

Another bolt of lightning streaked across the sky. The cows at the edge of the herd milled about, their calves bawling. A drum roll of thunder shook the skies as another bank of storm clouds moved in.

"Let's move 'em out," Con called, but before the cowboys could mount up, several of the cows bolted back up the trail from which they'd come, their calves running to catch up.

Jacob and Stub swung the children up onto the chuck wagon, while Con and three others mounted and rode after the cows. The other riders began to move the main herd up the trail to the east.

"Cut them to the left," Con shouted. "They're heading for the Kingston place." He dug his spurs into Hellion's sides and raced for the cabin. He saw Bethea open the door and start to step outside. "Get back inside," he shouted.

Above the shouts and bawling livestock, she heard him and slammed the door. The cows and their calves ran through the garden plot, two of the cowboys riding hard behind them. One of them circled behind the cabin and turned the herd. The cows stopped, confused, milling around in the middle of the garden before they loped toward the hillside. Another cowboy turned them into a widening circle and drove them back to the main herd.

As the cattle began to disappear over the crest of the hill on their way to the next valley, the cook Stub, the foreman Jacob, and Con Adler surveyed the damage to the Kingston property. The outhouse had been knocked over.

"We'll get it set back up, ma'am," Jacob assured her. He scratched his head. "But it looks like the garden is a total loss for sure."

"We'll make good on that, too, Bethea," Con said. Several rounded heads of cabbage ready for harvest lay split and broken, their solid cores covered with mud and manure. The lush tops of the carrots had disappeared under the trampling hooves. Somewhere under the packed mud the roots might be safe.

Small red potatoes not yet large enough for digging lay scattered about the yard, as if a giant pitchfork had been at work. They would be able to salvage a few, once the mud dried and they could hunt for them. The turnips and lettuce had disappeared completely.

Jacob was right, Con thought. His livestock, followed by his well meaning cowboys, had destroyed the food supply that would have fed the family all winter and saved them from starvation, bringing about one of Bethea's worst fears.

He looked across the devastation. She stared back at him. Her yellow dress was as cheerful as the sun now shining brightly in the sky. She had combed her hair and pulled it back into a prim bun. Not a speck of mud had touched the skirts she clutched in her fists, holding them half way to her knees, but her shoes were buried in the mud.

His heart grew heavy and he had to look away.

Despair and hopelessness had returned to her eyes.

CHAPTER TEN

"I WANT SEED and potato pieces," Bethea said. Staring at the destruction of her garden had planted a determination to conquer this harsh land.

Neither her insensitive husband, the land hungry Matthias Adler, nor the man standing on the other side of the plot could keep her from taking care of her little ones and surviving the coming months in this valley.

She may have hated it when she'd first arrived, but not now. Someday it would be known as the Lake Shore home ranch. She would show them all that she was made of stronger stock than any of them could imagine.

"The days are still long and the weather hot," she said, her voice as unyielding as her spine. "I have time. I want..." and she began to name off her demands.

She looked across the garden to Con, raising her chin defiantly. "And I want two loads of sawed wood. I want the pieces this long," she added, using her hands to measure the length that would fit into the voracious cook stove that would be their only source of heat during the winter. "If your cows hadn't been a distraction to my sons, they would have been able to do their work."

"Bethea, please."

She dropped her skirts into the mud, then yanked them up again. "That will be all, thank you." She turned away. "I'm going to the lake to clean my shoes. Thank you for watching my children, Mr. Foreman, but I can manage now. Come, children," she said, her posture stiff. "Good day, sirs."

She grabbed the bar of lye soap and led the children down to the water's edge and began to wash the gummy mud from her shoes and stockings. Her skirts fell into the water and she yanked them up and squeezed them, her anger growing with each twist of the material.

She had coveted Con Adler and God had dispensed his wrath quickly. "Guilty, Lord," she whispered, dropping to her knees in the water. Bowing her head, she did the only thing that could cleanse her soul by confessing her sin, the sin of lust, admitting to her Savior that she had lusted for a man other than her lawful husband.

Clifford would hardly look at her with her bloated belly, yet she had thrown herself into the arms of Conrad Adler and let him stroke her body. Waves of shameful heat swept up her cheeks as she recalled her reaction to his hands, his mouth, the pulse she'd discovered at the base of his throat, the moist heat of his tongue when it had found hers. Never in her life had she yearned for carnal knowledge of a man until now.

She took the bar of soap and attacked the soiled hem of her skirt with a vengeance. When her hands became covered with brown suds, she let the strong chemicals seep into the tiny cuts as if the stinging could cleanse her heart as well as her dress. She shifted to the next section of hem and rubbed the bar across the material harder and harder on the rock.

The material gave way, leaving a gaping tear several inches long just above the hem. Blinking away her tears, she stared at the damage. She couldn't shake the evidence of her abusive washing habits anymore than she could her guilt. She would be spending the evening repairing the damage in the glow of the coal oil lamp.

Esther shrieked and Bethea looked up. The two girls had fallen into the lake and were now splashing in the muddy water, tossing pieces of duck grass at each other and screaming with delight.

Bethea collapsed onto the sandy beach and buried her head in her arms.

Gabriel came to her and patted her shoulder. "Why are you crying, Mama? Are you sad?" he asked, his woebegone expression bringing new tears to her eyes.

"Yes, sweetheart, I'm sad," she said.

"Why?" he asked, touching the teardrop on her cheek with the tip of his index finger. "Mr. Adler found you."

"Yes, dear."

Gabriel smiled. "Mr. Adler is a big, big, tall up man, heah? He picked me up and I almost touched the sky."

She gazed into his eyes and they reminded her of Con Adler's piercing gaze. "I almost touched the sky, too, Gabriel." She squeezed him. "But now we're both down to earth, aren't we? And we have work to do. Girls?" she called.

Faith and Esther left the water, their dresses dragging in the sand, weighted down by the lake water.

She frowned down at their outfits, then at hers. "Girls, you and I need to find something other than dresses to wear while we're here alone. Can you keep a secret?"

"Sure," they chorused. "What, what?"

"Come with me," she said. A surge of new energy swept through her. "I'm sick and tired of doing the wash, and it's mostly dresses. As long as no one sees us, we're going to be practical. We'll keep our dresses handy and slip them on if someone comes, but while it's hot and we have work to do, how we dress is our business."

Several minutes later, in the back room of the cabin, Bethea leaned back on her heels and surveyed her daughters. If not for their long hair, they could pass for little boys. She had borrowed a pair of David's trousers and tried them on Esther, pleased to see they fit fine. A pair of his outgrown trousers she had been saving for Gabriel fit Faith to perfection.

Searching through the trunk of outgrown clothing, she found blue shirts for each of them and suspenders. Quick braiding of their hair took care of the constant combing and retying of ribbons. She plopped two of the straw hats she'd brought from Missouri on top of their heads. The two girls grinned as they sized each other up.

"Now you have six little boys," Esther said.

"What about when Papa comes home?" Faith asked. "He won't know who we are."

"We'll turn you back into little girls," Bethea said. "So keep an eye out for him."

"Can we go play now?" Esther asked.

Bethea shook her head and handed each child a bucket. "Not until you've filled this with all the red potatoes you can find on the ground. They'll turn green in the sun, so do your work first, then you can play."

"And will you bake us a peach pie?" Faith asked.

Bethea kissed her daughter's cheek. "I have several cans of peaches left, so yes, I'll stoke up that monster stove and bake us a peach pie, and some biscuits, too. If I'm going to heat up the cabin, we might as well enjoy the results."

The girls raced out the open cabin door, delighted with their new found freedom.

Now me, Bethea thought. She had seen women wearing trousers before, but they had been eccentric women who had thrown propriety to the wind. On the train ride through Nebraska, they had stopped at a tiny farming town and she had noticed three women dressed just like the men. They were sitting on the seat of a spring wagon, waiting, while two other trousered women loaded bags of seed onto their wagon.

"Lady homesteaders," a fellow passenger had remarked. "Although why they still lay claim to the word 'lady' is beyond me. Shocking, aren't they?"

Clifford may have purchased or won the property, but wasn't she living alone on a homestead just as much as those Nebraska women?

She tried on a pair of Clifford's trousers. If she had been slender, they would have bagged terribly, but with her belly to contend with, she made a few adjustments and was satisfied, then topped them with a loose shirt he'd discarded as a rag. For a moment, she was thankful that Con Adler and his cowboys couldn't see her now, and thank goodness, she had no mirror. She doubted she could accept her image in a looking glass.

When she adjusted a straw hat on her own head and stepped outside, she took a step. Delightful. Perhaps some practical good had come of this loss of her garden after all.

As darkness approached, they dipped out their bowls of cabbage, salvaged from the least damaged heads, and boiled beef and took them outside. Sitting on blocks of wood scattered about the yard, they discussed the work to be done in the weeks to come. Bethea slathered the biscuits with butter and service berry jam and gave two to each child. When their bowls were sopped clean, she slid in a generous piece of pie. The children's smiles warmed her heart.

When she returned to her own stump, she glanced at the block of wood holding the butter and jam. "The cow!" She jumped to her feet, catching her bowl of peach pie seconds before it hit the ground. "I forgot about Bossy!" She clenched her fists. "Did she get mixed up with the Adler stock? We'll have to go get her. How far is it to Alaska Basin? Dear Lord, how many things can go wrong?"

"Mama, look!" Ben sat his bowl and spoon down and ran to the edge of the wagon road, pointing toward the darkening eastern horizon. "Here comes Bossy now. See her behind that man on the horse?"

Bethea's heart lurched. Surely Con Adler wouldn't come back. She looked down at her trousers, awash with embarrassment.

"Look, Mama, it's one of the cowboys," Adam called, running toward the rider.

Adam retrieved the rope from the young man whom Bethea had not seen before. When the cowboy dismounted and turned to the people, she had to smile. Either he didn't recognize her or he was too embarrassed by her attire to speak.

She stepped forward and extended her hand. "I'm Mrs. Kingston," she said. "Thank you for returning our cow. We would have missed the milk. Adam, her bag looks full. Why don't you and David tend to the milking, then tie her up behind the cabin for the night."

The cowboy made no effort to leave. In the distance, the sounds of a wagon came to her and she searched the road.

"Ma'am, the boss said to bring you this wood. He says to apologize for it being only half a load and to assure you we'd be bringing you more as soon as we get it cut. Johnnie and me," he said, pointing to the other young man, "we'll stand up the...ah little house...back over its hole...if you know what I mean? The boss, he didn't want you folks inconvenienced any more than you already are. And he said to tell you the seed will be here within a week. He sent a rider to Virginia City as soon as we got the stock into Alaska Basin."

He took off his hat and clutched it against his shirt front at the end of his speech. She half expected him to bow.

"Tell your boss..." She could hardly tell this young man what she was really feeling. "Tell Mr. Adler we appreciate the promptness of the repairs. A week will be fine on the seed, but I would appreciate the rest of the wood as soon as possible. Tell him...thank you."

He glanced toward the empty pie tin. "I reckon I'm the culprit who started all this, ma'am," he confessed. "I go plumb loco hankering for pie when I see them. They reminds me of the pies baked by my dear sweet ma back in Missouri."

Her eyes lit up. "You're from Missouri, too? Where?"

"Fairport, in DeKalb County, ma'am."

"That's amazing," she exclaimed. "We're from Wilcox in Nodaway County. Please, join us. I baked three of them. I'll make a fresh pot of coffee and you two gentlemen can eat before you begin your work."

"If you're sure, ma'am. We wouldn't want to put you out none, but the boss made us come before we had dessert, not even the one we gave back to Stub."

For the first time in hours, she laughed. While the men ate, the children asked questions about the cattle drive and the young men seemed to enjoy being the center of attention.

The young man from Missouri, Broderick Harris, looked across the circle of diners and smiled at Bethea. "I reckon I can see why the boss was so concerned about you folks here. You seem right happy here and you've tried to make it a real Missouri farm. The boss, he was hard to get along with this afternoon, kept criticizing everything we did, even Stub."

He scratched his unruly thatch of blond curls. "I reckoned for a while you folks was kin, maybe on his pa's side, but he would have bit my head off if I'd asked. Usually he's more like his mamma's people, giving orders direct so's only an idiot could miss 'em, but today he said more than he's said in a month of Sundays."

She looked away. "Mr. Adler has been our friend...for months now. The children enjoy his company...as do I because...we get so few visitors here."

"Oh, does he come visit often?" the cowboy asked. "Sorry, ma'am, it's none of our business what the boss does when he takes off...only we figured he headed over to Lemhi to be an Indian for a while. I reckon deep down a lot of the men envy him being free like that, even if they act like they hate red skins."

She met his gaze directly. "Perhaps he's that rare individual who finds peace in both worlds. Some of us have trouble accomplishing that in one."

He nodded, his solemn expression making her uncomfortable. "Did you know he goes hunting with them in the fall?" he asked. "Rides all the way to the geysers and wears skins and moccasins like he was born to it, only now that I think on it, he was. Too bad that now that old man Matthias is laid up, he might have to pass this year."

Bethea nodded but didn't say a word, her own thoughts on the man being discussed.

Broderick stood up, blushing. "Gracious ma'am, I've been talking like a woman for sure." His face turned ruddy, highlighting the blond fuzz on his cheeks. "I'm sorry, ma'am, it's just that I have three sisters and they talk a leg off you. I didn't mean that you was a talker." He shrugged. "I reckon I didn't give you a chance to get a word in, did I?"

He handed her the empty pie dish and motioned to his partner. Now all business, he and the other man set about unloading the wagon of wood and returning the damaged outhouse to its proper position.

After the men rode off into the darkness, Bethea busied herself with the chores that always consumed the end of her day. When the children were all washed and tucked into their beds, she looked around the main room of the cabin. When her gaze fell on the bed, now cleared of toys and ready for occupancy, she sat down on its edge.

She caressed the worn quilt top. She had made the quilt when she'd come to grips with her plight as a pregnant fifteen-year-old. Anxious to make amends to her mother and spare her parents shame in the small town where they lived, she had worked diligently on this and three other quilts to prove her determination to face the responsibilities of married life. What other choice had she, except running away? She had rejected that as the coward's way out.

Con had asked her if Clifford left them alone often. Had he been asking something more? Did he want to know if he might be welcome again? Inside the cabin? After darkness?

The baby kicked, as if it knew her deepest thoughts and needed to bring her to her senses. But other than her commitment to her children, what else was there to consider? Her sham of a marriage? If this represented marriage, perhaps she would be better off a divorced woman.

But how would she survive and take care of her children? Could she possibly make a success of this small piece of land by herself? She could expect no sympathy from other married women. Some of the married men she had known viewed divorced women as easy targets for their own needs.

Retrieving her journal and the pen and ink, she grabbed a woolen shawl and tied it around her shoulders, then closed the door quietly behind her and stepped into the night. Sleep would be impossible until she had another soul searching discussion with herself.

Stepping carefully over the stones at the lake's edge, she worked her way to her favorite spot, a small clearing surrounded by cattails that would not turn green until late summer. Her shawl would keep the mosquitoes off, and if she sat very quietly, she could hear the soft sounds of the swans speaking to the cygnets. She had discovered the joyful sounds one night when she'd been extremely restless, but her curiosity had made her careless. Now she knew to keep perfectly quiet.

Pulling her legs up onto the next stone, she hugged her trousered knees, glad to be free of bulky skirts. Down the lake's shore line to the east, a glow began to appear above the horizon. As she waited, a full moon moved into the sky.

The cowboys had told them of the general directions and the distance to the next valley known as Alaska Basin. Con was there. Was he watching the same moon? Was he thinking of her? A comforting warmth filled her, and she bowed her head, praying that he would understand why she had changed into a hard negotiator after the damage to her garden. The expression on his face had been permanently etched into her mind. She had half expected him to demand that they pack up and leave immediately.

Of course, he had no right to ask. The deed in the cabin proved that. So just in case he might be thinking about it, she had insisted that he make reparation far greater than the damages done. No, that was untrue. The likelihood of a second planting reaching maturity was almost nil. Mrs. Burns had said snow could fall any time after August, and occasionally in that month. She had deluded herself to think that it would hold off until October. He knew about the seasons, yet he had promised her the seeds and never once challenging her plans.

As she thought back over the events of the day, she wondered if her senses had left her completely. She had asked him if they'd committed adultery after only a few kisses. She knew the biblical definition of the word.

He had replied, "Not yet."

Looking at the moon again, she took comfort in his response. At least one man cared for her. He couldn't come to her any more than she could go to him, but knowing that he, too, wanted more than what they had shared was sufficient.

Clifford would never know her inner thoughts, just as he would never read the revealing entries she made in her journal. Clifford could come home anytime now. He had been home twice since they had received Matthias Adler's offer to sell out. She had told him about the visit and her refusal. He had grown silent, and during the rest of the day he'd seemed withdrawn.

She had begun to wonder if he would have accepted the offer if he had been there, but she didn't ask. He had left early the next morning. "On business," he had said. She didn't understand why he made so many trips away from this valley when moving here had been his idea. He never talked about his business dealing and she saw little evidence of profit from his ventures. She had learned to exist without currency.

She concentrated on the deeply tanned face of Con Adler, allowing her heart to open to him in a way she'd never been able to do to her husband. She imagined him stretched out in his bedroll, his arms folded behind his head, staring at the golden orb that shone down on them.

For a moment, she felt his fingers on her heart, massaging it, opening it so both of them could peer inside. Had she fallen in love with this man she barely knew?

Did the spiraling emotion that seemed to begin deep inside her body and absorb every inch of her whenever he touched her represent lust or did it signify a deeper emotion? A thirst that could never be quenched, even if they could manage to be together just once? Would she be happier if she never saw him again or if she tasted his love once and then found herself deprived forever after?

As the moon rose in the night sky, her thoughts replayed again and again the ecstasy of lying in his arms, then the agony of being torn apart.

Carefully, she removed the writing equipment and untied the red ribbon on the journal. Dipping the tip of the pen into the ink bottle, she began to write.

"I've fallen in love with Con Adler. Today, when I needed him most, he found me near the lake. Before he came, I knew I would die for his kisses, but now I fear I shall die without them. They sustain me. They fill me with hope and also desire.

"His kisses came so fast I could not count them. They smothered my mouth. If only he could have kissed my throat, my breasts. Oh how I wanted him to touch my naked body. His lips were soft yet his mouth was hard. His arms were strong and I felt as if he had wrapped me in love. He wants me in the most intimate way. I know because when I leaned against him I could feel his manliness ready to fill and claim me as his woman.

"The baby saved us. I know that if I had been slim again I would have done anything...to know him. His hands were gentle yet his fingers burned my flesh. He is a well built man, tall and handsome, and when he sweeps me up against his body, the world spins. Someday, after the baby is born.... Whatever the future holds for us, I pray that God will watch over him and keep him from harm's way. If God has brought us together, surely He will help us to become true and everlasting lovers."

An hour later, she crept back to the cabin and crawled into bed, exhausted in body and but at peace in her soul.

ANOTHER WAGON LOAD OF WOOD arrived three days later. Broderick from Missouri, and his young partner, Johnnie, delivered it.

"Please thank Mr. Adler," she said, as they climbed onto the wagon to leave.

"I'll do that, ma'am," he replied. "He says for you folks to all take care."

A crushing sense of love brought tears to her eyes and she turned away. "Thank you," she said over her shoulder, "and we'll look forward to the rest of the wood and the seeds."

Bethea and the children worked from daylight to dark, making furrows in the garden and readying it for planting. A week after the garden had been destroyed, another cowboy dropped off a package containing the seeds she'd requested, three dozen seed potatoes, and several packets of flower seeds with a note to save them until the next spring. The note had been written on the face of the invoice from the seed store in Virginia City.

Saddened, she wished it had been written by Con.

Even Gabriel did his part by dropping the potato pieces into the holes Adam and Bethea made. They replanted peas, radishes, and turnips, and a row of greens. She doubted the carrots would have time to reach maturity and held those seeds back with the flower seeds for the next season. If the warm weather held out, they might be able to harvest some of the garden. If snows came in September, all would be lost.

When the second load of wood arrived, the green leaves of the potato vines had broken through the soil.

They carried buckets of water from the lake and carefully poured it along the furrows, compensating for the lack of rain. As the weeks passed, the garden turned into a plot of green promise.

Early in September, another rider stopped in and shared the noon meal with them. "Sure is unusual weather, ma'am," he said. "By now we should be having frost every night, but here we are still in the middle of summer. I reckon the whole world must be out of kilter. The spring was dry when we shoulda got rain, the summer was hot and baked us like an oven, and now the grasses are as dry as straw. We'll be moving the stock down later this month because there's nothing for the poor critters to eat up on the high valleys. You moving out soon, ma'am?"

She shook her head. "No, we're planning to winter here."

Unusual sounds came from the sky and they looked up.

Ben called from outside. "Come see the geese!"

Outside, flying from the north low over the lake were two long irregular Vs of large grey geese, honking loudly as they flapped their long wings to gain altitude over the Continental Divide to the south of the cabin. Behind Bethea and the cowboy, the geese on the lake grew restless and some took flight.

The cowboy took off his hat and scratched his head. "That's a sure sign of winter coming, ma'am. You rethink your plans, won't you? If your mister knows his business, he'll move you to Spring Hill until spring. Well, I'd best be moseying along now, and thanks for the grub. All the Alice cowboys say you're the best cook in this valley." He reached for the reins and swung into the saddle.

123

She laughed. "I don't know how much of a compliment that is, considering Mrs. McGyver and I may be the only women here."

"Oh, it's a compliment, ma'am," he insisted. "Mrs. McGyver is none too friendly to us cowboy." Brushing his hat brim with two fingers, he grinned and rode away.

Voices sounded behind her and she whirled around to the west, praying for Con Adler to be coming. To her dismay, Clifford Kingston, on a white horse Bethea had never seen before, was leading a caravan of three wagons, each with a driver on the seat, and a saddle horse tied to the rear of the last wagon.

He waved but she couldn't bring herself to respond. The children came running from the garden plot. When Clifford dismounted, surrounded by his children, he patted them absently on their heads and looked at Bethea. "Entertaining, Bethea?"

She frowned. "What do you mean?"

"That rider," Clifford said, waving his arm toward the east. "He was in a hurry to get out of here."

Bethea sighed. "He's an Alice cowboy on his way to Alaska Basin. They stop all the time, sometimes for a cup of coffee, this time I invited him to stay for dinner." She brushed a strand of hair from her eyes. "I get lonely."

"I'll just bet you do," he said. The wagons rolled to a stop near the garden plot and without a word, the drivers began to unload their assigned wagons.

"Not that one," Clifford yelled to the last man. The man replaced the two barrels and tied them down, then went to help the other men.

Bethea recognized the last wagon as the same one her husband had taken with him. "What happened to the sorrel gelding?" she asked, pointing to the white mare he now rode.

"Did a little horse swapping," he bragged. "The gelding kept going lame so when I found a newcomer in Virginia City, I worked a straight across exchange, as is. That old gelding is probably horse meat by now." He turned to settle with the three men. Two of the men climbed back onto the wagons and the third mounted the horse that had been tied behind Clifford's wagon of barrels. The three drivers nodded to Bethea, then the caravan turned back toward Monida.

Bethea went to the pile of boxes and sacks. "What's all this?"

"You tell me," Clifford said, grabbing her arm. "This was waiting at the mercantile. Sam Culver, the station master, said it arrived by train yesterday with orders to deliver to the Kingston place. You been ordering supplies while I was gone?" His finger nails bit into her biceps, bringing a cramp.

"How could I order supplies? I have no money and I'm stranded here. The only transportation I have is shanks' mares," she said, yanking her arm free and massaging it. She looked at the crates. "You paid for these?"

"It came prepaid from Kirkpatrick's store in Dillon, but it cost me to rent the damned wagons and the drivers," he complained. "It's mostly canned goods, and hell, we can always use an extra sack of spuds and cabbages. I don't turn down a gift horse."

"What if it belongs to someone else? Shouldn't we ask about that?" A feeling of uneasiness settled over her.

"Hell no, you stupid woman. Don't you know a thing? Possession is..."

She sighed and held up her hand. "It doesn't matter. If you'll help me put it away, I can make use of it." She turned toward the cabin, overcome with exhaustion. "Are you staying for supper?"

"Of course," he called. "I'm always willing to eat some of your good Missouri cooking. Who knows, if you act right, I may hang around for a while and then you won't get so lonely." He laughed as she closed the cabin door behind her, leaving him with his children. He never lingered once he saw the chores and repairs that needed doing.

This is the first time he's come back since Con kissed me, she thought, staring out the window. Strange how she had begun to gauge her existence in terms of Con Adler; before meeting him, between embraces, after his kisses. But now she would have to put those thoughts out of her mind.

On the dry sink sat two empty buckets. An excuse to sit by the spring or the lake would give her a chance to gather her will power to endure Clifford's presence until he grew tired of them and left again. She took a bucket in each hand and returned to the yard.

"I'm going for water," she said. "I'm walking along the lake shore so I'll be gone for about an hour. Clifford, will you keep an eye on everything?"

He gave her a smile that actually seemed genuine. "We're going inside," he said. "I have some presents for the children."

Adam scowled at his father. "What about my saddle horse you promised to buy me in Virginia City?"

"Son," Clifford said, massaging his son's shoulder, "there wasn't a horse your size to be found anywhere in Madison County, but I'll keep looking."

Bethea turned away in disgust. Why did Clifford bother to lie to his children? When would they begin to see him for what he was?

CLIFFORD LOOKED AROUND the cramped cabin. Every time he set foot inside, the walls closed in on him. Having six brats under foot didn't help. He wouldn't have come home this time, except he had had a string of bad luck at the tables in Virginia City. He'd gone by stage to Dillon where his luck had worsened.

At the station in Monida, he'd been forced to spend the last of his cash on transporting the goods. He would have left them sitting on the platform, but that nosy bitch Mrs. Burns had come out and stuck her nose into the whole affair. He'd shut her up by promising the drivers a bonus if they made good time. She had huffed her disdain and returned to the hotel.

Now he needed a stake to try again and somewhere in one of the trunks he knew Bethea had a stash of gold coins and maybe some greenbacks.

He sat down and pulled his oldest daughter down onto his knee. "Esther," he said, kissing her forehead, "how's my favorite girl?"

"I had a birthday. You were gone, Papa. I'm eight years old now," she said. "Did you bring me a present?"

"I ordered a special present just for you in Virginia City," he said. "I'll pick it up next time I go there."

She beamed. "Is it a dolly? The leg came off my rag doll and Mama tried to mend it but she said the cloth was rotten. Oh, I hope it's a new dolly."

"You'll have to be patient, sweet," Clifford, squeezing her. "Now then, I've got a secret for you. Can you keep a secret?" She nodded. "Well," he said, "I bought your mamma a special present and I want to hide it for her birthday, so she can find it and be surprised. Do you know where her special secret places are, where she hides trinkets or coins or jewelry?"

Esther shook her head. "Mama doesn't have any pretty jewelry, but she has a little sack of gold coins in the blue trunk."

"Show me, sweet," he said, following her into the back room. She pointed to the trunk and smiled up at him. "Fine," he said. "Now you go outside with the others while I hide your mamma's present."

Gleefully, she skipped from the room, whispered to the others about her father's surprise as they trooped outside.

Once he was alone, Clifford opened the trunk and felt among his wife's personal belongings. The light coming from the front room of the cabin was dim. He shoved several camisoles aside, lacy white garments that he'd never noticed before. She had preferred dressing alone and he had always taken her in the dark.

She acted as if her body was her private, secret gift to be given up only after he'd used force. She had turned out to be a cold, indifferent bitch of a woman. He doubted if she had an ounce of desire in her entire body. What had happened to the hot blooded fifteen-year-old who had teased him that Sunday afternoon in her father's barn?

His hand touched the grainy surface of leather and he grabbed it. Maybe it was a pouch or purse. When he pulled it from beneath the clothing, he frowned. He had been right about the leather, but instead of a box, it was a book. He'd always known she liked to read, but why secret away a reading book where no one else could enjoy it?

He stared at the book with its carefully tied red ribbon. His curiosity aroused, he yanked at the ribbons and used his index finger to flip the book open to its middle. It wasn't a printed book at all, but rather a blank day book in which she had made entries. Clifford Kingston began to read.

CHAPTER ELEVEN

WITH FREQUENT REST STOPS along the foot path, Bethea was able to lug the heavy buckets of water to the cabin, but when she reached the door, Clifford was nowhere in sight. She struggled inside, got the buckets as far as the dirt floor near the dry sink, and collapsed into a chair.

She dipped the corner of her apron into the nearest bucket and wiped her forehead, wondering if the temperature would ever cool. So much for the predictions of sub zero weather, she thought. This was more like Missouri. Maybe she could get Clifford to lift the buckets to the counter.

Before she regained her strength, her son David's shout came from outside. "Papa's leaving again. He just got here and he's going away." He shoved the cabin door open. "Why won't he stay?"

She pushed herself from the chair and followed him outside. The younger children were sobbing while Adam and Ben stood sullenly near the head of the horses, holding the reins. Clifford tied the reins of his new white horse securely to the back end of the wagon, then turned to Bethea.

"I'm not staying," he said.

"Where are you going?"

"Over to Henry's Lake then to Fort Hall, or maybe Eagle Rock," he said, not looking at her. "I got business in Idaho Territory."

A leaden weight halted her movements. "What's in the barrels? They look just like the old whiskey barrels back home."

He laughed. "They're trade goods for the Injuns. I'll make a killing this time."

"Selling whiskey to the Indians is against the law."

"Shut your damned mouth," he snarled. "You have your way with the Injuns, I have mine. They're trade goods, I tell you."

She was too weary to care about his business legalities. "I need money to send for medicine for the winter, and we need a horse. Please leave us a horse."

"I'm going," he said, climbing into the wagon seat.

Furious, she ran to the back of the wagon, untied the reins of the mare and led the animal away. "We're keeping the horse."

He stood up, bracing his legs against the wagon seat. "Take the damned horse," he shouted, his face filled with hatred. "It's just an old Shoshoni nag. I can get another one the same place I got that one." He reached into his trouser pocket and pulled out some coins, tossing them into the dust near her feet. "Cheap payoff at that. I won't be back."

A cold sense of dread drove her backward. "You're abandoning us? Here? Alone? My God, Clifford, I know you never loved me, but how can you just walk away from your children? And what about this next one?" She put her hand on her abdomen.

"I never wanted those brats, and I sure as hell didn't want that one. Every time I poked you, you had to make another brat. There are ways to stop 'em coming, but you wouldn't do nothing. Well, you're free now, you whore. Free to take up with that Injun you talked so lovy dovy about, free to go back to Missouri, or free to stay right here and freeze your asses off. After I sell these goods, I'm heading to Arizona Territory where it's warm." He slapped the heavy reins against the two draft horses and the wagon jerked ahead.

Adam and David jumped out of the way as the large hooves missed their bare feet by inches.

She ran along the wagon for several yards. "But the deed, the deed is in your name," she shouted.

He slapped the reins again. "You'll figure something out. You always do. You can write that trash in your book if you want to, but you'll have to squirrel away new money." He pulled on the reins and the team stopped.

She clutched her chest, out of breath from running alongside the wagon. His words began to sink in. When she looked into his face, she saw unbridled hatred.

"You're no better than the paid whores in Dillon or Butte City," he said, "only you take your pay in wagon loads of fire wood and canned food. Only a dumb Injun would pay such a high price for a piece like you. He could have gone to Fort Hall and got it for a jug of whiskey."

She reeled under his accusations. "I don't know what you're talking about."

"I've read your book," he said.

Her mouth gaped. "You had no right to snoop in my trunk."

"I could haul you into court for adultery and use your own writing as proof." He snickered. "I never knew you were capable of such passionate prose. If I hung around here, I'd beat the hell out of you, so count your blessing, like your nagging old mamma would say. I helped myself to the roll of greenbacks. I'd be careful if I was you. Only a woman who's lost her wits would walk about the lake in the middle of the night. Are you insane, Bethea? Don't tell your redskin lover. Injuns don't like crazy women. They're superstitious that way, I hear tell."

He spat upon the ground near her feet. "Seeing you in my pants instead of a decent woman's dress makes me glad I'm leaving for good. You can have the rest of my old rags. I've been wanting to buy some new duds."

He slapped the reins again, and without a backward glance drove away. Bethea watched the wagon disappear over the rolling hill to the east. Her children stood beside her, silent except for Faith's soft sobbing.

How did a mother explain to her children that their own father considered them all mistakes? That their father didn't love them and that he considered them intrusions in his life?

Adam turned away. "I'm glad he's gone," he said. "Now he can't tell me I'm always doing things wrong. Ben, want to help me milk Bossy?"

"It's too early," Ben murmured, unable to look away from the speck moving around the next curve.

She patted his shoulder. "We'll manage. Haven't we lived here by ourselves most of the summer?"

Ben looked at Bethea then back to the road. "I'm coming," he mumbled, trudging after his older brother.

Nine-year-old David leaned against Bethea. "We'll help you, Mama, and I promise to keep an eye on Gabriel so he won't get lost any more." She hugged him lovingly. He was her quiet child, lost in the middle of the large brood, a little boy who needed a friend. His older brothers often went about their business, excluding him because he was small for his age. Perhaps if his twin brother Caleb had not died, this child would be different.

Esther, a little mother in spite of her eight years, took her sister Faith's hand. "We'll go pick up our dolls, Mama, and Gabriel can help us. David, bring him along. I'll sweep the floor and then we can all go to see the baby squirrels we found yesterday."

Faith looked down at her scuffed shoes, then up at Bethea, her eyes round and tear filled. "Papa doesn't love us."

Bethea dropped to her knees. "He's angry. He wants to be free to come and go when he feel like it."

"Are you gonna go away, too?" Faith asked, her voice barely a whisper.

Clasping the petite little girl in her arms, Bethea broke into sobs herself. "Of course not, sweetheart. We'll stay together, right here, with Bossy to milk and the garden to hoe, and the baby squirrels and birds to watch over." She released Faith and got to her feet. "Speaking of the garden, if I don't get that hoe and get busy, we won't be able to tell the radishes from the weeds."

She found the strength to smile confidently at her children's worried faces. "Esther, be careful when you sweep. That dirt floor can make more dust than I ever imagined. Someday we'll put down some boards and build us a real floor. Why anyone would overlook a floor is beyond me. It must have been built by an old bachelor who had never done housework."

Bethea picked up the hoe and began to weed the garden. With each whack of the blade, she weeded Clifford Kingston from their lives. He'd hurt them for the last time. They could manage. She would go to Virginia City and file for a divorce come spring. Why should she care what other people would say? No one cared about them.

Con Adler's face materialized in her mind, but hatred for Clifford overshadowed it. Con was busy with his own affairs. They owed each other nothing. She would have to keep reminding herself of that. She had been on her own for most of the summer. They would manage through the winter. She raised the hoe high in the air and brought it down, severing a stubborn weed from the row of lush potato vines.

Two hours later the cabin had been tidied and the garden completely weeded. Adam and Ben returned with two sage hens they had snared. When the hens were cleaned and dressed, Bethea put them in the roasting pan she'd brought from Missouri, and began to peel potatoes.

They ate outside around a campfire, taking turns making up stories and watching the western horizon turn pink and golden as the sun announced the end of a long and traumatic day.

OVER THE NEXT WEEK, Bethea's ire cooled as did the weather. Broderick stopped by on his way out of the valley and they visited over coffee. When he was about to ride away, she touched the reins on his horse.

"Wait a moment, please," she said. "If...when you see Con Adler again, would you ask him to stop by? I need to talk to him. Tell him it's very important."

He dismounted and swept his hat from his head. "Why, ma'am, he passed by this way early this morning. I figured he'd stop in on his way out."

She clutched the ties on her sun bonnet.

"Didn't you see him, ma'am?"

"No." She swallowed the lump in her throat. "Will he be coming back soon?"

"Doubtful, ma'am," the young man replied. "He was headed to Alice, on to Dillon to transact some business, and then he was catching the train east to Boston."

"Boston? Whatever for?"

He shook his head. "The boss doesn't keep me informed of his reasons, ma'am, but old Matthias has two brothers there. They're partners in the livestock company. Have been since '75, I hear. Maybe they're needed out here for the winter. 'Course I'm speculating about all this, but I'm sure surprised he didn't stop here."

"Why?" Bethea asked, trying to hide her disappointment.

"He was talking about you folks to Stub and Jacob, our foreman. My ma always did say I had big ears, but I heard the boss give them firm orders to keep an eye on this place, and then I couldn't hear what else he said."

BRODERICK STOPPED AGAIN a few days later on his return and presented her with a bulky package. "From the Alice home ranch," he said.

"But why?"

He grinned. "The old folks just moved into their fancy new house, and Miz Victoria said you might be able to use this stuff. Old Matthias scowled all the while she was talking, but nothing stops Victoria Adler when she makes up her mind, so I'm just following orders." He rode away, whistling off key, leaving a bewildered Bethea standing in the middle of the wagon road.

Clutching the soft package to her bosom, she closed the cabin door and leaned against it. Con was gone, all the way across the country, thousands of miles, gone for weeks or maybe months. She laid the package on the foot of the bed and returned to her work. Late that night, after the children were settled in their beds and the tin bowls and spoons washed and put away on the open shelves above the dry sink, she put the kettle on the stove again and prepared for her weekly bath.

She longed to be able to sit in a tub and luxuriate in several inches of warm water, washing her hair and her body with lavender scented soap, then sitting in the sun while her long hair dried. She and her two sisters had made hair washing and drying a Saturday morning ritual at the farm in Missouri.

Sighing, she poured boiling water from the kettle into a small pan and added enough cold to bring the temperature just right. Unbuttoning the shirt and trousers, she let them fall to the dirt floor to provide a mat to stand on. Her underwear had become sweat stained and she added it to the pile. Standing naked in the dim light of the coal oil lamp, she dipped a rag into the water and lathered it with soap.

"Now I shall take my bath," she said to the empty room, pretending to be a rich matron about to soak in that imaginary tub. The tub would be sparkling white enamel, she decided, wondering what a marble tub might be like. Instead of standing and washing parts of her body with the strong soap and rinsing it away, then soaping another part, she would be lying almost prone, sticking a shapely foot out of in the air and flicking billowing bubbles into the air.

When she washed her face with the lye soap, she tried to ignore her burning cheeks. As soon as she finished, she'd use some of the precious glycerine and rose water her mother had given her. She worked her way down to her breasts, now heavy and tender from her advanced pregnancy. A little more than two months and she would be giving birth once more. She refused to think about that problem. She had more immediate concerns.

Her abdomen seemed to have enlarged significantly the last month but she knew it was merely a precursor of what lay ahead, and hoped she would still be able to work the garden and bend over to reach the ground. Her thoughts drifted to Con Adler as her soapy hand slid down the extended skin.

Savoring the cool breeze drifting though the window, she stood motionless, naked, staring across the small room. If life had been different, could this child have been his? Would that have made a difference? What would a child of theirs be like? Light skinned or exotic? Fair headed or dark? Green eyed or blue, or perhaps a throwback to brown.

She stared down at her belly. Her own father had brown eyes and black hair, inherited from his French mother. Con's hair wasn't black but a deep rich dark brown and a hint of a curl around his temples. She had noticed that when he'd laid his hat upon the ground at the spring house.

Clifford's body had been covered with downy brown hair. What would Con's body look like? Smooth and muscular, she decided, smiling sadly. He was on his way to Boston of all places. Boston! If only she had seen him ride by, she could have wished him a pleasant journey, or convinced him to linger, but what would they have done then? What if he had come a few days earlier and run into Clifford? She refused to speculate on what might happen if the two men ever came face to face.

Still, she was greatly disappointed in his failure to stop. Perhaps he had had time to think rationally. They hadn't thought so sanely when he'd found her behind the spring house, and the promise of those brief kisses had burned into her memory forever. But any rational man would think twice about getting involved with a woman who couldn't seem to stop producing children. He was single, unincumbered, wealthy and handsome. She stared thoughtfully across the room. Con Adler had all the things her husband desired but couldn't seem to obtain.

Clifford might be considered handsome if he didn't snarl and quarrel and belittle others but he could never be truly free and single. He had fathered these seven children. How could he deny that? She knew he couldn't handle money with thrift and he lacked the business acumen to become wealthy.

The bath water grew cool and she poured it carefully into the bucket beside the front door, then refilled the pan with a new mixture of hot and cold. Dawdling would chill her. She couldn't take a chance of getting sick now. Who would take care of the children? Her belly blocked her view of her legs more than once as she finished washing the lower portion of her body and legs.

Now only her feet remained to be washed. She put her soiled undergarments on a chair and sat down. Putting her feet directly into the pan, she wriggling her toes in pure joy. Her ankles were still slim, with no sign of the swelling that usually bothered her the last month. Perhaps if she stayed active as long as possible, she could keep any complication minimal.

Sometime in the next month, she would send one of the boys on the white mare to Monida and see if Mrs. Burns could help. Wouldn't Mrs. Burns be surprised at the news of another baby. Could her baby be the first white child born in the Centennial Valley?

As she swished her toes though the water in the enameled pan, a disturbing thought came. What if her time came during a blizzard, or if the snows were deep and Mrs. Burns couldn't get into the valley? Maybe she would have to think of an alternative plan. She had read that some Indian women delivered their babies alone, but could she? She hoped she didn't have to find out.

Once her bath had been completed, she found a clean blue flannel gown in her chest. In spite of the warm afternoons, the nights were chilly and the soft material gave her a sense of security she needed badly this night. She set about washing her hair and rinsing it with a few precious ounces of the cider vinegar from a gallon jug beneath the dry sink.

It would take hours for her hair to dry, but she planned to bring her journal up-to-date and that would help pass the time. If she combed it often and fluffed it out and ran her fingers through the waves, she would manage. Better now than in the morning with all the chores to do. She glanced over at the comb she shared with her children. Just that morning, she had broken out several teeth.

Retrieving the journal and writing materials from the trunk, she carried the coal oil lantern to the block of wood she'd garnered as a night table, and climbed into bed. The feather mattress sank beneath her weight.

When she reached to adjust the quilt, her gaze fell on the package from the Alice ranch, still unopened. Two feet by one foot in size, and almost of equal thickness, it was tied with a generous piece of twine. She tugged on the ends of the twine, being careful to keep it from tangling. She could put it to good use, and as it came free, she wound it around her fingers to form a ball.

Unfolding the crinkly brown wrapping paper, she gasped at the contents. Fabric; new fabric. Why would a woman give away new fabric? And to a stranger? A piece of pink checked gingham, enough for a new dress for herself, or maybe two for the girls. When she spotted the two pieces of wool sateens, one pale blue and one a darker shade that matched her daughters' eyes to perfection, she knew the selections had been no accident, and that the pink gingham had been sent for her personal use.

Several small pieces of plaid wool, in shades of blue and red and black, could only be destined for boy's shirts. Deeper into the package, she found scores of scraps that would be suitable for a pieced quilt top. Never in her life had she been able to make a quilt top from new fabric. Perhaps she'd sew the scraps into a larger piece and make something for the girls.

She crawled back against the log wall and stared at the fabric now scattered across the bed. She had brought the New Home sewing machine her mother had given her for her twenty-fourth birthday. Bulky though it had been to pack for the journey west, it now stood in the corner of the children's bedroom, covered with a small baby quilt. Tucked away in one of the trunks were several spools of white thread.

Now she knew how she would spend her evenings when the days grew short and cold. She loved to sew. Even making trousers for the boys from Clifford's worn out pants gave her satisfaction.

Her eyes filled with tears. How could she ever thank this woman she had never met? Wiping the moisture from her cheeks, she began to sort the fabric into stacks depending on their intended use. Her hand hit something hard between the folds of the pink gingham.

Excitedly, she pulled a silver and green metal box and held it in her hands. Her fingers trembled as she worked the tiny silver hook. When she lifted the lid, she gasped. A hand mirror of the finest glass lay nestled beside a brush and comb on green velvet. The floral design of comb's spine matched that in the handle and back of the brush and the mirror.

Only one person could have sent her this gift. Con Adler, the man others called uncivilized, had understood her need for these articles of a woman's toiletry. She lifted the brush from its resting place and put it to her head, then began to stroke her hair, feeling as if Con's hands were holding the brush. When her hair was dry and flowing about her shoulders, she cleaned the brush and put it away, and plaited one thick braid down her back.

Not until she placed the brush in its box and picked up the mirror, did she give into her full emotions, sobbing softly against her sleeve and clutching the precious mirror in her hand.

Con had given her a gift. Out of love? She wiped her cheeks with the sleeves of her gown and smiled, sensing his presence in the room. In the mirror, her green eyes were red from crying. Her cheeks had turned golden brown from the sun. She would have to remember to wear the sun bonnet more often. Examining her cheeks for wrinkles, she found none, but near her eyes, tiny lines had begun to form. From squinting at the bright sun on a clear day?

She sat on the bed staring at her image for several minutes, wondering what had attracted her to him? Had it been her face? He had said she was beautiful, but didn't most men pay such compliments just before they collected a kiss? He must have discussed her circumstances with his parents. Why? He couldn't have known of Clifford's plans. Her head pounded with confusion.

When the fabric had been neatly sorted into stacks, she carried them to the table, then folded the brown wrapping paper to use again. A small piece of white paper floated to the dirt floor of the cabin. She unfolded the stationery, admiring the embossed letters VAA in one corner.

"My son explained your circumstances," Victoria wrote in a script that reflected formal education. "We've moved into the house of our dreams. What irony I feel, for how I could have used this house when raising Con and his five brothers and sisters. I bought the pink gingham for my three daughters and never used it. Now, they are married and starting families of their own. The rest, other than the blue sateens, are from the years of sewing for our large family. Use it as you wish.

"I'm sure you know who the mirror is from. He purchased it in the county seat just before I saw him off for his trip east. My husband is not recovering from his accident as quickly as we had hoped. My son didn't want to go, but the circumstances required it."

She had scratched out the next several words, then continued. "My oldest son is special to all of us. I pray that he will find the happiness he so richly deserves. The Alice cattle will be in Alaska Basin until October. If we can be of help to you, send a message with one of the cowboys.

"None of us knows what the future holds. I didn't when I first met Matthias. He was married to the sister of Chief Tendoi and I respected that marriage. But that's another story.

"I have several readers for the children. One of the cowboys will drop them by. They are all trustworthy and loyal."

Respectfully,
Mrs. Matthias Adler (Victoria)
Alice P. O., Montana Territory

BETHEA AWOKE BEFORE DAWN, knowing how she would spend some of the money hidden in the trunk. As each child awoke, she made them step onto the brown wrapping paper, and with a graphite pencil she traced their feet, allowing room for growth. Beneath each set of prints, she wrote the owner's name and age.

She added her own feet to the templates of footwear. In a note, she asked Victoria Adler to inquire as to the cost of purchasing boots for all of them, suitable for the winter.

"Thank you for the dry goods, and especially the mirror. I've been without one for several months. Please let me know the charges for the shoes and I will send the funds in order that you might order them for me. We have one horse for the seven of us, so we remain close to the cabin most of the time. If anyone should ask about our welfare, please inform him that we are managing. With God's blessing, we will harvest our potatoes before the first snows.

"Also, please inquire as to the cost of a bar of lavender facial soap. One will do. The bars of lye I made last year in Missouri are harsh on my skin as well as that of my children.

"Thank you for your kindness,

Respectfully,
Bethea Kingston,
Lake Shore Ranch, South edge Upper lake
Centennial Vly, Madison Co., Mont. Ter.

A full set of McGuffie readers arrived a week later, followed by another package of outgrown children's clothes several days later. When a package containing the boots arrived, along with six bars of soap, Victoria Adler enclosed a bill for twelve dollars. Bethea made the cowboy wait while she retrieved the amount from the bag of coins.

The boots fit to perfection, and the children insisted on wearing them until blisters began to form, and Bethea convinced them to save the new boots for colder weather when woolen socks could be worn.

As the days went by, and another package arrived, Bethea became uneasy. The generosity of this woman was more than the Kingston family deserved. A thought nagged at her all day. Victoria Adler had made them charity wards of the Alice Ranch. When the next package arrived, Bethea refused to accept it.

"Please inform Mrs. Adler that I appreciate all she's done for us, but the Kingston family does not take charity."

October arrived with a slight dusting of snow, but it melted and the potato vines had already died down. She would wait two more weeks, then dig the potatoes and turnips and the garden could be forgotten until the spring.

At night the children complained they were cold. She stoked the stove and kept the bedroom door drape tucked behind a nail to allow the heat to reach their sleeping room. Two weeks of Indian summer gave her time to harvest her garden. Perhaps the purveyors of harsh winter stories had been tricked this year, for if the weather continued to be as mild as these weeks of October, they would have no trouble surviving.

When another load of sawed wood arrived, she swallowed her pride and accepted it, for Adam and Ben had fallen woefully behind on using the two-man crosscut saw, preferred instead to prowl the woods across the road. The stage coaches to the park stopped running. The last week in October she stood near the cabin door and watched the Alice cowboys trail the Adler beef stock out of the valley.

The foreman Jacob and cook Stub lingered to take tea with her after the herd had passed.

"Pie, gentlemen?" she asked. "We picked the berries just yesterday, the last of the season, I'm sure. The birds and bears cleaned many of the bushes before we found them."

Jacob and Stub exchanged glances.

"Ma'am, why don't we wait around here and help you pack your things?" Jacob asked. "You and the children can spend the winter in Spring Hill or stay at Mrs. Burns's hotel in Monida. Would you consider that? The boss said to tell you he'd take care of everything. He's already spoken to the Burns couple."

"We could never accept such a generous offer from Mr. Adler," she replied. She thought of the cost of renting a place for her family. "We'll be fine here." She stared at the straggling calves running to catch up with the herd. The calves had grown significantly since she had first seen them, as had her own children. The summer had been good for the children.

"And Matthias Adler?" she asked. "Is he up and about?"

Jacob shook his head. "He's hobbling around on a pair of crutches, but I doubt he'll ever ride a horse much from now on. On top of his broken leg, he got a bad case of erysipelas in his left arm and it left it almost useless. Miz Adler tries to convince him it's only temporary, but he's one bitter man right now and Miz Victoria has her hands full."

"Tell Mrs. Adler we send our greetings. She was very generous to us."

"Victoria Adler is a fine noble woman, ma'am," Stub said. "Count yourself fortunate when she becomes your friend."

Bethea recalled the terse note she had written to the woman. Other than the load of wood, no more packages had arrived. "I offended her," she said, explaining what she'd done.

Jacob chuckled. "It takes more than a case of misplaced pride to break the bonds of friendship with Victoria Adler, ma'am."

Bethea pursed her lips. "Is that what it is?"

Jacob shrugged.

"And Con? Has he returned from Boston?"

"He's due in on the evening train from Butte City," Jacob replied. "He's bringing one of his uncle and two cousins. Both of his brothers have quit the mines."

"I met Lee Adler once."

"I knew them boys would come home eventually," Jacob said. "The air in them mining burgs ain't fit for man or beast, and if you stay there for long, you'll either get caved in on, blasted with steam, or die of lead or arsenic poisoning. If one of those don't get you, you come down with a lung infection that cripples you for life."

Stub nodded. "You see, ma'am, the other Adler son, Quentin, was at Glendale in the smelter and the Hecla mines are rumored to be closing down in the next few years."

Bethea took a sip of her tea. "We all must plan ahead for our futures," she murmured.

Stub emptied his cup and stepped outside. "I'll get the horses, Jacob, then we'd best be moseying on out of this valley."

Jacob shook her hand, thanking her for the tea, and shoved his hat on his gray head, but before he made his exit, he took off his hat again and held it against his chest. "Ma'am, I may be speaking out of turn and maybe I'm jumping to conclusions about how you and young Con feel about each other, but I'm sure he'd be mighty relieved to know you was out of here. Don't forget those arrangements he made at the Monida hotel." He glanced up at the sky. "And don't be deceived by this weather."

"He's only a friend."

Jacob's mouth tightened. "I seen you two kissing and hugging, and I could tell by your faces you were more than that, ma'am. I've known him since he was twelve years old. He's grown up to be a fine man, a credit to both his mamma's and his papa's people. I reckon I can see the problems ahead, but if the Lord wills it, it will be. If you're dead set against leaving, can I take him a message? I'll be seeing him tomorrow morning."

"Tell him..." Her eyes grew misty and she blinked. *Tell him I love him*, she thought. "Tell him we look forward to seeing him next spring."

CHAPTER TWELVE

WHEN CON ADLER stepped down from the passenger car of the south bound Utah Northern, he scanned the Red Rock station platform.

The trip had been exhausting, partly because he couldn't get the Kingston family out of his mind. When he'd ridden past the Kingston cabin before dawn on his way out of the Valley, a dim light had shown through the window. A white mare had been picketed away from the garden. He didn't have to be hit over the head to understand that Bethea's husband had returned.

By now, her damned precious garden would be either harvested or froze out. They were probably snuggled in that bed he'd stared at, and making plans for the future. That thought alone emasculated him.

He'd done the right thing by volunteering to make the trip to Boston. His mission had been to explain the situation to the Adler family members who had invested heavily in the stock raising business in the early 1870s. After the panic of '73, the stock growers had met informally and worked out an agreement that had been sealed with handshakes that resulted in a pattern for usage of the public lands in the valleys of the area. His father had claimed major sections of the Centennial Valley.

While Con waited for transportation to arrive, his thoughts centered on his father. Shortly after his return from Omaha, Matthias Adler had been thrown from his favorite mount and lay in a ditch for more than a day, his lower left leg fractured, and his left arm gashed to the bone. Con had found him the afternoon of the second day, delirious with fever. Between the insects, the blow flies and stagnant water, the arm had become infected. When the doctor from the county seat came to tend him, he'd reopened the wound that ran from his shoulder almost to his elbow and scraped away the infected flesh and muscle.

Erysipelas, an infection that had turned his father into a screaming mad man, had lived up to its name of St. Anthony's Fire, and for three weeks his father had endured the pain. Now his left arm, still twice its normal size, hung almost useless at his side.

There had been no way to keep the large Alice operation going without help, and Matthias had insisted it come from within the family. Con had been summoned from the valley to bring the Adlers together once more, and he had deliberately avoided the only person who could have detained him.

A crystal clear image of the mirror and brush came to him. Why had he been such a fool as to buy it for her? His mother hadn't asked questions and he'd offered none. When he'd asked if she had any unused fabric or outgrown clothing, she had plunged into a search of trunks and sewing baskets.

He tried to concentrate on his surroundings. "I'm sure the buggy will be here any minute," he said to his Uncle Tyrone Adler.

Tyrone's two sons, both younger than Con and eager to experience the ranchman's life, looked around the depot until they spotted a pretty young woman accompanied by her parents. They stood together grinning at the blushing object of their attention, until Con reminded them of the luggage being unloaded from the train.

Through the glass window, Con saw a surrey with red fringe swinging in the breeze, pulled by a team of matched bay geldings, turn into the yard. Victoria Adler held the reins with Matthias at her side. *Probably giving her directions*, Con thought. The sight of his family warmed him. It was good to be home.

THE ADLERS SAT AROUND the dining room table talking late into the night, discussing the problems and Matthias's frustration at not being able to reassume the leadership of the business.

"I'll be honest with you, Tyrone," Matthias said. "Con should take my place. He has the experience, and he understands the men and the land. Quentin has come home, but he never took to stock raising until the smelter showed signs of shutting down. He's a cowboy, not a rancher, so he won't be much help in making decisions. Lee just had his seventeenth birthday. He's still wet behind the ears." He glanced across the table. "Con is the logical one."

Con rose from his chair, returning to the table with the coffee pot in his hand. "Father, we've discussed this already."

Matthias chuckled softly. "Cussed is more like it."

Con sighed. "Maybe in a few years. Bringing Uncle Tyrone out is the best solution for now. He's a good financier. It's time he learned the other end of the business." He turned to his mother. "Have you heard from the valley?"

Victoria smiled. "All is well. That's what Jacob Dingley said when they got home with the stock. They have three loads of wood and the two wagons of staple goods. With all that flour and canned fruit, she'll be baking pies all winter long."

Matthias scowled. "Are you talking about those damned squatters?"

Con let his father's question pass. "And the children?"

"Jacob says they've all grown like little weeds this summer," she replied. "Jacob insists there were six little boys running around in the yard." She waved a shapely hand in the air. "Maybe she's put her daughters into trousers, like I did a few summers. She must be a very practical mother."

"She's a devoted mother," Con said.

Victoria smiled. "Do you remember Rhoda, Sarah and Angeline in pants, Matthias? That was the summer they all learned to ride their ponies astride." She frowned at Matthias. "Their father warned me it was a mistake, making them think it was proper to act like their brothers. Well, they're proper ladies now."

She smiled reassuringly at Con. "I'm sure she's busy sewing up a storm now that fall is here."

"The silver box?"

"I wrapped it in the pink gingham."

"And the soap?"

She smiled again. "I forgot it the first time, but when she ordered winter shoes for everyone, I enclosed all six bars. She thinks she bought it herself. It's best that way, dear."

"What the hell are you two talking about?" Matthias asked.

"And the books? Did you get the readers and slates to them?" Con rubbed his temple. "We should have sent some tablets and pencils. They can't even go to school."

"Her damned husband is responsible for those matters," Matthias said, his tone cross and short.

Con and his mother looked at him.

"And if he doesn't, what then?" Victoria asked. "We had to start our own school after that terrible year at Red Rock. That's it! Next spring, we'll see about getting a teacher for them and start a school there. The cowboys can build a small school house in no time." She turned to Matthias. "Couldn't they, darling?"

"We pay those cowboys to help with calving or to cut hay," Matthias replied, "not playing carpenters." He reached for his cane as he grumbled, "They'd ruin more boards than they'd ever hammer."

"Matthias, don't be such a grouch," Victoria scolded. "It's unbecoming such a charming man as you."

"Are you sure she's well?" Con asked.

"She's a proud woman, my dear, perhaps too proud for her own good. We've done all we can. Now it's up to her."

"And her husband?" Con pressed. "Did Jacob talk to him?"

Victoria looked puzzled. "Jacob says there's no sign of him, and she and the children talked as of they expected to be alone this winter. All they have is a white mare and a milk cow. I worry about them, but I don't know what else we can do."

"She can't stay there all alone." Con began to pace the floor. "Good God, she's expecting another baby."

"Oh, Con, you never said she was going to have another child," Victoria murmured. "Is it...you wouldn't...would you?"

"You're fooling around with a married woman who's pregnant to boot?" Matthias asked, his handsome face flushing beneath the tanned lines.

"Yes, she's pregnant, but no, it's not mine." Con ran his fingers through his hair. "Wish the hell it was, then we'd get all this straightened out and she'd come here."

"With that brood? Not on your life," Matthias roared. "It would be the scandal of the century." He stood up and pounded his cane against the table top and everyone jumped.

Victoria took the tip of the cane between her fingers and daintily removed it. "You'll scratch the table, dear." As if she had answered all his questions, she turned to Con again. "Will you be going to see her?"

"I promised my uncle I'd go to Lemhi agency and see how their hunt went. On my way back, I'll swing by the cabin. I may be gone for months, so don't worry about me. Unless someone finds my body along the road, you'll know I'm fine.

"I'll be leaving early, before daybreak," he said. "I've missed the fall hunt to the geysers for the first time in years. Father, you understand about the hunt. It's important to their survival. I need to compliment my cousins on their success."

His father scowled and slid his good arm around Victoria's shoulders. "I'm sorry I get so riled up about the Kingstons. They'll work out their problems and we'll work out ours."

Victoria kissed her husband's cheek.

"While you were gone, Con, there was a ruckus about the Shoshonis violating hunting restrictions near the geysers," Matthias said. "Seems the local immigrants think the noble red man should stay on his reservation and starve. If the government won't keep its side of the treaty, what do the people expect?"

He looked at his brother Tyrone. "Those hunting excursions are in their blood. I've been on several myself and Con goes nearly every fall. They've been bringing back meat for the winter for centuries. They may never be farmers and ranchers the way the Indian agent wants them to, and why should they?"

Victoria patted his arm. "Don't get all riled up again, Matthias." She held out her hand to Con and he squeezed it. "Take care, darling, and we'll look forward to your return. Try to be home for Christmas. It wouldn't be the same without you."

CON TOSSED AND TURNED, waking with a jolt from a dream that Bethea needed him. Tears streamed down her cheeks as she reached out to him, but before he could take her hand, she slipped away.

The moon still hung in the sky when he packed his gear and headed toward the barn to saddle Hellion.

Tendoi had been chief of the Lemhi band since the death of Shag at Bannack in 1863. Now in his old age, he left the fall hunts to his young warriors, but he'd be wondering about Con's absence.

Many times, as a boy, Con had ridden over the mountain passes to seek solace in his uncle's encampment. Perhaps his uncle's ongoing efforts to live harmoniously with the encroaching white settlers had helped him to understand his mixed-blood nephew.

Lost in thought, Con let the stallion find his way up the well worn Medicine Lodge Trail, reaching the crest of the range that marked the Continental Divide as the sun broke into its full brilliance to the east. He stopped a few miles into the Idaho Territory and built a small campfire to prepare breakfast. He wasn't really hungry, but Hellion had earned a rest and time to browse the dried grasses.

He'd developed the white man's need for a fresh brewed cup of coffee before starting the day, and while the water in the pot heated, he put a cast iron skillet on the fire and dropped in two slices of bacon he cut from the slab of smoked meat he'd found in his stepmother's root cellar. After it browned, he pried open a can of succotash and dumped it into the skillet and let it brown.

After this meal, he would live off the land or from his Shoshoni relatives, until he reached the Kingston cabin. If Bethea's husband was there, he'd introduce himself and move on. If she was alone, he had no idea what he might do. No matter what his heart and body desired, he would never knowingly put her reputation in question. He simply wanted to know if she and the children were safe. Then he'd try to talk her into moving to Monida or Spring Hill until spring.

After breakfast, he washed the skillet out with sand and creek water, swished the coffee pot, and put the utensils away in the bulky saddle bags. One side contained food, the other a change of clothing. A bed roll, canvas slicker, and an extra coat were tied behind the bags. He traveled light because he knew his plans might change quickly.

He leaned back against a boulder and rolled a cigarette. The only other experience that energized him more than the rush of nicotine was the sight of Bethea Kingston, the softness of her lips on his, or the pressure of her body against his.

But enough, he decided. He was dawdling and there was no time for that. He finished the cigarette and crushed out the end with his boot heel.

WHEN CON RODE into Tendoi's encampment, he sensed sadness mixed with simmering tension. His uncle's features, weathered from a lifetime in the outdoors, was a mixture of grief and perplexity. Con dismounted in front of Tendoi's lodge and stepped up to him, clasping him on his shoulders.

"Uncle, what's happened?" Con asked.

"Chugan, welcome," Tendoi replied. "We have trouble."

"Can I help?"

"Only if you know a white man with brown hair and blue eyes who travels the land in a wagon with barrels of whiskey."

Con grimaced. "That sounds like many of the drummers who come from Corinne. Some still travel the old roads to the mining camps. Has he come here to Fort Lemhi?"

The chief shook his head sadly. "No, this one was near the geysers, where the young men were hunting."

"Did this drummer sell them whiskey?" When Tendoi nodded, Con felt his blood rise. "That's illegal."

"This man operates outside the law," Tendoi said. "Two months ago, he gave one of my grandsons and his friend whiskey in exchange for the white mare carrying a foal from your very own stallion. My son Jack had given her to his son. The fools traded her for a bottle of this man's rot gut. We found the friend dead in a ravine where he had stumbled, the broken bottle still in his hand."

"Did you report this to your agent?"

"The agent claims to have no power to bring justice for us." The bitterness in Tendoi's voice added to Con's uneasiness.

"Has the man come back to the area?"

Tendoi shook his head slowly, his long braids shifting across his broad shoulders. "The man came to the geysers where my young braves were hunting buffalo and elk." Tendoi took Con's arm and motioned for them to walk away from the women who were milling around the lodges.

Con explained why he had not joined them, then asked, "Was the hunt successful?"

Tendoi nodded. "Game was plentiful, but the band who loves whiskey fought with the band who never drinks it, and they divided into two parties for the return to our valley. The whiskey lovers met the drummer again and he gave them a small keg in exchange for six

149

horses. The men fought among themselves, then tried to get more from the drummer. He pulled a gun on them. 'For his own protection,' he will say. Three of our young men met death at the geysers."

"Damn the man," Con murmured.

"When the whiskey was gone and the hunters had recaptured their minds, they brought their dead brothers home. This morning, I sent two of my most trusted sub chiefs to report this whiskey seller to the agent at Fort Hall."

"Do you know the whiskey drummer's name?"

"King? Kingwell? Maybe Kingrock." Tendoi stared across to the mountains to the east. "My son Jack said the man bragged about going to sell to the Shoshoni women who live near the fort. They trade their husband's ponies when the men are away. Whiskey is a curse to my people. You have been wise to never taste it."

"Could the man's name be Kingston?" Con asked, feeling a foreboding that made him glance over his shoulder. "I'll track him if you can describe him. A man in a wagon can't be too difficult to find."

"He is much shorter than you," the chief said. "My grandson says his eyes are blue, pale and washed out, and behind his gaze, there is evil. His hair is as pale as the grasses of winter and as thin. My son says he has hair on his body, all over and thick like an animal's down!"

"I'll find him," Con said.

Tendoi got to his feet again. "Chugan, you are my sister's son. Go and find him, but do not bring grief upon yourself or your father or to me. Bring him to us."

Con arched a brow at his uncle. "What would you do to him?"

Tendoi chuckled. "Not what my grandfathers would have done. Those days are gone. I will question him, use what persuasive powers I possess, then deliver him to Fort Hall for punishment."

Con stared at his uncle for several seconds. "If the man is Kingston, he has a wife. She lives in the valley to the geysers."

"The woman has made a foolish choice."

"He has several children."

"They will need to find a new father."

"I want to be that father," Con murmured, startled by his own words. "I don't know if I can treat him fairly."

"Because of this woman, Chugan?" Tendoi asked.

"She's very special," Con admitted. "She has all the qualities a man needs in the woman he marries."

"You talk in riddles," Tendoi replied. "Shoshoni men can take several wives. I have three, even though some say I have fifty. But in the white man's world, no woman can have two husbands at the same time. The Mormon people to the south permit the men to have plural wives, but the agent at Fort Hall says the United States government has declared war on them, so my nephew, you have made a choice that can only lead to misery."

Con told the chief where Bethea's cabin was located and asked him to advise his braves to watch out for her and the children if they happened to pass by.

"We will frighten her."

"I don't think so," Con said. "I didn't seem to scare her."

Tendoi broke into a broad smile. "My daughters say that you have the eyes to charm any woman, regardless of her skin and hair. When they learn of your interest, they will envy this woman. Some of the young women here have had their eyes on you, Chugan, but you don't come to our encampment enough to give them hope. Now I can tell them why."

Con shook his head. "I'd rather you keep this to yourself. We have many bridges to cross before either of us finds what we're looking for."

"Have you spoken to her of your feelings?"

"No."

"And has she spoken to you of her feelings?"

"No."

"Then how do you know?"

Con make a kissing sound and pretended to hug himself. The chief chuckled, and together they walked back to Tendoi's lodge, the sadness momentarily gone from the old man's eyes.

WHEN CON ADLER REACHED Fort Hall, the official government operated reservation for the Shoshoni, Bannock and

Sheepeaters, he discovered that not only had no man fitting Kingston's description been seen in the area, but that the agent had only recently heard of the shooting in the national park.

"Then I'll go find him and bring him here," Con said to the man he'd met several times previously. "My uncle wants me to bring him to Lemhi, but considering the unrest I saw in the camp, the culprit might be safer here. Murder is murder, white man or Indian. If this man goes free, I wouldn't blame the Indians for rebelling. They have enough reasons already."

The agent ran his fingers through his graying hair. "I know. Tendoi and the other chiefs signed their last treaty in 1880 and Washington is still sitting on it. I'd like to bring the President and all his cronies out here and make them live for a year on one of these reservations, survive on the allotments, and see how they'd like it. Then maybe they'd take their pens in hand and live up to their promises. But that's not likely. You bring this Kingston fellow here and I promise I'll do what's right...to the best of my ability and authority."

Con spent the next several days searching for the elusive law breaker, still uncertain his prey was Clifford Kingston. He'd been positive the man was at the cabin when he'd passed by. Now that made no sense. The white horse fit the description of Jack Tendoi's mare. He'd even glanced over his shoulder as he rode past the cabin, thinking the mare had been vaguely familiar.

But there had been no team and wagon. He chided himself for not stopping. His pride had stood in the way of asking a few simple questions that would have saved him weeks of anxiety, for that was what he'd felt during the long weeks in Boston.

Darkness came early beneath the heavy clouds that had moved in since noon on the fourth day of his search. He spotted the glow of a campfire at the southern base of the mountains that had become known as the Centennial range.

Perhaps it was the fire of some lonely miner, or a cowboy who had gone for strays after the fall roundup. Snow dotted the peaks of the mountains. Now, several days into November, all stock would have been brought down from summer pastures. The snows had held off, adding to the drought that had cut the grazing time by several weeks in many of the high valleys.

As he approached the campfire, he saw an empty wagon, its front axle broken. A solitary draft horse was hobbled nearby, while off a hundred feet a band of Indian ponies searched for dry grass. A man knelt near the fire, his head bowed as he concentrated on the contents in a kettle hanging from a tripod over the fire. The top of the man's head was thinly covered with light brown hair. When the man got to his feet, Con could see that he was only a few inches taller than Bethea and thin, as if he had skipped many meals in recent weeks.

Was this Kingston? "Hello, friend," Con called, not wanting to provoke the man. The man jumped to his feet and grabbed a rifle Con had not noticed.

"Got enough in that kettle for a hungry traveler?" Con asked, keeping Hellion to a walk as they edged toward the fire.

The man continued to hold the rifle, his finger sliding in to rest against the trigger. "Reckon so. It's horse stew. Damned stupid animal broke its leg. Broke the wagon axle, too. I shot it. Ain't had meat for days, so why let it go to waste?"

Con dismounted. Holding the stallion's reins, he eased himself closer. "Whose ponies?"

The man stepped backward, his hand caressing the lever of the rifle. "I got 'em fair and square from some stinking Shoshoni."

"Shoshoni seldom part with their ponies," Con said, stepping closer to the campfire.

"These savages liked whoop-up juice better than ponies," the other man said, putting the rifle down against the wagon box.

"You a drummer?" Con asked. He looped the reins once around a dead juniper limb and stepped away.

"Sure as hell am," the man said. "Farmed some in Missouri, but no man can make a living farming in this country. I've decided to mine for gold my own way. The fools can dig it out and I'll sell them something for it. No man ever filled his gut with gold dust or quenched his thirst either."

"Then why the Indian ponies?" Con asked again, sure now of the identify of this man. Thoughts of the man in bed with Bethea sickened him. Together, they had created seven children. Angry at himself for letting his feelings for Bethea become a distraction, he concentrated on the man across the campfire. "Who do you intend to sell them to?"

"I figured I'd work my way to Utah. Them polygamist Mormons need horses and I hear tell they have money to burn."

"I hate to challenge your plans, but they need draft horses, not these scrawny ponies." Con stepped into the circle of amber light from the fire. "The Mormons are thrifty with their money."

"I can convince them to part with it," the man boasted.

Con shrugged. "Why don't you turn them in at Fort Hall?"

"Can't do that," the man said, reaching for a small sack and sprinkling a pinch of salt into the stew. "Almost ready now. Pull up a rock and sit. What did you say your name was?"

"I didn't, but it's Adler," Con replied, not moving.

The man's hand stopped in mid air. "Adler?" He looked up, as if seeing Con for the first time. His mouth tightened and his gaze swept over Con's face and body. "You're that half-breed son of a bitch whelped by that rich rancher near Red Rock."

"And you're Clifford Kingston," Con said.

Kingston's gaze raked Con's body again. "You've been fooling around my place, bothering my wife and kids."

"I've come to her aid a few times, but I've never..." Con bit the sentence off.

"You've done a hell of a lot more than that according to her," Kingston said, edging closer to the rifle.

Con accepted the other man's comment without challenge. If thoughts were of equal weight to deeds, he was guilty as charged. "If you cared about your family, why aren't you there now?"

Kingston laughed. "And put up with one more squalling brat? Hell no, I'm headed south."

Con closed his eyes for a split second. He'd sensed for days that Bethea needed him. He should have trusted his instincts. Had he waited too long? When he opened his eyes again, he found himself staring down the barrel of Kingston's rifle and he knew the answer.

Vile disgust twisted Kingston's features. "You've been whoring with my wife," he snarled. "I read all about it in her book." He tossed his head back and laughed like a mad man. "I reckon it's true about you bucks. She was always a cold piece with me, but whatever you did to her, she liked it. Did you teach her squaw tricks?"

"Shut your damned mouth, Kingston." Con's hand edged toward the revolver at his hip. Any plans to take the man to Fort Hall evaporated. Now his only thought was to get back to the woman in the valley. "I don't know what book you're talking about. I've never been with her. You're crazy, and a damned coward to leave her alone in winter. She deserved better than you."

"But that won't be you," Kingston snarled, aiming the barrel at Con's chest. "You've had her for the last time."

The explosion of the rifle deafened Con's ears as lead tore through his body. The sound of the rifle being levered again drove him toward the darkness. Another searing burst of pain hit his thigh. He turned, hobbling on one good leg.

Kingston jammed another shell into the chamber. Looking down, he didn't see Con's revolver come from its holster.

The rifle raised again when Con pulled the trigger. A circle of blood appeared at Kingston's mid section, hurling him against the freight wagon. He slumped, but the rifle didn't waver.

Another explosion rocked the darkness and Con knew he'd been hit again. The cold night air filled with the stench of gun powder and scorching stew. Time slowed as he lifted his good arm and took aim, then pulled the trigger again. Kingston flinched, then slumped sideways, his face calm and child-like in the glow of the campfire.

Con blinked to clear his vision, but darkness began to surge from somewhere inside his head. His unsteady hand touched the reins and he managed to untangle them from the juniper limb. Hellion whinnied softly.

"Stand still," Con mumbled, wondering if the words came from him or some stranger standing beside him in the darkness. He fought an urge to lie down and sleep, but he knew the searing pain in his chest wouldn't let him find peace. Struggling with the stirrup, he used the last ounce of energy in his good arm and pulled himself into the saddle, easing his bullet riddled right leg across Hellion's broad rump.

A cold wind came up, bringing with it a few flakes of snow. In the distance, he saw the dark outline of the Centennial mountains and pointed Hellion in that direction. "Go, fella, go to her."

The stallion broke into a trot for several miles, but as the narrow trail reached the timberline, it was littered with rocks and the horse slowed to a walk. Con retrieved a pair of fleece lined gloves from his coat pocket and finally managed to get them on. His head reeled, but the stinging icy sleet blowing at the higher elevation kept him awake. He knew there was a game trail in the area that had been followed for centuries and he hoped they were on it.

The sleet turned to snow and the stallion slowed his pace. Con adjusted the fleece-lined collar of his coat up around his neck. Had he been dozing? Or had he passed out and managed to stay in the saddle? He rubbed his gloved hand across his eyes and tried to clear his thoughts.

Hellion had found his way to the narrow pass that divided the waters. Con's vision cleared but the whiteness of the blizzard disoriented him. Had the animal turned around? Could he be going back down the mountain to where Kingston's body lay?

He tried to turn in the saddle, but a swell of warm blood inside his clothing told him that he'd made a foolish move. Using his teeth, he managed to pull one hand from its glove, then pulled a kerchief from a pocket and loosened his clothing enough the shove the cloth against the hole his fingers found.

When he tried to pull his glove back on, it fell to the snow. If he tried to dismount he'd never be able to get back in the saddle. The height of the animal he'd loved riding for years had now become one more curse against him. Draping the reins loosely around the saddle horn, he kneed the stallion, but that action sent a burst of pain shooting up his leg and threatened to sweep him from the saddle.

The stallion began to work his way down a narrow trail between the evergreens, following some instinctive need to seek lower ground.

Siren voices sang to him; rest, sleep, rest. The swinging gait of the stallion added the chords; rest left, sleep right, rest left, sleep right.

When he looked up, he spotted three dark gray timber wolves through the trees. He looked toward the sky. The blizzard had blown itself out and the clouds were breaking up. Dawn had come to the valley. And it was the Centennial Valley he was now in. The wolves crouched and crawled through the evergreens several dozen yards to his right. He had no desire to be fodder for those beasts, to let them tear his flesh, disembowel him and howl over his bones.

He was too close to his destination now to give up. He pulled his revolver from its holster, aimed at one of the wolves, and pulled the trigger. The blast ricocheted through the sub-zero air, but the bullet missed its mark. The wolves yelped and disappeared into the timber.

He looked around. Hellion had carried him half way down the mountain. In the distance, he could see the Kingston cabin, its roof covered with several inches of snow. A fine curl of smoke came from the stove pipe.

Two children were coming from the lean-to that served as a barn, carrying a bucket between them. At the sound of his shot, they stopped and looked around. One of them pointed up the mountain toward him. His mind clouded again when he tried to estimate the distance. Maybe they had spotted the wolves. Maybe they had seen him and recognized the stallion.

The boys turned to the cabin. He watched as they carried the bucket inside and closed the door.

They hadn't seen him, he decided, as he stared at the closed cabin door. His knees were as numb as his bare hand, and he'd lost feeling in his cheeks and ears, yet he felt warm, almost toasty. Before he could decide what to try next, darkness swept through him like a black whirlpool and he slid from the saddle.

He hit the ground with a thud and groaned. The snow burned his face. When he tried to lift himself up with his arms, the bullet wound in his upper left arm turned into a torch.

He had almost reached his destination. He'd almost succeeded in seeing Bethea Kingston's face once more. Now it was too late. He'd tried, only God would know how hard he'd tried.

Bethea's features hung over him momentarily. Groaning, he rolled onto his back. His bare hand slid off his chest and lay in the snow. The blackness faded and he thought about trying to move again, but he'd tried before and failed. Angels of darkness danced around him and this time he sought their comforting arms.

CHAPTER THIRTEEN

AN ICY BLAST announced the return of Adam and Ben from the morning chore of milking Bossy, now safely sheltered in the log barn behind the cabin. After several weeks of mild weather, snow had come during the night, bringing with it winds that shook the windows and kept Bethea awake for hours.

Wild creatures prowled the countryside and they frightened her. She'd heard the howling of wolves again, and the snap of a tree breaking under the weight of the snow. At first she'd thought it was a gun shot, then dismissed the idea. Her mind was playing tricks again. They were alone in the south part of the valley now. Adam and Ben were safely inside now.

She had begun to have misgivings about the wisdom of staying in the valley, but she couldn't let her children know. Even if she decided they should leave, how could they manage with only one horse to ride, and not a particularly gentle animal at that? The mare had shown a strange intolerance toward young children. Only Adam and Ben had managed to handle her with skill.

Maybe Bossy would be gentle enough that one or two of the children could ride her. If the two older boys rode the white mare, that would still leave two of the children on foot as well as herself. She doubted she had the strength to walk thirty miles in the snow in sub freezing weather to reach Monida. No, they would have to make the best of a bad situation.

The food seemed to be holding out. She had begun to ration the wood, putting the children two to a bed for warmth and heaping the quilts on them. As a last resort, they could all sleep in the big double bed in the main room. They would be safe for another three months or more and that would carry them into February.

By then she would be caring for a new baby. Her throat tightened and she swallowed hard. She'd come to grips a week ago with the reality that she would have to deliver the baby alone. The children were too young to help. She had talked the matter over with the older ones, withholding the more explicit details of a birth, and instructed them to leave her alone and keep the younger children occupied, and to not be upset if she made noises or even screams, that she wasn't really in pain. They had all seen calves and lambs being born on the farm in Missouri. She suspected the white mare would be foaling in the spring.

She turned to her oldest sons, anxious to get her mind off her own condition. Their blue eyes were wild with excitement.

"We saw wolves," Adam said, carrying the pail of milk to the dry sink. "And we saw a man."

She frowned. "A man? Where? On the trail from Monida? No one has traveled past here for a month."

"No," Ben said, running to the door and jerking it open. "Up there. In the trees. Mama, he was just sitting there on a big bay horse...like..."

Bethea felt as if a heavy anvil had fallen onto her chest. "Like...what?" An image of Hellion materialized. She must be loosing her mind for sure.

"Like the stallion Mr. Adler rides," Adam said, shoving his brother aside and running outside.

Bethea's heart stopped. "Mr. Adler? Here? But surely he'd take the road." She stepped out and closed the door behind her. In the distance, about three hundred yards up the rocky hillside, she spotted a riderless horse. "I don't see a man."

"But he's there," Adam insisted. "Those three gray wolves that have been hanging around old Bossy were stalking him and he shot at them and they ran into the woods. I swear it."

"Maybe he got off," Ben said.

A dreadful chill tightened her chest. "Go find out, boys. I'll get my coat and join you. Hurry!"

She ran back into the cabin and told the younger children to stay inside, then grabbed her heavy overcoat. Buttoning it on the run, she raced after her sons. As she worked her way through the snow, the horse became more visible. The bay stallion whinnied and shook his head when the boys reached him.

Stumbling through several inches of fresh snow, she almost fell, but her speed propelled her onward. Gasping, she reached her sons and the animal.

On the ground near the stallion's hooves lay Con's body. "Con?" His name froze on her lips. Dropping to her knees, she touched his cheek. It was icy old. "Con, can you hear me?" she whispered, leaning over him. He didn't move. "Con, wake up." She stared down at his closed eyelids. Panic curled its spiny claws around her heart. "Con, please speak to me."

"Ma, he's got blood on him," Ben said. "Coming out that hole in his coat."

A few inches below his collarbone, a round hole had torn the leather. She slid her hand inside the high buttoned collar and touched his neck. "He's warm. He's alive. We must get him to the cabin. Oh, God, how will we move him?"

"Let's take his arms and pull him," Ben suggested, but when he moved Con's left arm, the man groaned, the first sound he'd made since she'd reached him.

"He's got a hole in his coat sleeve, too," Adam said. "And in his trousers. Ma, he's shot up real bad. Is he gonna die?"

"No!" She got to her feet. "Where's the sled you boys made last month?"

"Under David's bed."

"Bring it. Hurry!"

The boys raced down the hillside, sliding on their bottoms part of the way. She dropped to her knees again, cradling Con's face in her hands. He groaned. "Con, can you hear me?" Her eyes filled with tears and the warm moisture dropped to his cheek. "Please, Lord, don't let him die." She leaned closer, brushing her lips against his mouth. "I love you, Con Adler. Don't you dare die. I won't allow it, do you hear me?"

His eyelids fluttered, then lay still again. His lips parted as if he were trying to speak. She kissed him lightly once more and smiled through her cascading tears. "You're going to be fine, Con, just fine."

His eyes opened and she could sense his pain. Their brilliance drew her closer. "Can you hear me?" she pleaded. An almost imperceptible movement came to her fingers as she held his face in her bare hands. "I love you, Con, don't ever forget that. Think of how much I love you if you feel yourself slipping away. I need you. We want you here. Oh, darling, please live." Sobs shook her shoulder.

When his mouth moved again, she leaned closer, putting her ear near his lips.

"I thought I wouldn't make it," he breathed. "But I kept trying, and I found you." Before she could reply, his eyes closed again, and his face fell heavily against her hand.

When the boys returned, tugging the crude flat sled behind them, she tipped it on its edge and eased Con's shoulder and hip onto it. "Help me, boys, but be careful. Don't hurt him."

Bethea and her sons maneuvered Con's unconscious weight onto the sled. Con's head rested against the wood, his arms trailing in the snow. His hips were on the sled but his long legs hung from the end. "At least we can move him," Bethea said, breathing hard from the exertion. She pressed her fists against the small of her back and waited for the tightening in her womb to recede, then reached for Hellion's reins.

He tossed his head and stepped away. "It's okay," she crooned, pointing to the unconscious man on the sled. "We'll take care of him. Boys, try to pull him but be gentle." She began to follow behind, her gaze clinging to the man on the sled.

Half way to the house, the boys stopped, puffing heavily. "He's heavy," Adam admitted. He waved toward the cabin. Bethea looked up to find her other children standing outside the door, their coats buttoned to their chins and their knitted caps pulled down over their ears.

Bethea motioned to the younger ones to join them, then dropped to her knees in the snow again. Taking Con's limp hand in hers, she rubbed it briskly. He didn't stir.

When the children reached the sled, they gathered around it, staring at Con Adler's motionless body. Bethea rose to her feet.

Gabriel leaned over and touched Con's cheek. "He's cold." He straightened. "Why, Mama? Is he dead?"

"He's hurt. He rode his horse all the way up the mountain and down here to us," Bethea murmured. Her eyes glistened as she studied Con's pale face. "He came to us because he knew we would take care of him."

"Is he gonna stay with us this time?" Faith asked.

Bethea brushed a fresh flow of tears from her cheek. "Yes, darling, he's going to stay." She looked across the broad valley. "At least until spring."

"I can help," Esther said, taking Con's large hand in hers and brushing the snow from his fingers. Without a word, Faith took his other hand.

"I can help pull," David said.

"Me, too," Gabriel insisted. His older brothers looked at him, but rather than argue, they made room for him at the rope attached to a hole at the front of the wooden sled.

Bethea walked behind them, leading Hellion down the hill to the cabin. When they reached the door, Bethea handed Adam the reins and he took the stallion back to the barn. Bethea and the others shoved the sled into the cabin and next to the bed.

Adam returned to the cabin. "I took his bridle off and gave him some oats and hay," Adam said proudly. "He's sure a fine looking horse, Ma."

She nodded absently. "Now comes the hard part." She looked from Con to the bed and back to Con. "I'll sit him up and take his coat off." Going to his right side, she put his arm around her neck and tugged. He didn't move.

"Help me, everyone." Between her pulling and the children's pushing, she got him upright.

"Now his overcoat."

That task proved easy, with one girl tugging on each sleeve while Bethea held his heavy head on her shoulder.

"Yuck," exclaimed David. "His shirt is all bloody."

Bethea ran her hand up his back, blindly feeling her way. When her fingers came into contact with a ragged hole filled with warm sticky blood above his left shoulder blade, her heart stopped. "The bullet passed through his body."

If no vital organs had been damaged, her primary concern would be infection. "Stand back," she cried. "I'm going to stand him up."

"We'll help you," the boys insisted. Suddenly Con was upright, propped between the bedstead and her own body. His arms hung limply down her back, his head turned toward her neck. The feathery caress of his shallow breathing was as welcome as his kiss had been months earlier.

They eased him to a sitting position on the feather mattress. Now his cheek rested heavily against her breasts. "Esther, put some wood in the stove and sit the kettle on to heat. Adam, get the whiskey jug from beneath the dry sink and the bottle of witch hazel and all the jars of salve you can find on that shelf. Ben, pull the covers down to the sheet. David, crawl between us and unbutton his shirt and underwear."

"I can't see," David whined.

"Then feel," she shouted. "Hurry. I had no idea Mr. Adler was so heavy. Faith, get that old pan and a bar of lye soap. Gabriel, bring me one of your union suits that won't fit you anymore. Adam, get a bucket of snow to cool the boiling water."

Within minutes, they had Con naked to the waist, his skin warm and golden copper against her pale hands. Esther and Adam worked with the tea kettle and snow until the pan of water was as hot as they could stand to touch, then handed Bethea a piece of underwear and the lye soap.

Gently she began to wash away the coagulated blood, but when she saw the ragged flesh of the exit wound, she feared for her stomach. Painstakingly, she coaxed the area clean. "Adam, put some of the whiskey in a bowl and hold it for me. I have no idea if I'm doing the right thing." She sopped the whiskey soaked cloth against Con's flesh, frustrated when most of it ran down his back. "Pour some of it on! Directly into the wound."

Adam's hand shook as he dribbled the amber liquor onto the raw wound. Con flinched against her, and she clutched him tightly in her arms. "Again." When she was satisfied with their treatment, she soaked a piece of linen in witch hazel and folded it into a thick compress, then spread a generous layer of Black Salve on it. Grimacing, she placed the patch on the wound, and with the help of Adam and Ben, laid Con on the bed.

Exhausted, she dropped into the chair, but one glance at his chest reminded her of the seriousness of his condition. When she examined the bloody edges of the entry wound, nausea rose in her throat.

"How come he's not bleeding much?" David asked.

"Maybe he's lost all his blood already," Ben replied, and Bethea sent him a warning look.

She cleansed the wound with soap and water and dressed it, then changed water and continued to wash the rest of his upper torso. The slight rise and fall of his chest brought comfort to her soul. His chest was devoid of hair, just as she had hoped it would be.

"Mama, his arm is starting to bleed," Esther said, leaning against the iron head rail, her little face pinched with concern.

Bethea began to cleanse the wound on his upper left arm. She asked Esther to bring one of her old petticoats from the trunk. After giving the wound a liberal dousing of whiskey, she ripped the undergarment into several wide strips, soaked one of the strips in the witch hazel and folded it several times. A generous application of Black Salve was applied before she pressed it to the wound and tied another strip around his arm. She felt the back of his arm for an exit wound but found nothing.

"Is he gonna get well?" Faith asked, joining her sister at the head of the bed.

"If we all say a prayer for him, and if we take good care of him, I think so," Bethea replied.

"He's bleeding all over your bed," David cautioned.

"I don't mind," Bethea said, getting wearily to her feet. She gazed at the unconscious man. He looked as if he was in deep slumber. A thin dark stubble on his chin disturbed his handsomeness. His head turned toward the window as if he were searching for the warmth of the winter sunlight coming through the small window near the bed.

Bethea bit her lower lip. "Now for the rest of him." She pointed to the back room. "Everyone but Adam and Ben, please go in there and play, or bundle up and go outside."

"Outside," they all said.

"Fine." She helped them dress for outdoors. "And don't come inside without knocking first. Understand?" They all nodded. She turned to Adam and Ben. "Help me take off his trousers and all the rest. Start with his boots and socks."

While the boys worked, she retrieved a baby quilt and draped it over his chest, fearing he might become chilled before they finished their work. She stood near the brass headboard and let the boys work, listening with half an ear to their remarks. When the woolen underwear started down his hips, she forced herself to stare out the window, yet she was aware of each inch of flesh that come into view as the boys peeled his clothing away and dropped them to the blood soaked pile already on the floor.

"He's got another one," Adam said, pointing to Con's right thigh. In minutes they had the third bullet wound cleaned, dressed, and bandaged.

Ben giggled and wriggled his thin brows at his brother.

"Shut up, Ben," Adam said, but he, too, couldn't suppress a snicker of his own.

"I see nothing funny," Bethea said, her hand and the soapy cloth lying on Con's uninjured thigh as she washed it.

"Are all men...like that?" Adam asked.

"Like what?"

Adam shrugged. "You know. Like that."

Ben spoke up. "He means will we be big like that when we're all growed up?"

How she had managed to avoid looking at the most private part of Con Adler's masculinity, she would never know. Now forced to give her sons an answer, her gaze fell to the mat of dark hair that surrounded his manhood. She was more than eight months pregnant. She had no right to stare at him, to imagine other times, to wonder... She took one more lingering glance at his body and reached for a larger quilt. "I'm sure all men are different in ways, but they're all the same, too."

She smiled, feeling almost light hearted. "You wouldn't want to grow up to be big and tall like Mr. Adler and still be the same...you know...size as you are now, would you?"

The boys snickered and shook their heads, then blushed deep rose and refused to meet her gaze. They joined her beside the bed, their brows furrowed with concern.

"I like him, even if he is an Injun," Ben said.

She turned to him. "Don't ever call Mr. Adler that again. Don't ever call any Indian man or woman that name. They're people just like us. They live differently. They live with the land while we try to change it to our fancy."

"But Pa always said...," Adam said.

"Your father is a little man with a little mind, and he is wrong." She began to clean up the area.

"How do you think he got shot up?" Adam asked.

165

She gazed down at the unconscious man. "I don't know, but it's a miracle we found him."

"I'll bet he met another gunfighter and they had a shoot out and the other gunfighter is dead for sure," Ben boasted. "Mr. Adler must be one of the fastest draws in the west."

"No more of that kind of talk, boys," Bethea scolded. "Help me with these bloody clothes, and then you can go outside."

THEY ATE THE NOON MEAL, but Con's sleeping body in the bed nearby cast a solemn mood to the usually jubilant mealtime conversation.

In the afternoon, Bethea gathered them around the table and they prepared their lessons from the readers and tablets Victoria Adler had sent them. Later the girls cut out figures from the mail order catalog and played with them. The boys browsed the book and discussed their plans and dreams for the summer to come.

During supper, no one spoke.

"Perhaps Mr. Adler needs to hear our voices," Bethea suggested, fearing he might be slipping into a coma. After chores, they sang choruses for the man on the bed, but he didn't open his eyes.

The children crawled into their beds earlier than usual, and Bethea pulled a rocker close to the bed and began her vigil. When the sun announced the new day, she got up and went through the routine she'd established. Chores were done. The children played. She pulled her sewing machine into the front room and began to work on the blue fabric for her daughters' dresses.

When darkness fell, she took a basket of quilt pieces and sat in the rocker again, talking to him as she pieced a new quilt top.

"These pieces are from your mother's gift package," she said. "Thank you, Con, for asking her to help us. Someday I hope I can meet her. Will you take me there and introduce us some day? Do you think she'll approve of me?"

He groaned, but she knew it was only in pain.

She cared for him whenever he stirred, but his eyes remained closed. She dozed in the rocker, but awoke whenever the bed shifted. During the night, he began to mumble but she couldn't make out any words. Could he be speaking Shoshoni?

On the third morning, he began to stir restlessly in his sleep. His brow felt warmer to her touch. She changed his bandages, grimacing when she eased them from the dried blood that held them. The chest wound appeared to be healing.

When she slid her hand beneath his arm, she felt a lump on the back side. His flesh was hard and hot to the touch. She called Ben and Adam into the cabin. "The ball is still in his arm," she explained. "It's infected. I need your help."

They nodded. She rolled Con onto his stomach to expose the back of his arm. She ran her fingers down his biceps, feeling the hard mass of inflammation.

She looked at her sons. "Hold his arm, Adam. Ben, you sit on his other arm in case he fights us."

"Whatcha gonna do, Ma?" Adam asked, his face pale as she went to the shelf and picked up a sharp paring knife.

"I'm going to remove the ball." She ran the blade up and down on a whet stone, tested it, wiped it, then dipped it in whiskey. "It's made of lead and it's poisoning him. We can't let him die."

Ben looked at her. "You like him, don't you?"

"Yes." She wiped Con's arm with whiskey and felt for the firmest part of the swelling.

"More than you did Pa?"

She stopped her inspection. "Yes, very much more. Your father and I were forced to marry for reasons other than love."

"Do you and Mr. Adler love each other?" Ben asked, adjusting his hold on Con's arm.

"I can't speak for him," she said.

"David saw you kiss Mr. Adler," Ben said. "He told us. Did you ever kiss Pa that way?"

She sighed. "I never wanted to," she murmured as she touched Con's skin with the point of the knife. She'd never cut open a man's flesh before. "Just like a chicken," she mumbled through clinched teeth and pressed the knife against his arm.

His flesh parted. As if she were another person, she saw the layers of skin and muscle separate. Blood and pus poured from the incision and she wanted to be sick. The tip of her knife touched metal and she slid the knife point under the ball of lead and worked it to the surface.

She looked at her sons. Their cheeks were pasty, the skin around their mouths pale green, but they never wavered from their assigned duties. Con remained unconscious as she cleaned the incision, massaging and squeezing the area until only bright red blood flowed from it.

"Whiskey," she said, and Adam washed the area.

"How you gonna close him up?" Ben asked.

"With waxed quilting thread dipped in witch hazel." Her hands were steady as she washed them with soap and threaded the sharp needle. Each time she pushed the needle into his flesh and pulled it out again, she flinched, but in a few minutes she had chained the two sides together until they formed a smooth narrow line beneath the thread.

"Ma, look at his leg," Ben said. "You gotta do it, too."

Not until both wounds were opened, cleaned and neatly stitched and the ends secured with knots did she take time to consider how she had managed. They changed the bed linens, rolled him onto his back again and put a clean salved compress on his chest.

"Let's pull the bed away from the wall," she said, "so I can tend to him from either side."

When the children went to bed that evening, she sat in the rocker, staring at the sleeping man. He didn't stir, but his fever had waned and with it the flush in his cheeks.

AS IF HE HAD AWAKENED from the sleep of a dead man, Con Adler opened his eyes and stared at the cheesecloth ceiling of the log cabin. His chest ached as if a dozen sledge hammers had crushed it. Something pulled at his thigh and when his hand slid down beneath the covers, he felt the ends of strings...no, smaller.

When he tried to moved his other arm, he flinched, afraid he would find threads sticking out of it as well.

He heard splashing and turned his head. Near the dry sink, Bethea Kingston was completing a sponge bath, her curly brown hair piled high on her head. Standing naked with her back toward him, her slender shoulders moved as she leaned a fist against the dry sink and soaped one foot, then the other. Her middle was gone, stretched by her advanced pregnancy, yet her hips and thighs were as enticing as he'd imagined.

How had he gotten to their cabin in the blizzard? He had a memory flash of the two boys looking his way, but they had closed the cabin door on him. He gazed at her for several more minutes, then respecting her privacy, he stared at the ceiling again. How long had he been lying in her bed? He touched his stomach beneath the covers and found it hollow. Then, as if a fog lifted from his mind, he realized he was naked. He closed his eyes.

He awoke when the bed creaked. Now Bethea wore a blue flannel gown. Her back was toward him. Unaware she was being watched, she began to brush her freshly washed hair. He could smell the faint traces of vinegar mixed with lilac and lavender and the fragrances seemed as wondrous as a spring day. Her hand drew the silver and green brush from her scalp, sweeping downward to make the ends bounce back into curls. Her hair turned to shinny copper strands as it dried and its luster caught the glow of the coal oil lamp on the log stump beside the bed.

He reached out, catching the curly strands as they fell free of the brush. She stiffened, then slowly put the brush down on the bed. When she turned, the sight of her face took his breath away. Her green eyes turned shiny.

She climbed onto the bed, crossed her legs beneath the gown, and clasped his outstretched hand in both of hers. "I feared for your life," she whispered.

He squeezed her hands. Suddenly he closed his eyes. He hadn't cried since boyhood, and he didn't want to embarrass himself in front of her now, but when her finger brushed the moisture from the corner of his eyes, he knew he'd failed. He turned his head away, his eyes still closed. "I was afraid I'd never see you again," he murmured.

The bed shifted again and he knew she had left him. In a few minutes she appeared on the other side, a steaming mug in her hands. She sat down in the edge of the bed. "I couldn't get you to eat a thing," she said. "You must be famished." She helped him sit up, propping the other pillow behind his head and shoulders.

"Be careful," she said. "There's a pad with some salve on your back, actually your shoulder. We've had trouble keeping it in place."

The sheet and blankets fell to his waist, exposing the purple wound on his upper chest. He stared at it. "Was I shot?"

She nodded. "Several times. I made a tincture of crushed Balm of Gilead buds and whiskey," she said. "It works miracles. It always does."

He looked down at his chest at the dark stain and up at her.

"I washed all your wounds with carbolic solution and whiskey and witch hazel and...oh, Con, I was so frightened for you, but the Balm of Gilead seemed to do the trick, and now you're awake, and my prayers have been answered. It's best now to leave your chest open to the air. I put a layer of Black Salve on it."

She looked around the room. "It smells to high heaven in here." She shoved the mug into his hands. "It's corned beef and cabbage soup. Your corned beef and my cabbage." She smiled bravely. "I thought you might be able to drink the broth. It's been snowing ever since you got here."

He took a sip of the broth. "And how long has that been?"

She glanced at marks on the wall above the bed. "Five days, almost six." She brought him a biscuit and he dipped it into the broth. "You woke up once after we removed the balls."

He frowned. "In my chest?"

She shook her head. "That one went completely through you on its own." She blushed. "We could feel the balls, one in your arm and one in your...thigh. I couldn't let you lie here and get gangrene and die, now could I?"

He spooned a piece of corned beef from the mug, and leaned back against the pillows, chewing as he admired her features. "You're a woman of many talents. You actually cut me open?"

She looked at her hands. "I pretended you were a chicken."

"A chicken?" He grinned. "Nothing more noble than that?"

She blushed. "You were a chicken when I cut you open. I pretended you were a handsome tom turkey stuffed for Thanksgiving when I sewed you back up."

He balanced the mug on the quilt top and reached out to touch her cheek.

She looked up at him.

"I owe you my life," he said.

She swallowed. "You'd do the same for me, wouldn't you?"

Centennial Swan

"And more." He took another sip from the mug. "Did you know that in many Indian societies, when you save a man's life, he's yours for the rest of your life?"

She started to smile but when her eyes turned shiny she bit her lip to keep from crying. "In my heart, you've belonged to me for some time," she admitted, looking away.

He emptied the mug and handed it back to her. "If you've stayed up for five days to care for me, you must be exhausted."

"I dozed in the rocker." She sat on the edge of the mattress.

"A woman in your condition needs her rest." Not knowing why, he put his open palm on her belly. She closed her eyes but didn't push his hand away. "When will the baby come?" he asked.

"About three weeks, but you know how babies can be."

He chuckled. "No, I'm afraid I don't."

"I had it all planned," she said, rising to her feet. "Now that you're here, I know it will work. You'll be well enough to take the children out for a long walk when my time comes. I'll take care of my own confinement, and then you can bring them back inside to meet their new brother or sister."

She set the mug on the dry sink and turned to him. "The snow is getting very deep outside. Adam and Ben keep paths open to the lean-to, we call it our barn, and the wood pile and the outhouse. Tomorrow they'll work on one to the root cellar. I'm beginning to understand why no one lives here in the winters. We have no sleigh and I doubt the horses could handle all the snow. It's quite deep."

"Hellion? Is he here?"

She nodded. "The boys have been taking care of him. We've inherited a beautiful white mare who's going to foal in the spring. If I didn't know better, I'd think Hellion and Snowflake know each other."

He shoved the blankets between his thighs and bent his knee to expose his leg, studying the entry wound and the line of stitches on the back. "Perhaps they do. Where did you get her?"

Bethea explained Clifford's arrival and departure. "Two wagon loads of food supplies were waiting at the station when he got off the train at Monida and Mrs. Burns insisted he bring them to us. Clifford wanted to keep them because he figured they had been shipped to us by mistake. My husband is not an honest man."

171

She looked across the room at his bare leg.

He slid it back beneath the covers. His head began to throb and he had to concentrate on what she was saying.

"They were from you, weren't they? They proved you were still thinking of us," she explained. "That was important to me."

"You're impossible to forget," Con said. When he'd first opened his eyes, he had no recollection of how he'd managed to find his way to the valley or the reasons why he'd let himself get shot up. Flashes of his visit to Tendoi materialized.

Bethea took a sip of water from the bucket on the counter and set the dipper down. "My husband has left us. We've been without transportation all summer, so I insisted that he leave us the mare. He did, but before he left he stole what little money I had...and read some passages in a journal I write in. He had no right!" She turned to him. "I plan to file for divorce as soon as the weather permits travel to Virginia City."

Another flash of memory filled his thoughts as the campfire roared to life, the man and the rifle, his own response. The corned beef sat heavy in his empty stomach when he looked at her. "Bethea, I met your husband. He's the man who shot me."

She covered her mouth. "Clifford shot you? The monster!"

"I was lax. He got off the first two shots."

"How did he recognize you?"

"He said he would have known me anywhere. He wanted to kill me when I said my name was Conrad Adler. My eyes didn't aid my disguise."

"But why?" she cried. "He had no grounds."

"He imagined you and I had sinned together."

She hurried toward the bed. "But we've done nothing. A few kisses are no grounds for accusing us of adultery."

He looked into her eyes. "He said you'd written things in your journal that proved otherwise."

Her hand trembled as she pushed her loose hair from her face. "I wrote about my feelings...my hopes and desires. They were inappropriate thoughts for a married woman, but he had no right to read them."

Con tucked a thick strand of golden brown hair behind her ear. "He despised me sight unseen."

"How did you meet him? Where?"

He told her of his uncle's complaint. "I tracked him down and he pulled his rifle on me."

"He's an evil man," she said. "He's a vengeful man, too. He holds grudges for years over some silly little slight. You're in danger, Con. I'd die if anything happened to you. This has been terrible enough. What if he tries again?"

His hand fell from her hair. "You have nothing to worry about and you won't have to file for a legal divorce. I killed him."

CHAPTER FOURTEEN

BETHEA OPENED THE DOOR on the stove and put in three pieces of wood. If the fire went out, they would all freeze within a few hours. All her diligence would be for naught. The children had remained healthy, not even a head cold, and she was thankful for that. Perhaps the isolation from other people had been a blessing, although at times she longed for the companionship of another woman.

Someday she would take the children and walk around the lake and visit the widow Mrs. McGyver. They would take tea and compare recipes and quilt patterns and discuss their children's progress. Perhaps the woman enjoyed reading novels and they could exchange books, except that at the moment Bethea had none to call her own.

The woman had a young son. How did she educate him when the valley had no school? If a school was available, no one could possibly get to it when the snow was four feet deep and getting worse. Drifts had covered the spring house completely.

Adam had climbed onto the roof of the cabin and shoveled the snow from it. They certainly didn't want the roof to cave in on them. Instead of freezing, they would die of suffocation. Wouldn't that be ironic?

The laughter that filled the room couldn't have come from her, nor the sob that followed it.

"Bethea?"

She looked across the room to the man whose life had hung in the balance for days. Gun shots, snow, no air to breath, and now this. *Murder.* What else could stand between them? Were they destined to never find the happiness she had written about in her journal? Had the journal become a curse rather than a sanctuary for her thoughts and feelings?

"Bethea?" Con sat up and held out his hand.

Hesitantly, she crossed the room. The bullet wounds would leave terrible scars, but her stitchery was as good as that of any doctor in the territory, and she was glad. His body was much too fine to be disfigured by her own needlework.

"It's late," she said. "You go back to sleep. I'll sit here in the rocker in case you need something."

His brow furrowed. "Is that where you've been sleeping?"

"I've slept very little since we found you."

He lifted the bed covers. "I have one good arm. I want to hold you, unless you prefer that rocker."

"No, but..."

"Humor me," he said.

In seconds she was nestled against him, his body heat warming her in a way the stove had never been able to. Her fingers sought his naked shoulder, touched tenderly the crusty scab on his wound, then slid down to his waist and around him. She kissed the smooth skin near his right nipple, her tongue tasting him for a moment before she fell back on her pillow.

He raised himself on his uninjured arm and gazed down at her. "If I wasn't feeling weak and you weren't pregnant, this could be a very different night for us."

She stiffened and tried to move away. "You find pregnant women repulsive, too?"

Grabbing her chin, he forced her to look at him. "Is that Clifford Kingston talking? Was he like that?"

She tried to break free, but his fingers tightened.

"If I didn't think I'd hurt you, I'd make love to you right now," he said, then one corner of his mouth curled upward. "But I don't have the strength." He released his hold on her chin and he stroked her cheek with the back of his fingers. "Clifford Kingston was a fool, Bethea. He didn't recognize his own good fortune. I do. I find you incredibly beautiful regardless of how you're dressed or how large you are with child."

She told him about wearing man's clothing and dressing the girls in trousers. He chuckled. "That explains why Jacob Dingley questioned whether you had four or six boys."

His gaze drifted to her mouth and she waited. When he didn't take the initiative, her heart began to pound and her mouth turned dry. She ran her tongue along the underside of her upper lip. "Kiss me, Con."

His head came closer and as if time had stopped, his mouth grazed hers. "I'm afraid to continue."

"Don't be."

"I still can't believe I'm here," he murmured.

"Believe it," she replied, pulling his head down and kissing him. Gently, she eased him back. "That's enough for now. I just needed to satisfy...this little feeling I have."

He dropped back to the pillow. "Damn, I feel so weak."

"Then rest." She touched the dark hair at his temple. His hair now covered his ears and the nape of his neck. Its tendency to wave was more pronounced, the texture soft and thick. "You haven't been to a barber for some time."

His eyes twinkled when he smiled. "Indian men don't cut their hair."

"But white men do."

"I'm both." The smile left him. "Does that bother you?"

"When I first saw you at the Monida depot, I didn't know what you were. I only knew something happened...here." She took his hand and laid it against her full breast.

"Bethea," he murmured, running his hand down her back. "No more rocking chairs for you. I want you to sleep next to me."

She turned down the lamp and lay beside him. In minutes he fell asleep, but she lay awake for another hour, thanking the Lord for enabling her with the power to heal him.

The next morning, as Bethea served the children their mush, she told them about his waking during the night.

"Can he play with us?" Gabriel asked.

"Not yet, dear," she replied. "We must be careful to not tire him, but a little exercise might do him good. We'll wait and see how he feels when he wakes up."

"I feel fine," Con said from the bed.

Her head jerked up. He smiled across the room and her heart skipped a beat.

She spooned some mush into a bowl and drizzled on maple syrup before topping it with cream skimmed from yesterday's milking and carried the bowl to him. "Eat your breakfast, like a good patient, and I'll find you enough clothing to make you decent."

He stared down at the bowl and after a few minutes began to eat. When the bowl was empty, she handed him his mended underwear and helped him into it. He leaned toward the window. "I don't know how you handled it while I was unconscious, and I don't want to know, but I want to try to make it to the outhouse."

With her hands on her hips, she studied him. "Put your socks and boots on and wrap yourself in a blanket. If you can manage to make it into the children's bedroom and back here, I'll trust you outside, but Ben and Adam must go with you."

"Yes, ma'am."

DURING THE NEXT NIGHT he grew restless and she returned to the rocking chair. An hour before dawn, he settled into a deep sleep. For the next three days, he walked from one end of the cabin to the other. Adam and Ben accompanied him to the outhouse and after making the eighth trip of the afternoon, she suspected he was using the out building as an excuse to test his stamina.

On the fifth night of his reawakening, he fell asleep immediately and she settled into the rocker for another uncomfortable night of half sleep. What she wanted most was to lie in his arms, but she knew his rest was crucial to his continued recovery.

"Bethea?" The tone of his voice drew her to the bed. "Come lie beside me," he said, holding out his hand.

She stood up. "I have no right."

"You have every right," he said. "We're alone here...well, other than six children, we are." He dropped the covers and slid onto his back, wincing before he found a comfortable position. "You must be chilled. You're the mainstay of our lives. The children...me. "

"I don't want to disturb you."

He took her hand. "You've been disturbing me for months." He lifted the covers.

She had been unaware of how chilled she had become until the heat of his body reached her. Her body trembled next to his. He rolled her onto her side and pulled her against his, tucking his legs up behind hers.

To her surprise, he slid his arm around her bulging waist and rested it beneath her heavy breast.

Warmth surrounded her. When the trembling subsided, she reached for his hand and kissed his fingers. "I've never been held like this."

"Oh? It feels so natural," he said, "except that I can't reach your mouth."

She turned in his arms. "Remember when you kissed me at the spring house?"

"How could I forget that?" he replied. "Bethea, I've never wanted to say this to any woman before, but I love you very much."

"Con, you needn't say that."

He leaned over her. "The first time I laid eyes on you, I wanted to know you better. When I held you that night, I didn't want to let you go. By the time I rode away from the hotel, I wanted to make love to you in the worst way. When I came with my father and brother, I felt as if I was coming back to my family. I found you crying behind the spring house and I wanted to take you away forever and protect you from all your hardships, and especially from that calloused bastard you were tied to."

"I don't want to talk about him...not now," she whispered.

"You were in my thoughts wherever I went," he replied, his lips grazing hers. "Only my mother knew how I felt about you."

"Maybe someday I'll be able to meet her and thank her for everything, especially for raising a son so fine." Her finger traced the outline of his lips, wonderfully made and pleasing to her eyes. His high cheekbones and firm chin reflected his mixed heritage, but it was some elusive inner quality she found most fascinating. "Would you kiss me? Really kiss me? Like you did behind the spring house?"

When his mouth touched hers, she arched against him, but her body became a barrier. She yearned to know his love, to be fulfilled, but she had never thought of being with a man at this advanced stage. Con seemed aroused in spite of her misshapen body. His fingers found the row of ribbons that held the front of her gown, untying them one by one and kissing her skin.

She forgot to breathe when he eased the gown down her shoulders and caressed her breasts. *No*, she prayed, *don't hurt me*. Clifford had never been satisfied until he made her cry.

She watched as his dark head lowered and his mouth found her nipple. Pain was not the emotion that filled her when he bathed it with his tongue and drew it into his mouth. *No*, she thought, *this can't be happening*. Unfamiliar tingling ignited low in her body, as if his mouth had found the source of all passion and now his gentle suckling was drawing it up, bringing it from its hiding place to burst into fulfillment.

She gasped for air as her fingers clawed at his head. "No, no, I can't." She panted, unable to get enough air to breath.

"You can." He raised his head and sought her mouth.

Hungrily, her tongue joined his, this warm moist part of him that could bring her pleasure, pleasure she'd never known. When his kiss ended, she moaned, wanting to press his head down to her breast again. He looked into her eyes, as if to read her soul. The lamp still burned nearby. Clifford had always taken her in the darkness.

"It's not fair to you," she whispered.

"What about you?" he asked, tracing her brow before kissing it.

She looked away. "I don't matter."

He took her chin and forced her to look at him. "Is that the way it was between you and your husband?"

She tried to pull free. "It always happened so quickly. I've learned to expect nothing."

His thumb brushed back and forth across her chin. "There are many ways for a woman to be satisfied, if a man will take the time to discover them."

"I don't know...what you mean."

He kissed her lips again, then began to explore the sensitive skin at the base of her throat. His kisses ignited a fever in her body. With the back of his hand, he lifted her breast, bringing her nipple upward. Circling around its fullness with his tongue, he seemed in no hurry to complete...what?

This intensity building in her held no pain, unless the throbbing in her nipples could be considered pain, but if it was, it had to be the sweetest suffering she could ever experience.

She waited for the sharp stab of his bite. When he took her nipple between his teeth, holding it gently as his tongue flicked across the aroused tip, conditioning from the past was swept away forever. Flames whipped across her body and up to her shoulders, then changed directions and began to crawl down her legs to the tips of her toes. She would surely die if he didn't stop. She couldn't breath and opened her mouth, gasping for air.

A moan slid up her throat to quiver on her lips. When he took her breast in his mouth and pulled on it, the flame exploded into an endless convulsion. Her nails dug into his shoulders and she clung to him, unable to talk or think, only feel.

NOT UNTIL SHE SLUMPED against the pillow, her eyes closed and her breathing shallow, did he kiss her mouth again. "I told you there were other ways," he whispered. He lay back, pulling her against his own aroused body.

He had had no intention of letting the situation go so far, but when he'd gazed into her eyes, seen the dilation of her irises and the desire they reflected, he had changed his mind. How could any man, fortunate enough to receive the love of this woman, not want to take the time to bring her the fulfillment she deserved? Now, as he held her, his own needs were overlaid with the knowledge that he'd awakened new emotions in her.

Carefully moving his injured arm, he brushed her hair back onto the pillow and shifted to look at her face.

"Are you all right?" he asked, kissing her cheek.

Her eyes opened. "I'm...not sure what happened to me...but I found it indescribably...wonderful."

"You've never felt such intensity before?"

Her head moved on the pillow. "Never, and I didn't know a man could be content...without..." She looked into his eyes. "I wanted to touch your body, but I didn't want to hurt you, and then I forgot all about you."

He nuzzled her ear. "I'm glad it happened and that I was part of it." She looked into his eyes. "Is it proper for the woman to touch the man? I mean like I want to touch you? Down there?"

"Be patient," he murmured. "Wait until we're together as man and woman, completely, then you can do whatever you want."

She kissed his shoulder and lay quietly in his arms. "There's more to being together than creating new life, isn't there? More than a wife doing her duty?"

"Much more."

Something moved against his hip, strange and subtle yet forceful and repetitive. He slid his hand down beneath the covers and touched her belly. He felt the movement again. He splayed his hand over her and the baby kicked again, harder. The thought of a tiny foot under his palm fascinated him. He'd never paid much attention to young children and hardly looked at babies in their mothers' arms whenever he'd encountered them.

His curiosity grew and as the lump in her abdomen moved, he followed it with his hand. Each time he pressed his open palm against Bethea's body, the baby responded with a kick.

He chuckled. "We have company. It's remarkable."

She turned onto her back. "I didn't know a man would care."

"I care, Bethea, don't ever forget that."

"When spring comes and you can get out of here, you'll be on your way to your ranch. Your family must be terribly worried about you. For us, it's different. My family knows we're in a remote place. We have no one to answer to."

"Do you want to know about his death?"

"No."

"People might talk..."

She reached for his hand. "They have no part in this. Clifford was an evil, abusive man. He married me because...my father forced him. I was a naive fifteen year old girl. He overpowered me. He started tearing at my clothing and I couldn't stop him. I liked his kisses at first, but he hurt me, and afterwards tried to deny it, but my brother had seen us go into the barn. Adam was born six weeks before my sixteenth birthday."

She covered her eyes with her forearm. "While all my friends were going to dances and parties, I was home nursing my first baby. I loved my baby, but I was incredibly lonely. Within three months I was with child again. By the time my friends were getting married, I had two little boys and another one on the way. Clifford wouldn't leave me alone, unless I was pregnant."

He squeezed her hand. "And that third pregnancy, did you miscarry? Was that the missing letter C?"

"Yes and no." She rolled onto her side and gazed at him. "I miscarried, but a year later I gave birth to twins. I had two tiny little boys, Caleb and David. They weighed four pounds each and no one expected them to live, but they did, for awhile. Little Caleb died when he was seventeen days old. David is still small for his age but as healthy as the rest of them. He's my quiet child. He never knew his brother but I believe he misses him none the less."

With his fingers he combed the lock of hair that had fallen over her shoulder. "You know your children very well."

"Clifford couldn't remember their names."

"Even I, with my lack of experience, have no trouble telling them apart, but you see the differences as special qualities, don't you?"

"Of course," she replied, taking his hand from her hair and pressing it to the mattress between them. "I despised my husband, but I love all my children."

They lay quietly for several minutes.

"I don't want to talk about Clifford," she said. "I'm glad he's gone. Now I'm free to make my own decisions. The boys want to find some maverick calves and start their own herd. I'm going to file on the land next to us. I can do that, since this piece was not a homestead claim."

"That's true."

"That will double the size of our place. The land on the other side of the lake has been surveyed as desert land and I can file for three hundred twenty acres there and if I'm willing to plant trees, I can get one hundred sixty acres more. This side of the lakes has all the trees. If we dig up the baby ones and transplant them and take good care of them, we can meet the requirements, and since it would be a timber culture, I wouldn't have to live on it. And in a few years Adam and Ben can file on their own land."

"How do you know all this?" he asked. "You sound like my father, Bethea. He knows every angle of homestead law. He might loan you a few of his cowboys to help you file."

"Don't tease me, Con, I'm serious. I've been reading this little booklet Mr. Burns gave me. So you see, we'll be staying right here. I do hope you'll stop by and visit us."

He propped himself on his elbow again. "I have something more permanent in mind."

"You do? You only come to the valley in the summer. You have your responsibilities on the ranch at Alice. Is there really a town called Alice? You must have lots of friends you socialize with. I can't imagine having time to socialize, although I used to. Do you know how to dance? I can just see handsome young Mr. Adler squiring his belle to a ball at some fancy ranch house. Do you have a special lady friend? Don't tell me if you do. I couldn't bear to hear about her. I haven't danced in years."

He laid his finger against her lips. "Listen to me. You're prattling. Yes, I know how to dance, and yes, I have a special woman in my life; you, Bethea."

"Don't say this if you're only trying to please me," she murmured.

"I'm telling you because I need to," he replied. "I fell in love with you when you stepped off the train at Monida. I have no doubt of that. Six months has passed, six miserable months of worrying about you, wanting to come to you, watching you struggle alone here. I knew your marriage was in name only. No man in his right mind would treat a wife the way he did you. I wouldn't be surprised if he beat you."

She rolled away and turned her back to him.

"Oh, God, Bethea, I'm sorry." He rolled her back into his arms. "The man deserved to die. Now you're free and I love you. Nothing would make me happier than for you to become my wife." He kissed her lightly. "Will you marry me?"

Her eyes widened. "Con, you don't know what you're saying. I come with seven children. It wouldn't be fair to burden you. I have very little money, only this cabin and the land, a horse and a milk cow and next year maybe some chickens."

"I didn't ask for your dowry, I asked for your hand."

She kissed his lips. "I love you with all my heart, but you're still a very sick man. A month from now you may change your mind. Two months from now you'll forget we ever had this talk. Now, before daylight comes and we've spent the entire night chattering away, you get some rest." She started to leave the bed.

"Only if you sleep by my side from now on."

"Is that a demand?"

He chuckled. "No, it's a plea from a very sick man."

She leaned toward the lamp and turned it down until the wick was snuffed out, plunging the cabin into darkness Curling up against him, she fell asleep immediately.

He lay awake listening to the wind. The snows of the Centennial had come in full force. His thoughts lingered on his proposal of marriage. She hadn't turned him down, merely suggested they wait

183

until both were well. If the snow continued to fall, he would need to regain his strength and help keep the paths outside cleared.

He rolled onto his side, and felt for her. "Come closer," he whispered, and the bed creaked as she wriggled toward him. Pulling her into his embrace again, he let the warmth from her back seep through him, knowing that someday they would recall this night as a turning point in their lives.

Just before dawn, warm moisture against his arm brought him awake with a start. Laying on her side, she'd buried her face in her pillow in order to hide the sounds of her crying.

He rolled her onto her back and pulled her hands from her face. "Are you crying for the loss of your husband?"

She rubbed her eyes with the heels of her hands. "Can't I shed tears of joy? You did earlier tonight. I'll have to tell the children."

"We have time," he said, kissing her mouth.

"I'm so thankful you're going to live," she murmured. I'm thankful the children are safe and warm, too, but I got up and looked out the window. It's snowed at least another foot and the boys will have much shoveling to do in order to reach Bossy for milking and I can't help them. I've become such a weakling these past few weeks and this is no country for weaklings. Most of all, I'm so happy at long last I can sleep in your arms."

"You have every right to not feel strong," he murmured. "City ladies in Boston would have taken to their beds long before this. You're an amazing woman, Bethea, don't ever forget that."

When Con awoke again, the room was flooded with glaring white sunlight reflecting off the snow outside the window. Bethea was still asleep beside him, only her hair visible above the quilts.

He looked around the room. Six pairs of curious eyes stared back at him. The children were fully dressed. The stove had been stoked and the tea kettle heating. He put his finger to his lips, then motioned to Adam, the oldest boy. When he came alongside the bed, Con whispered, "Where are my saddle bags?"

Adam pointed to them leaning against the dry sink.

"Bring them, please," Con said. "I have a change of clothes." When Adam unbuckled the pouch and pulled out the garments, Con motioned toward the other children. "Can you take them into the other room? I'll get dressed. Have you children had breakfast?"

Adam shook his head.

"Then I'll fix something," Con said.

Adam glanced at his mother's head. "Is she sick?"

"Just exhausted," Con assured the boy. "She needs her rest. We'll let her sleep. Carrying a baby is hard on a woman."

He pulled on woolen underwear, clean pants and wool shirt, but when he tried the socks, pains shot through his chest, so he carried the footwear into the back room. "Can anyone help?"

With three children working on each foot, he found himself dressed, although Gabriel was more nuisance than help. Con lifted the little boy onto his lap, ignoring the discomfort in his chest. "Can you do buttons?"

Gabriel grinned and began to work the buttonholes while the older children finished buckling his boots. He eased Gabriel to the floor again. "Now, let's see what's in the kitchen."

He followed them back into the main room. They gathered around the table and looked at him expectantly.

"Are you hungry?" he asked.

They nodded.

"What do you want?"

"Mush."

He'd hated mush all his life. "That's the devil's food." He stuck a few sticks of wood in the stove and looked around. "Where are the eggs?"

"We don't have chickens," Ben said.

"Bacon?"

"We got lots of bacon, but it's in the root cellar under lots of snow," Esther said. "We don't have a real smoke house yet. Mama has a little bit of sausage left from yesterday."

"Then how about biscuits and gravy?" he asked.

"You making the gravy?" David asked.

Con shrugged. "Sure." Several minutes later he put the bowl of milk gravy on the table alongside the platter of biscuits left from the previous day. He ladled gravy over the crumpled biscuits in each bowl, then sat down to eat. He took several bites. Slowly, he became aware of chewy gum balls in the gravy that he knew were neither sausage nor biscuit.

Gabriel stuck out his spoon to Con. "It's got lumps."

185

"But they're good," Esther added, showing her confidence in his cooking skills by taking another spoonful.

"Where did you learn to cook?" Ben asked, scraping the last of the gravy from his bowl.

"My step-mother taught my brothers and me," Con explained.

"How come you don't know how to cook mush?" David asked.

"Confidentially, I hate mush unless it's fried," Con replied. "I always gagged on it when I was your age."

"You mean like this?" Gabriel made sounds that were all too realistic, bringing giggles from his brothers and sisters.

Con glanced over at the bed, but Bethea didn't stir. "My stepmother said there weren't enough women to go around in the West, so we should all know how to fend for ourselves."

"Don't you got a wife?" Gabriel asked.

Con glanced at the body beneath the covers on the bed across the room. "Not yet."

"You gonna marry our mamma then?" Faith asked, smiling sweetly up at him.

He shrugged. "Too early to tell, children."

"You like her, don't you?" David asked.

He nodded.

"She likes you, too," David added.

Con peered at the boy. "How do you know?"

"Because whenever we would talk about you, she would smile, and we talked about it, all us kids, and we could tell."

His mother and father knew, Jacob Dingley had seen them kiss, Clifford Kingston had paid for his knowledge with his life, and all her children knew. So much for discretion.

When they'd finished eating, he bundled them up warmly and took them outside. Adam and Ben shoveled their way to the outhouse, where Con stood in line for his turn, then they shoveled the tunnel to the log barn and milked the cow.

Con checked on Hellion's condition. The stallion seemed well fed and contended as did the mare. "Do you have plenty of hay left?"

"It's under the snow and we keep digging it out," Adam said. "We have two sacks of oats left. Bossy and the horses sure can eat a lot of hay when it gets cold. Ben and I went to the swamps and cut it with my pa's sickle. We wanted to quit but Ma said we might need all the hay we could get later. She was right."

"You boys are born stockmen," Con said. "Did your pa teach you?"

"Nah, our pa says only fools use pitchforks and poke cows, but we like it. Our Grandpa Mayfield raises horses and mules back in Missouri for the cavalry and we helped him," Adam said, then launched into their plans to gain a foothold in the cattle business.

"I reckon I could find some unbranded strays for you," Con offered. "We always have some mavericks that need tending." He looked around for the other children, counting heads. The younger children had made a game of hiding and finding each other in the pathways to the different buildings, scooping out caves in the walls in which to hide.

He estimated the snow depth to be five feet on the level and didn't want to think about the ravines or the hilltops. He tried his hand at shoveling the snow and was pleased to see that he felt no ill effects from the exertion.

"I'll carry the milk pail," he offered. The boys gave it to him and he started back to the cabin. He got to within six feet of the door when a wave of dizziness turned his knees to water. The pail slid from his hand, bounced against the packed snow under his boots, and tipped over. The warm milk melted a large circle several inches deep.

Young hands steadied him.

"Get me a chair," he gasped. "Bring it out here."

Faith dragged one of the kitchen chairs outside and placed it a few feet from the closed door, then Adam and Ben helped him sit down.

David, his knit cap in his hands, stared at Con. "We thought you might die. Mama cried. She didn't go to sleep for days and days and days."

Con ruffled the boy's blond hair and put the cap back on his head, tugging it down over his ears. "That's why we're letting her catch up now." He leaned his head against the cabin logs and closed his eyes, resenting the weakness in his body.

Aware of warm dampness on his chest, he slid his hand inside his shirt and underwear. When he withdraw it, his fingers were blood soaked.

187

Sally Garrett

BETHEA AWOKE TO an empty bed and a quiet room. She heard Con's voice and the children's laughter coming from outside. She pulled her arms out of the sleeves of the billowy flannel gown and into her undergarments, then a loose gray woolen dress. Over wool socks, she laced up her boots and went to look at the wind up clock sitting on one of the trunks.

"Oh no," she gasped. It was almost noon. With the day half gone, she would never get the chores done that were waiting.

She heard a commotion outside and ran to the door. The children were around Con who was sitting in a chair.

Con's head rested against the logs at an awkward tilt, his complexion pasty, his eyes closed.

"Con?"

He stirred and his hand came out to her. When she saw his blood stained fingers, she screamed.

"I sprang a leak," he said. "All I did was shovel some snow and carry a little pail of milk. Will you help me inside?"

Sliding her arm around his torso, she motioned the children to clear a pathway. He leaned heavily against her until they reached the bed and she helped him sit down. She knelt between his legs, unbuttoned his shirt and pulled it from his pants, then unbuttoned his underwear and pushed it off his shoulders.

"Oh, Con, it was healing so nicely." She searched the faces and found Adam's, nodding. In minutes she had the whiskey bottle and witch hazel and salves, along with a pan of water and clean rags. The children surrounded the bed and watched her tend him.

As she cleaned the wound, he looked down at her. "You've done this before."

She concentrated on her work. "Yes, and I don't want to go through more days like the ones I've just been through."

His hand touched her shoulder. "And last night?"

She ducked her head but didn't speak. Without looking at him again, she asked Ben, "Is his back bleeding, too?"

"Nah, it's fine."

"Good." She got to her feet. "Now, please stand up."

He did. "Drop your trousers," she said.

"Ma'am?"

"Remove your trousers." Finally she looked at his face, hoping her no-nonsense expression that usually worked with the children would be equally effective with this man towering above her. "You're going back to bed. You may get up for an hour at a time two or three times a day, preferably at meal times. Other than that, consider yourself confined to bed whether you like it or not."

"And supposing I like it?" He grinned down at her.

"Conrad Adler, you're impossible."

CHAPTER FIFTEEN

OVER THE NEXT SEVERAL days, Con's strength returned as his chest wound healed again. Bethea snipped the stitches from his arm and thigh. The nights were spent in the same bed, always falling asleep on their separate sides, but somehow before morning she found herself in his arms.

He made no further attempt to arouse her, and that concerned her greatly. Although she argued privately that she didn't want him to, she knew his passivity was a more accurate barometer to his health than his manly appearance.

When he was able to be up and about for longer periods of time, he began taking over some of the chores and taking the children outside to slide down the hillside to the frozen lake. The snow had crusted over and only once did anyone fall through. Always eager to turn adversity into fun, they made a game out of pulling each other from the holes and stomping the snow down.

Pieces of wood boards were used as makeshift sleds and quite by accident, Ben discovered the excitement of guiding his sled into the holes and shooting out the other side, propelling himself into the air for several feet before landing with a thud and continuing down onto the lake.

Bethea's heart lurched the first time she watched her son fly through the air, but conceded it appeared to be an exciting ride. What else could she say after having her heart stop when Con displayed his own form on Ben's sled? She strictly forbade the younger ones from learning the stunt.

Peels of laughter spoke more than words to Bethea as she watched the children respond to Con's companionship. The snow had stopped for several days and if it stayed clear they would complete their tunnel to the spring house.

Twice Con and the three older boys had tried to make their way to the trees on the hillside to bring back saplings to replenish their dwindling wood pile, but gave up and returned.

She began to ration the pieces she used each day, going more than once to count the pieces in the pile, computing that the supply would last into January, if she was thrifty. If the temperature didn't drop below zero, they would be safe.

Each morning she would go outside and scan the sky, trying to anticipate the day's weather changes, knowing all the while she could do nothing about it except to plan for the worst, then hope and pray it wouldn't become a reality.

Their days fell into a routine. Con took charge of breakfast. After three meals of fried succotash, she insisted he learn to prepare oatmeal and cornmeal mush.

"Only if you have syrup and we can fry it," he said, kissing her cheek to show his willingness to compromise.

They never mentioned Clifford's demise or Con's proposal, and the children hadn't been told of their father's death, but both knew the subjects were simmering just beneath the surface. There would be time enough for those discussions when winter changed to spring. For now, Bethea had more imminent concerns to occupy her thoughts.

If the calendar nailed to the wall above the dry sink had been marked accurately, this was her birthday, but she said nothing. She washed the dishes from the noon meal and put them on the shelf, straightened the bed, then went into the other room and did the same to the children's bunks.

She examined the children's clothing looking for holes to mend but found none. She'd mended all day yesterday. Con had two changes of clothing. The one he'd been wearing when shot had been washed and mended.

Perhaps this would be a good day to sew. She tugged her sewing machine out from its corner and set it up. Now what would she work on? The pink gingham? A shirt for Con? Finish the blue dresses for Faith and Esther? Perhaps the quilt top she had been working on. She touched her abdomen. The baby hadn't moved since early morning.

She left the sewing machine and went to the shelves above the dry sink, scanning the boxes and cans on the two shelves. Would they last until they reached the root cellar where they had another sack of potatoes and several heads of cabbage? Would the canned goods in the root cellar be all right? Maybe she could go outside and help them with the shoveling.

No, she'd work on the pink gingham dress. Perhaps the color would cheer her. She wiped the already clean table and spread the material out, wondering where to begin. Gracious, she thought, she had made dresses since she was a girl. Why couldn't she start this simple project? But this dress had to be special. It would be the one she wore in June when Con came to visit when he returned to Centennial Valley with the Alice livestock. The thought of not seeing him for several long months brought tears to her eyes and she took the material in her fists, twisting it in anguish.

Her back ached. She tried to concentrate on cutting out the pieces of the dress pattern she knew in her mind. A pain shot through her from the bottom of her pelvis to her chest and she doubled over, resting against the table until it eased.

She put on her coat and made a trip to the outhouse, then returned to cut the skirt pieces out. Another trip to the outhouse followed. When she returned to the material, she promptly cut out two identical pieces of bodice, forgetting to reverse the fabric. "Darn," she hissed.

Her uterus tightened in a contraction that didn't ease for a full minute. Not until she straightened, did she realize she'd been counting the seconds. A third trip to the outhouse was followed by a fourth. Moisture on her legs forced her to change her clothing. When she glanced at her soiled undergarments, she wished desperately that she could turn back the clock.

She put on the tea kettle and a large pot of water to warm. She got out the clean white sheets she had brought with her from Missouri, her sewing scissors from the table, and a ball of white twine. She looked around the room. Extra blankets? They were all in use in the colder second bedroom.

The basket that would serve as the baby's bed. Used for storage and a tote between babies, the basket was now filled with canned good. She removed the cans and fluffed the pillow mattress, then covered it with a fresh flannel sheet and three small blankets, soft flannel against the baby and topped with two pieces of old woolen blanket she had cut to size.

Next she spread a large sheet of gum cloth on the bed and covered it with an old, clean blanket. On top of that she put a sheet. As she studied her handiwork, her hands supported her abdomen. She hoped she had managed to do the job right. She couldn't take chances on soiling the mattress. It was the only one she had.

The books! She waited for another contraction to pass, then retrieved the two books her mother had given her.

Almost reverently, she carried the first volume to the bed. *"Maidenhood and Motherhood; Ten Phases of A Woman's Life,"* the title read. She had read and reread the section on midwifery.

She laid the first leather bound volume on the night table and picked up the second book and scanned the birth section, then stuck a piece of fabric in the book and closed it.

Con and the children were outside on an expedition to find willow branches to use as frames for snow shoes. In spite of the depth of snow on the ground, the children had trampled it down into a hard, slick play area. Tomorrow they planned to break trail to the hillside again where they expected to find dead timber.

Her abdomen cramped again. She stared at the fabric and knew she should clear it away and set the table for supper. Stew again. If spring ever came, she vowed to never serve stew for a year. No one complained, but she didn't think she could swallow another bite.

When they trudged into the cabin an hour later, knocking snow off their clothing and muddying the dirt floor, she opened her mouth to scold them. Before she could say a word, a hard cramp doubled her over. Con rushed to her.

She clutched his coat sleeve. "It's time." She tried to breathe but her lungs didn't work right. "Take the children for a long walk. Now!"

"But we've been outside all day," he argued. "They're cold and hungry. You go lie down and I'll feed them."

She pulled away. "No! You promised to take them for a long walk. I'll tell you when you can bring them back."

"But it's getting dark."

"Take them outside!" she screamed, shoving his arm away. "I need to be alone." She forced herself to straighten. "Please," she said, finally able to make her voice sound normal.

The children stared at her. He whispered to them as he bundled them up again and they disappeared into the frigid late afternoon.

She looked at the empty tin bowls, the bubbling stew, the stale biscuits from three days ago. She hated the stew, the cabin, the winter, and if Con and the children hadn't gone outside, she was sure she would have added them to her list.

Her body became consumed by twisting, burning, grinding pain, and she felt as if her vital organs were being torn apart. Maybe she had endured too many labors. Maybe this one would be her final one. She would die in childbirth, then she would never have to go through this pain again. But who would care for her six dear little ones?

Con Adler had no obligation to them. They would be sent to an orphan asylum. Her poor little darlings; they deserved better than that cruel fate.

She had read newspaper accounts of such places. They were huge wooden buildings housing several hundred children, cared for by calloused indifferent matrons who never smiled. The buildings were fire traps waiting to turn into infernos. When the children burned to death because no one would try to rescue them, the officials expressed regret, but she knew they were relieved not to have to pay out their precious funds on paupers' orphans.

She turned away from the table and stared at the bed. Its comforting feather tick called to her and she removed her boots and socks and crawled beneath the covers. If she could go to sleep, the grinding pain might go away and she would wake up in the morning healthy and able to care for her children and keep them safely out of the grasping claws of the evil asylum matrons.

CON PEEKED THROUGH the small window. The cabin interior was lit by a single lamp. Bethea had gone to bed. They had been outside until dusk had been replaced by darkness, trying to abide by her ridiculous order, but unless she wanted to have six frozen offspring on her hands in addition to a newborn, she would have to accept his taking charge.

"Last trip to the necessary," he called. "Go whether you need to or not." When they all returned, he gathered them near the door. "We're going inside. We'll have supper, then I want you to all go into the bedroom and get ready for bed. You don't have to go to sleep but you must be very quiet. Your mother is going to have the baby tonight."

He looked from one face to another. "She may cry out, even scream, but she'll be fine when it's over."

"Will you stay with us?" Esther asked.

"No, sweetheart, I'll be helping your mother." He peeked through the window again. "Whether she wants me or not. Let's go, quietly now."

Inside, he lit several more lamps and placed them about the small room. Pink checkered fabric covered the table and he folded it carefully and stacked it on her sewing machine. Someday he'd take her to the meadow behind his parent's new house. She'd be wearing that dress.

No time for fantasies tonight, he thought, as he set one of the lamps on the table and dished up the stew. He was getting pretty tired of the same thing every night, but he'd choke it down rather than let Bethea know. He knew she had been feeling poorly the past few days.

Gabriel looked in his bowl. "Yuck, stew again."

"Eat," Con ordered, but when he saw the tears in the little boy's eyes, he winked, and Gabriel smiled back.

When the meal was over, he took a lamp into the back room and set it on a makeshift table. He shivered. The room was colder than usual tonight. He knew the temperature outside had dropped and the clouds had rolled in. He wasn't sure how much more cold weather they could endure.

They changed into their night gowns and shirts, dancing to keep their bare feet off the cold plank floor. He tucked them in two to a bed. "Snuggle up and keep each other warm and remember, no matter what you hear, you're not to leave your beds. Your mother will be all right by morning."

Something came over him as he surveyed their anxious faces. Even Adam looked young and vulnerable tonight. They had become precious to him, almost as precious as their mother. What a fool Clifford Kingston had been.

He kissed the younger ones' cheeks and smoothed the mussed hair of the older boys, then ducked around the blanket hung in the opening to the main room.

Bethea was still asleep. He shoved two more sticks of wood into the stove and opened the oven door. Pulling a chair close to the bed, he sat down and rested his face in his hands, concerned about his ability to handle what lay ahead.

She groaned and rolled onto her back. Moaning in her sleep, she curled up on her side, facing him. Perspiration dotted her brow and he wondered how she could stay asleep.

He spotted the books and reached for one. *"Dr. Chase's Third, Last and Complete Receipt Book and Household Physician,"* he murmured, scanning down the long title page. *"...including a Treatise on The Diseases of Women and Children."*

He flipped the pages. Between *"Medical Recipes"* and *"Food for the Sick,"* he found a chapter on nursing and midwifery and he began to read. When he finished the chapter, he started at the beginning and read it again, trying to imprint the information in his mind.

Bethea moaned again, straightening her legs beneath the covers before pulling them up. Her moans grew louder, tearing at his heart. If only he could help her. She seemed to settle into deep sleep again, and he returned to the chapter. Engrossed in the chapter, he didn't hear her stir.

"I hope you've memorized it," she murmured, and his head snapped up. "I can't seem to remember anything at all about having babies."

He moved to the edge of the bed and wiped her forehead with a dry soft cloth. "How do you feel?"

"Terrible." She looked around the room. "Where are the children?" When she glanced at the darkened windows, she frowned. "You didn't leave them outside? They'll freeze."

"You're right, my darling, I brought them back inside hours ago. They're asleep."

"Then you should go in there and sleep too," she said. "I can manage now."

He leaned over the bed and kissed her cheek. "Forget it, Bethea. I'm your midwife tonight."

"But you said you knew nothing about the birth of babies."

"But I've helped a lot of calves and foals into the world. Basically it's the same."

"I don't think so," she replied, shaking her head. "This is me, my body. We...don't really...know each other." She stopped, clutching her abdomen again. Between clenched teeth, she said, "Please leave."

"No," he said, wiping her brow again.

She sighed deeply. "I thought I could do it alone."

"I love you. We'll do this together."

"But it's not even your child."

"Yes, it is."

She clutched his hand again, her nails drawing blood before she eased her grip. "Read to me," she gasped. "From the book. We both need to know."

Holding her hand, he balanced the book on his knee and began to read the chapter aloud. After three pages, she tightened her hand and he waited for the pain to pass, then resumed reading.

They never finished the chapter.

She grimaced and he leaned over her. "Try to breath, Bethea, for God's sake, the book said to breathe easy."

"I can't." She strained again, harder. "Help me, Con." She panted, then strained again. "It's coming."

He swallowed the panic rising in his throat. She arched off the mattress, hissing through her clenched teeth. He shoved the blankets aside and pushed her gown up past her rock hard abdomen.

Between her legs, he saw a dark wet head appear. He ran to the dry sink and plunged his hands into the pan of hot water, washing them with the strong lye soap, dried them and ran back to the bed in time to see the baby's face appear.

"It's coming, sweetheart, it's a beautiful baby," he crooned.

She strained again and the narrow shoulders appeared. He cradled the baby's head in the palm of his hand and waited. What seemed an eternity turned into seconds as a perfectly formed baby slid into his hands.

Bethea's eyes were bright with excitement when she lifted her head from the pillow. "What is it?"

"A beautiful little girl." He wiped the thick mucus from the infant's face and turned her over in his hands. She wriggled, her tiny little behind turning pink before his eyes. "She's breathing," he said excitedly.

The baby whimpered, then filled the room with a sound unique to newborns, kicking in his slippery hands.

"Put her on my stomach," she said. "I want to touch her."

He smiled as she caressed the wriggling newborn. He needed a breather as much as she did and he dropped into the chair for a few minutes. "I've got to read the book again," he said, wiping his hands but before he could find his place, she began to strain again. He moved the baby to her side and put his hand on Bethea's abdomen and pressed, massaging with his palm and fingers, as the instructions became clear and precise. Together they concentrated on the next process of birth and when that, too, was completed, he smiled rather grimly at her.

"I told you this was just like calves and foals," he said, his confidence returning. "It's just a lot faster." He looked at the squirming baby again. "My God, she's still attached. Here, let me turn her over."

"My sewing scissors are on the night table," she murmured, her eyes never leaving the baby.

He tied off the umbilical cord and cut it. "I'll clean you both." As if he'd memorized the chapter, he took care of her, then washed the baby. Not until he had her in a clean gown and safely tucked into a clean dry bed, with the baby wrapped in a small blanket and tucked in her arms, did he relax.

"May I have a drink of milk?" she asked.

He laid the baby in the middle of the bed and raised Bethea's head and slid another pillow beneath her. She steadied his trembling hands as she lifted the cup to her lips.

He looked down at the baby whose cries had changed to whimpers again. "How is she?"

"She has your dark hair," she said, smiling at the baby.

He grinned. "Don't be silly." He touched the baby's small head, marveling at its perfect shape. The fine hair had dried and now formed a dark wavy cap. "She's pretty." He met Bethea's gaze. "Are you okay?"

"I'm fine."

"I'm a nervous wreck." He chuckled self consciously. "I'm sorry you had to bear all that pain."

"What pain?" She touched the baby's cheek with her finger.

"Is this a typical birth for you?" he asked.

She nodded. "I'm fine," she assured him. "Give me a few days and I'll be up and about. You see, Mr. Adler, one of the miracles of motherhood is that the birth is forgotten when a mother holds her child."

He shook his head. "I don't think I could forget it."

"That's why papas don't have the babies."

He laughed and leaned to kiss her lips lightly. The baby began to fuss. He laid the baby in her arms and watched as she opened the front of her gown and brought out one breast, then coaxed the baby to the nipple. The baby's mouth opened wide, frantically trying to find it, then latching onto it with surprising energy for so tiny a babe.

Bethea looked up at him again, smiling differently this time than he'd ever seen her smile before. They both watched the baby nurse at one breast then be moved to the other until she fell asleep in Bethea's arms. She nestled the baby upright between her breasts and rubbed her tiny back. The baby's mouth moved in her sleep and Bethea settled against the pillows.

Con dropped heavily in the chair. "What are you going to call her?"

"I don't know," she said, kissing the baby's soft hair. "I expected a boy. I thought of Hubert or Huxley."

He laughed. "Thank God she's a girl. No boy should ever go through life being called Hubert."

"I have a bed for her," she said, pointing to a basket near the wall. "I fixed it this afternoon. If you'll put it next to the bed, you can put her in it."

"The floor is too cold and drafty for her," he said, looking around the room. He shoved his arms into his coat and left the cabin, returning several minutes later to roll four round blocks next to her bed, then set the basket on the flat surface.

"There," he said, nodded his approval. "We don't want her to get cold her first night here."

When the basket was safely within Bethea's reach, he took the baby from her breast. It curled in his hands and he held it in his arms for a few minutes before carefully placing her on the pillow and covering her with the soft blankets.

When Bethea was satisfied all was well with her child, she settled back against the pillows again and yawned.

"Perhaps I should sleep in the other room tonight," he said, but she shook her head.

"I might need you during the night."

"Then I'll leave one of the lamps burning," he said. He went into the other room. The children had slept through the birth. He turned out the lamp and hooked the curtain back on a nail to allow the warmth of the stove to reach them.

Bethea was still awake when he turned out all the lamps but one, undressed to his underwear, and slid in beside her. "I know it has to begin with an H," he said. "How about Halona? It's an Indian name that means 'fortunate.' We could call her Hallie."

She turned from the baby and looked at his face. "We?"

He leaned over her. "I helped bring her into the world, I intend to be around when she grows up. If we can go through this together, we can survive anything. I want to know that you'll be my wife when we leave this valley,." He caressed her cheek. "Will you marry me, Bethea?"

She smiled, her eyes glistened with tears. "Yes, and I think Hallie is a wonderful name for her."

CHAPTER SIXTEEN

AS BETHEA REGAINED HER STRENGTH, she discovered a gentleness in the man who cared for her beyond any she had ever known.

"You should have been a physician," she said, as he completed her bath and slid a fresh gown over her head. Her hair had become matted, but she refused to let him brush it until it was clean, and she knew it would be unhealthy to wash it until she felt stronger.

He shrugged. "I have nothing else to do."

She smiled. "You've shoveled a path to the root cellar and brought wonderful variety to our meager meals. You've turned my sons into young loggers and sawyers. You've convinced the little ones they can do their school work at the table and not quarrel. You've shown Ben and Adam how to track and catch the snow rabbit and roast him over a fire. You shot that young bull elk and now we have something other than salted beef."

He chuckled. "I had to do that for my own survival. The stews are nourishing but..." He shrugged.

"You grew tired of them, too," she teased, "but no more than I did."

He gave her a light kiss. "The potatoes and carrots in the root cellar were fine after all your worrying. Didn't I tell you the snow would insulate them? The boys are stringing some of the elk meat now to dry it in the sun. If the sky stays clear, and the temperature warms, the snow will begin to melt, but we can't take it for granted. It's only mid December. True winter is still ahead of us."

He never complained about doing woman's work. Most of the laundry had been of her making, but the girls had been put to work hanging it over a rope he'd strung across the room where the warmth of the stove could dry it. The children seemed to relish not having to change clothes so often. Baths, other than her own, had been limited to every other week, with face and hand washing sufficing in between.

He insisted on carrying her to the outhouse whenever she needed to make the trip, waiting outside until she was done. He'd swing her up into his arms again and they'd return to the cabin. Early one morning, he carried her all the way to the frozen lake to see the sunrise. He sat on a boulder, holding her on his lap in the shelter of his arms, and together they watched the sky turn to golden pinks.

"I miss the swans," she said, leaning back against him. "They're so beautiful, and graceful too."

"Like you," he murmured, kissing her cheek.

"They're not like the swans we have back in Missouri."

He adjusted her slightly. "A naturalist who visited here three years ago on his way from the geysers called them trumpeter swans. He said they were uncommon and we should treasure them or someday they might be gone."

She nodded. "Those swans helped me get through the days when I first arrived here. I'd expected a fine house and I resented the cabin and hated Clifford for insisting we come here and then leaving us alone for weeks on end. I'd come down here to be alone and think, about home...and meeting you. I felt marooned in this wilderness. The swans never seemed frightened, even when they hatched their young. They make the strangest noises."

"That's why they're called trumpeters."

"No, no, I mean when they're in the reeds and talking to their little ones. You have to sit very quietly to hear them, and I was so discouraged I didn't want to talk to anyone. As long as the swans come to my lake, I'll protect them."

"Your lake, is it?" He chuckled and turned her sideways on his legs. "Just look out there, Bethea." His arm swept the horizon. "This lake must look the same way it's looked for centuries. If man ever truly discovers it and brings his guns, who knows what might happen?"

"But as long as we have control of the land surrounding it, we'll protect it," she replied.

"Alice Livestock controls much of it," he reminded her.

"I know and I worried at first, until I got to know you better. The shore is the key to the lake's survival," she murmured, gazing out on the expanse of ice. "That's why I've named it Lake View in my mind. At one time I considered calling it the Kingston home ranch, but I never want Clifford Kingston's name associated with it. Then I named it Lake Shore, but now it's Lake View." She pulled her glove from her hand and touched his cheek. "And it's our special place."

"Did I ever tell you that this is the cabin where my father and step-mother found me with my mother and baby brother?" He looked down the shoreline several hundred feet. "Their grave is through the quaky aspens. There's a small granite marker there with their names on it. I still go there sometimes."

He told her the story of his father's attempt to find help for his dying Shoshoni wife. "If he had known she was that ill, he would never have left her. It's preyed on him since. He rode to Bannack, the only town around here in those days other than Virginia City, and the only person who would go with him was my step-mother." He kissed the tip of her nose. "That was in 1863 and they've been together ever since."

The sky lost its brilliance as the sun broke through the thin cloud cover. "I'd better get you inside before you freeze and can't take care of that pretty little girl of ours," he said.

"You've spoiled me terribly," she murmured, gazing up at his intent features.

He looked down at her. "I have nothing else to do."

AFTER TWO WEEKS of lying about and sitting in a chair, she insisted on dressing. Then she sent him outside and went about surveying her pantry. Smiling, she brought down cans of blackberries and apricots and made four pies. There was a limit as to what she could expect Con to learn about her kitchen.

THE THERMOMETER that hung outside the door hovered below zero for days, yet the children had become so acclimated to the cold weather that they thought nothing of shedding their overcoats and working or playing in their woolen shirts and underwear. Bethea marveled at their healthiness.

Wildlife tracks were seen everywhere. The deer came down to the spring to drink as did the elk and an occasional moose. The children had seen several coyotes. Con had cautioned them to stay within shouting distance. Wolves were heard at night and as the winter progressed, they might become bolder in search of food. Bossy was a prime candidate because she was old, he warned them all, but he didn't want any of them to be in danger.

Bears and smaller animals were hibernating for the winter. Bethea had new respect for their solution to the cold.

Hallie was one month old when Bethea found herself able to fit into one of her woolen day dresses. The garment was still a little snug around her waist, but she knew it would be only a matter of days before she looked her usual slim self.

She decided to wash her hair. A month was all she could bear, so she scrubbed her scalp with the lye soap until it burned, then followed that with two latherings of lavender soap and a vinegar rinse. After drying it with a towel, she began combing and brushing. As she fought the tangles, her eyes fell on the scissors. How simple it would be, she thought, but what would other people think?

"Gracious, who would know?" she said aloud. Taking the scissors, she trimmed more than a foot of tangles, combing out what was left, and trimmed it again, bringing the tips up to the middle of her back. "Still respectable," she murmured, coiling it loosely onto the back of her head.

When Con and the children returned for the noon meal, she wondered if anyone cared about her new attire. The children began to eat with hearty appetites. Reluctant to meet Con's gaze, she turned toward the window, but when his hands settled on her waist and almost encircled it, she knew he had noticed.

He kissed her cheek. "I'll be back later," he said, and before she could ask him where he was going, he closed the door behind him.

A MONTH LATER, when the supper dishes had been cleared away and the children gathered around her, she opened the large Bible her mother had given her. Soon after Hallie's birth, she had made her entries, going back to the generation of her grandparents, then her parents, her marriage to Clifford Kingston and their seven children. In a moment of uneasiness, she added Conrad (Chugan) Adler's name to a new page.

Now, as she looked at the blank space where a date belonged, she wondered if their dream of marriage would actually come about. She turned to the Book of Genesis. "We have a long winter ahead of us and it's time you children received your scripture lessons. Remember how we used to go to church and Sunday School?"

The older children nodded, but Gabriel and Faith shook their heads. She smiled at them. "You were babies. We went with your Grandpa and Grandma Mayfield in their carriage and you'd be dressed in your finest suits and dresses that I'd made myself. We didn't have much money, but you looked very handsome and I was proud that you were my children."

"Did you wear a pretty dress, too?" Esther asked.

"Oh, yes," Bethea said, sighing and leaning back in her chair. "In those days, I had several pretty dresses and every year I'd go to the store in Wilcox and buy yardage for a new one and I'd make a bonnet to go with it. She closed her eyes, recalling that earlier time when money was more plentiful and the future brighter.

"Did Papa go with us?" Esther asked.

Jerked back to reality, Bethea glanced over their heads to find Con looking at her. "No, dear, he was usually gone. That's why we went with Grandma and Grandpa, but we had a wonderful time. Sometimes we would stay and enjoy a picnic on the grounds and you played with the other children and I visited my friends. We'd talk about babies and recipes. It would be a wonderful afternoon for all of us."

She looked at Con again, uneasy about talking of the past. He had been leaning against the dry sink, his features unreadable.

He came to her and rested his hand on the nape of her neck. "We all get nostalgic sometimes," he said, kissing her cheek.

"Why'd you kiss her?" David asked.

Con grinned at the boy. "Because I wanted to. Didn't you ever want to do something so bad you couldn't stop yourself?" When the children nodded, Con took up his station against the dry sink again, but she could feel him following her every move.

He had changed in the past week, becoming less talkative at meal time, eager to work outside. Maybe he was feeling the confines of the two room cabin.

She returned her attention to the children. "It may be years before we can have a Sunday school here at..." She looked over at Con. "...at Lake View, so we'll read each evening from our own Bible.

We'll start at the beginning." The baby began to fuss and she glanced over at the basket.

Con pushed himself away from his leaning post. "I'll take care of her." He motioned for her to continue.

She tried to concentrate on the creation story, but out of the corner of her eye she watched him tend to Hallie's needs. A dry flannel diaper replaced the soggy one. Clifford had never come near an infant in need of changing. A fresh gown was slipped over her head. He sat down on the bed, the baby cradled along his legs, her dark head on his knees and her tiny bare toes kicking in the air.

"Mama, you've stopped reading," David scolded.

"Yes, just when you're getting to the good part," Ben added.

Bethea forced her attention back to the page, but she couldn't resist one more glance. Con was actually making faces at Hallie, touching her chin, tickling her round little tummy. Suddenly he whooped. The baby screwed up her face and began to cry frantically, her arms and legs flailing the air. Bethea dropped the Bible onto the seat of her rocker and ran across the room, about to swoop the baby from his lap. He grabbed Bethea's hand before she could take the baby.

"What did you do to her?" she said accusingly.

He grinned from ear to ear. "Not a damned thing. She giggled. I swear, Bethea, she giggled. First she smiled, like she'd been doing, but then she looked right at me and laughed, didn't you, Hallie?" He looked up at Bethea again. "Didn't you hear her?"

He grinned again at the baby whose sobs had changed to hiccups. Hallie, her eyes moist with tears, smiled back. "I reckon I scared her, but damn it, it was exciting," he said. Taken by a wave of embarrassment, he looked away. "I guess I'd better finish the chores." He put Hallie in Bethea's arms and grabbed his coat.

"Do you want a lantern?" she asked.

He shoved his hat onto his dark head. "There's a full moon tonight. Don't wait up for me."

She wanted to go after him, ask him what was troubling him. Since she had been able to fit into her regular dresses, he had withdrawn. Con and the boys had improved the log barn for the livestock. For two weeks now, he'd taken to visiting the unorthodox structure in the evenings, giving the animals their last handful of hay for the night, checking to see how the hay stack was holding out. When he returned, she caught the faint odor of tobacco.

He would undress and go to bed without so much as a "Good night." He'd turn his back to her, staying on his side of the bed from night to dawn and not even touching her hand.

"Read some more," Faith pleaded, but Bethea ignored her. Perhaps Con wanted to leave the valley. Goodness knows they had all grown weary of the cold weather. Every night another inch or two of fresh snow fell. Through their diligence, they kept the paths to the outbuildings cleared and had added considerably to the wood pile once Hellion had been trained to pull dead trees down from the hillside.

"Please, Mama," Faith said.

Bethea sat down again and began to read. After an hour, Con returned and without a word, lit the coal oil lamp on his side of the bed, undressed and slid between the covers. She frowned. Usually he waited until the children were asleep. He appeared to be intensely interested in the pages of the mail order catalog on his knees, then tossed it to the dirt floor with a thud, raising a tiny cloud of dust.

He turned out the lamp on his side of the bed and she swallowed the lump in her throat. She began to read again, but once Abraham's son, Isaac, had been spared on the sacrificial alter, she closed the book and sent the children to bed.

After giving the baby a final feeding, she undressed and put on a new yellow flannel gown she had sewn a week earlier. If she had had some crochet thread, she would have made pretty lace to fancy up the gown, but the way Con had been ignoring her lately, the effort would have been a waste of time. Reaching for the brush, she pulled the pins from her bun and shook out her hair.

The brush tugged at her scalp, sending prickles through it. She sighed, enjoying the pleasurable sensations. Sweeping the brush down to the ends, she was glad she had cut off some of it. Hair could be such a nuisance, she thought.

She tugged the brush through a persistent tangle, but her thoughts focused on Con. It was only since the birth of Hallie that he'd grown cool. Had childbirth changed him? Maybe he was afraid that if they married, she would start producing children again at regular yearly intervals. There must be ways to prevent conception. She'd go see a physician in Dillon or Virginia City. Maybe they could advise her. Rich city women didn't have babies every year. In the back of her mind, she wanted to look forward to the day when her children were grown and she and Con could be alone.

She concentrated on her brushing. In the weeks to come, she would take extra pains to look womanly. Tonight it didn't seem to matter what she wore. Tonight she was a woman who wanted to lie in the arms of the man she loved. Maybe, if she turned out the lamp and joined him beneath the warm covers, touched his body in the right places to excite him, he would respond to her.

Clifford had forced her to touch him and she had hated it, but now, with Con, the idea excited her. Surely he would turn to her and at least hold her and kiss her.

She heard him turn over and her heart leaped. Had he merely turned in his sleep or had he read her thoughts? In spite of the chill in the room, her flesh felt feverish, her cheeks flushed.

Was Con awake, watching her? Was that the reason her mind had been filled with longing for him? Her body seemed to pulse, knowing he was there behind her. She fought the urge to turn around and throw herself into his arms.

In recent weeks, each time she saw him across the snow packed yard doing a chore, she had been reminded of his virility. She had taken to making up excuses to go outside, to lean against the cabin logs and watch him.

He must have his own needs. Clifford had never slept in this brass bed and now she knew that the loving hand of fate had prevented its defilement. This bed would only know the love making between her and Con Adler, with or without the bonds of matrimony. Did she dare speak of her desires?

Con took the brush from her hand. "I've wanted to do this for months." A knee and leg slid down alongside her hip and she knew he was sitting directly behind her. She had seen his entire body naked, bathed him in sickness, washing him as he had washed her. There were no secrets between them save one.

She sat quietly on the edge of the bed as he brushed her hair, putting his hand against her neck and running the brush down the mass of wavy hair. "It's shorter."

"I trimmed it a few weeks ago," she said, her voice breathless. Minutes passed as he continued brushing. She wanted to jerk the brush from his hand and fling it aside. He should be holding her, kissing her the way only he could, stroking her burning body and bringing it ablaze.

He laid the brush on the night table, then his long fingers touched the lamp, turning the wick slowly down to snuff it out. "Come to bed," he murmured.

The soft glow from the moon on the snow outside illuminated the room. Beneath the covers, she lay expectantly until at last she felt his fingers touch the ribbons on her gown.

"You're driving me out of my mind, Bethea," he murmured against her cheek. "I'm a desperate man." He ran his finger up and down the cleavage between her breasts. "You're a beautiful woman." His hand drifted down her gown and she could feel its heat like a white hot torch as it passed over her breasts, past her waist, and settled on the gown's hem and began to gather it.

His hand touched her flesh and began to slid up her bare leg, pushing the gown ahead of it. She tried to lie still but her body vibrated with desire.

Deftly, he removed the gown and shoved it against the brass head rail. His mouth grazed her naked shoulder, sending shivers down her spine. She unfastened the buttons down the front of his underwear and touched his chest, giving in to the yearning to explore him. He stroked the curve of her hip, lingering for a moment on her abdomen before settling on her waist. "You have an amazing body," he whispered.

"As do you," she murmured, her lips finding his skin irresistible. She showered his chest with tiny nibbling caresses as her hands eased their way inside his garment, desperate to explore him more fully. She felt herself turn into a stranger, a wanton. She pushed his garment off his shoulders and down his body until he was free. In her hands, he grew full, turgid and manly. He groaned, then buried his face against her throat, trying to muffle his voice.

"Kiss me, Con, make love to me," she pleaded.

"I've tried so hard to stay away from you. Oh, God, Bethea, what are we going to do?"

"I, Bethea, take you, Con, to be my husband in the eyes of God for all our remaining years," she whispered.

"And I, Con, take you, Bethea, as my wife in God's eyes forever and ever."

"No man but you has ever slept in this bed," she said. "Tonight it will be our marriage bed. I love you so much. I need you as my husband, at least for tonight." She pulled his head down to hers and drank from his lips.

A fever raged through her when he rose above her. His body touched hers, sending a tremor through her. When he slid into her, she arched against him, pulling him inward, deeper yet not deep enough.

His thrusts were cautions. "I don't want to hurt you."

"You could never hurt me. I love you so much, so much." Her voice changed to a moan as she met his thrusts. She imagined their bodies sliding in and out of each other and the image startled her. Her body seemed to swell around him, pulsating, throbbing. The uncoiling began again and she pulled his head down, claiming his mouth, gasping for air between his kisses, only to pull him toward her again.

Resting on his elbows, he clasped her face in his hands. "Look at me. I want to see your eyes." In the moonlight, she met his gaze and she knew destiny had brought them together and destiny would keep them safely in its arms. His arms slid around her body and he buried his face in her hair as she surrendered to the spiraling ecstasy, matching his passion and carrying him with her to fulfillment.

Later he loved her again, this time slower, almost lethargic until she drove him wild with her hands. Startled by the resurgence of her own passion, she cried out his name but he smothered her words with his kisses as he rolled her to the other side of the bed and carried her away to a new world where they needed no words.

She lay exhausted in his arms, stunned by her own spontaneity. "I don't understand how I can be this way," she murmured. "You touch me and I turn into some insanely wild woman. What have you done to me? What have I become?"

He kissed her forehead, then pushed her head down against his chest. "Maybe this is the real Bethea."

She thought about his words for several minutes. "Now have we committed adultery?"

"You're a widow, so no, I don't think so," he replied. "No one knows but us, and no one will." He stroked her shoulder. I've wanted to make love to you for a long time, Bethea. I knew it would be like this for us. As soon as we get out of here, we'll leave the children with my mother and take the train to Butte City. We can get married there without the attention it might receive in Dillon."

"I can't leave Hallie."

"Then we'll take her along."

He lay on his back in the moonlight and she looked down at him. "Are you sure? Are you really sure this is what you want?"

"I have a good income from the livestock company," he replied. "We'll build a house large enough for each child can have his or her separate bedroom"

She buried her face against his chest trying to muffle her giggle. "There's not a house in the county that large."

"Then ours will be the first."

"With heat for each room so the children won't be cold?" she asked. "And with running water in the kitchen? I get so tired of carrying water from the spring. Can we bring the spring to the house?"

"We can."

"A family back in Wilcox brought their necessary inside," she continued. "They called it a bathing room, but it had a build in chamber pot that flushed with water. They called it a crapper after the man who invented it. I thought it was the most luxurious room in the house. Can you imagine not bathing in a pan or a tub or not having to trudge to the outhouse when it's below zero outside?"

"I can." He winked. "I can even rig the tub so one spigot has hot water and the other cold. How would you like that?"

"Anything that pleasurable must surely be sinful," she replied. "I think you're teasing me, Mr. Adler." She brushed her lips against his. "You've given me everything but the stars and the moon, and I don't need them."

He chuckled but didn't say a word.

"But I want to keep this place and expand it," she continued. "someday I'll give it to Adam and Ben."

"Fine."

"Aren't you the agreeable man tonight?" she teased.

"Tonight I'm a satisfied man. Name it, and I'll see that you have it."

"All I really want is to live happily with you."

"We'll have that, too." His hand settled on her shoulder. "We can spend our summers here. We'll build a house here, too, right on the lake, with large windows so you can see the swans go floating by. I've been telling my father that we need a more permanent base in the valley. If you're willing, Lake View can be that place."

"But I won't sell it," she insisted.

"I'd never ask you to," he said. "You can lease the grazing land to him from season to season and pocket the funds for your future or your children's, but don't forget to include me in that future, Bethea. I can take care of you and the children. I want to, but I can understand why no one should feel completely dependent on another person. I have a friend who lives in Butte City. His name is David Addison and he's a lawyer. Perhaps he can help us. I want to share what I have with you and I don't know how to do it so no one can take it away from you if anything should happen to me."

"What could happen? Do you mean get hurt?"

"I carry a gun whenever I travel," he reminded her. "So do other men. Without my revolver and holster on my hip, I don't feel dressed. Having it has saved my life more than once." He stopped talking and looked at her. "This area has a long way to go before it's civilized. Some men still like to shoot first and ask questions later. But times are changing. If I'm going to become a family man, I'd best set an example for my ready made sons and daughters."

"That's sounds wonderful," she replied, stroking his cheek lightly with her fingertips before kissing his mouth.

His eyes grew dark, his chin firm. "There will be talk."

"Talk? I don't understand."

"There are some men in the county whom my father considers friends but I've seen their true natures. It's one of the few things we've argued about. Behind his back, they talk about him and my mother and that always ends with me. Maybe it's partly the fault of their gossiping wives, but they have never accepted my place in his family or his business. They think I should have been sent back to the Lemhi Agency and raised with *my own kind*."

"That's cruel, and it's none of their business."

"I wanted you to be aware of it. The residents of this county have driven most of the Chinese out, calling them Celestial heathens. Negroes don't stay long. The locals say it's because they can't stand the cold weather, but it's much more than that. They're always identified with their dark blood, never the amount of English or German blood flowing in their veins. If we have children, they'll be called quarter-breeds, never three-quarter English, just little redskins."

Disturbed by his bitter accusations, she lay in his arms, disappointed that the mood had turned unpleasant.

"And there's one more thing," he said. "People, especially the women, count on their fingers and when that doesn't work, they'll look at Hallie's dark hair and give me credit."

"That's vicious. You and I know the truth."

"They'll make up their own minds. They aren't bothered by the truth. Her skin is fair and they'll wonder about that."

"I'll tell them she *is* yours," she cried. The baby stirred, then settled again. "I think of her as yours. She'll know you as her father, but someday we'll have to tell her and the rest of the children what happened. It's all recorded in my journal, even Clifford's death." She shuddered. "He did terrible things to me. When we were...together, he hurt me. He never seemed satisfied until he made me cry. Is that why I'm so different now? When you kiss me or touch me, I shiver, but never in fear, only in anticipation."

He ran his fingers through her hair. "Anticipation will get us through the days and fulfillment will be our nights."

She laid her head on her pillow. "That's the most wonderful thing you could ever say. Truly, you are my husband."

He settled in beside her, his easy breathing caressing her hair, his arm draped across her waist.

"How can I tell the children what their father was really like?" she asked.

"Children need to have good memories about their parents," he replied. "We'll tell them he died in Idaho and leave it at that. It can be our secret until they're old enough to understand."

CHAPTER SEVENTEEN

CON ADLER GAZED into the distance. April had arrived but the Centennial Valley landscape seemed vast beyond measure under its deep blanket of white. Never a small valley in anyone's description, this afternoon its awesomeness threatened to intimidate him as well. He knew he had to get his loved ones out before it claimed them, as it had the three elk carcasses he had passed a quarter of a mile back.

After the noon meal, Con had ridden Hellion toward the west end of the valley to evaluate the snow depth and to determine if Hellion had the stamina to travel the thirty miles to Monida. Hellion had high stepped his way through belly deep snow for three miles before he had stopped, his sides heaving, and refused to respond to Con's heels. A week earlier, they had tried this trip and had managed to cover only a mile distance.

He looked toward the northwestern sky, trying to evaluate the heavy gray clouds that had begun to move in again. He wondered if the rest of the area had experienced as harsh a winter season as this valley. If so, the livestock losses could be substantial.

His father had been cutting hay for a decade and stacking huge loose piles in the meadows closest to the ranch near Alice, ignoring the snide remarks from some of the other livestock men in the area. But even with the stacks, if the snow depth prevented the workers from bringing the stock and the hay together, it would be for naught.

The usual Chinook winds of January had lasted only a few days and the snow that had melted had frozen again forming a sheet of ice that had since been buried beneath another four feet of snow. Now, three months later, he should have been able to see signs of the ice on the lake soften or hungry bears coming from their caves to forage. A bear would find little to eat this spring.

The elk had grown brazen. One afternoon, several had rammed their way through the fence surrounding what remained of their last hay stack and trampled much of it into the snow while eating their fill. He had seen it all from the hillside where he had been working in the timber with Hellion.

Adam and Ben had been frightened and powerless to drive them away and by the time Con had reached the stack, the damage had been done. The root cellar still held food but the selection had been reduced to cabbages, a half sack of spuds and three cases of canned peas.

Looking across the lake, he could see the tiny dot of the McGyver cabin and wondered if the widow and her son had survived. For the first time, he wished there were more settlers in the valley.

Between where he sat on Hellion's back and Monida another family had lived, building a log cabin and corrals but they had abandoned the place four months later. That was the only building between their cabin and the railroad town. Could they make it that far in a day?

Six young children, a woman carrying a four and a half months old baby, and himself? He had no doubt about himself, but Bethea wasn't as strong as she pretended, and the little ones would give out quickly. Ben and Adam could keep up, he was sure, as they were determined boys who wanted to prove to the world and themselves they were the fiber of which the West was being settled.

If Hellion could carry at least three, the mare two or three, they might manage, especially if the slow moving old milk cow could be put to use. If their very survival was at stake, the cow would either be put into service or meet her end. Two of her teats had suffered frost bite and milking had become difficult for Adam and Ben. Con had been wondering if the time had come when she would be better in a cooking pot than consuming the hay they would need for the horses.

Con looked back to the cabin in the distance. It had been his home for almost six months now. He and Bethea had dealt with birth and near death, building a deep abiding love for each other and an endless reservoir of passion. Her monthly flows had resumed at irregular intervals, relieving his anxiety about conception. He wanted her free for a few years before they had a child of their own.

She was more than he could ever want in a wife and lover. What would have happened to her and the children if he had not found his way to them? A chill went up his spine.

He reined Hellion around and dismounted. "Easy, boy," he said, stroking the stallion's nose. "You rest while I think about what we can do." The stallion tossed his head before nuzzling the snow. "No browse today," Con said absently. He turned back to the cabin, its spiral of smoke coming from the stove pipe reassuring. Their wood supply was shrinking in spite of their efforts to bring in more. The damned stove seemed insatiable.

He remounted and rode slowly back to within a quarter mile of the cabin. The door opened and one of the children came outside. He had never expected to enjoy the company of young children so much. At times they drove him crazy with their questions and quarreling but when Gabriel or Faith would crawl onto his lap and settle against him while Bethea read from her Bible, he understood the concept of family contentment.

As his affection for the children had grown, the mystery of Clifford Kingston's relationship to his wife and children deepened. Little Hallie's coloring was in sharp contrast to her sisters and brothers. Her hair had remained dark and had thickened with ringlets that formed a cap around her creamy face. Her eyes had begun to change to green.

Faith had expressed all their feelings one morning when Con had been holding Hallie. "She looks like you, Uncle Con, excepting your skin is darker. How come?"

"Only the good Lord knows," he had replied.

Faith had crawled up on his knee and kissed his cheek. "Hallie can call you Daddy. I mean when she'd old enough to talk like us. Sometimes I pretend you're my daddy." Her blond hair was still mussed from sleep. When she grinned up at him, his heart overflowed with love.

"Hallie can call me whatever she likes, and I think of you as my little girl, so if you want to call me Daddy or Papa, I'd be honored." He had looked up to find Bethea's eyes glistening. She came to him, laying her hand against the side of his neck and stroking the bare skin with her fingertips. He knew their lives had become entwined irreversibly.

Hallie could scoot across the bed, and he had fashioned a guard railing that could be removed at bedtime. Bethea has expressed her fear that if Hallie fell from the bed and hurt herself, they might not be able to tend to her injuries. He had agreed and begun work the next day with Adam and Ben giving him a hand.

Con wished he could snap his fingers and give them one of the plush room size rugs his step-mother had ordered for the new house.

The dirt floor was no place for a baby to crawl around. The ground frost had worked its way under the logs, sending waves of cold around their ankles.

The constant chill forced them to use more wood in the stove and the cycle had made the task of maintaining the wood pile almost impossible. His mother's people would have covered the floor with buffalo and bear skin rugs and they would have all been cozy and warm.

He had expressed his concerns for their welfare to Bethea, particularly the risk of their love making. She had shown him the pages in the two books that insisted a nursing mother seldom conceived. Torn between his passion for her and his desire to see her free of carrying a child for as long as possible, he arose each morning determined to stay away from her. Yet, each night when she came into his arms, he forget his morning vow.

Ironically, the bitter cold weather had brought abstinence that his own will power had not. Frost on the children's pillows from their own warm breath as they slept had forced them to make a drastic change.

"We can all sleep in Mama's bed," Faith said.

"We wouldn't all fit, stupid," Adam retorted.

"Let's move the beds into this room," Ben had suggested.

Crowding nine people, three sets of stacked beds, the brass bed and Hallie's basket into the twelve by sixteen foot room and still finding room for a table and chairs, dry sink, and stove had brought them all to tears of laughter until Esther had offered a solution.

"Faith and Gabriel and Hallie and I can sleep with Mama," she said. "You can sleep in David's bed with him, and Adam and Ben can sleep in the bed above you and David. We can play with our dolls on Mama's bed the way we did last summer." She beamed up at Con, then at her mother.

He had torn his gaze away from Bethea's ashen face and reluctantly agreed. With Adam and Ben helping, they pushed and dragged one of the heavy log beds into the front room.

Within a matter of hours, he had found himself with David's cold feet against his thighs instead of Bethea's warm body. That frustrating arrangement had been in effect for three long weeks.

He took Hellion's reins and began to walk back through the trail they had made. Halfway to the cabin, he looked up as Ben's shriek of pleasure filled the air. He had shown the boys how to make oval shields from the elk hide, lacing them to a rounded willow limb and using them in place of the sleds that had been turned into fuel for the stove.

During the evenings he had entertained the children by drawing symbols his mother's people used on their tepees, with a promise to help them paint them on the shields when spring came and the leather coverings were dry and reconditioned. The next elk hide had already been promised to David and Gabriel and if it proved large enough, for the girls as well. If a buffalo happened to wander through the valley he'd shot it for meat and the warmth its hide would provide.

Ben's shield sailed several feet into the air and with a graceful swoop landed on the snow and continued down onto the frozen lake. Why hadn't he thought of the shields before?

His mother's people had used travoises to carry their belongings for centuries. The shields were large enough to carry two children each. They could be lashed to poles and be pulled behind the horses. Hellion had pulled a travois several times, so had the white mare. If the horses were given sufficient time to plow through the snow, Bethea and the younger ones could be spared the exhausting walk out of the valley.

Had he been risking their lives in order to continue the isolation and prevent the intrusion of outsiders? The mare was due to foal anytime. Could they manage the trip before her time came?

He remounted and swung his heels against Hellion's flanks. If they were to get on with their lives, he had to get them out. His mind raced through the details of their escape. Not only would the children be safely housed in his parent's home at Alice, but he'd be able to make Bethea his bride in a matter of days and no one would keep them apart.

THE SKY DARKENED to a deep gray the day Con and the boys finished tying the riggings of the shields to the poles and the poles to the horses and took them on a short test ride with Gabriel and Faith on the shields.

During the night a blizzard struck and when they opened the door the next morning, they discovered two feet of heavy wet snow on the ground.

"We'll wait until the weather clears," Con announced at supper. Two days later Con turned to Adam. "We'll leave day after tomorrow, early in the morning. After you're finished eating, would you and Ben go to the root cellar and bring back a bucket of spuds for your mother?"

The boys nodded.

"We'll feed the horses, too," Ben volunteered. Grinning, he turned to Adam. "Betcha I finish eating first," he said, shoving a fork full of fried potatoes into his mouth.

"Boys, don't gulp your food," Bethea warned. "Chew it or you'll get a belly ache. I'm completely out of my stomach remedy so you'll just have to suffer or chew properly."

Con winked at the boys before scowling at them. "She's right, boys." But when he put a fork of potatoes into his own mouth, chewed twice and swallowed, she sent him a warning frown.

"You promised to set an example, Con," she reminded him. Looking at the grinning faces around the crowded table, she dropped her gaze to the dark head of her youngest. Hallie was balanced on Bethea's lap, trying to reach Gabriel's plate.

"I'm sorry," Bethea said. "I don't mean to nag, but I worry that one of you might get sick or hurt. I used most of my medicines on your Uncle Con when he was sick. The Black Salve tins are almost empty and the bottle of witch hazel is dry as a bone. I have one teaspoon of Balm of Gilead buds left but no whiskey to make a tincture. I used the last of it on Ben when the mare bucked him off and he fell into those briars."

She looked across the table at Con, then at the children. "I love you all too much to lose one of you over a belly ache."

Hallie reached for Gabriel's plate again. Since cutting two sharp lower front teeth, she had begun to put everything into her little mouth. Bethea blocked the baby's hand and handed her a cooked carrot to suck on. Hallie's tight grip turned the carrot into mush and it fell to the floor. She started to whimper.

"Try this," Con suggested, cutting a piece of elk steak into a long strip and handing it to the gurgling baby.

"But she'll choke," Bethea said.

"Indian babies suck on meat strips long before they're weaned," he said. "Give it a try."

While the others finished their dinners, Hallie's attention focused on the meat, her round little cheeks moving as she gummed the meat. Only when she had sucked all the flavor from it, did she let it fall to the dirt floor. She held out her carrot and meat soiled hands to Con and smiled a toothy grin, making sounds that only she and Con seemed to understand.

He took her in his arms and she immediately patted his cheeks with her hands, coating him with her dinner.

The children giggled. Sensing that she was the center of everyone's attention, Hallie patted Con's face again. He chuckled as Bethea cleaned the baby's face and hands.

"She's a little tease," Bethea said.

Con agreed. "She'll be the belle of the ball someday."

"And spoiled rotten," Bethea added. "You shouldn't encourage her when she starts to show off or you won't be able to stand her by the time she's two."

"By then she may have a little brother or sister," he said.

Faith looked at Bethea. "Are you gonna have another baby?"

"No, I'm not," Bethea replied, wiping the drying carrots from Con's cheek. "Maybe later," she murmured.

"Esther and I got up one night," Faith said. "We were cold and we stood by the stove to get warm. You and Uncle Con were all snuggled together. I think you were both asleep, but he kissed your ear and you smiled. Did you like sleeping with Uncle Con more than you do us girls?"

Bethea glanced up at Con and the desire she saw in his blue eyes unsettled her. "Yes," she admitted, "but for now, you girls are more important. We must stay warm."

"Didn't Uncle Con keep you warm?" David asked. "He sure does me."

Bethea looked at Con again.

He was trying his best to keep from smiling.

"Well, answer the boy, Mrs....Adler. Do I keep you warm or not?"

"You called her Mrs. Adler like she was your wife," Esther said. "But you can't get married until a preacher comes."

Con pulled Bethea against him and wrapped his arms around her waist. "Sometimes there's no preacher around and a man and woman say their vows to each other. That's what your mother and I did."

"But when we get out of here, we plan to go to Butte City and do it again," Bethea explained, hoping the children would understand.

Adam frowned. "But what about when Pa comes back? You can't marry two men at once."

Bethea stiffened in Con's arms. Had they waited too long to tell the children about their father? Before she could answer her son, Con stepped away.

"Sit down, children," he said. "I have something to tell you. It will make you sad, but it's best that you know about it before we leave here."

When they were all seated around the table, he took Bethea's hand. "Sit with me."

She slid onto the bench next to him, wishing this wasn't happening.

He turned his attention to the anxious faces of the children but continued to hold Bethea's hand on top of the table. "Your father is dead," he said, his voice soft and steady. Before anyone could ask a question, he continued. "He died in Idaho Territory. When we get out of here, I'll try to find out where he's buried and we'll put a marker on his grave."

Adam's features grew pinched. "How did he die? Did he get sick? How do you know he's dead? Were you there? Do you know our pa?"

Con's grip on Bethea's hand tightened. "He was shot in a gunfight. It was east of Eagle Rock, or maybe it was closer to Fort Hall on the reservation. I'm not sure."

"Who shot him?" Adam asked, wiping a tear from his cheek.

Con released Bethea's hand and rose from his seat to pace the small crowded room.

"Does it matter?" Bethea asked. "Your father is dead and we must think about the good times we had while he was with us."

"Papa was mean to you," Esther said. "He made you cry."

"Esther, you mustn't speak ill of the dead," Bethea said.

221

"But he did," David insisted. "He didn't like me and I didn't like him, and he never stayed with us like other papas."

"That's enough, David," Bethea said. "Your father tried, but he didn't know what to do with such a large family." She stared at her clinched fist on the table and covered it with her other hand. "Your father abandoned us in this valley. Without Mr. Adler's help, we would have all died."

The room became silent with only the sounds of their breathing disturbing its gloom.

"How do you know he died in a gunfight?" Ben asked of Con.

Con leaned against the dry sink. "Take my word for it. I know. He shot another man and the man shot back."

Adam bolted from his chair at the end of the table, knocking it over. "You were all shot up when Ben and me found you. You came over the mountain from Idaho Territory, didn't you? Did my pa shot you?"

Con laid his hand on Adam's shoulder but the boy shook it off and stepped away, bumping into Ben. "Did you kill our pa?" A stream of tears ran down the boy's cheeks.

Con took a deep breath. "Yes, but only because he was trying to kill me. He shot first."

Adam swiped the tears from his flushed cheeks. "You murdered my pa? You shot him down?"

"It was me or him, Adam," Con insisted. "I'd never met him before, but when I told him my name, he drew down on me. He hated me sight unseen."

"Why?"

"I can't tell you."

Adam's face screwed up. "I wished he hadda kilt you. He's my real pa and he was a good pa, too, and...and...you had no call to kill him. He woulda come home. I know he woulda. Come next spring when the snows melted so he coulda driven the team and wagon in, he woulda come back to us, and he probably woulda brought the horse he promised me. Ma woulda been glad and..."

"No, Adam, that's not true," Bethea said. "He was mean...to me, to you children. Have you forgotten so quickly?"

Adam turned away. "He woulda come back. He left before and always came back...until you shot him." He glared at Con. "I'm gonna tell the sheriff what you did."

"So am I," Con replied. "As soon as we get out of here, I'm going into Dillon and file a report with Sheriff Jones. He'll contact the authorities in Idaho and we'll get this straightened out. I promise, Adam."

Bethea would have given anything to turn back the clock to earlier in the day. Just when everything seemed so promising, their secrets had spilled out.

She went to the dry sink and brought a blackberry pie to the table. "This happened last November and maybe we should have told you right away but we were trapped here and nothing could have changed things." She slid a piece onto each plate and put the empty tin back on the dry sink. "Now eat your pie so I can do the dishes." She wondered how she could talk so calmly when her stomach cramped in misery.

Adam sat staring at his pie but didn't take a bite. "You hated him, didn't you?" he asked, glaring up at Bethea. "Why did you marry him if you hated him?"

A deadening weight of reality loosened Bethea's tongue as she looked at her oldest son. He, of all the children, resembled Clifford Kingston the most.

"I was careless," she said, knowing as the words were uttered that someday they would come back to haunt her. "He made me pregnant, and I had to marry him."

Adam stared at her. "Is that the only reason you married him? Women aren't supposed to have babies unless they're married, Grandpa Mayfield said. Am I the baby you had? Is it my fault you married him? If you hated him, do you hate me, too?"

"Adam, I love you as I love all my children," she said. "Sometimes men and women are careless. Babies come when they're not expected."

Esther's brow furrowed. "How do you make a baby?"

"You fuck just like horses and cows do when it's breeding time," Adam sneered.

"Adam, how dare you use that word," Bethea said. "It's vulgar and obscene and I won't allow my children to use it. Where did you learn a word like that?"

"My pa used it all the time when you weren't around," Adam bragged.

"Well, if I ever hear you use it again I'll wash your mouth out with lye soap."

Adam's chin raised defiantly. "Is that what you do with him?" he asked, pointing his finger accusingly toward Con. "I heard you making sounds and whispering in the dark. I used to listen to you and Pa, too, but you always cried and begged Pa to leave you alone. So do you like it when that Injun fucks you, Ma? Is that why you're gonna marry him?"

Con grabbed the boy by the back of his shirt collar. "You can't talk to your mother like that. I won't have you accusing your mother and me of that. Oh hell." He released Adam and turned away. "Go feed the stock."

"You can't tell me what to do," Adam said. "You can't give me orders ever, not anymore. I hate you. I'm gonna feed the horses and Bossy but not because you tell me to. Someday you'll leave here and..."

"When I leave here, you'll be leaving with me," Con insisted. "We're going to be a family, whether you like it or not."

"You're lying," Adam exclaimed. "You'll leave us alone just like he did." He looked away. "When you're gone, Ben and me, we'll take care of Ma and our brothers and sisters. We can do it, and without help from you or your pa or anyone." He grabbed his coat, mittens and cap and stormed out the door, slamming it behind him. Ben followed his older brother outside.

The other children finished their dessert and carried their dishes to the dry sink. Con kept the baby and the younger boys occupied while Bethea, Esther and Faith made quick work of the dishes. No one spoke about Clifford Kingston or the argument between Con and Adam. He read to them from the Book of First Samuel until Bethea announced their bedtime. She nursed Hallie and lay her in the basket that had been moved to the foot of Bethea's bed below where the girls slept.

When the children were asleep, Con cornered Bethea near the dry sink and took her hands in his. "I'm sorry. This wasn't the way we should have handled Clifford's death."

"I lost my temper and said too much," she admitted.

"And I got angry," Con said, pulling her into his arms. "I knew we were taking chances making love when the children were only a curtain away."

"I wanted it as much as you did."

"In my mother's world, love making is natural and parents do it with the little ones in the same tepee. No one thinks anything of it." He took her face in his hands. "I want to hear you moan or cry out my name again. It tells me so much."

She rested her head against his chest. "Living as a family isn't as easy to accomplish as it is to dream about, is it?"

He massaged her back. "No, but the effort will be worth it. When trouble comes, a family pulls together."

"Your father won't consider us part of his family," she said, rubbing her cheek against his shirt front to dry the tears that moistened her cheeks.

"He'll come around, but will Adam? Maybe they'll have something in common and they'll become allies."

She looked up at him. "We can manage by ourselves, Con. Adam is right. All we need is a way to make some money during the summers and I can earn that by cooking for the stage coach companies and if we can add a room, I can offer lodging. I can open a post office. The government pays for that."

He nodded.

"Good, and if I can get a loan from the bank in Virginia City, I can open a store. Goodness knows, the valley needs a store. When others settle here, they'll come to us to buy goods. I can get a freighter to bring a few wagon loads of supplies here and we can earn money to buy canned goods and staples for the winter."

"Now you're the one with second thoughts," he said.

"One should always have an alternative. Plans and dreams don't always work out. I learned that when Clifford rode out last fall. I never want to be totally dependent on another person ever again. It was only a stroke of luck that we found you and you lived to help us."

"I remember lying in the snow," he said, nuzzling her hair before kissing it. "I must have been delirious but I saw you leaning over me. You told me you loved me...and you told me to hold on to that thought...and I did."

"I was afraid you couldn't hear me," she said. "I was so frightened for you...and for myself if I lost you before I could tell you how I felt."

"These past few months have been a gift from God," he murmured, holding her against him.

She smiled bravely at him. "We'll stay here and you can ride out to Monida and let your family know you're alive. They must be frantic. I'll miss you terribly, but it's April already and the cows will be here in July and that's only three months. By then I'll have a garden in."

He laid his finger against her lips. "When we leave, we leave together," he said, then kissed her. His mouth was gentle at first, then deepened into sensual longing that turned her knees to jelly while his body hardened against her.

When their lips parted, she tried to catch her breath. "I don't know if I could survive being away from you for three months. I love you so much, but too many things could go wrong."

"Stop making matters worse by searching for more problems," he chided. "Tomorrow we'll be on our way."

An hour later, Con glanced over at Bethea. "The boys should have returned by now. I'd better go check on them."

Before he could reach for his overcoat, Ben's scream came from outside and the darkness beyond the window above the bed turned orange and an explosion rocked the cabin.

CHAPTER EIGHTEEN

THE ROOT CELLAR was ablaze, turning the night sky to brilliant orange in spite of the large snowflakes drifting to the ground.

Ben collided with Con. "What happened?" Con shouted, shaking the hysterical boy. "Where's Adam?"

"He's still inside," Ben sobbed.

"Are you all right?" Con asked, turning the boy's soot covered face toward him.

Ben nodded.

"Then get me the axe. Hurry!" Con said.

Bethea ran toward the blazing building but the heat drove her back. "Adam, Adam," she screamed. "Can you hear me?" She put her woolen scarf over her face and tried to approached the structure again.

Ben raced back to them with the axe. Con stomped his way through the thigh deep snow to the side of the building. "Stay back," he shouted. "It's mostly in the front. I'm going to try to break in here and get him out.

Terrified, she stood in the snow and watched as he swung the axe again and again until the logs collapsed and he disappeared through the smoke and flames.

Bethea covered her mouth to suppress her sobs. Con reappeared through the hole, carrying an unconscious Adam in his arms. Flames shot from Adam's coat when the fresh air fueled the smoldering garment.

Con climbed the snow bank behind the root cellar and lay Adam's limp body into the snow, rolling him over and over until the flames were extinguished. His own coat burst into flames and he shed it. "Bury it in the snow," he shouted, ignoring the blisters on his own hands.

Adam began to gasp and choke. Con removed the boy's coat and cap and tossed it to Ben. "Bury it in the snow until it's cooled down," he said. He lifted Adam in his arms and draped the boy's head over his shoulder and began to press on his back. "Breathe, Adam, breathe, boy, you're going to be fine. Breathe deeply, son. Your mother's here and so is Ben."

Adam choked and gagged, then began to struggle.

"Don't fight me, Adam, I want to help you," Con said, but Adam twisted from his arms.

"I'm gonna puke," the boy sobbed and the explosive loss of his dinner proved his point.

They waited until he had regained his composure and could breathe easier, but he began to sob hysterically and Con picked him up in his arms and carried him to the cabin.

They stopped halfway to the cabin and turned as the root cellar caved in on itself.

"We've lost most of our food," she murmured. Numbly, she turned to Con holding Adam. "Thank you for saving my son." Her voice was little more than a whisper. She took a deep breath, knowing this was no time to weaken. "Let's get him inside," she said. "His trousers are burned. His legs may be injured, too."

Inside the cabin, Adam tried to undress himself but his hands trembled.

"Ben, hold the blanket and I'll help him out of his underwear," Con said, spotting the holes in Adam's long drawers and the red blisters on the boy's legs. "Easy does it, son. We'll get some salve on these burns and you'll feel better." He wrapped Adam in a flannel blanket and held him on his lap as Bethea began to treat the burns on her son's lower legs.

"It's a miracle," Bethea murmured as she scraped the bottoms of the two cans of Black Salve. "I thought this was all gone." She leaned back on her heels and gazed at her son's legs. "My goodness, Adam, I didn't realize how much you've grown. If the rest of you ever catches up with your legs, you're going to be a tall young man in a few years. Twelve and a half and shooting up faster than I can make new trousers for you."

She smiled, shoving her shaking hands in her apron pocket. "When we get out of here, we'll take you to Dillon and buy you some new clothes."

Adam's cheeks blushed beneath the soot and he slid from Con's lap. "Why'd you save me?" he asked, turning to Con.

"Because I love you."

Confusion flashed across Adam's features. "But I ain't even your son."

Con accepted a warm soapy cloth from Bethea and wiped his face. "It didn't matter, Adam," he said. He handed the cloth to the boy. "Wash up so you don't get your bed full of soot." He looked at Bethea as she began to minister to his hands. "Where are our coats?"

"Outside in the snow," she murmured.

"Ben, could you bring them inside?" Con asked. The boy went out the door without a word. "Bethea, how about some hot cocoa? Maybe we can find out what happened."

Bethea went about making the hot drink in a pan, wondering as she worked how Con could remain so calm. When Ben returned with the coats and caps, she hung them over the rope clothesline to dry. Not until Con picked up his mug of hot cocoa, did she notice the trembling in his hands.

She sat down beside him, kissing his cheek before turning to the two pale faced boys sitting across from them. "We've lost all the food in the cellar, but we have you two. That's more important," she said, smiling bravely at them.

"What happened?" Con asked.

Ben and Adam exchanged glances. "You tell 'em, Adam. You found it. I told you we shoulda left it alone."

They waited until Adam's fit of coughing passed, then he began to tell his story.

"Ben and me, well especially me...I knew you were both mad at me, so I...we decided to count the cans and sacks and barrels real good, but when we moved a sack of cabbages near the back end of the cellar, we found a barrel. When I pried the lid off, it smelled just like whiskey. Ben and me, we even took a sip to make sure. It was awful and we choked.

"I bumped into it and it tipped over and when we tried to jump out of the way, I knocked over the lantern and the fount broke and the oil spilled out and the flame caught the whiskey on fire, and I told Ben to go for help, but I was behind the fire, and then something exploded. I'm not sure what 'cuz we hadn't finished counting the stuff but we'd found some boxes of black powder that Pa had stored there."

He stopped and glanced at Con before continuing. "We found some blasting caps that Pa used in the timber last summer and some other stuff that I think belonged to Pa...Ma, I swear I don't know

229

what happened, but the cellar filled with smoke and I couldn't breathe and there was this explosion and everything went black until...you came." He looked across the table at Con as his blue eyes filled with tears. "I was scared."

"You had every right to be, Adam," Con said. The room grew quiet for several minutes. "Why don't you two boys get to bed now?" Con suggested.

"If you put your drawers on carefully, the salve will stay on," Bethea said. "Would you like me to help you?"

"Nah, I can do it myself," Adam said, but when his brother offered to help, he accepted.

"Get some rest, boys," Con said. "Tomorrow we start for Monida. I've had it with this place for awhile, and now that the food's down to what we have here in the cabin, we'd better move out." He went to the bed and lifted Faith and carried her to the lower bed and deposited her where he usually slept. She never roused. He did the same with Esther, then rolled Gabriel to the far side of the brass bed.

"Whatcha doing that for?" Adam asked from the upper bed.

"Your mother and I are going to sleep together tonight," Con explained. "I'm damned tired of David's cold feet and his early morning questions, so for this one last night, I'm going to snuggle with your mother. Her feet are a hell of a lot warmer than your brother's." He undressed and slid to the middle of the bed. "Coming, sweetheart?"

THE NEW DAY GREETED them with bright sunshine and a gentle breeze that promised a warming trend. By the time they had the travoises assembled, icicles were dripping from the roof.

"Look," Esther shouted, pointing to the lake. "It's melting."

The children ran to the spring house and stared toward the lake. Con and Bethea followed them, holding hands until they reached the shoreline. Several inches of water lapped at their feet.

Bethea looked up at Con. "How could it change so quickly?"

He shrugged. "Spring had to come sooner or later," he said. "Next thing you know, the swans and geese will be nesting in the reeds, but don't ask. They've managed without us in years past. They can get along without us this spring, too."

Over breakfast, they explained to the other children about the fire and Adam's close call. Within the hour, each person had selected their most precious possessions, a change of clothes, and food for three days travel in case the trip took longer than expected.

Bethea put her journals and writing supplies in their leather pouches, then wrapped them in the pink gingham fabric and shoved it and the blue sateen dresses for the girls into one of Hellion's saddle bags. She turned to Con and handed him the large family Bible. "Is there room for this somewhere?"

He covered their bed rolls with canvass and tied them between the poles above the shields. "Sure," he said, loosening one roll and slipping the book inside before retying it. "Are you ready?" he asked, making a final adjustment to the leather thongs.

"Yes." A tinge of sadness brought a catch to her voice when she took one last look at the cabin.

"We'll come back before the summer is over," Con promised, draping his arm around her shoulders. He helped the girls onto one shield, the younger boys on the other one, cautioning them to sit still and hold on to each other. He turned to Adam and Ben. "Boys, do you want to walk or ride the horses?"

"We'll walk," Adam said.

"Then you can have Bossy's rope," Con said. "Bethea, why don't you and Hallie ride the mare?" Con asked.

"We'll walk, too," she insisted, but within the hour, she changed her mind and accepted Con's boost onto the mare's broad backside. "I'm surprised she hadn't foaled yet."

"She was showing a little this morning," Con said, going to the mare's rear and lifting her tail. "If we're lucky, she'll wait until we reach Monida."

An hour later, Adam called from the rear where he had been leading a reluctant Bossy at the end of a long rope. "My legs hurt," he called. "Could I ride Hellion for a while?"

"Ben, you're in charge of Bossy," Con called, waiting until Adam reached him. He gave the boy a boost into the saddle and the journey resumed. He stayed in the lead, breaking trail and coaxing the two horses through the knee deep snow.

They stopped for a cold lunch but didn't linger. The younger children curled up on the shields and napped. Bethea tucked a warm woolen blanket around them and rejoined Con.

"Want to ride again?" he asked.

"No, but you can carry Hallie," Bethea said. "She's wide awake and wants to look around, but my arms are tired. I believe she's gained twenty pounds since morning. "I'll take the horses."

Con took Hallie from Bethea and resumed his position in the lead. Hallie's little head bobbed as she peered over his shoulder and smiled at Bethea who struggled to get the horses started again. After a few miles, Con turned and walked backward for several paces. "Why don't you ride? You must be exhausted."

"I'm fine," she replied, determined to not let him know how tired she felt. "Come walk beside me," she suggested.

"Hallie hasn't moved," Con said, coming to her side.

"That's because she's asleep," Bethea said. "She's found the perfect shoulder to nap on."

With the sun sinking behind the western horizon, they reached the abandoned cabin which marked the halfway point of their trek. The wind had blown the snow off a small knoll, exposing patches of dry grass. Con hobbled the horses and turned them loose to forage, then staked Bossy nearby. From a gunny sack he'd tied above the bed rolls, he shook out hay onto the ground and stepped back as the hungry animals claimed it.

Inside the cabin, Bethea discovered a well build fireplace and a stack of wood next to it. "Thank you, Lord, and whoever used to live here," she murmured as she built a small fire and hung her cast iron pot on the rack that protruded from one side of the fireplace. Into the pot went a piece of meat she'd cooked the previous day. A few scoops of clean snow from outside added enough moisture to make broth. Within minutes they were sitting in a circle around the fire enjoying thick juicy meat sandwiches made from one of the loaves of bread she had brought along.

The children fell asleep in their bedrolls minutes after they finished their meal. Bethea nursed Hallie and put her in beside Faith, then spread bedding alongside her daughters for herself and Con.

When Con didn't return from checking on the livestock, she put a woolen shawl around her head, pulled on her thick coat and went outside. In the darkness, she spotted the glow of a cigarette and a man's silhouette leaning against the corner of the cabin.

"I knew you smoked," she murmured, reaching out to him.

He tossed the cigarette into the melting snow and crushed it out. "Only when I'm tense or extra happy," he said.

"And which do you feel tonight?"

"I'm not sure. Maybe both," he admitted.

"Having second thoughts about all this?" she asked, touching the front of his coat with her fingers.

"Never," he said, sliding his hands beneath her shawl to caress her neck. "If we can reach Monida tomorrow, we'll rest."

"And take baths?"

He chuckled. "And take bathes. Hot water and perfumed soap, sit-down tub baths, with soft towels and the works."

Her eyes filled with tears. "Goodness gracious, Con, I haven't been able to sit in a bathtub for almost a year. I won't know what to do."

"Want me to show you how it's done?" he asked, stroking her cheek and wiping a lone tear from the corner of her eye.

"Wouldn't that be scandalous?" she retorted. "We'll have enough explaining to do as it is when we show up together after all these months."

"We don't have to answer to anyone," he said. "We can ride the train to Red Rock and hire a team and buggy at the livery and if the snow is still deep, they can put runners on it. We should be home on the third or fourth day. We'll rest up again and then head to Dillon and see the sheriff. After that's taken care of, we'll catch the next train to Butte City where you can become Mrs. Conrad Adler in the eyes of the government and all the righteous souls of Montana Territory."

She stretched up and touched his mouth lightly with hers.

He pulled her playfully against him. "Mark my words, Bethea, you'll be my wife within the week, and this time no one can keep you from me. We'll stay there for a few days and who knows, maybe we'll head to Virginia City or the geysers."

"Won't the geysers still be snowed in?" she asked.

"We'll find out," he replied.

"Do we take the children with us?"

"They can stay with my parents at Alice," he replied. "I thought perhaps we would ask Mrs. Burns to go with us to Butte City and take care of Hallie. She has a sister who lives there and I'll pay her expenses if she'll accompany us. She's been trying to find an excuse for years to hop one of those passenger trains going north, so we'll make that possible." He cupped her cheeks in his hands. "I need a few days alone with you."

Her eyes widened innocently. "Why?"

"To show you all the different ways to love each other," he replied. He whispered three of them in her ear.

She gasped as each imaginary union blazed to life in her mind. "Can a man and a woman actually make love those ways?" she asked, her curiosity getting the best of her.

"We'll find out," he said, his voice low and husky. He began to kiss his way across her cheek to the corner of her mouth where he lingered until she turned her face into his and sought his lips.

"Sometimes you take forever to give me what I want," she whispered.

"And what do you want?" he asked. "Name it and it's yours."

"I want happiness with you."

EMILINE BURNS SHOVED another piece of wood into the stove and plopped two steaks onto the griddle.

A passenger train, marooned for three days south of Pleasant Valley Pass, had finally rolled into Monida at midday. They had run out of food the previous day and Emiline had spent most of the afternoon cooking for two cars of hungry passengers.

An hour earlier the train had pulled out and headed toward the county seat of Dillon, the passengers impatient to reach their destinations now that their bellies were full. But their generosity in payment had replenished the hotel coffers and made the work worthwhile.

She and her husband Bill has spent the rest of the afternoon washing dishes and cleaning the dining area of the small hotel. After all the excitement, they were now alone without a single guest for the night. Behind the hotel the mongrel dog began to bark. She tried to ignore the animal, knowing it was past time to give him some scraps from the tables. But first she and Bill deserved a sit-down meal themselves.

As she speared one of the steaks with a long pronged fork and flopped it over, the dog's barking changed to howls. "Bill, what's the matter with that darn cur? Can't you shut him up?"

Her husband took the can of scraps and headed toward the rear door of the hotel. She could tell by the set of his shoulders that he was worn out. At times such as these, she longed to lock the door, hang the "closed" sign, and coax him upstairs to their bedroom where they could make slow and easy love to each other. Later they would get an undisturbed night of rest. But at present, the sun still hung an hour above the horizon in the western sky.

The dog's barks changed to yapping and she resisted the urge to go kick him. The poor animal had been abused in some past life and cowed whenever strangers came around as it was. It had taken weeks just to get him to trust them.

"Bill, for goodness sakes give the bones to that dog so he'll be quiet." She pulled one of the steaks from the griddle and slid it onto Bill's plate, poked it once to make sure it was blood rare, then counted to fifty and removed her own.

A cold draft on her neck sent a chill down her spine. "Close the door, Bill, before this place freezes up again."

"God damn," Bill exclaimed, standing in the middle of the open doorway. "Emiline, you've got to see this for yourself."

"I'm busy, Bill, so quiet that dog and close the door," she said. "I'm bone weary and want to call it quits."

"Damn it, Emiline, get out here," her husband called as the dog's barking became frantic.

She set the plates on the back of the stove and wiped her hands. "I'm here so what's got you both so excited?" she asked, stepping outside and closing the door behind her.

Bill pointed toward the narrow wagon road that followed the rising hill toward the Centennial Valley to the east. The valley had been snowed in since November, but as she squinted across the glaring landscape, two horses worked their way down the unbroken snow covered road that sloped toward the hotel.

Even from this distance she recognized Con Adler's magnificent bay stallion. The other horse was an unfamiliar white animal.

"My God," she gasped, "we'd given up that boy for dead." She ran toward the trail to get a better look. Con Adler held the reins of the stallion, but in his arms sat the pretty Mrs. Kingston and in Mrs. Kingston's arms appeared to be an infant. "This can't be," Emiline murmured as Bill joined her.

The two oldest Kingston boys rode the white mare. Behind the horses were travoises on which rode the younger children. Slowly the caravan approached the hotel, a slow plodding Bossy cow bringing up the rear. The older boys slid off the mare's back, handed the reins to Con Adler, and raced toward the hotel.

"We made it," Ben shouted.

"All the way from the upper lake in two days," Adam boasted.

Emiline could think of nothing to say as Con dismounted, took the baby and put it in Emiline's arms, then helped Bethea Kingston from the stallion. The other children crawled from the travoises and began to chatter all at once.

Con disconnected the poles from the mare and led her to Bill. They had a whispered conversation, then disappeared around the corner of the hotel toward the livery. The mare tugged on the reins and acted as if she wanted to lie down, but Con dragged her forward. Blood and mucus ran from the mare's rear and Emiline realized the mare was in labor.

When she glanced down at the green eyed, dark haired baby girl in her arms, she knew the mare wasn't the only female pregnant in the valley. She still didn't know what to say when Bethea took the baby from her.

"Thank you for holding her," Bethea said.

Emiline's jaw hung slack while a thousand questions raced through her mind.

"I want to thank you for the use of Bossy and all the other things you sent to us," Bethea said. "I'm sorry I never got back to...you see, so much has happened to us." Bethea's eyes glistened and she choked down a sob. "The children are very tired and they're hungry." She smiled. "I believe I said the same thing the last time we met, didn't I?" Her shoulders began to tremble as her control slipped. "Oh, Mrs. Burns, you can't imagine how glad I am to see you."

"Honey, no gladder than I am to see you and Con and all these younguns," Emiline said, giving the younger woman a warm hug. "I notice your family's grown since I last saw you." She chucked the baby under her fat chin and the baby smiled. "She's a little doll. What's her name?"

Bethea gazed down at the baby. "Con named her. Halona, but we call her Hallie."

"How old is she?"

"She'll be five months May first," Bethea said. "She scoots everywhere and can almost crawl and she has two teeth and is working on four more and she can hold finger food and gum it to death." She smiled. "Con taught her that, and he made a board for the bed so she couldn't fall out and hurt herself. He's wonderful to her and good with all the children. We couldn't have survived without his help. Thank God he came to us when we needed him in the worst way."

"But he was almost dead," Esther added.

"Mama cut him open and took out the bullets," Ben said.

"We had to be very quiet," Gabriel said.

"'Cuz he was so sick and Mama cried because she was afraid he would die, but he didn't," Faith explained.

"I got to sleep with him," David said, "but that wasn't until he and Mama couldn't be in bed together anymore because Faith and Esther and Gabriel were there and it woulda been too crowded." He yelped when Adam kicked him.

"We're not supposed to talk about that," Adam said, scowling at all the others. "Are you all stupid?"

When Emiline glanced at Bethea, Bethea refused to look up, but her cheeks were pale and her hands trembled as she adjusted the baby in her arms.

Emiline did some quick calculations. "Then Con can't be..."

"No, he's not," Bethea said, smiling. "Do you have something for the children to eat? I don't need anything, but I'm sure Con is hungry. All I'd like is a hot bath." Reluctantly, she looked at Emiline. "I have a little money left to pay for it. If it's not enough, I don't know what I can do for now." Her complexion turned pasty gray as she swayed. "Take the baby."

Emiline grabbed the baby and caught Bethea as she began to crumble.

Con Adler and Bill Burns appeared through the hotel door. When Con spotted Bethea sagging in Emiline's arms, he ran to her and swept her up in his arms. "What happened?" he asked, his gaze centered Bethea's pale face.

"She fainted," Emiline said. "Bring her inside and lay her down. I have some smelling salts somewhere." She lead them all inside. "Put her on the settee," she directed, running up the stairs to her own bedroom. Still carrying the baby in one arm, she found the bottle and ran down the stairs again. She shoved Hallie into Con's arms. "She says you're good with babies. Watch this one. She looks enough like you to be yours." She knelt by the settee and passed the open vial back and forth under Bethea's nose.

Bethea's eyes flew open and she tried to sit up. "What happened?" Frantically she looked around the room. When her gaze fell on Con and Hallie, she sank back against the cushion. "I was tired."

"We left yesterday morning," Con explained. "She walked all the way today until an hour ago. Only when I got on Hellion myself would she agree to ride, too." He turned to Emiline. "Could you arrange for hot baths for everyone and a hot meal, too? I'll pay for it if you'll extend me some credit until I get to the ranch."

Emiline got to her feet. "I'll heat the water while everyone's eating. Then when the children are in bed, I think we need to have a little talk to clear the air. Con, your family thinks you're dead, but Chief Tendoi said you were alive because he had been given a sign."

"My uncle's third wife is a shaman," Con said. I hope my father believed him. The snows were deep. We couldn't get out."

Emiline nodded. "This has been the worst winter since we've been here, worst in decades according to the old timers. The snow has been heavy and the livestock losses unbelievable, between fifty and seventy percent by some estimates. The trains haven't been able to get through on schedule. The stockmen who are mortgaged are going to go under for sure."

At the stove, she took the two steaks and cut them into small pieces, added some vegetables and a jar of tomato juice and set it to simmering. In minutes she had a large batch of biscuits in the oven.

While they baked, she took charge of the children and made them line up at her sink and wash their faces and hands.

A half hour later, dinner was on the table. Gabriel climbed onto his chair and stared at the bowl in front of him. "Stew?"

The others giggled and Con explained the limited menu they'd had during the winter. "But this is fine. Right, kids?"

"Right," some of them replied.

"If you're sure," Emiline replied. "I could find something different." Con convinced her they appreciated her meal and she smiled, then turned her attention to Bethea. "You rest on the settee."

"But I feel foolish just lying around," Bethea said.

"You're still pale as a ghost," Emiline replied, easing a cup of fresh brewed herb tea into her hands. "And you stay with her," she said to Con. "The baby is asleep and the other children are fine." As she returned to the stove, she could hear their soft murmuring.

After everyone had eaten their fill, two tubs were set up in the bathing room and filled with water and they began to bathe, the boys two to a tub, then the girls and Bethea bathed. Emiline took care of the baby. While Bethea settled the children upstairs in separate beds, Con took his turn in the tub.

When Bethea came down the stairs, her hair loose about her shoulders as she tried to dry it, Emiline watched Con Adler's face. If ever two souls had become one, Con and Bethea had succeeded. Their love for each other was evident in every move they made and each glance they shared.

They gathered in the lobby area of the hotel, and Con took Bethea's hand and sat with her on the settee.

"Are you feeling better now?" he asked, leaning to inhale the fragrance of her freshly washed hair. As it dried, the curls tightened, framing her head and shoulders like a halo. The glow of the lamp on the end table highlighted the coppery strands. For a moment Emiline half expected Con to kiss the woman outright.

Bill joined Emiline, sitting on the arm of her over stuffed chair.

Bethea leaned against Con and he put his arm around her shoulders. When they looked up and realized they were being watched, Bethea blushed and Con smiled.

"It isn't what you might think," he said.

"And what do you think we think?" Bill asked.

"She found me. I was all shot up and dying," Con explained. "She saved my life."

"When I started into labor with Hallie, he helped me through it," Bethea said. "He took care of us both, you see. That's why he got to name her."

"I think I need a drink," Bill Burns said, going to the bar and bringing back a bottle of his best whiskey and four glasses.

Con shook his head as did Bethea, but Emiline accepted a double shot of whiskey and began to sip it.

"Why don't you start at the beginning and tell us all about it," Emiline said.

"I need a cup of coffee," Con said, moving to the table. "This may take longer than you expect."

CHAPTER NINETEEN

"SO YOU SEE, we did what was necessary to survive a winter in the valley," Bethea Kingston added after Con Adler had explained what had happened since he'd ridden away from the home ranch.

"And now instead of going to Virginia City and filing for a divorce on grounds of abandonment, we'll be going to Butte City to be married." She smiled at the Burns couple while Con held her hand beneath the table and squeezed.

"And that's where you can help us, Mrs. Burns," Con said. "We need a nursemaid for Hallie to go with us. We'd like that to be you. Could Bill run the hotel while you go with us? You could see your sister and have a vacation yourself."

Emiline's gaze darted to her husband's face and back to Bethea and Con. "Bill can't cook much beyond boiling water and making coffee, but Chester has a woman whose been staying with him. She's retired from doing business at Spring Hill..."

She stared at Bethea, then Con. "Well, anyway, Chester's been raving about her cooking. I've enjoyed having her as a neighbor. It don't make no never mind what's in a person's past. It's what they're doing now that counts."

"We'll be catching the train at Red Rock a week from today," Con said. "We'll spend a day in Dillon and catch the morning train out to Butte City. We...Bethea needs some time free of caring for the children. You'd be doing us a great favor if you'd come with us."

Bill Burns kissed his wife's cheek and grinned. "You'd be a fool to refuse, Emiline. I'll hire Chester, too. He can always use a few weeks work. We'll manage without you and when you come back, we'll tell you how much we missed you."

"Then it's settled," Emiline said. "Now, it's past midnight and you two must be exhausted. You're welcome to share a room. We're alone here tonight." She frowned. "Damn it all, honey, it's your decision. I have two empty rooms left and you can have your choice of either or both."

Bethea touched Emiline's hand. "I love Con with all my heart but we can wait a week to be together again. We have a lifetime ahead of us. Thank you for all you've done, and thank you for agreeing to accompany us to Butte City. Monida is the only town in the territory I've seen. Is Butte City larger?"

The other three burst into laughter.

"Believe it or not, Mrs. Kingston, there are larger towns and cities than this place," Bill Burns explained. "Butte City is a mining camp that kept booming instead of going bust. Why, I reckon there's several thousand folks living and working there. Yes, ma'am, it's a western boom town if ever there was one."

Bethea's hand brushed Con's shoulder as she rose from the table. "I'll look in on the children and retire to my room," she said. "Good night, Mr. and Mrs. Burns. Good night, C...Mr. Adler. God bless you all."

She turned away, unwilling for them to see her disappointment. What choice did they have, now that they were back with other people? Society had come between them, but not for long, she thought, as she climbed the stairs.

Faith had left her bed and crawled into Esther's. Gabriel's bed was empty as well and she found him wedged between Ben and David. Only Adam slept alone. She had become concerned about the lack of privacy for them all, but maybe she'd neglected to consider the benefits of companionship and security that the closeness of the cabin had given them. In the months to come, they would all have adjustments to make.

At the door of the room in which she would be spending the night with Hallie, she turned to find Con coming down the hallway. She paused, her hand lingering on the doorknob. He leaned against the far wall and held out his hands. She flew across the hallway and into his arms.

"I wanted to be with you, but I knew it wouldn't be proper," she mumbled against his shirt front. He smelled of fresh soap and tobacco and she knew he'd been outside for a smoke. "You smell wonderful," she murmured, looking up at his face.

Her fears and uncertainty evaporated when he took her face in his hands and brushed her lips with his.

"I'm afraid," she whispered.

"So am I and I don't know why," he admitted.

"Are you sure we're doing the right thing?" she asked.

"You keep asking me that. Why?"

She tried to pull free but he slid his hand around her ears and cupped her head. Aware of the strength in his hands and arms, she thought of how many times Clifford had hurt her with his hands. She'd never seen Con angry, but he'd had a gun strapped to his hip when they'd first met. He'd shot her husband with a gun, the same gun he'd used to bring down game that had enabled them to survive the winter. Had the Burns couple really understood Con's explanation of the shoot-out? They had seemed surprised, then perplexed, but hadn't asked for more facts than Con had been willing to tell them.

"Your hair is beautiful when it's free like this," he murmured. Without loosening his hold, his fingers stroked the curls near her ears.

"It's not very practical," she whispered.

"Wear it loose when we're alone together." His grip tightened, turning her head toward him. His tongue found hers and she didn't even realize she'd opened her mouth. *Our mating takes many forms*, she thought, sliding her arms up around his neck.

As she strained against him, she hungered for him as she'd never hungered for any man. Would she ever be satisfied for long, now that he had shown her the ecstasy of their union?

"God, Bethea, we've got to stop or I'll drag you into my room and make love to you in spite of everything."

She opened her eyes to find he'd released her head and now held her shoulders. Taking a deep breath, she tried to smile but couldn't. His face swam before her and she blinked, feeling a warm tear slid down her cheek.

"Don't cry, sweetheart," he crooned. "Everything is going to be fine." He eased her against him once more. "Why don't we catch the train tomorrow and head for the home ranch? Why waste a day here when we can get there by tomorrow night? I was going to send a messenger but why not let them see for themselves that we're alive and well?"

She brushed the tear away and smiled. "Does that mean we can move our wedding up a day?"

He kissed her again. "I'll talk to Mrs. Burns." He chuckled. "This is Sunday. I had to check a calendar and ask Bill Burns what day it really was. We can catch the train Wednesday and be in Butte

City the next day. By Thursday night, we'll be Mr. and Mrs. Conrad Adler, all legal and proper." He lifted her off the floor and whirled her around in the narrow hallway, then set her down at her door. "Now, woman, get yourself behind that door before I succumb to your charms."

She reached up, wanting to kiss his mouth again, but settled for a chaste kiss on his cheek. "Good night, Mr. Adler. Sleep well." She stepped away and turned the door knob.

"Doubtful," he complained, and the desire lingering in his eyes matched her own as she watched him turn away and disappear behind the door of his room.

Inside her own room, Hallie aroused and Bethea nursed her but the baby fell asleep again after a few moments. Her breasts ached with milk. Nursing had never been a problem for her. Motherhood came as natural as breathing, but as she wiped herself, she wished Hallie was old enough to wean to a glass. If the baby could be weaned, her milk would dry up, and she and Con... She shook the thought from her mind. How could she even think about sacrificing the health of her baby because she needed to be able to make uninhibited love with Con Adler?

After a half hour of expressing her frustration in her journal, she put it away and went to bed, but sleep was slow to come. Was Con still awake? Thinking of her? Were Bill and Emiline Burns awake, wondering if she and Con were together? She rolled onto her stomach and tried to close her eyes. Living in sin with Con Adler had truly turned her into a lustful woman.

EMILINE BURNS stretched and settled against the long warm body of her husband. Being in the company of Con Adler and Bethea Kingston had ignited desire between Emiline and Bill. No sooner had they undressed than Bill had pulled her gown off again and they had made love twice, something they hadn't done in years.

"That was wonderful," she whispered. "Who would have thought it from two old people like us?"

Bill chuckled and tightened his arm around her plump shoulders. "Just because we're gray haired and have been married for thirty-five years doesn't mean we have to act like straight-laced old fogies. I'm no saint and neither are you, Emi. Let's not ever take each other for granted. Seeing the looks passing between those two love birds reminded me of what we used to have and that it's still ours if we'll take the time to enjoy it. Remember that hell-fire and brimstone Methodist circuit preacher who used to ride through here?"

She nodded against his shoulder and gave in to the impulse to kiss his chest and run her palm slowly across his midriff.

He inhaled sharply before continuing. "He was wrong saying that loving was meant for procreation and that doing it for pleasure was fornication. The good Lord gave us these organs and He wouldn't have built them with so much pleasure if He hadn't intended us to enjoy them."

She tickled him playfully in his ribs. "You'd be a very popular minister if you expounded your beliefs from the pulpit."

"It would sure shake up some of those pious Methodists up north in Beaverhead Valley, wouldn't it?" His hand drifted to her breast before returning to her shoulder. "We never had any children. Does that mean we're never to enjoy being together like this? Hell, no. We've let this hotel become our child, but not anymore. Even if we have guests, we can still lock this door and play a little after hours."

"I think that's the best suggestion you've made in years, Billy. I'll hold you to your promise."

They lay quietly in each other's arms for several minutes. Bill's hand began to caress her upper arm. "I'm glad you didn't say anything about thinking you saw...Kingston last month."

She propped herself up on an elbow and peered through the moonlit darkness at him. "I would have sworn it was him looking out that train window at me, but he turned away and the train left a few minutes later. I reckon I was mistaken."

"You had to be," Bill replied. "Con shot him in the gut and somewhere else, he thought in the chest. I can understand why he didn't linger to verify his kill. Even for a mean bastard like Kingston, being gut shot is a painful bad way to meet your Maker. And if he didn't die from bleeding from his gut, he would have froze to death. Didn't Con say it happened at the start of that first big blizzard? No man could have survived that."

"It's a miracle that Con made it over those mountains," Emiline said, touching Bill's lower lip with her fingertip.

He kissed her mouth. "Don't say a word to either of them, honey. They've been through enough without you casting doubt on her widowhood."

Emiline settled against him again. "I reckon you're right, but if that wasn't him, it was his twin, and God help us all if there are two despicable characters like Clifford Kingston running around this country."

WHEN BETHEA carried Hallie downstairs the next morning, the children were already dressed and eating bowls of oatmeal and raisins topped with cream and brown sugar. She glanced around the room for the men.

"They're outside," Emiline Burns said. "The white mare foaled during the night. The children and I went to see for ourselves."

Adam nodded. "She had a colt. He's a chestnut, unless he changes later, and he has two white stockings on his front feet and a star on his forehead. He's a beauty."

"Uncle Con thinks he should be Adam's since he's been waiting for so long for his own horse," Ben said. "But why don't you get Adam a full grown horse and let me have the colt?"

David shook his head. "No, he's more my size, Mama. We can grow up together. Adam and Ben need horses to ride now. So can he be mine?"

Emiline Burns spooned bowls of oatmeal for Bethea and herself. "Let me hold the baby while you eat," she said, holding two spoons in one hand. "Have you tried her on oatmeal?"

Bethea shook her head. "We ran out a month after she was born, but she likes mush. She doesn't seem to choke on anything. Maybe I'll be able to...wean her early."

"Mama, what about the colt?" Adam asked. "Can he be mine?"

Bethea scanned the anxious faces of her sons. "Why don't we wait until the poor foal is strong enough to get around."

"But he's walking already," Gabriel insisted.

"Yes, darling, but..."

Con and Bill Burns came inside, shedding their coats and hats before they took chairs at the table. When Con smiled across the table at her, Bethea's heart skipped a beat.

"The children have been discussing the new foal," Bethea said. "Each boy makes a good case for claiming him."

"Why don't we wait and let him get stronger," Con suggested.

Adam let out an exaggerated groan of frustration.

"Bill has agreed to board the mare and foal until we get back to the valley," Con said. "We have more than a hundred horses at the ranch. We'll find mounts for everyone big enough to ride."

"Me, too?" Gabriel asked.

Con winked at the five-year-old boy. "Maybe after a few lessons and your mother's approval."

Bethea took a deep breath, feeling as if all their lives were about to take a significant leap into a different world, one of luxury and wants rather than the survival needs she'd lived with for most of her married life. "I leave the decisions about riding horses to you, Mr. Adler," she said, grinning at the formal use of his name, "as long as you include the girls and me in the riding lessons. I know how to ride a Missouri mule but not a fine saddle horse. As for the new foal," she murmured, looking at her oldest son, "I think he would make a fine animal for Adam to learn to work with...but only if you'll be careful and teach him the proper way to train him without getting hurt."

Adam let out a war whoop of pleasure.

"Mama, when do we leave?" David asked.

"On the morning train, stupid," Adam said. "Do we have to go to the Alice ranch? Why can't we go to Dillon?"

Bethea studied her oldest son, unable to interpret his actions. In spite of Con saving his life, she was sure he still held a huge grudge against him. "Today is Monday and yes, we'll be going to the Alice Livestock home ranch. On Wednesday, Mr. Adler and I will be catching the train. Hallie will be going with us but if Mr. Adler's parents are willing, you children will be staying there until we return. Mr. Adler will be your step-father when we return and you must show him respect. When he tells you to do something, you must obey. I'll no longer be Mrs. Kingston but Mrs. Adler."

"I ain't never gonna be Adam Adler," the boy said, shoving his bowl away and stomping from the room.

TWO HOURS LATER, wearing their only change of clothing, they boarded the northbound passenger train. Adam chose a seat by himself and stared out the window at the melting snow on the rolling hillsides. The car was crowded and the children argued over the window seats until Bethea cautioned them. As the train pulled into the depot at Spring Hill, fifteen miles from their starting point, Con stood up.

"I'll be back," he said, then left the car. When he returned and sat down beside her, his features were troubled.

"Where did you go?" she asked.

"To talk to the station master," he replied.

"About what?"

"Livestock losses." He pointed out the window as the train pulled from the station. "Pay attention to the dark lumps. They look just like huge rocks, but this area has no huge rocks."

Bethea peered out the window, trying to figure out what he was talking about. In the distance she spotted several boulders still covered with white patches of melting snow. As the train rolled along the track, the boulders became more numerous. "What are they?"

"Dead cattle." Con shook his head sadly. "The station master said the losses have been running above fifty percent for most of the herds and the stockmen are hard pressed to pick them all up. They've just begun to be able to get to the pastures. He said until a few days ago, the countryside was all but impassable. The trains stopped running, the stage coaches couldn't get through even with runners. Families have been snowed in for weeks in the valleys and for months in the high elevations. I hope my family is safe."

As the train approached Crabtree station, they watched as a group of men, working in the distance, hoisted a bloated cow onto a wagon bed mounted on runners.

"They're using a hay derrick," Con murmured. "It looks like they've got a wagon load."

"What will they do with the carcasses?" she asked.

"Bury or burn them," he said. "Good Lord, what's happened to this country?"

The man sitting behind them tapped Con on his shoulder and Con turned around. "Be glad you're not on the eastern plains, my good man," the stranger said. "Their losses have been as high as eighty and ninety percent. Those British investors are going down with the local stockmen. Mark my word, sir. This will change stock raising in the west."

"What do you mean?" Bethea asked, hoping the man exaggerated. Con's expression grew progressively more solemn as the man elaborated.

"I represent a banking firm in Omaha and Denver, ma'am, and we have significant loans in Montana and Idaho territories," he said, handing Con his calling card. "This is my third trip and each time the news is worse than before." He arched a dark brow toward Con. "And you, sir?"

"My father operates the Alice Livestock Company west of here," Con replied. "Last summer we had just under twenty thousand head. Now I'm wondering what's left."

"Ah, yes, I've heard of your operation," the man said. "Your two year old steers drew top dollar last spring in Omaha. I met the owner, Matthias Adler. Your father?"

Con nodded.

"You'll be among the fortunate if your losses hold at fifty percent," the man said, then reached for an eastern newspaper and began to read.

"Some good fortune," Con murmured under his breath.

"Will this change our plans?" Bethea asked as her wobbly confidence began to falter. "The children and I can always go back to the cabin in the valley if you'd rather."

"Nothing will change our plans, Bethea," he assured her. "A wedding, a honeymoon, a summer in the valley, then winter at the home place, and enough fire wood to keep us warm. Nothing will come between us now; nothing."

VICTORIA ADLER stooped to pet the head of the old female dog that had accompanied her on her evening walk. The bitch had been named Little Mama because she had had so many litters of puppies in her younger days. Now almost nineteen years old, she spent most of her days sleeping in the kitchen of the new house, close to the wood stove on a new horse blanket Matthias had bought for her. In spite of her stiffened hip joins, the dog always found the energy to accompany Victoria on her evening walks.

Victoria loved the longer days, the warming weather, and the flowering crocuses that heralded the melting of the snows. But the devastating destruction to the livestock herds and the grievous disappearance of their oldest son prevented this spring from being the enjoyable change of season she longed for.

When Con had failed to return by Christmas, Matthias had insisted on riding up the Medicine Lodge trail and over the pass into Idaho in spite of the deepening snow. At least he had had the wisdom to take his brother and his son Lee with him. After struggling for three days, they had reached the winter camp of Chief Tendoi's people. Three more weeks had passed before they had convinced Matthias to give up his search and take advantage of the brief chinook in mid January and return to the home ranch.

Tendoi had clung to the belief that his nephew was alive, but Matthias had accepted the possibility that Con was dead, lost somewhere in the wilderness of eastern Idaho.

As the months passed, a deadening sense of mourning had settled over the ranch. Whenever his name was mentioned, Matthias would leave the room to pace the hallways of the new house, its cavernous rooms echoing the emptiness of all their lives. The huge house seemed destined to become a monument to sadness.

When the snow had begun to melt, confirming a second devastation, Matthias had grown silent, distant and withdrawn. For the first time since she'd met him, she saw the spark of life begin to fade from his eyes and she knew the years were catching up with both of them.

He had regained partial use of his arm, but the disability had been difficult to accept. Now he'd lost one of the main purposes of his life. Even the return of his middle son didn't seem to help, and the two younger boys had fallen into the all too familiar routine of avoiding their father.

In a few weeks the roads to the other valleys would be passable. Perhaps if she sent messengers to their daughters, explained the problems at home and invited them to bring their husbands and new babies, the Adler family could have a Sunday reunion and all be together again. But how could they celebrate without Con?

If only someone would bring them news. A body. Someone who had seen him die. Anything that could bring a finality to this endless wondering. Con's horse or an article of clothing, even his gun and holster or his trusted rifle. The family needed to know once and for all that this beloved oldest child was gone.

Victoria stopped to admire the tulips that had begun to bloom, but the blazing red and yellow blossoms failed to lift her spirits. She stepped over the rivulets of melting snow to see if the daffodils had opened. The dog barked and left Victoria's side.

The shadows were long in the late afternoon. Rebecca Estes, the new cook, would be ringing the dinner bell within the hour. Victoria hadn't quite adjusted to having another woman in charge of the kitchen, and only when Matthias insisted she give up the cooking and spend more time with him, had she conceded.

The dog barked again and loped across the rolling lawn toward the wagon road leading from the ranch house. In the distance, Victoria saw a horse and rider still a quarter of a mile away.

"Hellion?" she gasped. What other stallion trotted so regally? No, it can't be. But this rider was a boy. No one but Con had a right to ride the treasured stallion. She ran across the lawn, unaware of the splashing of water against her skirts or the wetness that seeped inside her boots through the eyelets.

The unfamiliar rider reined the stallion to a stop several yards from Victoria. Her chest ached as she stared at the boy. She'd never seen him before. He took off his hat and brushed sandy brown hair from his forehead. His eyes were blue and clear, and she could see exceptional horsemanship ability when Hellion obeyed every touch of the reins.

"Where did you get that stallion?" she demanded.

The boy stiffened, his stubborn chin lifted in defiance. "Mr. Adler said I could ride him."

Angry over his cavalier manner, she reached for Hellion's bridle when the boy tried to pass. "Con would never give this stallion away. Where did you steal him? Where is my son?"

"They're coming." The boy turned in the oversized saddle and pointed. "They're in the buggy, but he had to stop and take off the runners 'cuz the snow was all melted."

Victoria stared down the road but could see nothing. "Con? Con's coming? He's alive?" Her voice quivered. "Don't lie to me, young man. You're not from around here. Who are you?"

The boy straightened in the saddle. "I'm Adam Kingston."

"Kingston?" She chewed her lower lip. "From Centennial Valley?" She stared down the road again. Two horses pulling a surrey passed under the cross beams that marked the entrance to the home ranch. The driver flicked the reins and the team broke into a trot. "If you're lying to me, I'll..." She covered her mouth, trying to suppress a cry.

"My ma's with him, and my brothers and sisters," the boy said. "He said we'd be staying here for awhile. He and my ma are getting married." Without a word, he reined Hellion around her and kicked him into a gallop, sending mud splashing onto her already stained skirts.

She stood in the middle of the road, unable to move. Con waved. Sitting beside him was a young woman, her bonnet hiding much of her face. She carried a bundle in her arms.

A baby? *Con, what have you been doing?*

Con pulled on the reins, stopping the team several feet from Victoria. He handed them to the pretty young woman and jumped to the muddy ground. His long legs brought him to her before she could move and she found herself wrapped in his strong embrace.

He kissed her cheek and hugged her again, then turned and walked her to the passenger side of the surrey. "Mother, I want you to meet Bethea Kingston and her family."

CHAPTER TWENTY

BETHEA KINGSTON TRIED to remain calm as the tall slender middle-aged woman approached the surrey. Hallie, fresh from a nap, struggled to be upright and Bethea sat her on her knee.

Hallie's round face broke into a smile as Con approached. Her chubby little hands waved in the air and he reached for her, resting her comfortably in the crook of his arm. He brushed a dark curl out of the baby's eyes and made a face at her. Hallie responded with a gurgle and a toothy grin.

The older woman's attractive face lightened with maternal affection as she observed her step-son with the infant. "Con, whose baby is this?" The woman's gaze skipped from Bethea back to Con. "She looks like you but..."

Con laughed. "This is Hallie. She's five months going on five years and truly advanced beyond the normal baby." He clucked at the baby again. "And no, she's not mine."

"When did you become an expert on babies?" the woman asked. She smiled and touched the baby's cheek, took her from Con, and looked up at Bethea. "And you must be Bethea Kingston. Welcome to our home. I've met your oldest son already."

"Bethea, this is Victoria Adler," Con said. "Let me help you up, Mother. I'll introduce the children and we can ride to the house together. Did Adam tell you what we needed?"

"He did."

Bethea slid closer to the middle of the cushioned seat, squeezed between the flouncing skirts of Victoria Adler and the leather holster on Con's hip. As Con introduced each of the children, she could think of nothing to say.

She stared at the house in the distance. *A grand mansion*, she thought. Sided with pale brown stained shingles, it was trimmed with numerous white shuttered windows. The two floors, plus the tall pitched roof with its five identical dormers that made it a three-story house, grew in size as the team and surrey closed the distance.

Stately white pillars stood like sentinels across the middle portion of the front, extending far out over the gravel driveway. Three steps lead to the portico and a veranda that ran the entire length of the house. Above the pillars, on the second floor French doors opened onto a sun porch. The house was intimidating in its size alone and she didn't want to think about the fancy furniture that probably filled every room.

Hadn't Con mentioned that the house had eight bedrooms? No house needed eight separate bedrooms. And what about their personal needs? A house with eight bedrooms would need several maids just to tend to all the chamber pots.

But she recalled Con's description of the flushing toilets; two of them, he had said, and hot water to the porcelain bathing tubs. She thought of the dirt floor of the cabin where she had lived for almost a year. She wanted to turn around and catch the first train south to Monida, hire a wagon and head for the security of the Centennial Valley where at least she knew to expect nothing and each small improvement had seemed a treasure. This house had so many treasures that the occupants probably took them all for granted.

They rolled along the circular drive and stopped beneath the portico. From the barn, Adam and a gray haired man using a cane approached. Bethea recognized Matthias Adler and her heart stopped as she recalled their angry exchange.

"I can't go through with this," she whispered.

"Of course you can," Con replied.

"That man hates me, and I don't exactly like him either." She took Hallie from Victoria's arms and hugged her tightly.

Con left the seat and ran to his father and embraced him. Bethea could hear their murmured conversation but couldn't make out the words. Another older man and two young men joined them.

The youth she remembered as Lee rode up on a dun gelding, accompanied by another young man whose family resemblance was undeniable. The sons of Matthias Adler leaped from their saddles with a whoop and almost knocked Con down with their greetings.

Victoria leaned toward her. "I think the men have forgotten us. Why don't we get down and go inside. Dinner is almost ready. I'd best tell Rebecca we have company."

Feeling as if she were trapped in a torrent and about to be sucked under, Bethea climbed down and helped the younger children alight from the surrey. Before she could instruct them in proper behavior, they ran to Con and Matthias and began to chatter all at once.

"Children, come back," Bethea called, but they paid no heed. "Mr. Adler hates my children as much as he does me," she said.

"Matthias has never hated a child in his life," Victoria replied, taking Bethea's elbow and guiding her toward the front steps. "When Con was young and Matthias would go to Lemhi to get him at the end of the summer, he would always bring two or three of Con's cousins back with them to spend several weeks with us. They would attend classes and become like our own. I loved having them and so did Matthias. Their fathers would pick them up on their fall hunting expeditions. This past Christmas was the saddest one we've ever had."

Bethea looked away. "We forgot Christmas."

"My husband could not accept Con's failure to return," Victoria continued. "When the searchers returned empty handed, I think he clung to a thread of hope but wouldn't talk about it."

"All the while he was with us," Bethea said. "But Mr. Adler was right in a way. He was at death's door when we found him. Con can tell you all about that later."

Victoria's gaze lingered on her husband and step-son. "Perhaps Con's return and the children will be the dose of spring tonic Matthias needs."

Bethea scraped her muddy shoes on a horse hair mat outside the huge white double doors, then followed Victoria into the house. An entryway, as large as the original room of the cabin in the valley, contained doors leading to the left and right. Directly ahead, a grand sculptured archway opened into a large room lined with bookshelves and a vast library. To the left of the library a wide staircase lead to the upper floor.

"That's Matthias's office," Victoria said, motioning to the left. "He and his stockmen friends and the buyers with their smelly cigars can talk business in privacy without tracking manure into the rest of the house. Beyond the stairs is a library and study, and in here is one of my favorite rooms." She opened a walnut door and motioned Bethea to follow. "It's too large to be a parlor. In the summer we'll open the French doors." She turned a knob and pushed the wall of doors to opposite walls, doubling the size of the room. "Won't this make a lovely ballroom? And look!"

255

Bethea followed her to a wall of windows. The windows overlooked a garden of flowers beginning to bloom. Several dozen yards away, a brook cascaded down the sloping meadow to empty into a larger creek.

"It's lovely," Bethea said. "You must be very proud to live in such a grand house. Our cabin..."

Victoria smiled. "I know, dear. That cabin was our summer place when the children were young. I'm sure it's just as crowded now as it used to be. I complained for years about that dirt floor."

Bethea nodded, unable to suppress a smile. "It's cold in the winter and dusty in the summer, and the bugs are so thick I couldn't keep the door open as much as I would have liked."

Victoria laughed. "We had to take turns just sleeping under a roof and when it rained or we had an unexpected summer snow storm, we were wall to wall people."

She took Bethea's hand. "My dear, you can't imagine how wonderful it is to have another woman to talk to. Rebecca insists that I call her 'Cook' and she won't call me anything but Mrs. Adler. I'm not used to such formality. It's wonderful to be able to tell you all about this house and when we have time, I'll tell you of the years we dreamed about it, and how it came to be built and what I want to do with it. It'll take years to finish furnishing it."

Bethea pulled her hand free, uncomfortable with the friendly warmth of Victoria Adler. "We have no right to simply drop in on you like this, Mrs. Adler." She swallowed the lump in her throat.

"Please call me Victoria."

"But..."

"Please, humor me. If I don't keep talking, I might start to cry. I'm so happy that Con is alive and well, and I'm glad you're safe and here with him."

Bethea fussed with the ruffle on Hallie's yoked dress. "I wasn't very nice to you when I refused your last package. My pride got the better of me. I'm sorry. And I was unnecessarily rude to your husband when he came to buy me out." She turned away to hide her tears.

Victoria's arm surrounded her stiff shoulders. Not knowing why she weakened, Bethea rested her head on the taller woman's shoulder and sobbed, overcome with loneliness for her own mother, her sisters, Mrs. Burns, all the women back in Missouri who had been her friends, and even the mysterious Mrs. McGyver still trapped in the valley.

Hallie began to fuss, being squeezed between the two women. "Don't be embarrassed," Victoria said, stepping away and smiling. "I've known ever since Con met you that someday you'd be here. He loves you and so will we. I must admit I'm curious about Mr. Kingston, and how you and Con can get married under the circumstances, but I'm sure that will come out later, too. Let's go upstairs and I'll show you where you'll be staying."

Bethea followed Victoria up the stairs. On the wall, just above a wide landing half way to the second floor, hung three large framed diagrams of the house. Two of the prints showed the interior floor designs of the main and second floors. The third showed a fully landscaped front view of the exterior of the house. They were all signed and dated by the architect.

As the women strolled the wide hallway of the second floor, Victoria touched the doors of the various rooms. "My younger sons share this room. Lee insisted on his own room, but when Quentin returned they decided the best way to get reacquainted would be to share a room. Next to them is their cousins' room. When they're not out working, they're usually all crowded into one or the other room."

She tossed her head and laughed. "Our Boston cousins are having the time of their lives *Out West* as they say in the Boston newspapers. Matthias's brother Tyrone is here," she said, tapping another door.

"And Matthias and I share this room," Victoria said, leaning against a door at the west end of the hallway. "It's a double room with a sun porch, but the weather has yet to warm up enough to enjoy it. We've filled the west wing, but we've been holding this east wing. There are three bedrooms large enough for two children each, and this would make a lovely suite for you and Con and the baby until she gets older."

"But..."

Before Bethea could refuse, she found herself inside a room that ran the entire width of the east end of the upper story. Dividing the front and back halves of the room was a wall of glass doors, separating the sleeping and sitting areas. The sitting area opened onto a sun porch overlooking the same garden and brook she had admired from the first floor. Several blue and gold Oriental rugs of assorted size were scattered across the parquet floor.

"This room is almost like ours at the other end," Victoria said, "but we don't have the view of the flower garden."

Bethea put the baby down on one of the rugs, hoping she would lie still, but immediately Hallie rolled onto her stomach and began to worm her way toward the sun porch.

"She'll be fine," Victoria said. "We designed it with children in mind. Until she begins to climb, you can rest easy."

Bethea scanned the room once more, overwhelmed by the sheer beauty and size of the room. "You could put the entire cabin inside this room and have space left over for furniture. No, Mrs. Adler, we couldn't accept your offer. It's too generous."

"Please call me Victoria."

"But we can't...I mean we're not...yet."

Victoria smiled. "But you will be in a few days. If you'd prefer, you and the girls can have this room until you return from Butte City, but then I insist that you and Con have it. Would you want this lovely view to be wasted?"

"But there's no furniture and I have no money."

"There's a huge storage building next to the barn," Victoria explained. "We had it built especially to protect the furniture. Many pieces were built right in the building by two men Matthias found in a saloon in Dillon. They were master carpenters down on their luck."

Bethea returned to the sun porch, then paced the distance of the empty rooms.

Victoria smiled from the middle of the room. "Matthias has been hinting rather loudly that if we'd get the furniture inside the house, he could convert the building into a second barn. He wants to try calving inside, at least with the two year old heifers. They calved in the open and some of the calves froze before we could get to them. Matthias has talked about trying a small band of sheep, too, and he says lambs deserve to be protected from the elements."

When Bethea started to shake her head again, Victoria continued. "Some of the pieces came from Boston last fall, and they've been stored out there all winter, cold and alone and unused. With this terrible winter and Con being missing for so long...well, you see? Matthias will be grateful to you for freeing up his barn."

Victoria stooped to pick up Hallie and went out onto the sun porch. Below them the Kingston children were milling about, talking with Con's two younger brothers and two cousins. The foreman, Jacob Dingley, had joined them as had the cook, Stub.

When a young blond man looked up at Bethea and waved, she remembered him from the pie episode. "That's Broderick. He's from Missouri, you know," she said, smiling as she waved back.

"You've been the center of many discussions this winter," Victoria murmured. "Jacob and Broderick wanted to try getting into the valley to make sure you and the children were safe. Matthias had arranged for them to go next week."

Bethea turned to Victoria. "Con and I have...lived together since last November. He couldn't live outside and we had the children with us. He was injured." She chewed her lower lip. "I was afraid he would die."

She blinked several times, determined to keep her composure. "When I had Hallie, he was my...midwife." She smiled. "He was so kind and gentle. I think he truly loves my children and he positively dotes on Hallie. She was born in early December and since that time...we've lived as husband and wife."

She felt compelled to clear away any misunderstanding. "We've...we tried to resist but the temptation...was great."

"Don't, Bethea," Victoria said, closing the doors to the sun porch and coming to stand beside her. "Matthias and I made love for the first time in that cabin and we didn't get married for another year. You and Con owe no one an explanation."

"Mr. Kingston...my husband is dead."

Victoria's eyes widened. "But how? When? Oh, Bethea, should I say I'm sorry? No, because now you and Con can find your own happiness. My prayers go with you both." She walked into the hallway. "Let's go downstairs and let Rebecca know about our change in dinner plans. She's a grandmother herself and loves little ones. The youngsters can eat together while Rebecca cooks a second dinner for the rest of us. While we're waiting, we can have some of the cowboys bring in the furniture and get it set up. We can have a late dinner and you and Con can explain everything."

"THE HELL YOU SAY," Matthias exclaimed when Con finished recounting the events of the past months.

"I'm going to talk to the sheriff in Dillon," Con said. "By the time we come back, he should have some news for me that will put it all to rest. I shot the man defending my own life, Father. He shot me twice before I could draw my gun."

"Do you have witnesses for the wedding?" Matthias asked.

"Mrs. Burns," Bethea said. She turned to Con. "How many do we need?"

"Usually two," Matthias inserted. "When are you going?" he asked again.

"Wednesday."

"I have some business to take care of in Butte City," Matthias said. "I've been putting it off. I could ride along and be your second witness, but I'd have to catch the next train back."

Con and Bethea exchanged glances.

"We wouldn't want to impose," Bethea said.

Matthias ignored her. "Visiting the sheriff is more important to me than witnessing this damned wedding, but if I go half way, I might as well finish the job. Young woman, do you think you and I can be civil for a day or two in each other's company?"

Bethea tried to speak but only a squeak sounded.

"I reckon I'll interpret that as a yes," Matthias said, shifting his attention to his half empty glass of brandy.

"Thank you, Father," Con said. "I want you two to get along. I want you and Mother to learn to love Bethea and the children the way I do. Is that asking too much?"

Matthias pursed his lips. "You're taking on quite a load. Having your own children arrive one at a time gives a father time to adjust, but you're taking on seven young ones who will be under foot for years to come."

"It's my choice."

"She could be marrying you for other reasons."

"My wealth?" Con laughed. "We fell in love before she knew I owned a single cow and before I knew she had six children."

"People will talk."

"They've been talking all my life."

Matthias rubbed his chin. "Is Bethea aware of the prejudice in the county?"

"We've talked about that too, and the fact that Hallie looks like she might be my daughter."

"Why don't you convince me she isn't," Matthias said, a hint of a grin beginning to show.

Bethea stiffened in her chair. "I was three months pregnant when I stepped off the train in Monida. I'd never laid eyes on Con. Count on your fingers if you insist."

"I've already done that," Matthias admitted, taking another sip of his brandy.

"My father is French and English. He has black hair and brown eyes. My daughter's hair is dark but mark my words, her eyes are clearly going to be green. Suspicious souls will make up their own minds, regardless of the truth. Con wants her to grow up as Hallie Adler."

Matthias nodded several times. "You've talked this out?"

"What else is there to do when you're snow bound in the valley for six months."

Matthias choked on his brandy. "You tell me."

His wife slapped at his hand. "Matthias, shame on you."

When Con looked at Bethea, her complexion was flushed a pretty pink and she was staring out the window, her spine stiff and proper. He took her hand and they rose. "We accept your offer to be our witness. Now, if you'll excuse us, I want to take Bethea for a stroll outside. Mother, call us if the children get to be a problem."

"Yes, dear, and welcome home." Victoria rose from her chair, brushed both of their cheeks with a light kiss and waved them from the room.

MATTHIAS REMAINED SEATED, a heavy scowl spoiling his handsomeness. He held his tongue until his son and the Kingston woman retrieved their coats and left the house. "I knew from the beginning that woman and her brood would be trouble. No one is going to buy that story."

"Matthias! Are you saying he lied?" Victoria dropped into the empty chair next to his. "How could you?"

"I believe him, but will anyone else?" He emptied his glass.

"She says he almost died," Victoria said. "Do you doubt her story as well?"

Matthias shook his gray head. "No, Vickie. We talked while he changed clothes. Those scars are proof enough for me. One went straight through his chest and missed his heart by inches. The ones on his arm and legs are worse. Did you know she actually cut the lead balls out with a kitchen knife?"

Victoria covered her mouth. "Is he badly scarred?"

"Surprisingly not. She must be a hell of a good seamstress." He refilled his glass and took a long draw. "But damn it, what are you going to do with all these children underfoot while they're gone on a damned fool honeymoon? Con wouldn't even say when they'd be back or where they were going."

She smiled. "They deserve an extended honeymoon."

"But this house isn't large enough for all these people," Matthias argued.

"Darling, we've always found room for guests when we lived in the cabin. If I thought living in this huge house had turned us in begrudging misers who couldn't share their hospitality, like those pompous rancher friends of yours living up Horse Prairie, I'd ask you to tear it down shingle by shingle and help you do it."

His jaw tightened.

"It will be just like the old days, darling. You can take the boys with you. Keep one for yourself and assign one to Jacob, one to Broderick, one to Mexican Pete, and if the men get tired of them tagging along, rotate them one at a time to Stub. Surely he can keep little boys occupied in the cook house. They can help him roll out those sugar cookies all the cowboys love."

"He'll quit if I try to make him a nursemaid," Matthias argued.

She laughed. "We'll see. Try it for a week and if that doesn't work, we'll discuss it. I'll keep Faith and Esther busy in here. Later in the week, we'll take the train into Dillon and look at the new spring fabric at Kirkpatrick's or Eliel Brothers. Would you like to stay over and shop with us?"

"Fawning over dress fabric isn't my idea of excitement," he said. The rest of his response was lost under the thunder of six pairs of running feet as the children filled the dining room. Ben and Esther began to argue over their respective versions of why Gabriel and David had gotten into a fight and how Ben's lip had gotten cut and his blood splattered all over the skirt of Faith's only clean dress. From the kitchen where Rebecca had offered to tend Hallie, the baby's whimpers escalated into a gusty wail.

"This is your idea," Matthias said, wagging a finger at his smiling wife. "You sort it all out."

"I had nothing to do with it," Adam insisted.

"Good," Matthias said, "Then you come with me and we'll feed the mares about to foal."

IN THE GARDEN, Con and Bethea stopped at the edge of the brook. She pulled the collar of her coat up around her ears.

"Cold?" he asked.

"Summer is still a long way off, isn't it?"

He nodded. "Did my mother show you the house?"

She nodded. "I'm afraid it's much too fancy for me to ever feel comfortable in."

"You'd prefer dirt floors to that plush Oriental Rug?"

She smiled. "I'll admit I wanted to take off my shoes and stockings and run my bare toes through it, but Con, what if the children have accidents or break something, or quarrel."

He chuckled. "They've probably already done that." He put his arm around her small shoulders and guided her alone a stone walk that followed the brook. Behind the solid trunk of an old cottonwood tree, he stopped and leaned against it.

"I know I'm asking a lot of you, Bethea, but this is my home. Where else can we live, especially in winter? My work is here. I've already told my father that in exchange for our living quarters, I'd become the manager of the beef stock section of the operation. He's been after me for years and I've refused, but now the time is right. My uncle and his sons need to return to Boston."

"How extensive do they think the losses will be?" she asked.

"Between fifty-five and sixty percent," he said, looking off into the distance. "It's hard to imagine eleven thousand head of dead stock out there. They're still not sure about the horses. Maybe it's a miracle that we had two horses and a cow and they survived."

She reached out to touch his cheek. "I'll do my best."

"What more can I ask?" he said, pulling her into his arms and kissing her. "We wish we could sleep together tonight."

She shook her head. "Not until we're husband and wife."

"But what about the vows we shared in the cabin?"

"I'm afraid they count for little now that we're here," she said, resting her cheek against his chest. Suddenly she smiled up at him. "Remember what you said about anticipation and fulfillment?"

He nodded.

"We must endure three days of anticipation," she said.

"Then I'll expect three nights of fulfillment," he said.

EMILINE BURNS was on the train when they boarded at Red Rock station. Victoria Adler had decided she and the girls, along with Gabriel, might as well accompany Matthias to Dillon and do the shopping for dress material. They would stay in Dillon until he returned from Butte City and meet them for the train ride home.

She greeted Emiline Burns with open arms and they sat together, entertaining Hallie on their laps.

Gabriel insisted he needed a boost to see out the passenger car window, and before Matthias could discourage him, the boy was settled on his legs and asking questions about the passing scenery. Esther and Faith sat next to Matthias, smoothing their freshly laundered dresses down over their petticoats and conducting themselves like little ladies who had traveled to the city many times.

In Dillon, the men escorted the women and children to the Corinne Hotel to freshen up while Con and his father spent an hour with Sheriff Jones. On the way back, Con visited the local bank and made a large withdrawal. The entourage met for lunch in one of the local chop houses.

Con gave Bethea a bundle of bills. "You'll want something new to be married in," he said. "And we saw a white wicker baby carriage at Eliel Brothers. Hallie can get very heavy if you have to carry her in your arms. Since we can't get a cradle board for her, try the buggy. My father and I have some business to take care of. Meet us at the hotel at six for dinner."

The women spent the afternoon shopping. Bethea purchased two dresses and shoes to match. New undergarments were added with the older women insisting on paying for them. Victoria found several bolts of fabric for herself and the children, added material for boys' trousers and shirts. "Bethea, my dear, you must choose at least two pieces for yourself. We can spend the summer sewing."

"But my sewing machine is in the valley."

"Then we'll send someone after it," Victoria said.

They visited Mrs. Hackett's popular millinery shop where Victoria added lace and ribbons for bonnets she insisted the girls couldn't be without.

"I haven't had such fun since my daughters married and left home," Victoria said. The owner of the shop showed them sketches of the latest fashions and colors. "Do you think the day will ever come when we won't have to be covered down to our ankles. I get so tired of muddy hems."

"Sometimes I slip into a pair of Mr. Burns's trousers when I have to work outside and no one is staying with us," Emiline Burns confessed. "I'd be so embarrassed if anyone caught me."

Bethea exchanged warning glances with her daughters and they moved to a counter case filled with laces and ribbons and imported dolls.

Outside the millinery shop, the women decided to return to the hotel. Hallie, riding in her fancy wicker carriage, was almost buried beneath the brown wrapped packages that had been deposited at the foot of the carriage one by one.

A diaper change and short nursing of Hallie made Bethea and the baby the last to return to the hotel lobby. The other women and her daughters were pacing the floor.

"Mama, what took you so long?" Esther said. "We're going to a toy store now. Grandma Adler said we could each choose our very own doll if it's all right with you."

She suppressed an impulse to decline. The heightened color in Victoria's cheeks reflected the enjoyment she was having.

"Yes, if you promise to take care of them *and* keep their clothes on."

265

Faith grinned. "Grandma Adler is going to show us how to make doll clothes. Remember you promised us you would after the baby came, and then Uncle Con came to stay with us, and you forgot."

Bethea felt her cheeks warm and she looked away.

"Bethea, did you find bonnets to go with your new dresses?" Victoria asked.

Bethea frowned. "Yes, but I forgot shoes and gloves, too."

"This way, ladies," Emiline Burns said, pushing Hallie's buggy ahead of her. "There's a new shop that's been advertising in the Tribune. Mrs. Hackett must be furious, because it's run by her cousin. Isn't that exciting?" They headed south along the boardwalk to the new millinery shop.

When darkness fell, Bethea was weary. She had spent the entire day away from Con, and the evening would be spent at the opera house where they had tickets to see a touring drama group. Mrs. Burns begged to be excused and took the children upstairs to her room for the evening.

Exhausted from a day of walking the boardwalks, Bethea found her head nodding more than once against Con's shoulder when the lights of the opera house were dimmed. After the show, he escorted her to her room and she went inside, falling asleep still dressed. Hallie's wail awoke her during the night. Bethea nursed her in bed and they fell asleep together. The next morning they boarded the north bound train to Butte City.

By early afternoon, they were at the court house obtaining a marriage license. The clerk seemed hesitant to issue the license until Matthias threatened to call the sheriff and Con paid the clerk an extra fifty dollars. The man mumbled under his breath about "breeds marrying white women."

Bethea looked at Mrs. Burns who was holding Hallie.

"They'll work it out," Mrs. Burns whispered.

Bethea wasn't so sure. She feared Con was on the verge of losing his temper while Matthias threatened to call the governor in Helena if the man didn't perform his duties. After a half hour of bickering and bribery, the license was issued.

Within the hour they were in the office of a justice of the peace and exchanging simple vows. Mrs. Burns wiped a tear from her cheek and hugged Bethea.

Matthias surprised everyone by kissing both women.

"May your marriage be as satisfying as my own," Matthias said. "I'll go get a carriage and take Emiline to her sister's, and then I'm meeting a couple of stock buyers for drinks at the Crystal Palace." He looked at Con. "I don't suppose you'd like to go along?"

Con smiled at his father. "Doubtful."

Matthias shrugged. "Would you like to meet for dinner?"

Con gazed down at Bethea and she nodded. "How about seven at the McDermont?"

While the men went to get carriages, Mrs. Burns and Bethea found a private alcove where Bethea gave Hallie a final nursing that would have to hold her until the evening.

When the men returned with two carriages, Matthias escorted Mrs. Burns and the baby to one and they drove away. For the first time in two days, Con and Bethea found themselves alone.

"And your destination?" the driver asked.

Con gazed down at her. "Are you tired?"

She smiled. "Yes, terribly."

He squeezed her hand. "To the McDermont and hurry. My wife needs to rest."

CHAPTER TWENTY-ONE

THEIR ROOM was on the third floor of the newly opened McDermont Hotel, dubbed the queen of the lodging houses in Butte City.

Con closed the door, turned the key in the lock and removed it. Tossing it once in his hand, he dropped it into the silver bowl on the high boy nearby. "Are you really tired?"

She smiled. "No, but I am a desperate woman. I hope you're a desperate man."

"And why are you so desperate, Mrs. Adler?"

Her heart skipped a beat at the sound of her new title. "For one thing, you forgot to kiss me when the justice of the peace pronounced us husband and wife."

He scowled. "Could I have done that?"

She nodded.

He obliged her with a light kiss.

"Are we really alone until seven this evening?" she asked.

He grinned.

"No children? No babies? No one knocking on the door?"

He shook his head in answer to each of her inquiries. "Is there something special you'd like to do?"

The skirt of her lime green silk mull gown sashayed as she strolled toward him. "Yes. First I want you to kiss me like you really mean it. I would hate to find out that your kisses can no longer curl my toes."

"Is that what they've been doing?" He swept her into his arms and when his mouth claimed hers, her concerns evaporated.

He stepped a few paces away. "Is there something else, Mrs. Adler?" His mouth tightened as if he were trying to suppress a smile. His eyes were deeper blue than she had ever seen them.

She stepped backward until she found herself against the bed post of the huge maple bed. "Yes," she said, fighting to keep her voice steady.

"Name it and it's yours." He removed the unfamiliar derby hat he'd worn to the wedding and tossed it onto one of the hooks of the hall tree, then unfastened the buttons on his black jacket. Slipping out of it, he draped it on the hall tree and removed the stiff collar that he'd been tugging on most of the afternoon. "Damned civilized men's suits. They're the devil's creation to punish us for thinking we're so superior."

"But you *are* superior," she murmured, admiring the way the fine linen shirt covered his broad shoulders. She had never seen him formally dressed until he had met her in the lobby of the hotel. "Look into the mirror and you can see for yourself."

"I'd rather look at you," he said, taking a step toward her. "You should wear silks and laces more often. You're as regal as any woman in Boston society."

"I don't look at myself in a mirror very often," she said.

"Then let my words be your mirror." He found the huge pearl end of the pin that held her hat in place, slowly pulling it free and tossing the oversized gauzy chapeau onto the dresser. "A year ago I was tying your bonnet, but I wanted to loosen your hair and bury my face in it."

Her feet seemed glued to the carpet as his fingers sought the numerous pins that held her hair in a stylish upswept arrangement, a creation of Emiline Burns. When the mass of coppery brown curls tumbled around her shoulders he ran his fingers into her hair and lifted a handful to his nose.

"I'm in love with the fragrance of your hair," he said, releasing the strands to fall free down her back.

"I love to run my fingers through yours," she admitted. "When I first saw you, I thought it was black, but it's not." She touched the wave at his temple. "It's like mahogany on fire in a moonlit night."

His lips curled into a grin. "No one ever said that before." He removed the gold chain and pendent watch he'd given her as a wedding gift and carefully placed it beside the hat, then unfastened several of the tiny buttons at her throat.

Her heart began to thud. "We've never had to undress before, have we?"

Several more buttons came free. "Another form of anticipation." His hands slid inside her dress to rest on her waist. "You're not wearing a corset. I'm glad."

"Those contraptions are the devil's design for women," she said. "I can't breathe when I wear them. I took mine off when I left

269

Missouri and haven't worn it since. I think it's in one of my trunks at the cabin."

"Leave it there." He eased the lacy strap of her camisole down her shoulder and followed it with his mouth.

"Oh, Con," she moaned.

He nibbled the sensitive skin below her ear lobe. " We have four hours to be alone."

She hiked the back of her skirt and found the ribbons and buttons of the three petticoats the dress maker in Dillon had insisted must be worn with the sheer material. Wriggling her hips, the dress and petticoats slid down her legs and settled in a billowy pile about her ankles. Stepping out of the garments, she retrieved them and tossed them impatiently onto the nearest armchair.

When she turned to face Con again, she wore only an embroidered camisole, lace edged mid-calf length drawers, the first pair of silk stockings she'd ever owned, and high-buttoned pointed-toed patent leather shoes. She sat down on the edge of the soft bed and stuck out her feet. "Will you take these off? They're pinching my toes. My mud boots are much more comfortable." She wriggled the toes. "But not as pretty." She handed him the long slender button hook.

He removed his shirt and undershirt, then flexed the muscles of his shoulders as he knelt at her feet. "And when these are removed?" he asked, looking up at her.

She leaned back on the heels of her hands and stared directly into his eyes. Two of the ribbons that held her camisole together had come loose, revealing a few inches of lush cleavage. She watched his gaze drift downward. "I want you to make love to me, in the daylight, with the sun warming our bodies."

"And after that?" he asked, using the hook to unfasten her first shoe.

"I want you to do it again."

"Now I'm the desperate one," he said, as the button hook flew down the opening of the second shoe. When the shoes had been tossed aside, he slid his hands up her legs to find the garters that held the silk stockings. She shivered as his fingers reached the top of the stocking and lingered, caressing her skin as he drew the stockings and satin garters downward.

Centennial Swan

When he reached for the ribbon on her drawers, she stopped him. "It's my turn to help you now." Pushing him onto the chair that held her dress, she unbuckled his boots and tugged them off, then his stockings. "Up now," she said, grinning as she reached for his trouser buttons.

"When did you learn to undress a man?"

"I've been undressing little boys for years, my darling. The only difference is..." She dropped her hands when his trousers slid partially down his trim hips. She turned away. "I'm not doing this right, am I?"

He didn't reply, but time hung heavily when she heard the rustling of his clothing. His hands caressed her slender waist, then slid to the edge of her camisole and slowly eased it from her shoulders before dropping it to the floor. A single tug on the ribbon tie of her drawers released them to slide downward.

The warm afternoon sun shone in the window and she glanced out. Could anyone see them? She turned, about to ask him if they should pull the velvet drapes across the glass. His vision swept all concern about the window view from her mind.

Naked in the sunlight, they admired each other openly for the first time. "Bethea, you are the loveliest woman in the world, and I'm so proud that you're my wife." His index finger encircled her breast.

She hoped she wouldn't start to feel the milk come down, for that had been one of her greatest concerns. How could she separate the feelings for her baby from the deep burning desire she felt for this man?

Her gaze swept down his body. His coppery shoulders glistened under a light sheen of moisture and she knew his desperation was equal to her own. The scars from the bullet wounds were still vivid. They were the only imperfections on his magnificent body. She reached out to touch his ribs. Pressing her palm against his chest, she could feel the thudding of his heart. She looked up at his face.

"I want you," he said.

She suppressed the desire to step into his embrace. "I'm not ready yet. I want to...see you, to touch you. May I?"

Her hand trailed down his body to the dark line below his navel. Her gaze followed her fingers until she found him, encircling him, admiring his size and his readiness.

His sharp intake of air revealed the effect of her fingers when her other hand slid between his thighs to caress the source of his virility. "Is this...all right to do?" she asked, risking a glance at his face.

"God, yes," he groaned, his hands gripping her shoulders.

"I've never wanted to touch a man before. Can a man be beautiful? I mean in this way?" She looked up at his face again.

His gaze burned into hers as he eased her hands from his body.

"In the cabin, we were always in the dark, and never alone," she murmured.

"I know, sweetheart," he said, sliding his hands through her hair. "Now we can find out what loving can really be like. It was wonderful before but this will be more unforgettable. You're my wife now and nothing can take you away from me." He swept her into his arms and carried her to the bed. Gently he laid her on the bed, covering her body with his own. She slid her arms around his neck. "Kiss me, Con, kiss me like you've never kissed me before. I want to experience all the ways you've whispered to me. I want to be all the women you've ever been with and more."

"What women? I can't remember them." His mouth hovered above hers.

"My husband, Con Adler," she whispered, touching his lower lip. "You're the man I've always needed. I love you so much." Her thighs opened to receive him. "Teach me, Con, to be the woman you want."

"You already are, my love. You've always been."

A LIGHT CARESS of his fingers on her cheek roused her. The shadows were long across the carpet and the corner of the bed, but she didn't care.

They had loved again and again, each fulfillment swept away by the touch of his finger or a feathery kiss on a newly discovered sensitive spot on her body. They had discovered an endless number of ways to make love, yet they had always found their ultimate release clutched in each other's arms.

And in his arms, she had finally fallen asleep. Now, as he leaned over her, she reached out and touched his chin. "You look different," she whispered. "The storm has left your eyes."

He kissed the ring on her left hand. "When I first woke up, I wasn't sure why I was here," he confessed. "I couldn't justify all this privacy." He chuckled. "Sleeping alone with you behind a locked door will take some getting used to, but I think I'll manage." Playfully, he rolled her on top of him and kissed her mouth. "Do you want to try again?"

She giggled, burying her face against his chest. "Did we miss one of the ways?"

"I'm sure we can find a variation," he replied. "Or we could start repeating them. Do you have a suggestion?"

"I don't think I have the strength." Her hair fell across her face and she brushed it away. "But could we try again later tonight?"

He laughed and pulled her down against him. "Yes, but first we have a dinner engagement with my father and Emiline Burns."

She touched the scar on his chest with the tip of her tongue, then slid it slowly toward his left nipple. "Couldn't we send them a message to go ahead without us?" she pleaded, splaying her hand across his flat abdomen.

He grabbed her wrists and rolled her onto her back. "You little vixen," he hissed, pinning her arms above her head and lowering his hungry mouth to hers. She arched against him, wrapping her legs around his to coax him closer.

She heard a sound. "Con, someone's outside our door."

He propped himself on his hand and strained to see the windup clock on the bureau. He groaned, rolling away from her and sitting up on the edge of the bed.

"What time is it?" she asked, rubbing her hand over his back.

"Seven-thirty."

"Oh, no," she cried, leaping from the bed and grabbing the lounging wrap she'd bought along with the new dresses.

The knock sounded again, augmented by a baby's cry.

Her breasts tightened at the sound of Hallie's cries and she knew it was time to return to reality. Her engorged nipples began to leak milk and she pressed lace hankies against them and tied the belt around her wrap. With each cry from her baby, her breasts responded until by the time she reached the door, all she wanted was relief.

"Who's there?" she asked, knowing who would answer.

273

"Just me and a very hungry baby," Mrs. Burns called from the other side of the closed door. "Mr. Adler is getting impatient about dinner and your daughter is starved."

"Just a moment," Bethea called, frantically trying to fit the bulky key into the lock. When she pulled the door open, she blushed with embarrassment. Her hair was still loose and disheveled about her shoulders.

When the baby was safely in Bethea's arms, Mrs. Burns smiled. "Why don't you come down when the baby is fed?" she suggested. "I'll keep that good looking grandfather occupied. He was young once, and I'll bet he still have some fire in his furnace. I'll tell him you took a nap and overslept. We'll go ahead and order our dinners and when you get to the dining room, I'll take Hallie for the rest of the evening." Her smile disappeared. "Don't you dare apologize for being in love." Before Bethea could reply, Mrs. Burns disappeared down the hallway.

Another hour passed before they were dressed, the baby fed, and they confronted a scowling Matthias Adler. No explanation was given for their tardiness, and after Mrs. Burns and the baby left, Matthias ordered a bottle of champagne. Over a sumptuous dinner they discussed the effect of the winter on the livestock company, their plans for the valley land, and the imminent departure of Tyrone Adler and his sons.

"How soon are they leaving?" Con asked.

"Middle of May, if not before," Matthias replied. "When will you be home?" He glanced at Bethea who avoided his gaze.

"Our plans depend on the weather and whether the stages are running to the geysers."

"Don't stay away too long, Con," Matthias said. "We need you. I'll try to talk Tyrone into staying another week or two, but he's determined to return to Boston. Says he misses the damned place. Can you imagine?"

"Champagne, sir?" the waiter asked.

"No thank you," Con said. "Do you have sparkling water with a twist of lime?"

"Of course, sir," the gentleman replied, filling the other glasses before bustling to fill Con's request.

"Why don't you ever drink wine or whiskey...or champagne?" Bethea asked.

"My mother's people don't have a good history of handling liquor," he explained. "I've seen it decimate too many of them, so I've never touched it."

She twirled her glass and took a sip. "When I had to cut you open?" She looked at Matthias then Con. "After I got the balls out, I forced you to drink an ounce or two of strong whiskey each time you would arouse. You fought me, but I knew you were in pain, and I didn't know how else to help you. I had no laudanum."

Matthias scowled at her. "Did you really perform surgery on my son? Most men I know couldn't have done that."

She concentrated on the smoked oysters on her plate. "I loved him and he was dying. I had no choice."

The rest of the main course was finished in silence. Over dessert and Matthias's brandy, he asked about their more immediate plans.

"We'll drive to Virginia City so Bethea can take care of some legal matters," Con said. "If we visit the geysers, we may come home through the valley and bring some more of their things. Most of the children's clothes are still there."

"And my sewing machine," Bethea added.

Matthias laughed. "Women and their blasted sewing machines. I do believe that if a wife had to choose between her husband and her sewing machine, she'd have to give it some serious thought before making up here mind."

"Why can't she have both?" Bethea asked.

EARLY THE NEXT MORNING, they met Matthias for breakfast and said their good-byes when he boarded the train for home. At mid morning they dressed in their wedding attire once more and went to the newest photo art gallery for photographs to commemorate the event.

Con left the two women and the baby to shop the stores of Butte City while he visited a business acquaintance during the afternoon. They enjoyed a quiet dinner in Mrs. Burns room that evening. Con seemed unusually quiet.

"Who did you see this afternoon?" Bethea asked.

"A man named David Addison."

"That bright young lawyer who practiced in Dillon for awhile?" Mrs. Burns asked, rocking the baby carriage gently.

"Yes," Con replied, offering no further explanation.

"A social call?" Bethea asked.

He looked at each woman for several seconds. "I told him about the shooting. I wanted him to play devil's advocate. He checked some of his law books and promised he'd look into the matter some more. It may not get settled as quickly as I'd hoped."

"Why not?" Bethea asked.

"People often see a given situation from different view points and they don't always agree on either the motive or the outcome. I want to be prepared for the worst." He smiled at her. "We leave tomorrow morning on the Virginia stage. If the stage office attendant is correct, we might get to see the geysers after all."

THE COACH RIDE to Virginia City was rocky and bumpy, with the road little more than a game trail in places. They spent the first night at the Silver Star Hotel. Traveling south, they stopped at Laurin to admire a magnificent Catholic church recently constructed by the town's founder.

"I'm losing track of the days," Bethea said, as they boarded the stage again.

"The next stop is Virginia City," Con said. "We'll lay over there for several days if you'd like."

They rumbled into the mining camp that had evolved into a full fledged city. Bethea's eyes widened at all the people, the teams and wagons being loaded with supplies, the men and women on the streets. She turned to Con. "It's almost as large as Butte City."

"Since it lost the territorial capital to Helena it's been on the decline," Con said, "but it still has good hotels and eating establishments. Let's get rooms and rest up, then I'll take you to the court house and you can get the deed transferred into your name."

"Good," she said, smoothing her hair and tucking a wayward strand beneath the brim of her bonnet. "I want to see about filing on the land just west of me, too." She squinted up at him. "It doesn't belong to you, does it?"

He visualized the pieces of land in the valley controlled by the Alice operation. "Nope," he replied. "It's yours for the taking. Excuse me, those days are gone, aren't they? It's yours if you want to file. Are you willing to live on it for five months out of the year? Mind if I file on the piece next to it?"

She pursed her lips. "Would you be a good neighbor?"

"The best," he replied, grinning. "I clean up after myself. I can hunt and track game. I'm a good wood chopper, and I'll come take tea with you in the afternoons occasionally."

She frowned. "But you'll be in Alaska Basin. I'd be alone again most of the time."

"I'd come over the pass to your place every few days," he replied. "Would you find time for your husband?"

She smiled. "Always."

CON ACCOMPANIED BETHEA to the clerk of the court and waited while she explained her purpose. She removed the deed from her purse and laid it on the counter. The clerk adjusted his eye shade, mumbled to himself, and went to consult with another man who carried the deed upstairs. Several minutes later he returned with two pieces of paper.

"If you'll sign this affidavit of your husband's death, we'll issue the new deed, ma'am," the first clerk said. "It's a good thing he signed it before his untimely demise. Otherwise it would have been tied up in probate."

"Probate?" Bethea asked.

"To settle his affairs," the clerk said. "You being his widow and all, and having lived in the county for a year, the judge might be willing to appoint you the administrator of his estate."

"What estate?"

"Well, ma'am, didn't your husband own property in addition to this land he deeded to you?"

She looked at Con, then back at the clerk. "I don't know. He had a team and wagon and some supplies. Does that count?"

"Did he leave heirs?" the clerk asked.

"Heirs?" she asked, feeling like a dunce.

"Children," Con whispered near her ear.

"Well, yes, he has seven," she replied, hating the shaky sound of her own voice. "The wagon was old and the team not very good. He left us with a horse, some food, a run down cabin and 160 acres in the middle of the Centennial Valley. He rode away."

"Beg pardon, ma'am?" the clerk murmured.

The clerk's face began to swim before her and she blinked.

"He abandoned us with winter coming on. I don't know or care what he has. I don't want it. He left us to die, all of us, but we didn't, so what does it matter? He never told me about his business affairs. If he had wealth, he never shared it with us."

The clerk frowned. "How did he die? Do you have proof of his death? A statement from the attending physician or someone else who was with him."

Her spine stiffened. She refused to look at Con or the clerk. "I know he's dead because someone came to our cabin and informed us. The man couldn't write." Another lie, she thought. "So I couldn't have him write it out." Anger surged through her. "If he had nothing, and I don't want it, why do I need to probate an estate that doesn't exist?" A tear trickled down her cheek and she took a lace handkerchief and wiped it away.

"I'm sorry, ma'am, I didn't mean to upset you," the clerk said. "You can take care of it some other time, but can you leave us your mailing address in case the judge wants to get in touch with you."

She wrote her address down and handed it to the clerk. His gaze jerked up to Con as he held the paper. "Are you one of the Adlers at the mouth of Horse Prairie?"

"Yes, and Mrs. Kingston is now Mrs. Adler, my wife," Con said, stepping forward to stand beside her. "If there's a problem, please consult David Addison in Butte City. He handles our legal affairs. Now, if you're finished and Mrs. Adler can have her new deed, we'll be on our way. Is there a fee?"

The clerk mumbled an amount and Con paid him.

"What about filing on the land next door?" she asked.

Con inquired about taking up two pieces and the clerk directed them to the proper office down the hall. An hour later, they returned to the clerk and picked up the newly executed deed transferring title to the cabin and 160 acres to herself as a widowed woman. When the legal papers were safely back in her purse, Con took her arm and escorted her from the building.

Outside, he tightened his hold on her elbow. "When did Clifford sign that deed over to you?" His eyes were dark and angry as he peered down at her.

She looked away. "He didn't." She hated herself for being trapped by her own actions. "The night he left us, I forged his name." She whirled around and stared up at him. "I wasn't going to let him trap me that way, with him owning the property and us having nothing."

"Bethea, that's illegal," Con hissed.

"Not if you don't tell anyone," she retorted.

CHAPTER TWENTY-TWO

THE TRIP CONTINUED but the ghost of Clifford Kingston had come between them.

During a layover at Ennis, they learned they could take a stage to Riverside, a few miles from the park entrance and there learn the condition of the roads to the geysers.

Their hopes were fulfilled when they reached Riverside.

"The first coach of the season leaves at eight tomorrow morning," the stage company agent said. "We have room. Would you like to book passage, sir?"

Con purchased their tickets and they took two rooms in a boarding house that adjoined the stage station.

The next morning, the driver explained the route they would be taking and the scheduled stops along the way. "The east side of the park is still snowed in, folks, so this trip will be to the Upper Geysers then on to Old Faithful where we'll spend the night. We'll be running as long as the weather lets us. Climb aboard, ladies and gentlemen, for a trip into Wonderland."

The sparkle returned to Bethea's eyes when they stood next to the coach, its wheels replaced by runners, and she saw for herself pools of boiling water gurgling, hissing, spurting and gushing, their colors reflecting all the hues of a rainbow. Her favorite was a pool of clear violet and white, shaped like its namesake, "Morning Glory."

A short side trip took the travelers to bubbling pots of mud. The driver told them the material had been used to paint some of the newly built structures within the park.

They reached Old Faithful and settled into their rooms at the hotel. Dubbed "The Shack" by would-be competitors, its beds were comfortable. After enjoying baths in water warmed by the natural hot geysers, they reassembled in the dining room to enjoy a sumptuous meal.

"Con, this is marvelous," Bethea exclaimed. "Who would have expected such luxury in so remote a place."

"Thirty years ago, only the Indians valued this place," he said. "People in our county have been coming here for years at the end of the season, but they had to rough it, coming in on horseback and sleeping in tents if they had them, and cooking over an open fire. Now anyone with time and money can visit it." He looked down at the pink slab of prime rib on his plate. "I'm not sure the changes are for the best."

She gazed across the table, touching the elegant white linen cloth and the fine table setting. "Are we wealthy?"

Emiline Burns's gaze darted from Bethea to Con, then down at the sleeping baby in the white carriage. When Bethea met her curious stare, Emiline shrugged.

"We're comfortable," Con replied.

"I could get accustomed to all this," Bethea admitted. "But I don't want to forget the cabin and how we struggled." She turned to Emiline Burns again. "I had nine tin bowls and four plates. The plates were enamel ware. I didn't have enough forks or knives to set a table for guests. I cooked all our meals in a skillet and two pots."

Con grinned. "What she's not telling you is that near the end we had stew, day in and day out." He winked at Emiline. "But it was delicious."

Bethea frowned. "You never complained."

"Stew was better than going hungry," he replied, chuckling. "It was great stew, but a man would get tired of prime rib, too, if he ate it every day."

Late that night, in the privacy of their room, Bethea shook Con's shoulder.

"Don't wake me, Bethea, I'm exhausted," he mumbled.

"If you didn't make love to me all the time, you'd regain your strength," she teased.

"I have a head ache," he admitted, rubbing his temples.

"Are you telling me that our honeymoon is about over?"

"Doubtful," he said, sleepily running his hand across her stomach.

"Listen." She sat up, cocking her head toward the window. "You can hear the geysers shooting off. They make different sounds. If I lived here all the time, I could get to know them by their voices."

"Mmmm."

When his arm pulled her down against him and his lips found hers, she forgot the music of the geysers.

THE NEXT MORNING, their driver met them after breakfast. "Ready to see more of Wonderland?" he asked. They nodded. "We'll be traveling in a coach with open sides. You'll be able to see the sites better that way, but you'd best bundle up."

Con and Bethea, Emiline carrying the baby, and three other visitors boarded the stage on snow runners and they were off.

"This is called Geyser Basin," the driver said, grinning proudly as if he was responsible for it's beauty. "I reckon this is the best time to see them, in my opinion. If you come back in the summer, I could show you more boiling mud pots and the waterfalls, and I hear tell they're planning to build some more lodges, too. Won't this be a vacationer's delight someday?"

Many of the trails were still impassable, but by the time they had spent three days visiting the park, Bethea was duly impressed.

THE STAGE TO HENRY'S LAKE, IDAHO traveled through Shot Gun Valley, where a friend of the Adler family operated a ranch. The owner and his wife convinced them to spend the night.

Late that night, Bethea undressed, turned out the lamp, and slid between the covers of their bed.

"Con?" she whispered. "Are you asleep?"

"No," he said, rolling onto his side to face her. "Are you ready to talk about that little spat we had in Virginia City?"

"Yes. How did you know?"

"We've talked about everything but that," he said. "I don't want you to get into trouble, Bethea."

"I apologize for snapping at you," she whispered. "I did wrong by signing Clifford's name, but I don't know how to make amends. When this trip is over and we're all settled in at Alice, could we go see your friend Mr. Addison?"

"I don't think we can do anything about it until the summer is over," he said. "We take the herd to the valley in July."

"Alone?"

He grinned and kissed her lightly. "Maybe, maybe not. If you don't come right away, you can bring the children later in the summer. Maybe I can get some of the cowboys to rebuild the root cellar and add another room or two."

"And put a floor in the main room?"

"Spoiled by carpets and rugs, are you?" he teased.

She snuggled in his arms. "No, just spoiled by being your wife. I've had so much loving these few weeks. I don't want to give it up, even while you're in Alaska Basin."

"We haven't made love for two days," he said, running his finger between her breasts. "Are you desperate again?"

"Yes," she murmured.

THEY BORROWED A TEAM AND WAGON from the ranch owner, promising to return it when the Alice livestock was brought to the valley.

"We need to move some trunks from a cabin in Centennial Valley to Alice," Con told the man and his wife over breakfast. He paid the couple an ample sum and the man slapped him on the shoulder.

"You can consider it yours to keep for this price," the man said, and he and Con shook on the agreement.

As they drove along the north side of Henry's Lake and watched the swans landing on the water, Bethea smiled. "It's like home, isn't it?" She turned to Con. "Do you think the swans have returned to Lake View?"

Mrs. Burns looked puzzled. "Where's Lake View?"

Hallie smiled from Mrs. Burns's lap and Bethea shook her chubby little hand. "That's what we named the cabin where we lived. Someday we'll have a post office and a store and a hotel there...maybe." She looked at Con. "Maybe a school in the summer, too."

When they reached the cabin, after camping out under the stars for one cool night, they loaded the sewing machine and two of the trunks, but left their other belongings there as well as the canned goods and a few items in the spring house.

Mrs. Burns looked around the room with its dirt floor. "Well, I'll be," she said. "You folks all crowded into this little cabin? That's what I call close, even with the other room. I reckon if you could still love each other after six months of this, you'll make it for the next fifty years. Frankly, I need room to breath and move my elbows."

"We had the entire valley for that," Con said and Bethea nodded.

The next morning they continued west toward Monida, reaching the hotel that evening.

Bill Burns greeted his wife with wide open arms. "Hell, Emi, I thought you were never coming back," he said. "You've been gone for almost a month."

Con and Bethea exchanged glances. "I reckon we lost track of the days," Con admitted.

"Did you miss me?" Emiline asked her grinning husband.

"Well, that woman of Chester's is quite a cook, but not as good as you, Emi," Bill said, kissing her cheek. "Welcome home."

"Any news from the county seat?" Con asked over dinner.

Bill Burns shook his head. "I heard rumors of a possible murder trial, but none of the details, and the man who told me about it had a whiskey soaked brain. We haven't had a paper for weeks now, and I've been too busy to read it anyway. Con, you won't believe the livestock losses around the country. Leeds lost over half his stock. They froze right in the fields where they stood. God, the smell around here in a few months will be unbearable if they don't get them buried or burned. Horse Prairie Livestock is so snowbound in its upper pastures they can't even estimate. I hear tell the big outfits in the eastern part of the territory lost over eighty percent. Damn, it's hard to imagine."

"You said you hadn't read the newspapers," Con said.

"I heard about the stock losses from the conductor on the Utah Northern and G. L. Leeds stopped in on his way to Eagle Rock but that was a month ago," Bill explained. "I reckon this will put a lot of stockmen out of business. Those British investors are going to rethink their strategy for sure. Serves the arrogant bastards right, if you ask me. Anyone with money thinks he can come to this territory and rake in the profits and then head for home."

Emiline Burns and Bethea Adler exchanged a tearful good-bye early the next morning. Con took the reins and they headed north, taking the Beaverhead Wagon Road that wound along the river grade not far from the Utah Northern Railway tracks.

"This layover at Red Rock will be our last," Con said, carrying Hallie's buggy into the hotel.

"It'll be good to be home and see the children," Bethea said as they settled into their room and she nursed the baby.

"Any regrets about being away so long, Mrs. Adler?" he asked, watching her and Hallie.

"No, Mr. Adler," she murmured. "This was truly a honeymoon to remember. I hope the children obeyed your parents."

AS THEY DROVE THE TEAM AND WAGON into the yard at Alice the following day, Con frowned. "That horse belongs to T. W. Jones," he said.

"Who is Mr. Jones?" she asked, clutching Hallie on her lap.

"The sheriff. I wonder what's wrong."

She looked ahead. "Does he only come when something is wrong?"

"Not necessarily," he replied, his frown deepening. "But this is a long way to ride to make a social call."

Before they could reach the colonnade, the children raced out of the house and down the steps. After hugs and kisses, Bethea coaxed them inside. "Now, tell me what you've all been doing?" she asked. "I swear, David, you've grown a foot and Gabriel, your hair is darker. Adam and Ben, have you been good boys?"

Adam shrugged. "We've been doing chores."

"And Grandpa Adler is teaching us how to ride the broncs," Ben added. "I got bucked off twice, but I got right back on."

She glanced at Matthias, whose face was somber. "Did you get hurt?" she asked her second son.

"'Course not," he insisted, "Grandpa Adler thought Adam broke his arm once, but it wasn't."

"How did that happen?" Con asked.

"He tried to ride a bull."

"Oh, God," Con groaned. He forced a smile at Bethea. "But you can see he's all right now," he assured her.

He introduced the sheriff to Bethea. The sheriff nodded but didn't speak.

"Grandma Adler is teaching us how to sew dresses for our dolls," Esther said.

"And I only poked my finger three times," Faith reported. "But once it bled all over my skirt."

"From a needle poke?" Bethea asked.

"Well," Faith explained, "I wanted to punch a hole for a button and Grandma Adler and the cook were busy talking about supper, so I got a knife from the drawer and..."

Bethea gasped.

Faith's mouth tightened. "...and when Grandma Adler saw the knife she screamed, and I got scared and poked myself. It was sharp and my finger bled all over my skirt, but the cook stuck my finger in cold water and Grandma Adler put some medicine on it and wrapped it up and now it's all well. See?" She held up her index finger displaying a narrow scar running from the tip down to the first joint."

Victoria laid her hand on the girls' shoulders. "Other than that little mishap, we've had a delightful time. Right, girls?" They nodded. "They're very bright," she added. "So are the boys, and we've studied our lessons without too much complaining, and the boys now know not to ride bulls. Right, boys?"

Gabriel grinned, displaying a newly missing tooth.

David nodded sagely.

Ben said, "You betcha."

Adam looked away. He had yet to give a greeting to his new stepfather, and Bethea sensed his slight had been deliberate.

"Are you our new papa now, Uncle Con?" David asked, as if reading her thoughts.

"Yes, boys and girls," Con said, "but you can still call me Uncle if you prefer."

"I want to call you Papa," Faith said. She grinned over at Con's two brothers. "I already have two uncles and a new grandpa and grandma, but you're my favorite and I want you to be my Papa."

Sheriff T. W. Jones remained on the outskirts of the conversation. He joined them for dinner but said little.

Victoria glanced at Matthias and the sheriff, then to the children. "Time for afternoon naps and rest," she said. "Adam, you and Ben can go to the barn if you wish." The older boys raced from the room as she hustled the younger children upstairs.

The sheriff got to his feet.

"Do you have to do this now?" Matthias asked.

"It's the law," the tall angular man said, reaching into his pockets and removing a folded piece of paper and a pair of handcuffs.

"What's the law?" Con asked.

"Oh, Con, it's terrible," Victoria exclaimed, rushing down the stairs to rejoin them. "We've kept it from the children and we've contacted Mr. Addison. We tried to find you but lost track of you after you left Virginia City."

"We went to see the geysers," Con said. "Why did you need us? The children are fine. You two aren't sick. Is Uncle Tyrone still here?"

"Tyrone and his sons left last week," Matthias said. "They offered to stay on, considering everything, but I told them we could manage, that this was all a mistake."

Con looked from Matthias to Victoria. "Are Lee and Quentin in trouble?"

"They're fine," Matthias said. "They've been bringing in the stock for branding and cutting. They came in just yesterday."

"My sisters and their families?" Con asked.

"They're fine," Victoria said, dabbing at the moisture in her eyes.

Bethea slipped her hand into Con's. "Then why is the sheriff here?" she asked.

The sheriff handed Con the folded piece of paper. "It's a warrant for your arrest, Con. I'm sorry to have to do this, your family being friends and all."

Con stared at the folded legal document but didn't open it.

"While you were gone, we found a body," the sheriff explained. "They held a coroner's inquest in Dillon. Two men who knew Clifford Kingston from the gambling tables in Butte City identified the body."

Con's cheeks paled. "Where was he found?"

"Between Spring Hill and Dell," Sheriff Jones replied. "That puts it in Beaverhead County, Montana Territory."

"That's not where it happened," Con replied. "We were in Idaho Territory."

"Maybe you were mistaken," the sheriff said. "You said it'd been snowing and you'd been tracking him for several days. His face was blasted away with a shotgun."

"I shot him in the gut," Con said, his voice rising.

"I reckon at this point the details don't matter," the sheriff said, opening one of the cuffs.

"The hell they don't," Con said, stepping away from the sheriff. "I don't own a shotgun. Ask my father. He can verify that."

"Naturally, your father is on your side in this," the sheriff said. "I have no way of knowing if you're telling the truth, son, and it's not my job to judge the case."

Bethea took Con's elbow. "You have no right to doubt my husband's word. He's an honest man. He told you what happened."

"The coroner's jury found evidence of foul play and turned the matter over to the grand jury that met the following week," the sheriff said, snapping one of the cuffs on Con's left wrist. "Step away from the prisoner, ma'am," he said to Bethea.

Con's brother, Lee, took her elbow and pulled her away.

"Turned what over to a grand jury?" Con asked, a muscle in his jaw twitching as he stared at the silver cuff pinching his wrist. "What the hell is going on here, T. W.?"

"The grand jury was more biased as any I've ever seen," Matthias shouted.

"Now, Matthias," the sheriff said, his revolver drawn to show his authority. "You're not impartial in this matter."

"The evidence was rigged, I tell you, rigged as sure as the sun will come up tomorrow. They won't get away with it. I'll see that everyone of those men pays." Matthias stopped his tirade when Victoria came to his side and took his hand.

"Mr. Addison will know what to do," she assured him, then nodded bravely at Con.

The room had become divided, with Con wearing one of the handcuffs and the sheriff with pulled revolver on one side while Con's parents, Bethea, and Con's brothers on the other.

Bethea clutched Lee's arm to steady herself. "You have no right to do this to my husband," she pleaded. "He's innocent. Clifford shot first. My husband came to you willingly. He thought you believed him, or we would never have stayed away for so long. What is that paper?"

The sheriff retrieved the paper and gave it to Bethea. "I'm sorry, ma'am, but I have a warrant for your husband's arrest for premeditated murder." He turned to Con again. "I've got to take you in, son. You'll be held in the jail in Dillon until the probate judge comes to town for court. Normally it wouldn't be until October, but he might make an exception for this case."

"No, you can't do this," Con shouted, his right hand edging toward the revolver still hanging at his hip. "I'm not going anywhere." He started to pull the gun.

The sheriff shoved the barrel of his revolver against Con's ribs, wrenched the gun from his hand and snapped the cuff onto Con's right wrist in a series of fluid movements that indicated he'd done it many time before. Shoving the revolver beneath his belt and into the waistband of his pants, the sheriff shook his head sadly. "There's no need for violence, folks."

Con stared down at the chain restraining his hands, then to Bethea.

She ran across the room and grabbed the handcuffs, tugging on them frantically. "He's innocent. You can't do this to him. Take them off! I swear he's innocent. Don't you understand?" She looked up at Con. The stoical expression of his features belied the disbelief in his eyes. "Con, they can't get away with this," she sobbed, yanking on the cuffs again.

Lee and Quentin pulled her away, but she kicked at them, twisting free to run to Con again.

Clinging to his waist, she pressed her wet cheeks against his shirt front. "I love you, darling," she sobbed. "I'll make them free you."

She felt his mouth touch the top of her head before she was wrenched away again. Through her blinding tears, she watched as the sheriff stuck his gun against the small of Con's back and marched him out the front doors and down the steps.

"I want to ride Hellion," Con said, the tone of his voice revealing his renewed resistance.

"Saddle the stallion," Matthias said to Lee, who released his hold on Bethea's elbow and raced to the barn.

"I'd rather we borrow the wagon," Sheriff Jones said.

289

"No," Con shouted. "Either I ride my own horse or you can shoot me here and get this crooked business done with."

"I'll arrange bail," Matthias said, striding to confront the sheriff while they waited for the stallion to arrive.

"Doubtful the judge will go for that," the sheriff said. "Capital offenses are serious business and he might high tail it to his mamma's folks and we'd have an Indian war on our hands. Would you want to endanger the lives of all the good citizens of this county?"

"Good riddance for the ones who served on the grand jury," Matthias said. "Don't worry, son, when Addison gets here, we'll come see you and get this straightened out."

"Bring Bethea, too," Con said.

The sheriff shook his head. "That jail is no place for a lady, Con. If she saw that iron cage, it might upset her."

Bethea pulled free from Quentin's grasp. "And you think this injustice doesn't upset me? You are the most despicable man I've ever met. You're more despicable than Clifford ever was and he was evil and unbearable. If I had a gun, I'd use it."

Quentin jerked her back into his arms and muffled her mouth with his hand. "Threatening the sheriff won't help matters," he murmured. "Don't take her seriously, sheriff, she didn't mean anything."

The sheriff scowled at Bethea. "I always take the threat of being shot seriously, ma'am. I don't like this business either. The Adlers have always treated me fairly, but I'll have to report your threat to the presiding judge who'll be hearing this case" he said, stepping closer. "At the worst, you could find yourself a widow again if he's at the end of a rope."

A wave of dizziness swept through Bethea, leaving her wobbling in Quentin's arms.

"If the judge shows mercy, he'll go to the territorial prison at Deer Lodge," the sheriff continued. "That hell hole might make you both wish he'd been jerked instead."

"For how long?" Bethea asked, her gaze clinging to Con's.

"Ten, twenty years to life, ma'am," the sheriff speculated. "Hard telling. Depends on the judge's mood. If it's Judge Cornwall and he's lost at the gambling tables and had too much whiskey the night before, he might get time at hard labor.

"On the other hand, if Judge Meader hears the case, he might temper it at five to ten years. He has a big family of his own and he might feel sorry for you and the little ones, but he's none too partial to half-breeds. A Nez Perce killed his uncle back in the seventies. The law gives a judge a lot of leeway. The prison is full and the judges are under pressure to ease up."

"But I'm innocent," Con said, as Hellion was led to him. "The evidence will prove that. Father, go to Butte City and bring David Addison down here."

"I'll catch the train tomorrow morning," Matthias said.

"And I'll go with him," Bethea promised.

"Time to leave," the sheriff said.

When Con was in the saddle, the sheriff lashed the handcuffs to Con's saddle horn, attached a chain leash from the cuff to his own saddle horn, then handed Con his reins. "Don't try anything foolish, son. I'd hate to have to shoot you."

Bethea wiped her cheeks and watched as the two riders disappeared over the first rise in the trail leading toward the Horse Prairie road and east to Red Rock. The horses broke into a ground swallowing cantor near the second rise, then the horizon swallowed him.

"Oh, God, what are we going to do now?" she sobbed.

Matthias stomped past her. "If he'd never met you, he'd be a free man right now. This is all your doing."

"Matthias, you can't mean that," Victoria exclaimed.

Quentin refused to release Bethea, but she turned in his arms, glaring at her father-in-law. "My husband admits to shooting Clifford, but it didn't happen the way the sheriff said. I don't expect you to believe me, but don't you believe your own son? He came from Idaho. There were no tracks from the west, only down the mountain side."

Matthias scowled. "It's hard enough coming over those mountains in the summer. In a blizzard, it would be impossible. You made him lie. You had all winter to concoct up your stories."

"You're wrong, Mr. Adler, and I'm going to prove it," she cried. "He wasn't at Dell. He was in Idaho Territory."

Matthias ran his hand through his graying hair. "Damn it, if he shot him at Dell, he was closer to home than to the valley. Why didn't he come on home? We could have handled this."

291

"Because he wasn't at Dell," she screamed. "He would have died without my care. Doesn't that mean anything to you? He came to me because he loved me, and I saved his life."

"Saved him for what?" Matthias asked. "To swing at the end of a rope? You'll be a widow again. You may think you'll be wealthy this time, but don't start making any plans yet, young woman. I'll do everything in my power to see that you don't get a dime of my son's money. If he'd stayed away from you like I told him to, he'd be a free man right now, not on his way to that iron cage and waiting to be hanged."

CHAPTER TWENTY-THREE

"I'M SORRY ABOUT LAST NIGHT," T. W. Jones said, as they reined in their horses in front of the livery stable in Dillon.

"It wasn't your fault," Con said. He'd expected to spend his first night home alone with Bethea in his arms, loving and planning ahead for their new life together. Instead he'd found himself trying to sleep sitting up against the inside wall of the dilapidated building at Red Rock whose owners called a hotel.

He had been a paying guest the previous night, but the owner had refused to rent him a bed when he'd seen the handcuffs. The sheriff had argued but to no avail and as a last resort had hand cuffed and shackled Con to the bed post.

The next morning, after Con had paid the owner three times the usual cost of breakfast, the man had served him some under fried bacon and runny eggs. He'd tried to ignore the mold on his bread, suspecting he'd be given worse before he saw freedom again.

Now, well past noon, a crowd began to gather as Con and the sheriff dismounted.

"Finally run him down, did ya, sheriff?" a man in the crowd called.

"Ignore him," Jones murmured as Con waited for Jones to unshackle his hands from the saddle horn.

"I'd rather bash his head in," Con replied under his breath, after glancing over his shoulder to search the crowd for the source of the familiar voice. "He's one of my father's business associates."

"Don't let them hear you talk like that," Sheriff Jones warned. "They lynched Jessrang a few years ago, and I suspect several others, so don't do anything to rile them. A lot of the Bannack vigilantes live around here now, and I reckon once a fellow takes the law into his own hands and tastes blood and vengeance, it's hard to stop. This jail isn't the safest from either the inside or the outside. Every year the grand jury condemns it and every year the good citizens turn their heads the other way."

The handcuffs stayed in place as the sheriff called out to open a pathway through the milling men and boys. Con held his head high, ignoring the slurs mumbled by the crowd. A chant of "Injun, Injun" began to escalate as they reached the small log building that served as the county jail.

Inside the twenty by thirty foot log structure, they stopped in the small entry room that held the jailer's desk. Two men were playing cards.

"Open the cage," Sheriff Jones instructed.

"It's too late for a meal," the jailer said. "It was last night's stew. You didn't miss much."

"You cooked it, so skip the small talk and let us in," Sheriff Jones cautioned.

The deputy acting as custodian of the prisoners grabbed the ring and shoved the door open. "This way," he said, as if the sheriff didn't know his way around the building.

Con stepped into the room and stared at the facility. Over the years, he'd bailed out dozens of ranch hands who had come to town to celebrate after payday, but he'd never given the jail more than a cursory glance.

In the middle of the room stood an iron cage no larger than thirteen feet by thirteen feet square. He counted fifteen men already crammed inside. The room stank of urine, unwashed bodies, sour whiskey and worse. Two honey buckets set unattended near the back door.

"Where do they sleep?" he asked.

Sheriff Jones avoided Con's gaze. "Three of them get released later today, and four are going to the pen at Deer Lodge as soon as the U. S. Marshall gets here. They leave on the evening train, so if you're lucky, you'll get to sleep sitting down. Sorry."

Jones turned to the jailer. "Didn't I tell you to empty those piss pails first thing each morning? This place stinks worse than a pig sty. I don't care if these men are guilty or innocent, Homer. No man deserves to have to breathe this vomit and worse."

"But..."

"Just do it, before you find yourself on the inside."

Several of the men in the cage chuckled. One was brave enough to give a cat call to the jailer.

Jones scanned the prisoners, finally settling his gaze on one of the youngest. "Johnnie Bridwell, do you want to get out of here two days early?"

The young man, hardly out of his youth, brushed strands of stringy blond hair from his eyes. "Sure do, sheriff."

The sheriff beckoned him to the iron door. "If you're willing to mop this place down with some lye soap and hot water, you can be out of here by supper time."

The young man's face broke into a grin from ear to ear. "You'd be making my mamma right happy, sheriff."

"Remember what the judge said?"

The young man looked puzzled.

"Has liquor soaked your brain permanently, boy?" Jones scolded. "You stay out of the saloons and never let whiskey pass your lips again. Is it a deal?"

Johnnie nodded vigorously. Jones motioned for the jailer to unlock the cage and Johnnie slipped out. He stretched his arms and took a deep breath, immediately choking on the foul air.

"I'll have this place looking like my mamma's kitchen floor, sheriff," the boy promised.

"Good," Jones said, waiting until the jailer had the iron cage secured again. "Homer, I want those honey pots emptied before we get back. Con, come this way."

Instead of being shoved into the cage, Con found himself in the rear room that served as a kitchen. In addition to a table with two benches, a cot was pushed against one wall where the night jailer could get some sleep.

"Can I trust you if I take those off?" Jones asked, motioning to the handcuffs.

"I won't try to escape," Con promised, and for the first time in twenty-four hours he found himself unshackled. He glanced at the sheriff. "Why?"

"The regulations say prisoners get three meals a day," Jones said. "I saw the slop that bastard at Red Rock served you, but it wasn't worth causing a ruckus at the time. Let's mosey over to the Magnolia Chop House and have a decent dinner." He looked over his shoulder to the jailer. "You know where to find me if you need me. Sign Johnnie out after he finishes his work."

Con Adler and T. W. Jones walked the few blocks to the Magnolia House, appearing to the casual observer to be two friends on their way to dinner. Con considered breaking away, but eliminated the possibility as quickly as it formed. He was unarmed. The sheriff wore two fully loaded revolvers, and he had a reputation for seldom losing a prisoner.

He didn't relish the feel of bullets ripping through his body again. Once the circumstances were brought out, he'd reclaim his freedom and return to Bethea and the children.

Inside the restaurant, they began to eat generous portions of roast beef and whipped potatoes.

Halfway through the meal, Con laid his fork down. "If I hadn't come to you a month ago, you'd never have arrested me. This case makes no sense at all."

"It's not my job to make sense of it," Sheriff Jones replied. "Leave that to the court."

"Hanford Mellon has political ambitions," Con murmured.

"I'm afraid so. He hates to blemish his record with a loss, so expect a hard and dirty trial."

"What about bail?" Con asked. "I have money on deposit at the bank. Let me see Mr. White."

Jones cast a dubious eye toward his prisoner.

"I came in voluntarily. Doesn't that count?"

"You tried to draw down on me. I can't forget that."

"I admit that was a mistake," Con said.

"And your wife was none too peaceful, either."

Con chewed his roast beef thoughtfully. "She was upset." The reality of living in the iron cage loomed within the hour. "I can put up deeds to some of my land? That should cover bail."

"I've already spoke to Judge Cornwall on behalf of your father," the sheriff said. "He said, and I quote, 'that half-breed should have stayed on the reservation where he belongs.' So don't expect sympathy from him. Judge Meader is hearing cases in District One to help out old Judge Toole and won't be back for another month."

"Ask Judge Cornwall again," Con insisted. "Damn it, I was born near here..."

"You were born at Lemhi Agency in Idaho," the sheriff said.

"Montana didn't exist then. This land was part of Idaho Territory," Con argued, feeling his temper rising. "There was no agency when I was born. My father is a citizen of the United States.

Damn it, I vote and I've served on the grand jury. Treat me like the other men around here."

The sheriff cut a piece of roast beef off and balanced it to his mouth on the end of his knife, chewed slowly, and swallowed. "Truth to tell, son, you're not like the other men. Did you know there's a move on to remove citizenship from all residents of mixed blood?"

Con's eyes narrowed. "You're joking."

Jones shook his head. "Seems some folks want to clear up the matter before Congress gets serious about making this territory a state. I doubt it would ever become law. If you do it to Indians and mixed-bloods, do you go after the Italians next? Maybe Catholics, or those odd-ball Methodists that parade around town banging on their tambourines. Stranger things have happened. I thought you ought to know. Con, there's a hatred for the red race in these parts that runs deep for some of these sanctimonious white folks."

"But my uncle is equal to any white man," Con argued.

"Chief Tendoi is the exception to the rule as far as the good citizens of this county are concerned," Sheriff Jones said. "Just keep your guard up and know what's going on here. Some of the more powerful men have plans to make Dillon the largest city in the territory, maybe even the capital. But the good Lord has a way of tempering the plans of arrogant men. Mark my words, son, this town will never be more than a cow town on the way to somewhere else."

Con chuckled. "I reckon you don't voice your opinions when you campaign."

Jones grinned. "Not if I want to get reelected. If I had it to do over, I'd never have admitted you came to me."

They ate in silence for several minutes.

"Who identified Kingston's body?" Con asked.

"Two gamblers at Spring Hill," Jones replied. "They came down from Butte City to play the workers from the railroad. They claimed to be riding along the river near Red Rock when they found him in the ditch."

Con frowned at the congealed grease at the edge of his plate. "I shot him more than seven months ago. Was the body decomposed?"

"It's been colder than hell this winter, Con," the sheriff argued. "I reckon the snow kept him...preserved."

Con shook his head. "If he made it into our county after I shot him, he died months ago," Con continued. "If he didn't die months ago, then I'm not the one who killed him and you have no right to hold me."

The sheriff took another bite of beef. "He's been identified as Kingston. What more do you want? Even if his face was blasted away, the rest of him was confirmed as Kingston."

"I never touched the man's face," Con murmured. He looked at the sheriff. "Where did you bury him?"

"We didn't. He's rolled in a tarp and stored over at the ice house, only don't tell anyone. People wouldn't take kindly to drinking lemonade made with the same ice that's been keeping the body cold. I reckon I won't be satisfied until his closest kin identifies the body."

Con glared at the sheriff. "You'd have Bethea come look at a body that's been dead for seven months? Jones, you can't do that to her. Bury the bastard."

They finished their meal in silence and within the hour, Con walked into the iron cage, turning in time to see the door slam shut. Two hours later, the four prisoners heading to the territorial penitentiary were passed into the custody of the federal marshall and his deputy, chains running from the handcuffs at their wrists to the shackles around their ankles.

As night fell, Con Adler settled into a corner of the cell. He wondered how Bethea was coping, if his parents were treating her well. Did the children understand what was happening? He visualized seven-months-old Hallie on her mother's knee; Hallie with the dark curls like his own and eyes that promised to be as intensely green as Bethea's.

Ah, Bethea, he thought, leaning against the cold bars, *this isn't the way our honeymoon was to end.*

Maybe he should have left well enough alone and not gone after Kingston, but his uncle had been on the verge of taking the law into his own hands. He was a man of peace and integrity, a proud leader who had done more than most tribal chiefs to adjust to the white man's ways. Yet in the end, Con knew that Tendoi would live his final years on a reservation just as Con's mother would have if she had lived.

But if his mother had lived, he would never have grown up on his father's ranch and then he'd have no reason to be at the station in Monida. Bethea would have been alone until her wayward husband had decided to show up, and she'd still be living with him, suffering at his hand, being forced to submit to his abusive will, probably another child on the way.

Con wanted to be the father of her next child, but he knew he was being selfish to want her to go through a pregnancy again just to satisfy his own desire to see their child. Was he also being unfair to bring a mixed blood child into such a prejudicial world?

He shifted his thoughts to Clifford Kingston, reliving each moment of the encounter, analyzing his actions and those of his opponent, the terrain and the hour. When he'd managed to reach the saddle and turn Hellion away from the campfire, Clifford Kingston's face had been almost boy-like in its repose. If it had been blown away, someone else did it.

He pushed back the stale blanket he'd been issued and began to pace the cage, taking four paces before reaching the bars and turning around. Ten other prisoners shared the cramped space with him. The cell seemed to have a revolving door as men came and went on a regular basis.

The room cooled and he grabbed the blanket from his corner and draped it around his shoulders, trying to ignore its odor as he continued his pacing. Deep in thought, he stepped on the foot of one of the men. The man rolled over, cursing in his sleep, then began a bone rattling snore. On Con's next pass, he nudged the man's ribs with the toe of his boot. The man rolled onto his side and the snoring changed to a soft steady rumble. Con resumed his pacing.

Who would want to frame him for murder? He'd gone out of his way to treat the Alice workers fairly, even getting his tight fisted father to loosen his purse strings and give an end-of-season bonus to each man who stayed with them throughout the summer. He owed no man and managed his financial affairs in an equitable manner.

At sixteen, he had been sent off to school in Boston. Returning only during the summers, he'd kept his vow to his father to graduate from an eastern university. His uncle Tyrone had introduced him proudly as his nephew, so he'd not suffered the stigma of his mixed heritage until he'd returned to his homeland. He had left the county a gangly boy and returned an educated man, cultured when the situation required it, but more than able to enjoy the way of life of his mother's people.

He stopped his pacing. He knew some considered him an "Uppity half-breed." Surely, his Boston education wasn't the cause of his problems. He'd never been romantically involved with women of the area. He'd seduced a few in Boston but only after they had made the first overture. He'd visited a few of the houses of ill-repute in Butte and Eagle Rock but had avoided similar establishments in his own county.

The young ladies of Dillon strolling along the boardwalks with their parasols and summer dresses had always reminded him of the pigeons in the Boston Common near where he'd gone to school. Knowing their fathers would have been outraged if he'd shown any interest in the young ladies, he'd kept to himself, concentrating on the cattle operation at Alice.

He'd kept in touch with his mother's people and had been fawned over by the unmarried young women. Many were his relatives. There was one pretty Shoshoni maiden, his third cousin according to his uncle, who had shown a definite interest in him. His manly ego had responded in a casual way.

One summer, during his twenty-second year, he'd come to the band's camp needing a sympathetic female companion. On the ride over the pass to Lemhi, he'd decided to pursue her actively, only to learn upon his arrival that she had married a distant cousin.

He made mental lists of the men he'd encountered over the years who might hold a grudge. True, he'd worn a revolver since he had turned eighteen, and had not hesitated to draw it if a situation threatened to get out of control, but only twice had he pulled the trigger. There had been witnesses to both altercations and no charges had been filed. The two enemies had left the area soon after their recovery but they both had relatives still living on outlying ranches. Kingston had been the first man he'd ever killed.

In spite of his love for Bethea, he would never have shot first. He wore a gun for the same reason most men did, to keep the peace, not to disrupt it, to protect himself against the occasional highwayman still operating in the territory, or from wild animals that didn't always distinguish between man or beast when they were hungry and on the prowl.

He stopped his pacing when the door to the anteroom opened and the jailer's silhouette filled the entry way, a large ring dangling from one hand.

"Time to take a trip out back," the jailer shouted.

Con glanced toward the small window. The sun wouldn't be up for another hour. He'd paced the night away.

The jailer dragged the ring of keys across the bars, then rattled the iron door, bringing the sleepy prisoners to their feet. After each prisoner had been hand cuffed and shackled, they were marched outside to the single hole outhouse, then marched back into the jail.

"Why so early?" Con asked.

The jailer grinned. "Wouldn't want to offend the good citizens by letting them see you scum on parade." He left their handcuffs and ankle bracelets on and pointed to the tables in the small kitchen.

"Breakfast is served," he said with a bow. "Take what you want." He set a large bowl of mush on the table, a pitcher of cream and a bowl of syrup.

Con looked across the table to the jailer.

"That's it," the jailer said before Con could ask. Con filled his bowl. As he tried to eat the lumpy mush, his thoughts drifted back to the mornings in the cabin after Bethea had given birth to Hallie and he had been in charge of breakfast. Those memories were becoming more precious day by day.

He bit into something crunchy and bitter and spit the mush out. When he spotted the legs of an insect he couldn't identify floating in his bowl, he fought down the impulse to gag and started to leave the table.

"Coffee?" the jailer asked, grinning.

Con dropped onto the bench and waited. One swallow of the scalding black brew confirmed it hadn't been made that morning.

After breakfast, the prisoners were supplied with a pan of cold water, a bar of strong soap, and a single towel. "Wash up, gents," the jailer said.

"Do we ever get a clean one?" Con asked, as he searched for a clean place to dry his face and hands.

301

The jailer chuckled. "You'll be here long enough to find out, half-breed. If you know how to count beyond your fingers, you'll figure it out in about two weeks."

Con bit the retort he wanted to make and handed the soggy stained towel to the next man, trying to ignore the odor of his own body and those around him. Thank God Bethea didn't have to see him like this, he thought. Maybe he could get a message to his father to bring him a change of clothes.

The iron door clanged behind him and he turned, gripping the bars in his fists. "When the sheriff comes in, would you tell him I want to see him?" Con asked.

The jailer fumbled as he picked up the pan of dirty water, splashing some of its contents down Con's trousers. "I ain't no messenger boy," he said and walked from the room.

A drunken card shark from Eagle Rock arrived just before noon. After a meal of fatty bacon and brown beans, the men settled into their places along the bars. Several men stretched out in a row on the floor and dozed. The gambler sobered enough to pull a deck of cards from his vest pocket and invited the others to join him in a game.

Four of the prisoners accepted the challenge, using pebbles picked from the dirt floor of the cage as ante. Con declined an invitation to join the game.

The cage was anchored in the middle of the room, depriving Con of a window to stare out. The afternoon passed slowly. The sheriff never appeared.

The next morning, Con asked again to see the sheriff.

"He ain't here," the jailer said. "He'd gone after two prisoners being held at Fort Shaw." He grinned at the inmates. "That's up on the Sun River."

"When will he be back?" Con asked.

"'Bout four days if he don't get sidetracked."

Con's knuckles turned white as he gripped the iron bars of the cage. "Can you send a message to my father?"

"You think I got time to go gallivanting around the country for the likes of you, just so you can get out of here and commit some new crime against the citizens of this fair burg?" The jailer guffawed at his own remark.

Con ignored him. "Can I see a judge? I have money for bail. Why can't I be released on bail?"

"I ain't no judge and I can't set bail," the jailer replied.

"Is the justice of the peace here? He can set bail."

The jailer grinned. "Ain't it strange the way everybody's out of town just when you need 'em most? Ain't nobody with no authority within seventy miles of here, so shut up and don't be bothering me. I have enough to do around this place with all you scum to clean up after."

Con glanced at the untended honey buckets still in the room. He'd already antagonized the jailer enough.

Two of the prisoners were discharged in the afternoon. Con accepted an invitation to play cards with the gambler from Eagle Rock and listened with half an ear to the man's stories of his wandering life.

The population in the iron cage decreased to three the next day. They played several rounds of stud horse poker until the older man withdraw to a corner for a nap. Con and the gambler took time out to replenish their pebble supplies, then resumed the game.

"What are you in here for?" Con asked.

The gambler shrugged. "I won a great deal of money from the mayor of Boise and the good citizens of that burg decided I cheated at cards. Can you imagine that?"

"Dealing from the bottom of the deck?" Con asked casually.

The man's gaze darted around the room. "You noticed?"

Con arched a brow but didn't say a word.

The gambler shook his head. "I must be losing my touch. Why didn't you call me on it?"

"They wouldn't let me out of here long enough to file charges," Con said, grinning at the other man. "And I can always pick out some more pebbles for ante."

"I reckon you're right," the gambler said. "Maybe I'll head back to Missouri and help my pa on the farm when I get out. My ma is none too healthy and my pa is getting old." He glanced up from the soiled deck of cards. "Want to play a few more rounds if I swear to play straight?"

"Why not?" Con said, settling down to serious play. He won the next two games.

The gambler shuffled the deck. "What are you in here for?"
"Murder."
"Damn, that's serious."
"It was self defense," Con said.
"Aren't they all? Who'd you kill?"
"A man named Kingston."
The gambler glanced up from his hand. "Kingston? I ran into a man named Kingston, a little bastard who couldn't control his mouth. I cleaned him out and he didn't take kindly to it. He kept complaining about all the injustices of life."
Con nodded. "That sounds like Kingston. Where did you meet him?"
"Down in Eagle Rock," the gambler said.
"When?" Con asked.
Before the man could answer, the door opened and the jailer unlocked the cage. "Okay, Samson York, you're on your way to Boise," the jailer said, opening the cage door with a flourish. "Stick your hands out, so Idaho Territory can cuff you for the trip."
"Wait," Con called as the gambler was hand cuffed and shoved toward the anteroom. "When did you meet Kingston?"
The gambler, ignoring Con's question, listened to the marshal from Boise, nodded, and stepped into the anteroom.
"When?" Con shouted.
"February or March," the gambler called over his shoulder. "I'm not sure which."
"Wait!" Con shouted but the door slammed shut, leaving Con alone with the sleeping old man. The silence was deafening as the departing words of the gambler rang in his ears. He had to get word to his father and to David Addison, the attorney who should have come days earlier to arrange his release. Someone had to listen to him.
Two more days passed before Con learned that Jones had returned to the county seat, but the sheriff seemed to be avoiding him, or else he hadn't received the messages Con had left with the jailer.
A few hours after he'd forced down a bowl of under cooked lima beans and venison, he settled into the corner of the cage to think again. For the first time since his incarceration, he was alone in the cage.

Who was the gambler? York, Someone York. He had to find out for sure. Could there be more than one arrogant bastard named Kingston running around the west? Glowering at the tips of his boots, he began to play the mental game of listing all the inconsistencies in his plight.

The door to the cage room opened and Con got to his feet. Maybe he'd have someone to talk to again. Sheriff Jones appeared with the key to the cage in his hand.

"Am I glad to see you, Jones," Con said, clutching the bars near the door.

"All you had to do was leave a message," Jones said.

"Messages? I sent them twice a day for hell's sake."

The sheriff shook his head. "I reckon Homer has been playing sheriff again. He likes the power of running this place when I'm gone. His brother is a county commissioner and I'm stuck with Homer until I convince his brother that he's unfit."

"Then why are you here?" Con asked. The sheriff unlocked the cage door and held it open. "I have no intention of being shot in the back while I chance a hasty exit." He stepped away from the door. "I'll stay here, thanks."

"Suit yourself, but you have visitors," the sheriff said.

"You're crazy."

"Your father and that attorney Addison are here," the sheriff said, a strange smile tugging at the corners of his mouth. "Want me to tell them they wasted their time?"

Con looked around the room, took in the honey bucket still unattended, the grimy hand towel and scummy pan of water setting next to it. "They'll pass out when they get a whiff of this stench," he warned.

"I'll get Homer in here to clean up while you're out. Your guests are waiting in the kitchen," Jones said. "Do you want to see them?"

"Of course."

"You'll have to wear the cuffs," Jones said.

Con held out his arms and accepted the now familiar restraints as they clicked around his wrists.

"Do you want to take time to clean up?" Jones asked. "Sorry you can't shave those three whiskers on your chin. Want to put on clean clothes?"

Con snorted. "I have five whiskers. I washed my face and hands this morning, and unless you bought me new duds, they'll have to see me like this."

Jones shrugged. "This way," he said, drawing the revolver and waving it toward the door leading to the kitchen.

Con knew he looked wretched, but he could do nothing about his appearance until he'd talked with his father and David Addison. He'd ask for fresh clothes. No razors were allowed so the scruffy beard on his chin would have to stay unless he could pluck out what was there.

He stroked his chin. He'd seriously considered letting it grow into a goatee just to have something to do. Running his fingers through his hair, he tried to smooth it. His eyes felt gritty from too many nights of pacing the cage.

What the hell, he thought, stepping into the shadowy kitchen. His father nodded silently, as did his friend from Butte. "We'll be outside having a smoke," Matthias said, as he, the attorney, and the sheriff exited out the back of the building. *My father doesn't smoke, neither does Addison*, he thought, staring at the closed exterior door.

He turned. His heart lurched when he spotted the slender woman standing next to the stove, her back to him. She was wearing a jumper dress of dark green chambray. The long sleeves of a white batiste blouse came to her wrists, accenting their smallness. Her waist seemed more slender than he'd ever seen it. Had she lost weight? On the table lay a green sun bonnet. Her hair fell in a thick coil down her back, caught at her nape with a green satin ribbon.

She'd always been small but now she looked fragile enough to shatter.

"Bethea?" He blinked twice, unable to maintain his crumbling composure. The past several days had taken their toll. When she turned and faced him, he knew he'd been pushed beyond his breaking point.

She stared at him from across the room, tears streaming down her cheeks as she held out her arms to him.

CHAPTER TWENTY-FOUR

BETHEA ABSORBED the essence of her husband as he hesitated, then came across the room. He'd changed, she could see that. He'd lost weight and he needed a change of clothes and a shave, but what disturbed her most was the loss of dignity in his eyes.

"Con, my darling," she cried as she clutched him in her arms, holding him securely against her, cradling his head against her shoulder as she stroked his back with one hand, soothing him while the fabric of her dress turned wet from his tears. "We've come to help you, Con. You're innocent. We all know that, and now we're here. Don't loose faith, my darling."

She felt him wipe his eyes on her shoulder and waited until he'd regained his composure. *No man should be pushed to this*, she thought angrily. She would sell her soul to free him.

She clasped his face in her hands, stroking his cheeks with her thumbs. "If you aren't a sight," she declared, gazing into his bloodshot eyes. Forcing a smile, she drew his head down and kissed his mouth.

"Put your arms around me," she murmured.

"I can't."

They both looked down at his wrist restraints.

"Lift them up," she directed, and when he did, she slipped inside and leaned back against his hands. "I've missed you terribly. I was worried and lonely and wanted to come to you days ago, but I couldn't. Your father and I...well, he'll tell you all about our trip, but for now, kiss me, Con, like you used to." She slid her arms up his chest and around his neck, burying her hands in the hair at the back of his head.

"I must stink something awful, living in that pest hole," he said, hesitating.

"I don't care." Another wave of convulsions moved up her throat. She didn't want to cry again. Enough tears had been shed since she'd watched him ride away.

His hands pressed against the small of her back as he tried to bring her firmly against him. Only when his mouth settled on hers, was she truly convinced that they were together. Her emotions crumbled as his lips lifted from hers and she sobbed against his chest.

"Please, sweetheart, don't cry," he whispered. "I never expected you to come to this place. I'm in such a sorry condition. God, I love you, Bethea. But I keep thinking if we'd never met, you wouldn't be going through all this."

"You're the one being treated unjustly. Shame on you for worrying about me. It's you we must think about. That's why we've brought Mr. Addison with us." She slid from beneath his arms, then reclaimed his hand and clutched it tightly. "Let's ask your father and Mr. Addison to come back in. I cleaned that terrible coffee pot and brewed some fresh coffee for us. I swear it hasn't been scrubbed for weeks."

"Did you find anything crunchy?"

"Crunchy?" Puzzled, her gaze darted to the steaming pot.

"Never mind," he said.

She patted her hair. "Do I look all right? Are my eyes red or swollen?"

"You're beautiful," he assured her. "You always are."

She smiled, touched by his compliment. "And you're the handsomest man in this county, most intelligent, too, and more honorable than those men who are trying to railroad you. Keep your faith tightly clutched to your heart, Con. We'll be together again in Centennial Valley before the year is out, maybe even the summer."

She hurried to the back door and opened it a few inches. "Mr. Adler, Mr. Addison, come in, please. You, too, Mr. Sheriff. You may come inside now."

MATTHIAS ADLER entered the room and promptly embraced his son. "You look like hell. What have they done to you?"

"This isn't the Corinne Hotel, that's for sure," Con said, waving them gallantly to the benches on either side of the table.

"You folks can use this room until supper time," Sheriff Jones said. "I trust you, Matthias, but if anyone skips out on me, you'll be the one to pay."

Matthias nodded but avoided meeting any of the curious gazes directed his way.

Bethea filled the cups, then joined them, sitting next to Con and holding his hand. David Addison, a small stature man with impeccable taste in dress, doffed his derby and placed it carefully on an empty chair after brushing the surface.

The damned man was fastidious to the point of irritation, Matthias thought, but his reputation in the territorial courts was beyond reproach. Matthias was thankful his son and this man, with so little in common, had become friends over the years. They had met in Boston while his son was finishing his last year of university. Addison had been in his second year of studying law with a friend of the Adler family. Their friendship had been resumed when Addison had opened a law practice in Butte City.

David Addison opened a leather case and withdrew a small pad of paper and a pencil. "Now, let's start at the beginning," he said, his piercing blue gaze shifted from one person to the next. "Mrs. Adler, tell me exactly how you and Con first met, the times you saw him during last summer, how you found him again and where. Don't leave anything out. Con's confession is going to be used against him. They have a body and a confessed killer and Hanford Mellon is the prosecuting attorney. He wants to wrap this up with a neat and tidy conviction so he can get on with his campaign for district judgeship."

"But that's an appointed office," Con said.

"There are many types of campaigns," Addison countered. "This man is clever. He'll twist the facts to suit his purpose, and his motives always involve his move up the judicial ladder."

When Bethea had completed her recounting of the events the previous year, Addison turned to Con. "I want to hear it from your side," he said, thumping the end of his pencil against the table. "Why did you get involved with a married woman?"

"Damn you, David, I thought you were on our side," Con said.

"I am, but if you can't tell me, how are you going to explain it to the opposition? Now, try again. Why did you get involved with her?"

Matthias watched as his son and Bethea Kingston gazed at each other. Damned woman, he thought. If she'd stayed in Missouri, his son wouldn't be in this predicament. Yet, as he watched them, he recalled those early years with Victoria. Perhaps he had been too harsh in blaming the Kingston woman.

"We did nothing wrong," Con insisted.

Addison rearranged his papers. "Let's try it from a different direction. Why did Clifford Kingston want to kill you on sight?"

"He thought Bethea and I had become...more than mere friends. But he was wrong. Not until after she had the baby did we..." He stopped and looked around the table. "We fell in love. Is that a crime?"

David Addison arched a brown brow. "No, but ill fated love can lead to a crime. Is that what happened?"

"No," Bethea insisted. "Clifford was mean, abusive to both me and his children. Con tried to help us. Clifford would leave us alone for weeks at a time."

"And that's when Con would come to see you?" Addison asked.

Bethea's eyes widened. "No...well, he came twice, but he had no way of knowing Clifford was gone." She turned to Matthias. "He came with you. Explain to Mr. Addison why you came, that it was no rendezvous. After I left Monida, we only saw each other twice during the summer."

Addison chuckled. "They must have been powerful meetings to turn your husband against you."

Bethea shot from her chair. "You're wrong, Mr. Addison. We kissed. That was all. And without Con's help, we would have starved unless we froze to death first. Con saved the lives of my children and I'm grateful to him. But I fell in love with him in Monida." She looked at Con. "He didn't know how I felt. Maybe I didn't either, not until I began to put my feeling down in the journal."

"Journal?" Addison asked, leaning toward her across the table. "What journal?"

"I keep a day book, a diary," she explained. "When I first met Con, I described him."

"You mean his height, his eye color? Things like that?" Addison asked.

"Yes, and what I thought of him as a person," she said.

"And that's all?" Matthias asked.

She glanced at Con but refused to meet Matthias's gaze. "Sometimes I'd wrote about...how it might be...if Clifford were gone and Con took his place."

"God damn!" David Addison pounded the table with his clenched fist. "Who knows about this book? You, Con?"

"Kingston mentioned it, but I didn't believe him."

Bethea rose from the table and fiddled with the coffee pot on the stove. After a few minutes, she turned to the men. "Clifford read it." She lifted her chin. "He had no right."

"As your husband, he had every right," Addison said. "The law gives him total control over his wife and her belongings."

"Then it's an unfair law," she exclaimed.

"It may not be fair, but it's the law nonetheless."

"Where is the journal?" Matthias asked.

"I have it," Bethea said. "I write in the second book now. I try to record my thoughts and feelings every day. It's the only way I have of trying to make sense out of all that's been happening. It's personal and no one has the right to read it without my permission. I meant it to be a travelogue for my children, but it's become...much more."

"If Mellon gets word of it, he may want to enter it as proof you and Con planned this whole sordid affair."

"Con and I planned nothing," Bethea replied. "As long as Clifford was my husband, I knew I could never find happiness with Con. For my children's sake, I planned to keep my wedding vows no matter what, but when Clifford walked out on us, I changed my mind. I planned to go to Virginia City and petition for a divorce as soon as the snows left. Clifford was a despicable man and I'm glad he's dead!"

"Lord, don't say that where anyone can hear you, Mrs. Adler," Addison cautioned. "Remarks such at those add fuel to the fire of a love triangle. Now, perhaps you can tell me why your husband would think you and Con were more than friends. Did he catch you during those kisses? Embracing? What?"

"Of course not," Bethea insisted, dropping back onto the bench alongside Con. "But he did know that Con's cowboys had taken to stopping by, but so did the stage coaches to the geysers. Does that mean I was wicked with all the travelers who passed by?"

"No, but Mellon may try to imply that very thing," Addison explained. "These juries are made up of righteous men who deal harshly with immoral women."

"I'm not an immoral woman," Bethea exclaimed. "And I'm not on trial here. I was attracted to Con from the moment I first saw him, but that doesn't mean I seduced him or that he seduced me. We both tried very hard to conduct ourselves in a proper manner."

David Addison nodded. "I know that, Mrs. Adler, but I want you to be aware of how unpleasant these proceedings can become. Prepare yourself for the worst and for God's sake, hide that journal and don't show it to anyone, not even your husband."

"Yes, sir," she murmured.

Addison turned to Con. "Describe once more exactly what happened when you finally met up with Clifford Kingston, and don't leave out anything."

An hour later, David Addison shuffled his papers, scanned his notes once more before putting them neatly into his leather case, and smiled grimly. "The trial will begin a week from next Monday. The court had seen its way clear to hold a special session due to the nature of the crime. Actually, the judge has business to conduct here, so he's consented to hear the case, with or without a jury."

"A jury," Con replied. "Surely good men will see the evidence in the light of truth and reason."

"Or at least better than old Judge Cornwall alone," Addison added. "I hope he's sober enough to stay awake. He's been known to imbibe during a trial and give the wrong sentence for the crime involved."

"What are the possible outcomes?" Con asked.

David Addison surveyed the concerned faces around the table. "Innocent, self defense, second degree murder or worse."

"How worse?" Matthias asked.

"If they find him guilty of first degree premeditated murder, they might decide to hang him immediately. Hanging is carried out in the county where the crime took place."

"Then build the gallows in Idaho," Con said.

"Don't joke, Con," Bethea said, taking his hand.

"What's in between?" Matthias asked, fearing the potential seriousness of the coming weeks.

"I've seen second degree murderers given anywhere from five years to life, depending on the circumstances of the case," Addison explained. "Why don't we wait until we're into the trial and I'll have a better idea."

Con stared at his hands. "Can I get a change of clothes and clean up?"

"Better than that," Matthias promised. "I've made arrangements for you to spend Sunday night at the Corinne after you've soaked at White's bathhouse. We'll have dinner in one of our rooms and discuss the case, then you can get a decent night's sleep, son."

Con ran his fingers through his unwashed hair. "What took you so long to come here?"

Matthias exchanged glances with Bethea.

"When you left, we had...words," she said, her voice barely above a whisper. "He said it was all my fault."

"At the time I felt it was," Matthias confessed.

"I searched my trunk and found my coins," Bethea said. "I didn't have very many, so I asked your father to loan me enough to go to Butte City to see Mr. Addison."

Matthias shook his head. "She insisted on going alone. She told me a thing or two, that's for sure. In Butte City, she found out he was in Miles City. At home, Victoria was making my life pretty miserable, so I went to Butte City to find her. When I learned David was gone, I suggested we leave a message and return home to Alice, but she'd have none of that. We rode the train to Miles City and finally tracked him down in Deadwood, Dakota Territory. That little lady can sweet talk a man into doing the impossible when she sets her mind to it."

Bethea's chin lifted slightly. "I didn't sweet talk Mr. Addison at all," she said, turning to Con. "I simply explained the unfairness of you being accused of a crime that didn't take place where they said it did, along with all the other inconsistencies, and that you were locked up in this despicable jail. He accompanied us here immediately." She stroked the back of Con's broad hand, tracing the cords alongside the veins. "I must get back to the children, but I'll be here for the trial."

Con grabbed her hand. "Maybe it's best if you stayed away."

David Addison grimaced. "She can't. She's being called as a witness by Mellon, and he wants to put Adam Kingston on the stand as well. He'll be coming in with Jacob Dingley."

AS THE PRISONERS WERE BEING CUFFED and led to the kitchen for their Sunday evening meal, the sheriff motioned to Con to follow him into the anteroom.

"I'm trusting you again," Jones said. "Your pa put up his ranch as collateral for your release from now until nine o'clock tomorrow morning."

"He put the ranch up as bond?" Con asked, stunned by the willingness of his father to risk so much.

"Had to do a might of talking to old Judge Cornwall, too," the sheriff explained. "Went all the way to Deer Lodge and bought him several rounds and got the judge feeling so good that he signed the bail agreement. Can I trust you to behave if I turn you over to him?"

"Of course," Con replied.

The front door of the jail opened and Matthias Adler, accompanied by David Addison in his usual derby hat, entered.

"Is he ready?" Matthias asked.

"Just sign here and he's your responsibility," Sheriff Jones said, pointing to the form on his desk.

Within minutes Con was soaking in a full tub of hot water, leaning back against the sloping wooden back and trying to avoid thinking of why he was here. He had endured a month in the jail, a month without a bath or hair cut or shave. He scrubbed his hair three times before he became convinced that all the filth had been washed away, then worked the bar of soap vigorously down his neck to his chest, armpits, and the rest of his body.

Splashing the soapy water onto the floor, he stuck his feet out one at a time and began to work on them. Never had a bath felt so satisfying.

Several minutes later, his father called from behind the screen. "Are you going to sit in that tub all night? We have dinner coming at seven. We'll meet you outside when you're dressed. You'll find some fresh clothes on the chair."

When Con stepped outside the bathhouse, dressed in a finely tailored dark brown, summer broadcloth suit, he felt like a new man, but when his gaze drifted down the street toward the little log jail, the reality of his situation dampened his spirits.

He adjusted the derby on his head and nodded to David Addison. "Do I look respectable enough to be a guest at the Corinne? I've been sleeping with one to fifteen men every night. I hope I have a room to myself. Nothing personal against you gents, but I'd prefer privacy tonight."

His father and David Addison exchanged glances.

"You have a room to yourself, but you won't be alone," Matthias said.

Con frowned.

"Your wife is waiting for you," David Addison explained.

"I DIDN'T THINK THEY'D EVER STOP TALKING," Bethea said. A soft gas light on her side of the bed cast a shadow across his features. His eyes were closed, but she didn't think he could be asleep. His cheek bones were sharper than usual, accenting his Indian heritage. His skin glowed a coppery tan, smooth and fine, and she suppressed the urge to touch him.

If she thought they could carry it off successfully, she would convince him to slip out of the hotel and go to his uncle's camp at Lemhi, or hide out along the Snake River with other bands of his mother's people. She would gladly give up her life with him to see him free.

She untied the ribbons at her throat and slid the dressing gown off her shoulders. Should she remove her gown as well? Would he make love to her? Would she have to ask? Yes, if necessary, she thought, as she decided to leave the gown on.

The room was warm and stuffy. Perhaps if she opened a window, they could enjoy a breeze from the small creek that flowed behind the hotel. She walked to the window and looked out. Their room faced southwest on the second floor but from the shadows below, she knew a full moon hung in the eastern sky.

She tugged on the window, trying without success to open it. If she let her guard down, she would crumble. She couldn't do that, not in front of Con or his father, or any of the members of the court or jury they would confront tomorrow. These men represented the power of society. In their eyes, she would appear weak and female.

She tugged at the window again and managed to get the window up a few inches. The silhouettes of two men walking along the creek bank toward a row of tiny log cabins caught her attention. One man leaped across the creek, then the other man joined him.

Listening to the night sounds, she could hear laughter coming from the two men who had disappeared into the darkness. She jumped. One man's laughter reminded her of Clifford. How cruel for her own mind to play tricks on her. Her heart and hopes had grown heavy as the weeks had passed.

"It isn't fair," she murmured, leaning her forehead against the pane.

"No, it isn't," Con murmured, his breath stirring her loose hair near her ear as his hands slid lightly around her waist.

Her heart pounded as she turned in his arms. "I didn't hear you get up," she whispered as her hand stroked the smooth muscular skin of his chest.

"We may never have this opportunity again," he said.

She tried to swallow the lump in her throat. "I have no regrets about any of this. I treasure knowing you."

He gazed down at her. "I have regrets."

She stiffened in his embrace. "About you and me?"

He shook his head. "No, never about us, but I should never have gone looking for him. I knew I was walking into trouble. I was a fool for shooting him and a bigger fool for reporting it."

She bit her lower lip to suppress a cry. What good would it do to bemoan the past? It was the here and now that counted. Her hands caressed his cheeks. "Will you make love to me, Con? I need you tonight." Leaning against him, she felt his arousal through the thin lawn fabric of her nightgown.

"I'd planned to just hold you, Bethea, but I reckon that's impossible now," he murmured. "I need you, too."

She pulled his head down. "Shush, my darling, love me instead. Don't waste time."

THREE TIMES THEY MADE LOVE and after each union, whispered to each other, never promising what they knew might never be.

His fingers stroked her back, stopping to caress each rib. "I fear what lies ahead for us."

"We're being tested," she whispered. "Our love will be our strength until we can be together again. David Addison is confident. "He'll make the jury realize you were only defending your own life. How can they come to any other conclusion considering the evidence?"

"Maybe."

She rolled onto her back. He propped himself up on an elbow and gazed down at her. His hand encircled one breast, trailed down past her slender waist to her abdomen, then caressed the curls at the vee of her thighs. Three times he had emptied his seed into her and three times she had received him with the ultimate response to his love making, yet her body began to stir beneath his touch.

He leaned down to kiss one nipple. "Your breasts have changed." He kissed the other nipple. "They're smaller. Have you lost weight?"

"I stopped nursing Hallie," she said, touching his chin with her fingertip. "I knew with the trip to Butte City and with the trial that I had to make a choice. She can drink from a cup. You taught her to eat from the table long before my other children did. Your mother and Rebecca fix her soft foods and she loves them. She pulls herself up and stands. She'll be walking long before any of the older children ever did. She's a handful, but your mother doesn't seem to mind."

"I miss the children," he said. "Do they ask about me?"

"Yes, but it's hard to explain what's happening," she said. "We don't talk about it much."

He gazed down at her again. "Maybe we shouldn't have made love, Bethea. This is no time to take chances."

"I want to have your children," she murmured.

"But not now," he said, dropping back to his pillow.

"No, not now." She put her head back on his shoulder. "I had my monthly flow over a week ago. I'll be fine. Now, let's get some rest. Tomorrow will be a busy day."

317

ON THE FIRST DAY of trial, the jury was selected to hear the case from a pool of eighteen men, followed by the opening statements of the two attorneys. Hanford Mellon, the prosecuting attorney, described Clifford as a hard working, devoted husband and father, scorned by an unfaithful wife who had plotted his murder with her half-breed lover.

Twice Con had to be cautioned by David Addison to keep quiet, to let the prosecutor rail his outlandish remarks.

At the end of the day, Con was led back to the jail, his walk hindered by ankle shackles chained to his handcuffs. Bethea's heart broke each time she watched him shuffle away, enduring the indignity of the crowd of men and boys who gathered outside to listen and partake of the gossip and speculation of what had gone on inside the building.

The courthouse had once housed the public school, and only in recent years been converted into a full-time courthouse. Circus arena would be a better name, Bethea thought, as she closed the door to her room the evening of the second day of the trial. She was staying in the same room she had shared with her husband, but now it became her sanctuary away from the gazes in the dining room, the whispers as she walked the short distance from the courthouse. She had begun to fear for Con's life.

On the third day of the trial, Bethea was called to the witness stand. The trial had not gone well. Mellon had twisted every bit of evidence to suit his will.

She answered his questions, being careful to avoid elaboration and watching David Addison to see if she had made any mistakes. The courtroom was filled to capacity and the bailiff had turned away spectators, while the judge cautioned both attorneys to avoid sensationalizing the trial.

"Mrs. Kingston...excuse me, Mrs. Adler, when did you and the defendant first become lovers?" Mellon asked.

The color drained from her cheeks. "What does that have to do with the shooting?" she asked.

Mellon turned away, his disgust obvious to the jurors. "Your honor, please direct the witness to answer my questions. This *woman*," and he dragged the word out as if it left a bad taste in his mouth, "has been evading my questions repeatedly. I suspect Mr.

Addison has been coaching her. Any woman wicked enough to plot the murder her own husband would not hesitate to lie to this court. Perhaps we should have two defendants on trial."

Bethea shot from her witness chair. "You're the liar, trying to make my husband into a saint and Mr. Adler into the villain. I...I mean...my deceased husband. Mr. Adler is my husband and legally so."

The judge pounded his desk with his gavel. "Young woman, I'll have no outbursts in this court."

Bethea flinched and dropped limply back into the chair. "I'm sorry, your Honor, but that man is despicable." She glared at Mellon, trying her best to suppress the threat of tears burning the back of her throat.

"Mr. Adler and I were married in Butte City in May. If we are lovers, we are legitimate lovers, and it's no concern of yours. I love Mr. Adler with all my heart and I shall stay by his side. He's a fine and man of high principles. I have no more to say to either of you."

Without a backward glance, she rose from the chair and strode from the courtroom.

After court adjourned, and Con returned to the jail for the night, David Addison knocked on Bethea's hotel room door. "We have dinner waiting in my room, Mrs. Adler. Please join us. We must talk about this."

Bethea took a deep breath. "I'll be there in ten minutes."

"Promise?" he asked through the closed door.

"Yes." When she opened the door a few minutes later, she peered out to make sure no one was lurking in the hallway, then tiptoed to David Addison's door and knocked lightly three times.

Matthias Adler and David Addison were sipping glasses of wine as she entered the room. They stood until she joined them at the table. "Did I spoil everything for Con?" she asked.

"Please eat something," Addison said. "You'll make yourself sick and then you won't be any help to your husband."

She took meager portions from each serving dish. "I was outside before I realized what I'd done. Will the judge throw me in jail for walking out of the courtroom?"

David Addison smiled. "I doubt it, but you have the dubious distinction of being the first witness to do that to Judge Cornwall. I assured him you'd be back tomorrow morning, rested and cooperative."

Bethea's shoulders slumped. "Please, no."

"If you want to help your husband's case, you must bear up under the questions. Refusing to answer gives validity to the speculations."

THE NEXT MORNING, she joined David Addison at a table in the hotel dining room, and they ordered their meals.

Matthias stormed into the dining room and took his seat. He tossed the latest edition of the weekly paper onto the table. "This is turning into a circus," he said, pointing an accusing finger at the paper.

"Adulteress in Love Triangle Storms From Courtroom," the headline screamed above the front page article. Bethea scanned its contents.

"It's filled with innuendos and half truths," she insisted. "This reads as if they've already convicted Con, and me along with him. How can the editor publish lies?"

"He can and he will if it sells papers," David Addison said. "Try to ignore it."

But Bethea couldn't. The food on her plate turned cold as she reread the article and its accompanying side bar about escalating immorality in modern marriages. Her thoughts darkened. If she had access to a cannon, she'd wait until the judge and the prosecutor, along with the biased jury were in the courthouse, aim the cannon directly at the upstairs window of the wooden building where Con's trial was taking place, and blow them all to smithereens.

But she couldn't do that. Con would be inside the courtroom. She'd have to think of another way to rescue him. She took a bite of her breakfast. With each taste of the cold food, her hatred for the prosecutor grew. How could she and Con expect justice when this man specialized in injustice?

An hour later Bethea took the witness chair once more. When Con smiled at her and nodded, she felt a surge of confidence and resolved to maintain her composure. His neatly tailored brown suit had become rumpled and she suspected he'd been forced to sleep in it, but his posture was straight and proud.

She glanced at the jury of gray haired men. Would Con's pride be held against him? Did they resent his handsomeness, his success, his intellect, even his eastern education? Did his very presence disprove the accepted bias toward the Indians in the county? She studied each of the jurists. Several of them avoided her direct gaze.

Judge Cornwall took a sip from his china cup and motioned for Hanford Mellon to resume the examination. Mellon, a tall thin man with a bobbling Adam's apple below his white goatee, stalked across the creaking floor of the second floor of the building and glared down at her. He slowly stroked his tobacco stained goatee. She glanced toward the men in the jury box again and was startled to find most of them grinning at her.

He continued to stare at her for several minutes.

David Addison stood up. "Your honor, if my worthy opponent can think of no questions to ask the witness, then please excuse her."

The judge flinched, opened his eyes and cleared his throat, then straightened his robe. "True, Mr. Addison," he said. "Mr. Mellon, move along now. We have other witnesses scheduled."

"Of course, your honor," the attorney said, bowing slightly in deference to the judge's instruction. But he continued to peer down at Bethea for several seconds before pointing his finger at her.

Bethea draw back from his accusing finger only inches from the tip of her nose. It smelled of sour tobacco juice.

"Mrs. Kingston," the attorney said, pausing for effect as he glanced at the jurists, "Is it not true that Conrad Adler is the father of your youngest child?"

CHAPTER TWENTY-FIVE

MR. MELLON LEERED down at Bethea. "The infant in question has black hair, dark eyes, and her skin...is different." He turned away and scanned the crowded courtroom. "The infant's skin is certainly not fair."

"How do you know so much about my baby?" Bethea asked. "Have you changed her diaper?"

The crowd roared.

Mellon turned back to her. "I saw the defendant with you and the infant shortly before you boarded the train about two months ago. No one but a father would fawn over a child the way the defendant did that morning. His conduct was most suspicious to say the least, Mrs. Kingston. Do you deny the baby's hair is just like Mr. Adler's?"

Bethea stuck out her chin. "Actually, her hair is darker than his and more like my father's. Her eyes are turning green, and her skin is as fair as my own but you'll never be able to prove that fact because you'll never see her bare bottom. A man's love for a child is not grounds for false charges. The grand jury was wrong to bring these charges against my husband and you know it."

Her shoulders were rigid and she continued her assessment of him. "Mr. Mellon, you are a bigot. God help us all if you ever become a judge. If I could vote, it would be against you. You have no case against my husband so you're making one up. Isn't that true?"

He sputtered at her outburst, then changed his tactic. "Are you through with your suffragette statements, Mrs. Kingston?" he asked, smiling at the all male jury.

"My name is Mrs. Adler," she corrected him. "Mrs. Conrad Adler, and someday we will have children, but Hallie is not his. I arrived in Monida in late May. Hallie was born December first. Count on your fingers, Mr. Mellon. Mr. Adler could never have been her father unless you know something about procreation that I don't. I've had seven children, all created the old fashioned way with Clifford Kingston."

She turned her gaze to Con and David sitting at the small table on the left side of the courtroom. Con's features were unreadable. David Addison's lower face was hidden behind his hand.

Her confidence swelled. "Do you have more questions, Mr. Mellon, or am I excused?"

THE TRIAL RESUMED after a dinner break. Jacob Dingley took the stand and gave a terse description of the time he found Con and Bethea wrapped in each other's arms.

"But he was just comforting her," Jacob insisted, casting a pleading glance at Con. "He's a good man."

Immediately after Jacob Dingley was excused, Mellon turned to the bailiff. "Bring in Adam Kingston."

Adam, his blond hair slicked back, followed the bailiff to the witness chair. He avoided looking to either Con or Bethea.

"Young man, please identify yourself," Mellon said.

"Adam Kingston. I'm almost thirteen. I'm my pa's oldest boy." His voice croaked and he coughed.

"And who is your pa?" Mellon asked.

"Clifford Kingston, and that man shot him," Adam said, pointing a finger at Con. "He told me so."

Mellon smiled encouragingly at Adam. "Tell the jury what you told me about after our defendant came to live with your mother. Where did he sleep?"

Adam's gaze skipped past Con to Bethea, then back to the attorney. "He slept with my ma in the brass bed my pa bought for her. And they made noises in the middle of the night."

Mr. Mellon leaned close to Adam. "What kind of noises? Snoring? Groaning?"

"Yeah, groaning. Moaning, too," Adam said. He looked across the room to where Con sat. "He had no right to do that to my ma. I woke up in the night and I'd listen to them. My ma acted like she liked what he was doing to her. They'd whisper and laugh only not very loud."

"Did you ever get out of bed and go see what they were doing?"

"Once," Adam admitted. "At first I thought they were wrestling, like my brother Ben and I do sometimes. But I was wrong. They were doing it."

"Thank you, Adam, for being an honest boy," Mellon said. "I won't ask you what it was that they were doing."

David Addison asked Adam to tell about Con's saving him from the burning root cellar, then tried to get him to recant his accusations. "Why do you hate this man?"

"Because he murdered my pa," Adam said, his eyes wet and shiny. The witness was excused.

One of the two gamblers who had found the body testified as to the identity. The local mortician who had acted as coroner described the body's wounds and testified as to the cause of death. When asked by Mr. Mellon, the mortician speculated on how Kingston had managed to get to where his body had been found.

"I doubt the defendant is telling the truth," the mortician said. "No man could travel that far with those wounds."

"Thank you, and you're excused," Mr. Mellon said. "Your honor, the prosecution has no more witnesses."

"About time," the judge mumbled and took another sip from his cup. "Mr. Addison, be ready for your defense first thing tomorrow morning. Tomorrow is Friday. Maybe we can wrap this up before the weekend. I need to get back to Deer Lodge. Court's adjourned until nine o'clock."

THE NEXT MORNING Bethea took the stand to describe how she had found Conrad Adler close to death, how she had nursed him back to health. She elaborated on his recovery and his assistance at the birth of her daughter. Two of the jurists huffed their disapproval at such intimacy. She tried to ignore them, then dwelled on the importance of his helping them to survive the winter.

She waited for Addison to excuse her. "Mrs. Adler, describe your marriage to Clifford Kingston."

Caught off guard, she tried to reorganize her thoughts and gave account of their marriage, their children, why they had moved to Montana Territory, and how he had often left them to fend for themselves in a harsh and unfamiliar country.

"Did Clifford Kingston ever mistreat you?" Addison asked.

Her eyes widened. "How...how do you mean?"

Addison touched her hand reassuringly. "As husband and wife? Did he hurt you?"

"Yes."

"How?"

Her mouth tightened. She had tried to forget Clifford's cruelty and neglect, but the degradation she had suffered at his hands was too strong. Her chin trembled. "I can't describe it." Tears trickled down her cheeks. "He was terrible. He never left me until he made me cry. He...he hurt my body." She turned accusingly to the men in the jury box. "You all know what a man can do to hurt a woman. Decide for yourselves." She buried her face in her hands.

David Addison handed her his white handkerchief. "Mr. Mellon, your witness."

"No questions, your honor," the prosecuting attorney said.

"You're excused, Mrs. Adler," the judge said, taking another sip from his cup.

Addison called Con to the stand and asked him to describe the events of his only meeting with Clifford Kingston.

Con avoided the jury box and Mellon as he described what had happened. He told of his promise to his uncle to find the culprit who sold whiskey and murdered the band's young men. He insisted that in the beginning he didn't know the whiskey seller was Clifford Kingston.

Bethea listened, her confidence strengthened by the reality that his story never changed. He had to be telling the truth.

The judge dismissed the court for dinner.

"Stay here," David Addison said. "I have food coming in for Con and Bethea. You, too, Matthias. It may be our last chance to talk." When ham sandwiches and a small kettle of soup arrived, they ate quietly, as if they were eating a final meal.

"What do you think?" Matthias asked, staring into his bowl of soup.

"I can't tell," David admitted. "We're hearing two unrelated cases. The jury members are all old cronies and business friends. Five of them are from Bannack and I know for sure that at least three of them were Vigilante members. They think alike."

"They're my friends," Matthias countered. "At least I thought they were. Maybe I've misjudged them."

"Two of them have used Mr. Mellon to represent them in other cases I've been involved in," David said. "I'd just set up practice in Butte City. I lost one case, but won the other. They could hold a grudge." He scanned the faces of the men gathered around the small defense table. "Those men go back a long way together, some all the way to vigilante days. I just don't know."

WHEN COURT RESUMED, Mr. Mellon recounted the evidence that supported his assumptions of a love triangle, the body found, Con's confession to the crime. He covered the range of statutes and penalties that could be meted out for such a crime. He never mentioned the possibility of innocence.

David Addison began the summation of his argument with a list of proofs that his client was innocent of murder, that Con had defended himself from a man determined to kill him. He pointed out the inconsistencies and cast doubt on every facet of the prosecution's case.

"If justice is to prevail," he concluded, "give credit to the integrity of an upstanding citizen of this county, a man who came forward and admitted to shooting a man in another territory, and discovering the man's identity only during the last few seconds before Clifford Kingston shot the defendant in the chest.

"Yes, gentlemen, we admit Conrad Adler loved this woman," and he turned an open palmed hand at Bethea. "But it was love beyond the physical or mortal. They knew their love could not bring them happiness, so they each, separately, chose to go their own ways, to live without each other.

"Conrad Adler's meeting up with Clifford Kingston had nothing to do with the woman he loved. He tracked the man down because he loved his uncle and felt a loyalty to him. Many of you know Chief Tendoi personally. He, too, is an honorable man. Clifford Kingston had broken the law by selling whiskey to Chief Tendoi's band. Mr. Adler did us all a favor by eliminating one more scoundrel from causing trouble between the white and Indian populations.

"This case isn't a love triangle. See it for what it is; an unfortunate altercation during which a good man defended his life against evil. Con Adler insists Kingston's face was unmarred and I believe him because he is an honorable man. If the body identified as Clifford Kingston is his, then someone else killed him and we have the wrong man on trial here. If the body has been falsely identified as Kingston, we must ask ourselves why? My client is innocent of all charges except that of protecting his own life, as is the custom and tradition of the west. Thank you for your attentiveness, gentlemen. Thank you, your honor."

David Addison wiped his brow and sat down beside Con, who sat staring at the handcuffs at his wrists.

They listened as Judge Cornwall instructed the jury. He described the statues the territory functioned under and their respective penalties. He omitted the possibility of innocence in his final instruction.

After the jury left the room to deliberate, the judge scowled at the crowd, then nodded to the attorneys. "This won't take long. Why don't we all stay right here and we'll wrap this up. The evening train leaves at eight. We can all be on it."

David Addison pulled his watch from his vest pocket, letting it dangle at the end of a gold chain. "Four o'clock," he murmured. "Judge Cornwall had been nipping from that cup all day. He'll need help to climb on the train if he keeps it up." He glanced up to see the judge tip the cup up as if to drain the final drop of brew.

Bethea leaned forward and touched Con's shoulder. He turned and looked into her eyes. "I love you," he whispered. "Remember that." He turned around and resumed his wait.

Forty-five minutes later, the jury returned and handed their verdict to the judge. He read it carefully, smiled slightly, then asked, "Every man agrees?"

"Every last man," the foreman said.

"Then read the verdict," the judge directed, handing the folded piece of paper back to the foreman.

The foreman of the jury rose, stroked both sides of his bushy mustache, and puffed out his chest. "We, the jury, find the defendant, the half-breed Conrad Adler...guilty of murder in the second degree. We leave his fate to the mercy of the court."

Hanford Mellon smiled and stroked his goatee.

A gasp rose from the courtroom, but Bethea heard none of it. She started to get to her feet to challenge the jury's findings, but Matthias pulled her down beside him.

"Wait until we hear the rest," he whispered, refusing to release his vice-like grip on her clenched fist.

Judge Cornwall stared into his empty cup and sighed, then turned his attention to the jury. "Thank you, gentlemen. You've taken your responsibilities seriously and rendered a just verdict. The court sees no reason to prolong this trial. Conrad Adler, will you rise?"

Con got to his feet. The chain that connected his wrists to his ankles clanked then hung slack. His jaw clenched and his eyes narrowed.

"Conrad Adler, I hereby sentence you to serve ten years in the territorial penitentiary at Deer Lodge," Judge Cornwall shouted above the murmuring of the spectators. He leered at David Addison. "And if your attorney thinks he can get you moved because you're Indian, forget it. That's the federal prison for this entire area, so you'd be sent there regardless of where you committed the crime. I'm signing the papers and instructing Sheriff Jones to accompany you on tonight's train. The sooner we get you locked up in Deer Lodge the better. Next time you'll think twice before you pull the trigger on a white man or fool with another's man's wife."

Judge Cornwall scowled across the bench at Con. "After a few years there, you may wish we'd hanged you."

A SANDY HAIRED MAN standing at the outskirts of the crowd nudged the man beside him. "What's going on?"

The man grinned and extended his hand. "Name's Wilbur Sebree, and yours?"

The man hesitated, then accepted the show of hospitality. "Claude Kruger." The train rolled into the station in a cloud of steam and cinders and the man named Kruger waited until the noise subsided. "What's all the excitement?"

"A jury convicted some half-breed of murdering a white man in cold blood," Sebree said. "The judge is shipping him out on the evening train." The man chuckled. "Otherwise the Vigilantes might ride again."

"You mean lynch him?" Kruger glanced at the local man.

"It wouldn't be the first time."

"Sounds like first degree murder to me," Kruger said. "Why didn't they hang him?"

"Hard to tell," Sebree retorted. "This half-breed conspired with a white woman to kill off her husband. Justice prevails." He shook his head. "But the evidence sure was mixed up." He launched into a recounting of the trial. "That's exactly the way I heard it and I was there in the courtroom every damned day."

Kruger listened attentively, and as the tale unfolded, he removed his felt hat and wiped his forehead. "Sure a warm day." He replaced the hat, adjusting it low over his brows. He stroked his reddish blond beard. "Quite a scandal for a burg this size."

"I 'spect after the stock losses this spring, the townsfolk needed a diversion," Sebree replied. "First the smell of rotting beef carcasses and now the stink of this case. It's going to be hard to settle back into what we usually do. Hell, other than an occasional fire on a windy day, nothing much happens around here now that the gold has been hauled away. Say, mister, I was on my way to the Palace to wet my whistle. Want to accompany me?"

"Thanks, friend," Kruger murmured. "Let's wait a moment to see if the half-breed actually boards the train. Maybe someone will settle the matter before he leaves town."

Sebree's eyes narrowed. "You reckon someone hates him that bad?"

Kruger shrugged. "Vengeance has its way of leveling the score."

Sebree glanced down at his own gun. "I got no score to settle with him, but you never know about others."

"Did you know him?" Kruger asked.

"I spoke to him once," Sebree said. "He's the son a high falutin rancher south of here," Sebree said. "A place called Alice. His daddy's money couldn't save him this time." Sebree scratched his head. "His daddy's own past may have caught up with him. You see, he used to be a renegade and a squaw man himself. Folks don't forget that around here." He wandered into a tale of Bannack in its birth which had little to do with the current case.

329

"What about the woman?" Kruger asked.

"I hear she'd holed up at the Corinne," Sebree replied, glancing at the two-story hotel behind him. "I'll be damned. There she is now, standing on that balcony and acting like a grieving widow."

Kruger's head jerked around. His gaze centered on the woman standing beside a tall, robust middle aged man. She wore a navy blue gown, the design accenting her slender waist.

"Ain't she a pretty thing?" Sebree said.

Kruger shook his head. "A man can never tell by looking at a woman's face. Inside she can be as wicked as Jezebel."

Both men shifted their attention back to the train.

Sebree nodded. "Putting on airs for the crowd won't do her much good. That Injun won't be back for years, maybe never. Injuns don't do well in that hell hole, I hear tell."

The crowd grew noisy as the sheriff and his prisoner made their way to the first passenger car in the six car train. The prisoner's height brought him head and shoulders above most of the spectators. He mounted the first step, the sheriff urging him to board. He paused and turned, glancing up at the balcony of the hotel.

The noise subsided as if the crowd sensed an unspoken message had passed between them. The prisoner turned away and scanned the crowd. His blue eyes seemed out of place in his tan face.

From across the platform, Kruger turned away. "Let's get that drink," he said, leaving the crowd to its own amusement.

Sebree followed him into the Palace saloon on Main and ordered a double shot of Scotch whiskey from the bar. After the second drink, they took the bottle to a table.

A third man joined them. "Mister, do I know you?" the newcomer asked.

"Doubt it, sir," Kruger said. "I don't linger in a place for long. Tell me more about the people involved in this trial. What's going to happen to the woman? She loses both way, doesn't she? Husband and lover?"

"I hear tell she has a passel of younguns," the newcomer said. "The only way for a woman with lots of children to make it in this county is to..." He teetered. "Well, you know what I mean. If she would take up with a half-breed, she'd take up with just about anyone. But I don't know if a white man would want to pay much for her services after she'd been with a savage."

Sebree stared thoughtfully into the amber liquid in the partially empty bottle. "I hear bucks teach their women how to please a man. If she sets up business in the Green Tin Can and she's cheap enough, I'll her give a try."

Morris nodded. "Those gals in the Red Brick think they're too high and mighty for anyone but the big shots." He laughed. "I heard that the last time Judge Cornwall was in town, he fell down the stairs coming out the alley exit and almost broke his leg. The girls had to help him to his buggy." He stuck out his hand. "I'm Lou Morris from Silver Star, and you?"

"Clyde King," Kruger replied absently. "How many children does the woman have?"

"Seven," Wilbur Sebree said. "Mellon did his damnedest to make it look like the half-breed was the youngest one's papa, but if what she said was true, then the 'breed couldn't be, but how the hell can you tell who's doing the lying in all this." He slammed his glass down on the table, indicating for Kruger to give him a refill. "Hey, you said your name was Claude Kruger."

"Claude? Sure, I meant Claude," Kruger said. "My tongue doesn't work right after a few drinks. Claude King Kruger. How's that for a moniker?"

The three men laughed and refilled their glasses, and began speculating on the availability of the evening's entertainment.

Morris emptied his glass and squinted over the rim at Kruger. "Are you sure we've never met? How about Eagle Rock? I know I've seen you before. Maybe without the beard?"

Kruger ignored the question and stood up. "Here's for the bottle, and thanks for the company, gents." He tossed a double eagle onto the table and sauntered from the saloon.

At the livery, he paid his bill and cautiously saddled up and mounted. The gelding had bit his shoulder more than once since he'd traded a jug of whiskey for it, but it was better than riding his own shanks' pony, and he'd resorted to that more than once.

When he rode down Main street, he glanced across the railroad tracks to the Corinne Hotel. The balcony was empty. Maybe the

331

old man was comforting her in one of the rooms at this very moment. *Keeping it all in the family,* he thought.

Without a backward glance, he rode from the town, heading south, revising his plans as he kicked the horse in the flanks to make the animal cross the shallow river that curved around the town. He had a stop to make before returning to Eagle Rock.

BETHEA WATCHED THE TRAIN roll from the station. From her position on the balcony of the Corinne, she had seen Con board the train, the glint of the sheriff's drawn revolver pressed against his back to convince him there would be no delay. He had turned once and glanced up and she had wanted to wave but then changed her mind.

She wiped her eyes again. How could tears continue to come when they had been falling all evening? When the finality of the sentence had sunk in, she had ran to Con and thrown her arms protectively around him, praying silently for a miracle. For a fleeting moment, she had felt his lips press against her hair, but two men had dragged her away, shoving her into Matthias's arms while the sheriff and a deputy forced Con from the courthouse.

She had pleaded with David Addison and Matthias to get permission for her to visit Con in the jail one last time. Their requests had fallen on deaf ears. Breaking free, she had raced along the dirt street to the jail and pounded on the door, but it had been bolted from the inside.

Before Matthias could grab her, she had run to the side and shouted toward the high window. "Con, speak to me," she had screamed. "Are you all right? We'll get you out. Don't lose hope. They can't do this to you!"

Matthias had pulled her away but not before Con's voice had come from the interior, faint but audible. "Go home, Bethea. Go home and forget me."

Shouts from inside had drowned out his voice, and in defeat, she had let Matthias lead her back to the hotel. He had put his arm around her, shielding her from the curious onlookers and not releasing her until they had reached the second floor landing.

"The sheriff says David Addison can visit Con," Matthias said. "He's there now."

"We've got to keep fighting, Mr. Adler," Bethea said, between sobs.

"We'll find a way." He patted her shoulder. "Let's go out onto the balcony," he had suggested. "We can watch the train leave from there."

She'd ignored the stares of the milling crowd below her, and now, as she stared at the caboose as it disappeared when the track curved along the creek, she wanted to die. When she turned to Matthias, she saw the moisture in his own eyes. "Oh, Mr. Adler, what can we do?" she cried.

He shook his head. "At the moment, not a damned thing." He held out a hand to her.

Feeling her composure crumbling, she let the strength and warmth of his arms comfort her. "I love him, Mr. Adler, I love him more than life itself. I can't go on without him."

He patted her shoulders. "It's not over, Bethea, not by a long shot. Addison will be back any minute now, and he'll help us. He did a fine job, but he was playing against a stacked deck." His arms tightened around her. "These men won't get away with this. I'll get them if it takes the rest of my life and every last penny I have."

When David Addison arrived, they gathered in his room again and shared a light meal. After the men finished eating, she looked the attorney. "I have some unfinished business, Mr. Addison. Can you help me?"

"Of course," David replied. "A change from this case will do us all good. What can I do for you?"

"I've never settled Clifford's affairs," she explained. "Con suggested I ask you to handle it."

He retrieved a pad and pencil from his leather case and began to make notes. "Where are his bank accounts?"

"I don't know."

His head jerked up. "You don't know where he kept his money?"

"He refused to tell me about his legal affairs, and frankly, I didn't want to know," she explained. "If a man sells whiskey illegally, wouldn't he make a sizeable amount of money? Now that Con is gone, I'll need money to live on. I have a few greenbacks left from what Con gave me on our honeymoon."

"Bethea, that isn't be necessary," David said.

"Of course not," Matthias said. "We'll provide for you and the children. Victoria and I wouldn't have it any other way."

"That isn't necessary either, Mr. Adler," Addison said. "When I visited Con, he signed some documents that turned all his assets over to you, Bethea. You're a wealthy woman. They let him take ten dollars with him. The rest is yours...after we settle the legal fees."

He glanced at her. "This is damned awkward, ma'am, talking about him as if he were dead. He'd not, and I haven't closed his case. Even if you couldn't pay me, I'd keep working on this. He's my friend. I don't forsake my friends, not one as fine as Con, so don't you loose heart. Now tell me what you know about Kingston's affairs."

She told him of all the towns and cities Clifford had boasted about visiting. "I know he gambled and spent time with women. What should I call them?"

David leaned forward. "You mean the whores?"

She nodded.

He studied his notes, then smiled. "I know many of the sporting ladies in Butte and Virginia City and I've represented my share when the police wanted to get rough with them. Some of them are very clever business ladies. I'll visit the banks and ask around up there, then take a trip to Virginia City and Eagle Rock and see if I can scrounge up some financial assets. Considering how he died, he couldn't have had time to settle his affairs. Can you think of any other places he may have visited?"

She named two more towns Clifford had mentioned upon his infrequent returns to the cabin in the valley.

When David was satisfied he had enough information, he put his pad and pencil away and patted her hand. "Anything else?"

"Yes," she said, shoving her plate aside and glancing toward Matthias. "I want to see Clifford's grave."

David looked away and studied the wall behind Bethea. "That's impossible, ma'am."

"Why?"

"He's never been buried," David said.

"What the hell?" Matthias glared at David. "This is no time for jokes."

"After I visited Con, the sheriff asked me to stop and see him," David explained. "He wanted to know if it was all right to bury the body now. They've kept the body on ice ever since they found it, but the ice supply is getting low and the body...well, it won't keep forever...God, I'm sorry about all this, ma'am."

"Of course, we'll see that he's buried," she said.

"The sheriff needs someone to take financial responsibility for the burial. I can tell him no if you prefer."

"I'll pay."

Addison nodded. "He said he'd take care of the details as soon as he got back from Deer Lodge."

"There's one condition." Bethea's eyes closed for several seconds. When they opened again, they reflected a determination neither of the men could challenge. She looked from David to Matthias. "I want to see the body."

CHAPTER TWENTY-SIX

"NO, BETHEA, I can't allow you to do that," Matthias said.

"He's right, Mrs. Adler," David Addison said. "A dead body is not a pleasant sight. No woman should have to endure such a thing, and this one has begun to...decay. I'd never forgive myself if I allowed you to do that."

She rose from her chair. "I'd never forgive myself if I didn't. You've both been most helpful, but it's my fault Con has been taken away. I should never have told him how Clifford treated me. I should never have fallen in love with Con."

Her breasts heaved as she took a deep breath. "I've lost him now for ten years. I'll wait for him, but I couldn't live with myself if there was a thread of doubt."

"You're grasping for straws, Bethea," Matthias said. "The body has been positively identified, and my son had admitted killing him."

She turned to him. "Yes, and that was his major mistake. He assumed he did. He could hardly stay around and make sure. He was dying himself. We had the entire winter to talk about it. How many men who were gut shot could travel forty or fifty miles on foot, in the winter over mountains, and without help?"

Matthias snorted. "My son did almost that."

She shook her had. "He was riding Hellion. The distance was about twenty miles, we've guessed, and we found him the next day. And without my help, he would have died. That's the point, I helped him. Who helped Clifford? And why, then, did that helper leave him to die?"

"She makes sense, but nothing we haven't already considered," David said.

"Who identified the body?" she asked.

"Two gambler who had played cards with him."

She put her fists on her hips. "I lived with him for eleven years." She dropped her gaze. "He came to me naked. I touched him. Clifford had two scars on his lower back from a wagon injury shortly after we were married."

"A lot of men have scars," Matthias argued.

She looked up at the men again. "His body was...hairy, even on his shoulders. I never liked to touch him because he had hair everywhere." She covered her mouth. "I must put my soul to rest if I'm to make it through the next ten years. I don't want to live with this doubt in my mind. Tomorrow morning, before we leave town, I want to see the body. I'd be grateful if you would arrange it and accompany me."

WHEN CON ADLER STEPPED inside the twelve-foot high wooden fence that surrounded the prison, the finality of his sentence sunk through his body and into his bones, sucking all hope from him. He hadn't even been allowed to say good-by to Bethea.

Sheriff Jones escorted him through the door of the three-story stone building and into the warden's office.

William Wheeler, the federal marshal in charge of the facility since 1874, looked up at Con, then nodded at the sheriff. Wheeler nodded. "'Evening, Will, how's the law down south?"

Jones grimaced. "Could be better." He handed the official papers to Wheeler. "I've got a train to catch," he said.

Wheeler accepted the documents. "See you again soon, I'm sure." The door slammed behind Jones, leaving Con alone with the marshal. Leaning back in his chair, Wheeler's gaze wandered from the top of Con's hair down his frame to where the desk blocked his view, then swept back up to his face. "You're a big man."

Sheriff Jones had warned him to answer only when spoken to.

"Yes, sir," Con said.

"Sit down, Adler. We'll have a chat."

Con took an uneasy seat in the high backed chair across from the marshal.

"You a breed?"

Con closed his eyes for a moment. "My mother was Shoshoni. My father is English from Boston."

Wheeler glanced at the papers before him. "Your kind don't do well here. They can't handle the confinement, but this is a federal prison so we get a lot of them. Think you can?"

"Yes, sir."

"It says here you killed a man over a woman."

"I shot a man who was selling whiskey to Indians in Idaho Territory."

Wheeler studied the papers before him. "Doesn't say anything here about that. What happened to the woman?"

"She's my wife," Con replied.

Wheeler's gaze shot upward. "You shot a man who was fooling with your wife?"

"She was his wife when I shot him," Con said.

Wheeler chuckled. "Well, the details don't matter now. You're here to stay for ten years, so you need to know the rules. If you abide by them, you'll get time off for good behavior and you'll see her maybe in about six years. Otherwise, you'll serve every damned day. If you cause trouble, you'll go to the hole. That's a pit underground with a door on top. You'll get fed once a day while you're there. That's the only way you'll know another day has passed, so stay out of trouble."

"Yes, sir."

Wheeler scratched his ear and rocked the chair a few times. "We operate under the Auburn System. Know how that works?"

"No, sir."

"It's simple, there's no talking," the marshal said. "No talking when you work, no talking when you eat or shower, no talking unless a guard speaks to you first. You work all day and you're alone all night. You get two meals a day. Breakfast is mush and corned beef hash, sometimes bread, and always coffee." He smiled. "I like my morning coffee. I figure the inmates do."

Con didn't reply.

"Dinner is better," Wheeler said. "Meat, potatoes, vegetable, bread and tea. Sound delicious?"

"Yes, sir," Con replied. At least it wasn't mush twice a day.

"You educated?" Wheeler asked.

"I graduated from Boston University," Con replied.

"Damn, an educated Indian." Wheeler wagged his finger at Con. "You make sure that doesn't get you into trouble, hear?"

"Yes," Con replied. "Do you have books?"

"We have a library, compliments of the Library Association here in Deer Lodge formed a few years ago. When the guard comes with your food, you can ask him for a book. When you've finished it, give it back and he'll bring you another. Of course the inside cells get dark early."

"Do we ever go outside?" he asked, hoping he wasn't getting himself into trouble by asking.

"To work, and it's hard labor," Wheeler said. "I'm going to use convict labor to replace this damned wood fence with stone. You'll do your share. Each cell has a honey bucket, so if you learn to regulate your business, you won't stink up your cell for too long. Any other questions?"

Con clenched his fists and the marshal's gaze dropped to them. He forced himself to relax. "No, sir."

"Good. We'll get you to the barber for a head shave and then issue you two pairs of prison stripes so you'll feel at home. We have a new fangled procedure here now. A photographer from the town takes pictures before and after for the record. Don't waste your time thinking about climbing over that wall. We have a photograph to show everyone what you look like."

He rose from his chair and motioned Con to precede him through another door. "Welcome to Montana Territorial Prison. Make the best of it so you can get out of here."

AT THE JAIL in Dillon the next morning, Matthias Adler retrieved the legal documents that he'd pledged for his son's temporary release. Extending a ten dollar greenback, he announced their intention to examine the body.

"The coroner has charge of the body," the jailer said. "You know, that new mortician who came to town last summer."

"Then get him," Matthias insisted. "I want witnesses and I want someone to record everything that's said. Now!"

"I ain't got no one to relieve me," the jailer said, staring hungrily at the paper money.

"Fine," Matthias said. "We won't have you interfering." He shoved the money back into his pocket. "We'll make the arrangements ourselves. Come, Bethea, let's get this over so we can get home."

An hour later, B. F. Greene, a prematurely balding young man with a nervous flutter to his hands, unlocked the ice house and motioned to his assistant to bring the body, wrapped in canvas, out into the secluded area behind the building.

The odor of decaying flesh wafted through the air and Bethea covered her nose with a lace edged handkerchief.

"You don't have to do this," David Addison said.

"I must," she insisted, and gingerly stepped over some trash and approached the table that had been hastily brought to the alley. She closed her eyes as the canvass was unrolled, exposing a ghostly pale human body, its underside purple as if the body had been beaten.

"The blood pools," the mortician murmured. "Ma'am, if you'll describe the scars, we'll look for them."

Bethea whirled around, turning her back on the corpse as the impulse to gag grew stronger. She took several deep breaths. "On his lower back, just above his left hip."

The mortician, Matthias, and David Addison leaned over the body, each holding a cloth over his nostrils.

"Maybe they faded over the years," the mortician murmured.

"She said his body was hairy," Matthias said. "Does hair fall out of a dead body?"

The mortician shook his head.

"This man doesn't even have hair on his chest," David Addison said. He went to Bethea and put his arm around her shoulders. "Do you think you can look at him? Just for a moment? It's terribly important, Mrs. Adler."

She edged forward and tried to look at the body through narrowed eyelids. Suddenly her eyes opened wide. "Look! No body hair." She looked past the corpse's mutilated face. "And his hair is blond. Clifford's is sandy brown with a reddish cast and thinning." She turned to the coroner. "Who is this man?"

THEY MET THE SHERIFF in the small office of the local justice of the peace when he returned late that evening. Sheriff Jones listened attentively to the events of the morning.

He shook his head. "Ma'am, you had no right to take matters into your own hands like this," he said. "I hated to take Con to that hell hole, but you can't just come up with evidence out of the blue and expect me to get him released. I have no way of knowing if you've made up this whole story."

She shot from her chair. "But this proves he's innocent. They've convicted an innocent man. Mr. Mellon twisted the facts to get a conviction and the judge was drunk during the trial."

"Cornwall is always drunk during his trials," Jones said.

"Then he should be removed," Matthias said, his voice rising an octave. "The jury railroaded my son. They'll all pay."

The justice of the peace raised his hand. "We need more proof than Mrs. Adler's statement about the body. If you can come up with evidence that proves Mr. Kingston is alive, you can ask for a new trial."

"With this judge?" Matthias shouted.

"Let me finish, sir," the justice said. "You can also take your evidence to Helena and see if Governor Leslie will sign a pardon. Do you know him?"

"You damned betcha," Matthias said.

The justice of the peace smiled. "He's gotten quite a reputation for being lenient on prisoners sent to Deer Lodge."

"I can understand why if others are railroaded like my client has been," David Addison said.

The justice of the peace shrugged. "All I'm trying to do is warn you all that Mr. Mellon and Judge Cornwall can twist Mrs. Adler's statement and make it look false. Judge Cornwall likes the prestige of his office and Mellon wants a judgeship of his own. Don't get your hopes up."

"You don't believe me," Bethea said, her stomach churning as her newly found hope collided with despair. "Why would I lie?"

"Ma'am, I'll be honest with you. Some men around here don't take kindly to white women becoming involved with Indians."

She wanted to slap the man across his pox-marked cheek. She clenched her teeth and began to tap the tip of her green silk parasol against the floor. She couldn't think of a single civil word to say to him. Yet she refused to let him think he and others like him could have their way.

"My husband is one of the finest men in the territory," she said, forming her words carefully. "He's warm and loving, considerate and fair, a fine Christian man. He's a devoted husband. He's

341

willing to be a father to children who aren't his own. He's a hard worker. He's intelligent and wise. He's handsome and strong and tall and he stands proud."

"Standing proud like he's equal to a white man? That isn't so good when he's a breed," the justice replied.

Bethea's eyes narrowed. Before she realized what she had done, she swung her parasol with all the force she possessed, catching the justice of the peace across his cheek and ear and knocking him to the floor.

Matthias lifted her bodily off the floor and whirled her away from the downed man. "Bethea, keep your wits about you," he hissed, and tried to march her from the room. When she balked, he lifted her over his shoulder and carried her out of the building.

From her perch, she spotted the wiry built justice scramble to his feet, pushing David Addison's offered assistance aside. "If that woman ever sets foot in here again, I'll press charges of assault with intent to commit murder and she can join that savage of hers at Deer Lodge. Mark my word, I have some power around here, too."

The door closed in Bethea's face before she could hear David Addison's response. He was probably trying to convince the man she'd simply been a hysterical woman. Well, he was wrong. She wasn't hysterical at all.

The soles of her high buttoned shoes touched the boardwalk in front of the justice's office when Matthias let her slide to her feet. He started to chuckle and she turned to stare at him.

"I see nothing funny about all this."

He grinned, and his smile touched her deeply.

"My son would be most impressed with his wife's conduct in there," he said, removing his felt hat and wiping his brow. His hair had whitened considerably over the summer, but the change had enhanced his features. Perhaps there was more of him in Con than she'd admitted.

"He'd be mortified, I'm sure," she countered. "I've turned that man against us, too." She held out her hands. "What are we going to do, Mr. Adler?"

"Call me Matthias, or Father, or Papa," he suggested. "Anything but that damned formal Mr. Adler."

She gazed up into his blue eyes. "You didn't approve of me at first, did you?"

He looked away for several seconds, then met her gaze directly. "No. I didn't want to see my son hurt by getting involved with a married woman. He had enough strikes against him. He was treading in deep waters when he started talking about taking on a ready made family."

"You meant well. You wanted to protect him."

"Come walk with me," he suggested.

She slid her hand beneath his elbow and they began to stroll toward the edge of town. "Why did Con stay home while the others all left Alice?" she asked.

"I asked him," Matthias said. "He's a good manager. He understands livestock raising. He knows the land and how to treat it. He's intelligent and educated and can deal with businessmen back in the states."

"But that's not all, is it?" she asked.

He didn't answer. They stepped off the end of the boardwalk and continued walking down the dirt trail still called Main Street. The buildings changed to small clapboard houses. Saplings lined the path where they walked. Someday these saplings would provide shade but she doubted if either of them would live to see that. A few blocks from town, the houses were left behind and one-room log cabins took their places. They reached a bend in the creek and stopped.

"Someone should build a bridge," she said absently, staring at the churning waters. "Tell me about you and Victoria in the early days."

Matthias leaned against a huge cottonwood tree trunk. "I've had a foot in two worlds for three decades and I brought Victoria into my problems. Maybe she deserved better. At times it seemed like the three of us against the rest of humanity," he confessed. "This country was settled by many southerners with all their ingrained prejudices. Mix that with those Puritanical New Englanders and you've got trouble and intolerance."

"You're from Boston," she said.

"But born in Kentucky," he replied. "The New Englanders who come west are more subtle about their beliefs. Maybe they're more dangerous because they hide beneath their religious piety, but they're part of the picture, too, I reckon."

Bethea closed her parasol and joined him beneath the shady limbs of the tree. "Tell me about Con's mother."

Matthias smiled sadly. "She was a half-sister to Tendoi. He wasn't the chief then. Back in '56, I was on my way back to Boston. I'd tried the diggings in California and done some trapping but that business was dying. I was thirty years old and still at loose ends, a graduate from Boston University who had been expected to go into his family's tobacco business. All I wanted was room to breath. The Lewis and Clark Expedition was still in the news. William Clark had laid out the city of Paducah where I was born. He was a friend of our family."

He chuckled. "As a little boy, I can remember sitting on his knee and listen to his stories. Can you imagine that? The lure of the west was in my blood from the beginning. After graduation, I talked my father into a grubstake for two years and promised him I'd return if I failed."

"Did you give up?"

"I lost my tote with all my money and food in it trying to cross a river. It was spring time and I almost drowned myself. Tendoi found me and took me to his camp. Maliyah was fourteen when I met her. I liked their way of life and stayed. We were married when she was sixteen and I was thirty. It sounds scandalous now but I loved her and she loved me."

He gazed back at the small town. "My son was born the next year. His grandmother named him Chugan. I couldn't believe it when his eyes lightened to blue, but then a damned old shaman said it was a sign of evil to come and warned me to protect him because his life would be endangered.

"I was proud of Chugan, but I knew he could never be a full member of the Lemhi band, yet the color of his skin would mark him in the white man's world. When gold was found on Willard Creek and Bannack City swelled, I used to take him there to give him a taste of city life."

He smiled. "That's when I met Victoria. I reckon if a man can love two women, I was guilty, but Maliyah was my first love. When we were camped by the lake in the valley, she went into labor ahead of her time. The rest of the band left us behind at her insistence. Our tepee leaked and I didn't have the materials to patch it so I used some of the dead timber on the side hill and build a one-room cabin. I never had time to put in a floor, as I'm sure you noticed."

She smiled. "It's hard to overlook."

"She had the baby, a son," he continued. "Then she started to hemorrhage and I knew she needed help. I left her and the baby and told Chugan to stay next to her and not leave the cabin. Bannack City was the closest settlement. Victoria was the only person in the camp who seemed to care and she went with me, but by the time we reached Maliyah, she and the baby were dead."

He bit the tip off a cigar and lit it, drawing in the aromatic smoke. "I was literally sick with grief and Victoria took care of me as well as my Chugan. She talked me into returning to Bannack City where she became my housekeeper."

"How romantic, but scandalous, too," Bethea exclaimed.

He grinned. "She didn't care. She would take Chugan's hand and parade down the street to the store for supplies, daring anyone to say an unkind word. I've never told her or Con, but I was terrified for them both. I worked a small claim by day and protected them both at night. I asked her to marry me twice and she refused."

He tossed the half smoked cigar into the water. "Finally I took up some land at the mouth of Medicine Lodge and I told her she couldn't come with us unless she agreed to marry me. She did and the rest is history, but I've always known deep down inside that I was taking my son away from the white man's world so he could grow up whole and confident."

Bethea touched his hand. "You succeeded."

"But for what?" he asked. "The old shaman's warning has come true. Damn it, he's become a sacrificial lamb on the altar of this sanctimonious county after all. Why did I ever bring him here? If we'd returned to Idaho, would things have turned out differently?" His eyes turned shiny when he gazed down at her. "Bethea, have we both lost him?"

"No, no," she pleaded. "Don't say that. I would never have met him. You would never have met Victoria. This is all meant to be, and it isn't over yet. Have faith...Matthias." She smiled up at him through her tears. "You are like a father to me, but I'd rather call you Matthias."

345

"And you've become my daughter," he said, touching her shoulders. "My son and my daughter. I love you both, and I'm proud of you both. You're right. It isn't over yet."

"MY DEAREST CON has been taken away from me," she wrote in her journal book late that night. *"The dead man is not Clifford. Matthias Adler and David Addison believe me. I'm not positive about Sheriff Jones. No one else does. How can I endure the months and years alone?*

"I shall return to the valley and try to make the days pass by working on my new land. If I do nothing to improve it, I'll lose it. I must think of my children. We cannot live on the charity of others, especially not Matthias and Victoria Adler. They have treated me like a daughter, but deep down I know it is up to me.

"I'm so alone. I need Con's arms around me to tell me this is all a terrible dream. I fear Con will never be free. If he does not survive the years in prison, I shall never love another man. I am twenty-seven years old. Twenty years from now, Hallie will be grown and married, with a life of her own. After that, I do not care what becomes of me."

WHEN THEY RETURNED to Alice, Matthias and Bethea were met by Victoria Adler and Jacob Dingley.

Victoria broke into sobs when told about Con's conviction.

Jacob shook his head sadly. "I reckon I'd best get on back to the valley and let the crew know. This summer won't be the same without the boss."

Bethea gathered the children around her and tried to explain Con's conviction to them.

"Is that why Adam got to go to town?" Esther asked.

Adam refused to look at Bethea. "The judge said I had to tell the truth and I did."

"But you got to ride the train," David said. "I tell the truth, but I don't get to ride the train."

"That's because you're a baby," Adam said. As if the matter had been settled, he stared at his mother. "I get to go on the fall roundup," Adam said, "but Mr. Dingley says I have to get your permission first. Can I go?"

"We'll be moving to the valley," Bethea said. "You're old enough to ride to Alaska Basin where the crew stays, but I need you to help me build a fence first." She loved this oldest son, but couldn't understand why he had said the things he'd said from the witness chair for all the courtroom to hear.

"Can I work the fall roundup, too?" Ben asked.

"Maybe next year," she replied.

"Mama, I..." Faith sidled over to Bethea, then tucked her blond head. "I know a secret."

"What is it, darling?"

Esther grabbed her sister's skirt and yanked on it. "Grandma said you had to be wrong, and to not worry Mama."

David looked at his sisters. "What secret? You never told me."

"Faith told me the secret, but I promised Grandma I wouldn't tell, either," Gabriel said. "Can we play now?"

"Mr. Adler shot our pa, and I'm glad he's in prison," Adam said. "I'm going to the barn."

"Adam!" Bethea scolded.

Before she could get to her feet, her two oldest sons were out of sight.

INSIDE THE HOUSE, Matthias climbed the stairs, weary from the strain of the weeks past. Victoria followed him to their bedroom and sat on the edge of their four-poster bed while he changed into work clothes.

"Matthias, something happened while you were gone."

He stopped buttoning the front of his chambray shirt.

"A man came to the door, a stranger," she explained. "He asked about Bethea and Con."

Matthias frowned. "Did he give his name?" He slid his trousers down and stepped out of them, then into a pair of well worn denim trousers and began buttoning the opening. "Victoria, damn it. What was his business?"

"He didn't say. He wore a floppy hat and coat. He had a beard but I'm sure I've never seen him before. After he rode away, Faith came running into the house in tears." She came to stand close to him. "Matthias, Faith said she'd seen her father but when she called out to him, he ignored her as if he'd not recognized her. Esther had been with her, and she said it wasn't him. Esther said her sister saw a ghost. I know it's crazy, but is it possible? Or did Faith simply see a man who reminded her of her father?"

Matthias told her about Bethea's insistence the body in Dillon was not that of Clifford Kingston. "Would he really be so brazen as to come here, if in fact he is alive?"

"I told the girls to keep it our secret," she said.

"I'll get word to Sheriff Jones," Matthias said, "but I doubt if that man would try to come back and play husband and father, even if he is still alive." He nodded his head and put on his hat. "If you ask me, Kingston's body is still in Idaho, his bones picked bare by the vultures."

BETHEA WAITED for word from David Addison, but her hopes faded with each passing day. Judge Cornwall refused to review the case and she knew the territorial rules required that any appeal begin with the judge who had rendered the sentence.

Each morning she searched for strength to leave her bed, the bed she and Con had never shared. She would open the glass doors and go to the edge of the balcony overlooking the brook and wonder if she would ever see her beloved husband again.

She wrote weekly letters to Con, but received nothing in return. Keeping busy at her sewing machine, she made dresses for her daughters and shirts and trousers for her rapidly growing sons. The pink dress for herself lay abandoned beneath three bolts of calico. She refused to work on the dress until Con was free to see her in it.

Matthias received a letter from David Addison. "He's received permission to see Con. He wants me with him."

"I want to go with you, too," Bethea pleaded.

Matthias shook his head. "That prison is no place for women. Write him a letter and I'll deliver it personally. David says he can't have official family visits yet."

Centennial Swan

She wrote Con a long letter filled with news of the children dwelling on Hallie's latest accomplishments, then closed it with a vow of everlasting love.

MATTHIAS ADLER and David Addison waited in the visitor's reception room of the prison while one guard examined David's leather case, then both men were thoroughly frisked for weapons.

Thirty minutes later, Con shuffled into the room, his hands manacled and his ankles shackled.

Matthias's heart ached for his son's condition. He'd trade places with him if the officials would allow it. "It's only been four weeks, Con. What the hell happened to you?"

Con sit down on a bench near their chairs. A guard stood at each door. Con touched the purple bruise turning to green on his forehead. A wicked abrasion running the length of his cheek had scabbed over. One of the guard sent him a warning glance.

"I'd forgotten they shaved heads in this place," David said.

"I don't mean the hair," Matthias steamed. "What happened to your face? It looks like someone beat the hell out of you."

Con glanced at the grinning guard. "Here they call it discipline. I stumbled while I was emptying my cell bucket. I got some on the guard and he knocked me down with his club. I lost my head and struck back. I spent three days in the pit."

"What's that?" Matthias asked.

"I'll tell you later, Mr. Adler," David said. "Let's not use up all our time on what's past. We can't stay here all day. Rules won't allow that."

"You're right," Matthias said, pulling an envelope from his vest pocket. "This is from Bethea, and she wanted to know if you got her other letters."

Con glanced up from the white envelope. "She wrote?"

"Weekly," Matthias said. "I took them to Red Rock myself."

Con fingered the envelope. "It's so clean." He glanced up at his father and friend. "I'll read it later. Tell her I can't write letters until I've been here two months. Tell her..." His voice broke. When he spoke again, it was a soft whisper. "If I can figure out how to do it, I'm going over the wall. It's been done before."

David held up his hand. "Don't do anything rash. A man from Silver Star visited me in Butte. Sheriff Jones sent him. Seems he thinks he had a drink with Clifford Kingston right in Dillon the night you left town, only he wasn't sure until he got back home. He says they watched you board the train. Con, could that be?"

"Impossible," Con said. "He's dead in the wilderness in Idaho, I tell you. Did you take Bethea back to the ranch the next morning?"

"Almost," Matthias replied. "We paid a visit to the justice of the peace after she learned about the body in the ice house. She looked at it and insists it's not Kingston's."

CHAPTER TWENTY-SEVEN

"I TOLD SHERIFF JONES to forbid her to see it," Con insisted. "He had no right to force her."

"It was her idea," David explained.

Con stared at David Addison. "But the body was positively identified as Kingston's."

"Bethea insists it's not," Matthias said, and described the outcome. "She's talking about moving to the valley again."

"Don't let her," Con said.

"That's one strong-willed woman you've married," David said, shaking his head. "We also had a letter from a gambler who spent a few days with you in the Beaverhead County jail."

Con leaned forward. "The man from Boise?"

"Yes, Samson York."

"But he was on his way to jail himself. What did he say?"

"That he'd played cards with a man who called himself Calvin Kingston in Eagle Rock in the late spring. He made a statement in front of a judge and witnesses and signed it before he left for Missouri. He said it was the decent thing to do, since you were responsible for him cleaning up his own life."

"Then get me out of here," Con insisted. "Father, I won't survive ten years in this hell hole. They look for any excuse to send me to the pit." He looked away. "It's because my skin is darker than theirs. That's the only reason. Even when I follow the rules, the guards use those clubs. The white prisoners shower first, then when they're out, the guards get rough with the Indian prisoners, and the mixed bloods get it worst."

Con looked at his scabbed hands. "If I can't escape or you can't get me out, I'd rather be dead. We can't talk."

Matthias frowned. "You can't speak? To anyone?"

Con shook his head. "Never to another prisoners and only to the guards if they speak to us first, and they seldom put themselves out. I think I'll go crazy if I can't have a civil conversation with another human being."

"You were always a man of few words," David said.

"But I had the freedom to say them," Con explained. "It's so quiet in that cell I begin to think I'm the only man left in the world. Sometimes the men scrape their chair or table in their cells just to hear the noise. It sounds good knowing someone is in the cell next to you. I'm beginning to think the silence is worse punishment than being locked up."

David fidgeted in his chair.

Con straightened. "But they can't keep me from thinking. I have these little conversations with myself. It helps. I keep my lips together so the words don't come out."

David touched Con's arm. "Friend, I hate to bring this up, but if these sightings of Kingston are true, then Bethea is not your legal wife, or she's guilty of bigamy."

"Oh, God," Con said, starting to run his fingers across his skull. The bristly growth couldn't be more than a quarter of an inch. "Sometimes I want her to come visit me so much it hurts, but I don't want her to see me like this. I'm surprised they let you in."

"Attorneys are the exception," David said. He touched Con's arm again. "Don't give up. I'm on my way to Virginia City. I'll be settling Clifford Kingston's affairs for Bethea. Only now I'm wondering if it's not premature. Then I'm going to Eagle Rock to visit some of the gambling dens there. For now, I'm proceeding as if he's dead. I don't care if Bethea is your legal wife or not. You two belong together. Even a blind man could see that."

"Tell it to Judge Cornwall, the damned drunken incompetent," Con replied. "Tell me about the children, the ranch. How bad were the losses? It seems like an eternity since I was there."

They spent the rest of the visit discussing affairs at Alice. Matthias pulled two photographs mounted on cardboard from his pocket. "We took the children into Dillon for a photograph sitting. The other one is a reprint of your wedding photo taken at Butte City. Bethea wanted you to have them."

Con stared down at the photos, his eyes misty at the sight of them. "Thanks, and tell her...well, she knows how I feel about her, about everything. I just wish I could undo all this and we could start over."

David and Matthias rose to leave but Con motioned them to sit again. "There's one more thing. Bethea signed Kingston's name to the deed to her property the day after he abandoned her, indicating he had given it to her. She was desperate, but I don't want her up here, too, and the way the jury treated us both, if she went to trial, she'd fare no better than I have."

"Is there no end to this business with Kingston?" Matthias asked. He turned to David. "Can we keep this to ourselves until we find out what's really going on with Kingston?"

David sighed and retrieved his note pad again, jotting down what Con had said. "I'll do some research, but this is not the time to clear this up. I'll restrict my business to Kingston's bank accounts if he had any."

AN HOUR LATER, Matthias threw his arms around his son. "We'll have you out of here soon. We'll see you next month. Maybe we will have good news. Your mother sends her love."

David shook Con's hand, squeezing it reassuringly, then they were escorted out of the prison building, through a short grassy yard to the double doors in the wooden fence.

When the train rolled into the station at Red Rock hours later, Matthias was met by a cowboy driving a matched team and a surrey.

"Good to have you home, sir," the young man said.

"Good to be back, Broderick," Matthias replied. "I thought you'd be on your way to Missouri to visit your mother. How's everything in Alaska Basin? Have the herds been moved yet?"

"Moving them now, sir," Broderick said. "The young Mrs. Adler is waiting for you. She's all fired up about moving back to that cabin of hers. She made me promise to help her. I told her I was taking the train to visit my folks, but she made me promise to get her settled before I left. That woman is a powerful persuader, sir."

When Matthias reached the ranch, two fully loaded wagons were parked in front of the main house. He hurried up the steps, resenting having to use the cane for support. He found the women inside parlor. "What the hell is going on here?" he shouted. "Bethea, you can't just leave us. That's crazy."

Victoria rose to her feet, her summer cotton skirts swaying around her as she approached him. "It's just until the end of summer," she explained. "Then why two wagon loads for hell's sake?" he asked.

"Bethea didn't want to run out of the necessities," Victoria explained. "But she promised to be back in two months." She smiled at the younger woman. "Didn't you, dear?"

Bethea rose to her feet. "I'm accomplishing nothing here, and I'm so lonely I can't bear to endure another day. I need to see the lakes and the valley and the swans before they leave again. Please try to understand."

Victoria smiled. "If Mrs. Taylor, the new county superintendent of schools, can arrange for a teacher to stay with us this winter, she'll authorize an official school. She stopped by on her way from Amesville. Won't that be wonderful?"

"Did you give Con my letter?" Bethea asked.

"Yes, I did, and he said he'd not received your letters," Matthias said. "I asked Wheeler to check into it."

"Was he all right?" she asked.

Matthias thought of his son's bruises and abrasions, the jolt of seeing him without hair, his trouble with the guards. "He looked fine, honey, just fine. He's reading every night and getting two good meals a day."

"Only two meals?"

"That's all they issue," he replied.

"I want to go there and storm the walls and make them release him," Bethea said. "If only I had a canon."

EARLY THE NEXT DAY, the small caravan left the Alice Livestock home ranch. Con's youngest brother, Lee, drove one wagon while Broderick took the reins of the other one. Bethea rode beside Lee, holding Hallie on her lap and Faith and Esther between the adults. Gabriel and David climbed up alongside Broderick. Ben and Adam rode their own horses, gifts from Matthias.

At the last minute, Matthias joined them. "I'll go with you as far as Monida."

They spent the night at the Burn's hotel where they talked long into the evening. Bethea poured out her woeful experiences of the trial. Matthias slouched in the corner of the sofa.

"Emiline, we've had two men come forward insisting they'd talked to Kingston this spring," Matthias said.

Emiline Burns jumped from her seat and ran outside. In a few minutes she returned dragging her husband Bill with her. "Tell Bill what you just said."

Bill's eyes narrowed as Matthias described the reports. When he turned to Emiline, he wasn't smiling. "Then maybe you were right, honey."

They sat down together and Emiline recounted how she had seen a man on the northbound train months earlier.

"It made no sense when she told me," Bill said. "Could he still be alive?"

"We need more proof. Keep your eyes open when the trains come through," Matthias said. "If you see anyone who looks even remotely like him, send a man to Bethea and send him armed."

"I'll be fine," Bethea said.

"I'm asking the Alice cowboys to stop each time one goes by the cabin," Matthias said. "You'll never be alone for more than a day or two."

"I'm going there to be alone," she insisted.

Emiline chuckled. "You and seven children. That's alone?"

When they left Monida the next morning, the milk cow they'd left stabled at the Burn's livery since spring was tied to the rear of one wagon. Bethea paid up the board bill for the white mare and foal, then gave Bill an ample advance payment for the rest of the summer.

"I'd be glad to buy her," Bill said, as she settled the bill. "She's a fine mare, and that colt of hers looks more like Hellion every day."

Bethea smiled sadly. "Then you know why we can't part with either of them. Someday I'll have time to ride her. Adam and Ben both have their own horses now and they've agreed that David deserves the colt. He's getting to be a big boy."

She smiled at her middle son and he grinned back.

"Thank you," she said, extending her hand to Bill Burns. She gave Matthias an impulsive hug and whispered in his ear, "We'll be fine."

THE ROCKING AND BOUNCING of the wagons seemed to grow worse with each mile. Suddenly Bethea turned green around her mouth. "Stop the wagon," she shouted, shoving Hallie into Esther's arms and jumping to the ground before the wheels had rolled to a full stop. She ran into the sage brush and bent over, heaving her breakfast onto the ground.

When she had to stop again several miles later, Lee and Broderick held a quick counsel and agreed to stop at the abandoned cabin for the night. Bethea didn't argue.

They reached the aspen grove at mid afternoon the following day. Lee reined in the team and pointed. "We have company." Four tepees had been set up near the cabin. Indians milled about and a band of ponies were picketed nearby. A tall man came from the cabin and paused, holding something in his hand. He had to stoop to pass under the doorjamb overhead.

Lee grinned. "It's Tendoi." He slapped the reins against the team's rumps and they cantered the last quarter mile.

Bethea stared at the men, women and children in her front yard. "Whatever shall I do?" she asked.

"Enjoy their company," Lee suggested. "If I know Tendoi's wives, they'll have a meal ready for us all. I wonder how they knew we'd be coming?"

When she climbed down from the wagon, the tall man left the doorway and approached her. His skin was leather brown, his handsome features bearing a slight resemblance to Con. Black braids hung over his shoulders and feathers fluttered near his ear. Although his trousers were from the white man's world, his shirt and footwear were of traditional Shoshoni leather and beadwork. When Bethea stared at him, she sensed why the white man who knew him considered him their equal.

Tendoi nodded to Lee who grinned and threw his arms around the older man's shoulders. Tendoi returned the embrace, then turned his full attention to Bethea. He glanced at the photograph in his hand. "Is this Chugan's woman?"

She recognized the photograph as one she had left in the cabin when she and Con had passed through the valley from the geysers. She waited, afraid to move for fear of offending him.

Finally his mouth moved at one corner and a twinkle shone in his black eyes. "My nephew chooses well."

She exhaled a sigh of relief.

"Yes, sir, that's her," Lee said. "Bethea Adler, meet Tendoi, Chief of the Lemhis and a longtime friend and relative of our family." He waited while they exchanged greetings. "Who's with you, Chief? Did you bring all your wives?"

"Young Leander, I have only three wives," the chief scolded good naturedly. "Do not make it sound like more. Cora and Laura are with me. Sarah has many aches in her bones so she stayed in our camp at Lemhi. Some of my sons and grandsons are hunting north of the lakes. They left yesterday and will return tomorrow before the sun sets. We will be taking down the tepees in two days. My wives have much food in their pots." He turned to Bethea. "Will you join us?"

"What...is it," she asked cautiously.

Tendoi grinned. "Shoshoni do not eat dog."

"I'm sorry, I didn't want to offend you," she said. "I have seven children with healthy appetites."

"I have had sixteen but only ten now live," Tendoi said. "Young children, especially boys, are always hungry."

Lee and three of Tendoi's grandsons joined Broderick in unloading the wagons. Bethea scooped up Hallie in her arms to keep her out of harm's way.

Tendoi smiled when he saw Hallie, reaching out to touch her black curls. Hallie held out her arms to the man and Tendoi took her, holding her high above the ground in the crook of his arm. The baby entertained herself with his braid.

"This girl child cannot belong to my nephew," Tendoi said.

"No," Bethea murmured.

"She bears a resemblance." The chief touched the baby's pale cheek. "Someday my nephew will hold a place of great honor. You will be proud to stand by his side. He told me of his love for you many months ago."

She felt the heat of a blush on her cheeks. "I was married when we met. I knew I shouldn't fall in love with him, but..."

He smiled. "But you did and he did and all will be well soon. Stay at his side. He needs your strength."

The chief stood directly in front of her, his eyes piercing as he examined her features. "When will Chugan's child be born?" he asked, his voice low and meant for her ears alone.

357

A wave of nausea churned in her stomach. "In the spring," she admitted.

Tendoi handed Hallie back to her but his gaze never wavered. "My nephew will be with you to see the birth of a son."

Her eyes widened. "You know...that it will be a boy? How?" Tendoi nodded then reached into a pouch on his belt. "This is a medicine ball," he said, handing her a small pouch of leather pulled tightly around some unseen contents and tied with a thong. Colorful beads decorated the pouch. "Keep it for your son and trust my words. Your son will know his father well."

She accepted the gift but still shook her head. "But he's in prison for ten years."

"When we heard of Chugan's punishment at the hand of the white man's justice, the old crone opened her medicine bundle and examined it for my nephew's fate. He will be with you when his son arrives. She always speaks the truth. That is why we are camped here, to tell you of her message."

DURING CHIEF TENDOI'S visit, Bethea seldom saw her children other than when they brought a new friend into the cabin to meet Bethea. After a quick introduction, the young ones would race outside again to meet with other children for games and to explore the countryside.

Two of Tendoi's grandsons took David under their guidance and by the middle of the second day, he returned to camp with a cottontail rabbit he'd snared all by himself. As he squatted over a small fire roasting the skinned carcass to be shared with his friends, Bethea could see the boy's confidence soar.

Gabriel came to her late in the second day with a slender brown-skinned boy in tow. "This is my friend Jack," Gabriel said. "Can he sleep in here tonight? His tepee is too crowded because Ben is sleeping there. Jack has never slept inside a cabin. Can he, heah?"

Bethea tossed her head back and laughed. "Of course," she said, realizing how good it felt to be able to laugh once more. She vowed to kept Tendoi's words tucked away in her heart.

"Can we sleep in your brass bed?" Gabriel asked. "Jack has never slept in a brass bed before."

Bethea kissed her son's cheek, then impulsively bestowed a kiss on the other child's cheek as well. "The brass bed is yours. I'll use Adam's bunk."

But when the camp had settled in the for night and Gabriel and his friend Jack were nestled in the brass bed, sleep escaped Bethea. She wrapped her knitted shawl around her shoulders to ward off the chill of the cool August night and left the cabin to follow the trail past the springs to the lake's sandy edge.

A half moon provided enough light for her to see the outlines of swans and other water foul down the shoreline. Could Con see the same moon glow? Did his cell have an window? He was a man used to the freedom of climbing the magnificent mountains, riding the rolling hills, stopping to drink from an icy stream at his leisure. Did he have enough blankets or was he cold? Did he think of her often? Had he reconciled himself to the length of their separation?

The last words he'd spoken haunted her. He'd told her to go home and forget him. Surely he didn't think she could ever do such a thing.

An animal howled in the forest behind her. Was it a wolf or coyote? She tried to remember what Con had told her about telling the difference. Was she hearing a howl or a yapping sound? It sounded like a little of both, she decided. Maybe they interbreed. Con had taught her the differences between edible plants and those that would poison her and the children, how to dry the berries for winter tea, which ones could be made into healing potions. She had learned so much about life and love from him.

The howling sounded again, further away. Probably a wolf protesting the intrusion of humans into its territory, she decided. Glancing down, she spotted the rock on which she'd ruined her dress the previous summer in a futile effort to wash away her guilt and sin of falling in love with a man whom society would not approve.

Memories of the first kiss they'd shared swept away what little control she had. She stood alone, silhouetted in the moonlight, her shoulders shaking as she cried her grief. Tears streamed down her cheeks as she stood hugging herself. Crying seemed to be the only balm she'd found that enabled her to face the empty days ahead.

A twig snapped behind her, but she didn't turn. A shadow fell across the water's edge.

"You still don't believe?" Tendoi asked.

She turned to face him. "I miss him so much. If it weren't for the children, I'd go into the mountains and curl up and die."

"Think of his child."

"We didn't want a child until we were together again."

"Does he know?" Tendoi asked.

She shook her head. "He'll be very upset."

Tendoi took his hand and lifted her chin, forcing her to look at him. "Tell him. He needs to know. He's a man of deep convictions, but he has the weakness of his father's blood. White men give up. Chugan must never give up. Tell him of the child so he can hold it to his heart and know that soon he will be free. Tell him of our visit."

Sobs racked her again and she found herself in the chief's arms. He comforted her like his own daughter, murmuring words in his own language as she cried against his chest. The odors of burnt sage and tanned leather blended with the camas root and roasted venison surrounded her. This man from a culture so different from hers understood her loss.

For several moments her pain eased as he murmured more Shoshoni phrases and she wished she could understand this language of her husband's people.

She stepped back. "I'm sorry. I cry too much, but when I stop, I get so angry I want to go to the prison and demand they free him. If only I were a man, I'd...do something."

Tendoi chuckled and spoke in Shoshoni, then smiled down at her. "I think Chugan prefers you as a woman. Remember what I told you about the old woman's words. I know my nephew. Tell him about the child."

THE NEXT MORNING the Lemhi band broke camp. The chief came to say farewell to Bethea and the children, then mounted and led the procession over the trail to the east.

"They were great," Adam said. "I never knew Injuns would be so smart. My pa always said they were just savages."

"Your father spoke out of ignorance," Bethea replied.

"But why would Pa say those things if he didn't know?" Adam asked, frowning as the procession disappeared from sight.

Bethea sighed. "I don't want to talk about your father, Adam. Maybe later. Con is my husband now. Frankly, I don't care if you accept him or not. He's my husband. When he comes home, we'll be a family again. Until then, we have work to do."

She began to describe what they needed to do in the months to come. "We won't be spending the winter here, but I've filed on land and I want us to build a fence around it. Con and Mrs. Burns and I marked it off on our way home from the geysers. Remember the fences at the Alice ranch?"

The children nodded.

"Those are jack-leg fences and two of the cowboys are coming tomorrow to help us get started, but they won't be able to stay more than a few days, so we must learn to do the work ourselves." She peered at her oldest son. "Adam, may I borrow a pair of your trousers?"

"Sure, but why?" he asked.

"I've got work to do, and these skirts are a bother," she said. "Now let's get started."

A MONTH LATER Victoria arrived in a surrey, a young woman sitting beside her. "This is Miss Polly Dotson. She's from Illinois and has been hired to teach at our new school."

"What new school?" Ben asked.

"The Alice School," Victoria exclaimed. "I've wanted an official school at Alice for twenty years and at long last it's a reality. Miss Dotson and I have discussed the children's needs and she wants to begin next week. We've come to bring you home."

Adam stepped back. "I'm too old for school. I'll be thirteen in October. I already know how to read and do ciphers. Ma, you can't make me go to school."

"I wanna go," Gabriel said. "I'm six years old and I wanna go to school." He beamed up at his mother.

She ruffled his sandy brown hair absently. "He already knows his letters, but we still have a lot of work to do here. I wish I had known you would be coming so soon."

"Bethea," Victoria said, taking her arm and leading her away from the children who were questioning Miss Dotson about the new school. "Bethea, there have been sightings of your husband."

"Con?" She swallowed a moment of panic at the possibility that Chief Tendoi's words had become a reality so quickly.

"No, Clifford Kingston," Victoria said. "If they're true, you might be in danger." She described David Addison's findings during his trips to Virginia City and Eagle Rock.

"He found three bank accounts and closed them out. The money has been deposited in the First National Bank of Dillon in your name. In Eagle Rock, he visited with two men who insisted they played cards with him. And once a man came to the house asking about you." She described the man's features and body built. "Faith insisted it was her father. Esther said no, and I believed her at the time, but could Faith have been right?"

Bethea chewed her lower lip. "The body in Dillon was not his. His body is still in the mountains in Idaho."

"The U. S. Marshal in Idaho led a search," Victoria said. "They found the wagon with a broken axle and two horse carcasses, but no body. Someone must have helped him, Bethea."

"Maybe the wolves dragged his body away," Bethea said.

"There would have been bones scattered, something."

"But he must be dead," Bethea replied. "If he *is* alive, then I can't be married to Con." Her voice was little above a whisper. "This cannot be."

"It's no longer safe for you to stay here alone," Victoria insisted. "Please come home with us."

Bethea paced the shoreline, then turned to the older woman. "I need a day or two to think about it."

Victoria nodded. "We thought you might feel that way, so we've come prepared to rusticate for a few days. Miss Dotson is from Chicago and she doesn't know much about rural life. She wants to experience it for herself so she can understand the children better."

They began to walk up the pathway toward the cabin, but Bethea stopped. She'd intended to tell Victoria about her condition. Now she couldn't. The child was Con's, yet she might still be married to Clifford. Victoria would insist she return, and she couldn't leave yet. They had work to finish.

"Have you heard from Con?" she asked, keeping her voice steady.

"Not yet," Victoria said, a sadness in her blue eyes. "Matthias will leave in two weeks to meet David Addison in Butte City. They'll go to Deer Lodge by train to see him."

Bethea hesitated, mulling over her options, then made up her mind. "You can take Ben, David, Esther, Faith and Gabriel back with you, but I'm staying here with Adam and Hallie. Adam had been working like a man on a fence around our new property."

"But Hallie will be underfoot," Victoria argued. "Please, let us take her, too."

Bethea shook her head. "No. I've been gone from her too much this summer. I need to be with her." She smiled. "She took her first steps yesterday. Con would be so proud. I want to write him a long letter. Will you give it to Matthias to deliver to him?" She looked off across the lake. "I hope he's healthy. I've stopped..." *Crying*, she thought. Instead she added, "missing him quite so much."

It was a lie, but what else could she say? If she returned to the Alice ranch, she would be surrounded by well intended people who would try to boost her spirits. Matthias and Victoria Adler would do their best to entertain her, to give her hope, to involve her in activities that held no importance.

Adam had grown quiet since they'd returned to the valley. His introspection matched her own and they'd settled into a cooperative spirit in the fence building project that met her need for privacy. Hallie's laughter continued to be the balm she needed now. Nothing else mattered.

Deep in her heart, she felt a sense of relief that the other children were leaving. Their high spirited behavior had begun to grate on her nerves. Never before had she resented her own children, but now their rambunctious energy had pushed her patience more than once.

The ache in her heart had grown stronger in the past weeks, pressing against her chest wall as if she were dying, and she wanted to die alone.

Three days later, the surrey left carrying the middle five children out of the valley. Bethea had written a six page letter to Con, describing his uncle's visit. In a final paragraph, she wrote of her deep feelings for him and closed with a pledge of love and a prayer for his safety and health.

She reread the final paragraph, then added a postscript. "I didn't want to tell you this news," she wrote, "but your uncle, the chief, said I was wrong to keep it from you. He said you needed to know. I carry your child. Tendoi insists we will have a son and that you will be with me at the birth."

CHAPTER TWENTY-EIGHT

THE SHACKLES AROUND CON'S ANKLES clanked as he shuffled down the long gray stone corridor toward the visitor's reception room. The officials were wrong if they thought they had broken his spirit. One more trip to the pit had convinced him he had to escape and soon. No man deserved such degradation.

The barrel of the guard's shotgun poked at his back, but he refused to quicken his step. If he stumbled and fell, as he'd done before, the guard would use his clumsiness as an excuse to use the butt. He wasn't the only inmate who went through the shower room with bruises on his backside and endured the unseen healing of broken ribs.

They had to strip off their soiled black and white striped prison garb and stand naked, forming a line to wait in the cold stone anteroom to move single file through the shower room. The room could handle only three men at a time and there were more than eighty men in the prison. Each man wet himself down at one of the three shower heads, stepped aside to soap himself, and rinsed himself at the single shower head near the exit.

It was a once-a-week ritual he'd begun to look forward to, even if the half dozen towels provided were soaking wet by the time the Indian inmates used them. The mixed-bloods were at the end of the line. Occasionally the water was warm for the first several white prisoners, but the icy spray that awaited him was welcome because it reinforced his determination to break out.

The isolation and silence had taken its toll. Once he's found himself whispering to a fly that had made its way into his cell, but the guard had heard him and threatened him with a third trip to the pit. Con had lost his control and spoken without permission and to make matters worse, had reached out through the bars of his cell and grabbed the guard's coat sleeve. One blow from the guard's shot gun butt had left him with a broken finger.

For some unknown reason, the warden had seen fit to limit his stay in the pit to only a single day.

In order to keep his sanity, he'd begun to hold internal dialogues with himself, as if he were two distinct persons. He'd named his other self Chugan. Was this proof that he was going crazy after all his efforts to keep his sanity?

Several of the prisoners had been declared insane and had been transferred down the road to the newly enlarged insane asylum at Warm Springs. Maybe they were the clever ones.

He felt an itch behind his ear, and without thinking, raised his arm, only to have it jerked down by the chain that connected his cuffs to his ankle shackles. *Warm Springs.* Just the sound of the asylum's name comforted him. *I can act as insane as the next man.* He'd talk it over with Chugan. He would take the side for going. Chugan could handle the opposition. His alter ego was amazing in analyzing the opposition.

Two days earlier he had been allowed to write his first letter to Bethea. A single sheet of paper had been given to him, slipped beneath a bowl of greasy stew with stringy bull meat. A large circle of grease had soiled the paper, making it incapable of taking the lead from the stubby pencil he'd been issued. Finally, he'd written, "I love you," and signed his name.

He'd decided against entrusting it to the guards and held it, hoping that his father would come soon. As he reached the door of the reception room, he patted his shirt, reassured the folded piece of greasy paper was safely tucked inside.

"Inside, breed," the guard said, shoving the barrel brutally into Con's ribs, still healing from a fall on the slippery floor in the shower room a week earlier.

Con gripped his own hands and waited for his anger to subside. His father was waiting. He didn't intend to be beaten right outside the door. Maybe his father had news from Bethea. He stepped into the visitor's room and the door slammed behind him. A new guard appeared at the other door leading toward the administration offices.

He wanted to touch his father, to hold his hand, anything to erase the feelings of abandonment, but he pushed the impulse down. Just as well, he thought, doubting that his ribs could handle any display of affection.

"Father," he said, nodding. "David, good to see you both. Excuse my lack of hospitality. They have a rule about touching."

Matthias scowled. "My God, what have they taught you here?"

Con exhaled sharply and regretted the impulsive act. "That hard work and silence are the foundations of survival. It's supposed to teach us something more profound, but I'm not sure what it is, other than hatred for the sadistic guards that work here."

The guard grinned and stroked the butt of his shotgun as if it were a woman's thigh.

"What kind of work do you do, son?" Matthias asked.

Con glanced at his father. "Repairing the very wall that keeps me in here, but when we do hard physical labor, we get three meals a day. Isn't that considerate of them?"

"Well," David said, shifting nervously. "Let's sit down. We have good news for you."

"I'm being released?"

"Not yet, but soon," David said. He launched into an accounting of his trips to Virginia City, Eagle Rock and Boise City, the finding of the bank accounts and how he'd turned them over to Bethea.

"That's all?" Con asked, his hopes sinking back into their customary pit of defeat.

"No," David said, smiling. "Finally we have the proof we need that Kingston was alive this spring."

"The sightings weren't enough?" he asked.

"The judge implied that I had paid the witnesses to say they'd seen Kingston. When that didn't work, the court insisted the statements were hearsay," David explained. "The judge said the witnesses lacked credibility. Gamblers, jail inmates, drunkards, the dregs of humanity."

"Strange, isn't it, that a drunken judge can't believe a drunken gambler?" Con shifted his position. The hand cuff on his left wrist pulled a scab off an old injury and he watched, disinterested, as blood trickled down his hand.

His father whipped a handkerchief from his coat pocket and wiped Con's wound. The guard stepped toward them and Con pulled back from his father's ministration. "Don't," he growled. "They don't allow touching of any kind." He tried to ignore the pained expression on his father's face. "What is the proof you've found?" he asked.

David pulled a folded legal paper from his inside jacket pocket and handed it to Con. "This is a sworn statement from a probate judge in Virginia City. When I went to close out the accounts, I asked to look at the entries in them. I did it out of curiosity, because I wanted to see how much a whiskey runner could make." He whistled. "It was sizeable. Con, you won't believe this but the bastard made a withdrawal from each of the accounts; one in March and two in April of this year. We have his signature on the withdrawal requests."

Con frowned. "Someone forged his name."

David shook his head. "The name on two of the accounts had been changed to Claude Kruger, but he left the last one as Kingston. The man was careless but it's worked in our favor. The signature matched that on the original forms that opened the account. That damned tightwad had over five thousand dollars in one account alone."

"He left his family to starve." Con's mind absorbed this new evidence. "That means he's still her husband."

"I'm afraid so, but I'm going to see her after we've been to Helena. I have the divorce papers all drawn up and she can sign them and you two can marry again."

Con stared down at his hands. Would she feel they'd been fornicators after all?

"Con, I want to do the ceremony," David said, poking himself in the chest. "I've been asked to fill the vacancy of old Judge Landon, the justice of the peace in Butte City. I've accepted the position, effective next Tuesday. I would consider it an honor to perform the ceremony at your convenience."

"It's not convenient at the moment," Con murmured.

"But it will be soon," David insisted. "Don't you see? We have proof that you are innocent."

"But Judge Cornwall refuses to hear the case again," Con reminded him.

"That's why your father and I will be going to Helena as soon as we leave here. Your father and Preston Leslie go back a long way. I know Leslie, too. I worked with him before on mining claim disputes. He's a good Democrat and your father has assured me...well, he's going to present the evidence and ask for a full pardon."

"If I'm innocent, why do I need a pardon?" Con asked, his mind playing tricks on him. Maybe it was all this talking. He was out of practice, but his rational side had begun to function.

"We'll get you released on a pardon for now, then apply for a full acquittal later," David explained.

"When?" Con asked.

"Within the week."

Con lowered his voice. "If I don't hear from you in a week, I'm going out my own way."

"Don't do anything to spoil all this, Con," David whispered. "We've been working very hard to come up with this evidence. Please be patient and wait a little longer."

"For seven days," Con replied in a soft whisper. "I've been working on the wall. I know where it's still weak. Get me out of here within the week or I'm breaking out." He glanced at the guard and raised his voice. "Do you have word from Bethea?" He pulled his own letter to her from his shirt and exchanged it for three from Matthias.

He started to open the earliest one. "Is she settling into living at Alice?"

"Five of the children are home so they can attend school," Matthias said. "Adam and Hallie are still with her in the valley. She's coming home when the boys bring the cows down."

Con looked up from Bethea's letter. "She shouldn't be there alone."

"Jacob and Broderick check on her regularly," Matthias said. "Broderick visited her folks while he was in Missouri. The fat really hit the fire when she found out he'd told her family about her problems. They want her to move back to Missouri."

Con ripped into the second envelope. "Is she?"

"She wrote them that she's not setting foot outside the territory until she has her husband with her, and then it will be to visit only."

Con smiled and opened the third letter and read the first few pages. "Uncle Tendoi paid her a visit. Great. I wanted to take her to Lemhi." He continued to read the letter. His eyes scanned the last page and the color drained from his face. "No," he growled. "This can't be. She must be mistaken."

"Con, what's wrong?" David asked.

Con handed him the sixth page of the letter and buried his face in his hands.

"Oh, God, Con," David said. "This should be a time of joy, but I know how you must feel." He handed the page to Matthias.

Matthias read the page and handed it back to Con. A deathly pall settled on them. "A new grandchild." Matthias stared at Con. "I suppose congratulations are in order."

"It's the worst thing that could have happened," Con said.

"Then we'll turn it into the best," David Addison said, rising from his chair. "We'll get you out of here first, then get you married to that pretty little woman of yours again."

A WEEK PASSED and Con heard nothing from his father or his attorney. They had failed in their efforts to free him. They'd done their best, but had held out hope based on grains of sand that must have shifted unexpected.

He made his decision during another trip to the pit. Learning of Bethea's condition had shattered his ability to concentrate, but in the pitch black of the hole, he saw the situation in a new light. She would not go through this pregnancy alone. He wanted this child. The hope of sharing this time with Bethea was the incentive he needed to seek his freedom.

On his fourth day back in his cell, he stared at the lumps in his bowl and the clabbered cream that smelled sour. "This is the last bowl of mush I'll ever eat in this hell hole," he said silently to Chugan.

Because of his strength and willingness to work hard, he had been reassigned to the fence repair crew. They worked from before dawn until darkness. The guards had speculated on his endurance. They would never know that the white man Conrad Adler worked the morning shift, his Indian brother Chugan took over for the rest of the day.

He'd been able to hide a piece of iron to use as a weapon if they tried to stop him. It was buried beneath debris in the grass near the fence they'd been working on. In the confusion of quitting work and gathering their tools, he would slip through an opening he'd left in the fence and head to the willows. If he reached the willows, he knew he could reach the trees, and then the hills.

Darkness would be falling and they wouldn't be able to track him until morning, unless they had a pack of dogs. Did they? Chugan should have thought of the possibility of hounds. He would be without a jacket but exposure to the elements would be a minuscule price for his freedom.

The prisoners finished the morning shift on the wall and went inside for the noon meal, then returned for the next seven hour shift. While Chugan worked, Con wondered if other inmates would try to follow them. He hoped not. Others would have to make their own plans, he decided.

He planned to travel the old stage route from Deer Lodge to Bannack City. Abandoned since the coming of the railroad, the trail was identifiable to a person who knew the lay of the land.

His stallion had been returned to Alice, so he would skirt Bannack and head over the hills to Alice, get Hellion and ride like the devil to Centennial Valley. If they caught him, they'd have to kill him, because he wasn't coming back.

The sun edged toward the horizon. One more hour and he would be a free man or a dead one.

A young man from the administration office ran across the yard and showed a piece of paper to one of the guards, but the convicts knew better than to stop their work.

"Conrad Adler, over here," the guard called.

Damn it, Con thought. Had someone found his piece of iron? He dropped his shovel into the rack and walked to the guard, but didn't say a word. This was no time to get into trouble.

"Wheeler wants to see you," the guard said, his voice sounding civil.

"What?"

The man in street clothes took his arm and led him toward the building with the shower. "Shower. I'll get your clothes," the man said.

Dumbfounded, Con stripped the white and black striped baggy shirt and trousers from his sweaty body and let them drop to the floor. He turned the controls to the shower room and stepped inside. The water was icy but his body had become immune.

His mind raced over the possibilities.

This was a mistake. They knew of his plans and were taking him to the pit again. But why would they have him clean up and change clothes?

He had been declared insane and he was on his way to Warm Springs, Chugan countered. *Wasn't that what he'd been wanting?*

He planned to take matters into his own hands, Con argued.

They wanted another inmate with a similar name, Chugan teased.

He wouldn't tell them of their mistake, Con insisted.

Be patient, Chugan cautioned. *Either way, he'd be outside the walls and he could make his getaway.*

After he reached the rinsing shower, the showers were turned off and he glanced over his shoulder. The man who had brought him inside tossed him a clean towel.

"Can I talk?" Con asked.

"Sure."

"This is the first clean towel I've used since I came here. What's the occasion?" He pulled on his underwear and trousers, then shoved his arms into the sleeves of a soft chambray shirt that he had never expected to wear again. Next to a chair were his boots and a pair of woolen socks.

"You're about to become a free man, Mr. Adler," the man said, handing him his familiar felt hat he'd worn on more roundups than he could remember.

"Free?"

The man motioned him to follow him. In minutes they were in the U. S. marshal's office.

Wheeler motioned him to a chair.

"Am I really free?"

Wheeler nodded. "I don't know how your family pulled it off, but Governor Leslie says that you're to be released, pending a retrial."

"I didn't murder the man," Con said. "He's still alive."

Wheeler scratched his head. "Damned confusing if you ask me, but I reckon I'll read all about it in the newspaper someday. Hey, what does that make the woman you married?"

Con squinted to the marshal. "She's still the woman I love and we're going to be married again. May I go now?"

"Not yet," Wheeler said. "Do you have money?"

"I came with ten dollars."

Wheeler handed Con an envelope. "This money is from Governor Leslie's office. I don't understand it, but my instruction are give you a travel authorization. Buy yourself a ticket on the evening train to Dillon. Your father and attorney will meet you there. In Dillon, you're to go see the sheriff. He'll give you a paper authorizing an official release. Then you're a free man."

Con got to his feet. "Are you sure?"

Wheeler came around his desk to the outside door. "Have you grown so fond of this hell hole that you want to go back to your cell?" he asked, holding it open and speaking to the guard outside. "Get the hell out of here, Adler, and don't come back."

CON WAITED at the door of the passenger car when the train rolled into the depot in Dillon, but before he could get off, Sheriff Jones shoved him back into the car. Matthias Adler and David Addison followed close behind the sheriff.

"We're meeting Mrs. Adler at Red Rock," the sheriff said.

"Bethea?" Con asked.

"Victoria," Jones said. "She sent a wire a half hour ago that a man who fit Kingston's description had come to the ranch looking for Bethea. She's meeting the train at Red Rock."

The four men rode south in silence for several miles. "Glad to see you out, Con," the sheriff said.

"Good to have you home, son," Matthias said.

The smile Con managed to find was fainthearted. "I was planning to break out tonight. Tonight! Damn, I could have gotten myself killed and all the while been a free man."

David motioned to Con's head. "Other than your hat that doesn't fit, you look good."

"His hair will grow back, but he looks thin," Matthias said.

"I never felt so bad as when I had to take you to Deer Lodge," Jones said. "Cornwall and Mellon are the ones who belong there."

"Do they know I'm out?"

Sheriff Jones shrugged. "I haven't had time to make the proper announcement. Do you want to do it?"

"I'd like to kill the bastards, but I don't intend to return to Deer Lodge. Hell Hole is a rightful name for that place."

At Red Rock, Sheriff Jones asked the engineer to delay departure for a few extra minutes. They left the train and Victoria Adler ran to them.

"Con, you're free," she exclaimed, throwing her arms around his neck and kissing his cheek. She turned to the others. "I'm so frightened for Bethea."

"Tell us what happened," Matthias said, putting his good arm around her shoulders.

"A stranger came to the door asking for Bethea," she explained. "I told him Bethea wasn't home. He wouldn't give his name, but when he turned to leave, Faith and Esther saw him. I was alarmed when they waved and ran to him as if they knew him.

She turned to Con. "He knelt down and actually talked to them. My heart stopped when I realized he was the same man who'd come before but now he wore a beard. I was so stupid, so blind. I tried to get the girls away from him, but they were thrilled to see him and told him Bethea was in the valley before I could stop them. I grabbed your shotgun and ordered him off our property. I must have been crazy to confront him. He's a mad man."

"How long ago?" the sheriff asked.

She looked at the clock on the wall. "Long enough to catch the earlier train. I left the children with Rebecca and Stub and rode here as quickly as I could and wired the sheriff. If he gets off at Monida, surely the Burns will recognize him. Maybe Bill will keep him there."

"If not, he's on his way to the cabin already," Con said. "Can't we get moving? Her life is in danger."

"I brought Hellion with me," Victoria said, giving Con a quick hug. "I knew you'd need a dependable horse."

"Thank you, Mother," he said, then went to load the horse into one of the freight cars.

Matthias kissed Victoria. "Go to the children and keep them inside. Lock all the doors and get some of the cowboys to stand guard. He might decide to double back for the children."

The sheriff waved to the engineer and the train rolled from the station. At the depot at Monida, Emiline and Bill Burns were startled to see Con alight from the train, but insisted they had not seen Clifford Kingston.

"I'd know that son of a bitch anywhere," Bill assured the sheriff. "I'd shoot first and ask questions later."

"I'm riding to the cabin," Con said, running to the freight car and leading Hellion down the ramp in minutes. "Get some saddle horses from Bill and catch up with me."

BETHEA SHOOK THE LAST laundered bed sheet out and hung it over a bush to dry. She'd finished a large wash, the first she'd done since the children had returned to Alice to attend school. The sun began to set as she completed the laborious task of finding places to spread the items. How she longed for a clothes line and poles.

The imaginary picture of her children attending an official school pleased her immensely. Only the four older children had ever had any formal schooling. She had done her best to keep their skills progressing, but she knew she'd grown lax as her pregnancy with Hallie had advanced.

She smiled as she looked around her at all the laundry draped bushes. Once the sun went down, the cabin would look as if it was surrounded by ghosts. The grasses had begun to turn brown and several mornings she had awakened to frost on the ground outside the cabin.

Within a month, the lake would begin to ice over and the swans would leave. For now, she would enjoy these final few weeks of serenity. A pair of swans had nested in the old rushes and raised five fine cygnets. The thought of their leaving saddened her.

"If only Con were here," she murmured. She had so much to tell him. Later in the evening, after the dishes were washed, she planned to write in her journal.

Feelings for Con had run strong all afternoon, almost as if he were calling to her. When the journal entry was finished, she would write him a long letter and tell him about the spirits she had felt during the day. He would think she was losing her mind for sure.

By now he knew of the baby. She hadn't seen Matthias since he'd taken the letter. Doubts had assailed her after writing him the news. He had enough concerns without taking on hers.

375

As the weeks had passed, she'd had a chance to adjust to the reality of another child so soon. Hallie would be seventeen months old. She was already walking from the table to the bed without losing her balance.

Bethea felt a warm glow come over her. She had never minded being pregnant, but in the past she had used her condition to keep Clifford at bay. Now she wanted to lie in Con's arms and have him make love to her again and again. Knowledge of their child within her seemed to heightened her physical need for him.

She would visit a physician once she left the valley. Out of curiosity, she would ask him if being intimate with one's husband was advisable for a woman in her condition. Perhaps not for this pregnancy, but once Con was released, she would want to have another child. His children would be nine and a half years apart, she thought, almost like raising separate families.

She gathered her wicker basket and trudged up the pathway. *It's a good tired*, she thought. Con had been gone for more than two months and she still missed him terrible, but the pain had receded to a dull ache in the quiet of the evenings.

In the distance, a rider appeared. The horse was unfamiliar. She knew most of the horses and riders from the Alice ranch. They always stopped in for a meal or a cup of coffee. She knew they were following orders, and the thought that someone cared was comforting.

From inside the cabin, she heard Adam scolding Hallie who had decided to play during supper. Bethea quickened her steps in order to meet the horseman before he reached the door. She didn't like strangers coming to the cabin so late in the evening. She tossed the basket inside and turned to greet the horseman.

CHAPTER TWENTY-NINE

CLIFFORD KINGSTON, WEARING a scruffy reddish blond beard, dismounted and smiled as he approached her. "Dinner ready?" he asked. He rubbed his dirty hands together and stepped closer. "I haven't eaten all day, honey. Are you glad to see you bone weary old husband home again?"

"What are you doing here?" Bethea gasped. "You should be dead. You have to be."

He grinned and stepped closer, rubbing his hand across his beard. "You seem surprised to see me, Mrs. Kingston."

She stepped away. "I'm Mrs. Conrad Adler now."

He smiled. "Not as far as I'm concerned. I had a devil of a time tracking you down. I stopped here in early June but no one was here. It looked as if you'd packed up and moved. I found a picture of you and that breed. I almost threw it in the fire, but I figured what the hell, someday we'd all get a laugh out of it."

She stepped to the door. "You have no right to be here."

"Says who? That half-breed lover of yours?"

The expression on his face reminded her of a rabid wolf she'd seen once. She stiffened. "He's my husband now."

He leered at her. "You may have been fucking him, but you're my wife. Now invite me in. I rode all day to get here."

A flicker of hope surfaced as she looked at him. "Did you get off at Monida?" If the Burns couple had seen him, they would send a message to the sheriff in Dillon. Maybe Jacob Dingley would stop by to visit her. Her heart sank. Jacob had passed by on his way back to Alaska Basin the previous day and she had assured him all was well.

"I got off at Spring Hill and cut across the hills," he said, stepping closer. He grabbed her shoulders and jerked her against him, pressing a wet kiss on her mouth. His breath smelled of whiskey and sharp cheese. "Feed me," he ordered, shoving her inside.

Adam whirled from the dry sink where he'd been washing the supper dishes. "Pa?" The boy dropped his wet cloth, his mouth gaping. "Pa, you're supposed to be dead."

"Be quiet, Adam," Bethea warned. "Your father is hungry and we'll feed him, then he can leave."

Clifford chuckled. "I'm spending the night, maybe longer." He sauntered to the stove and peered into a roasting pan. "A slab of this beef on some of your fine bread will do. Good looking meat. Where'd you get it?"

"It's Alice Livestock beef," Bethea said. "Con's father insisted we take it."

"Living on charity?"

She bit the retort on her tip of her tongue. "Adam, where's Hallie?" she asked, looking around the room.

"Climbing in and out of her box," Adam said. "She's a monkey. Pa, you should see our new sister. She's real pretty and smart, too, right, Hallie?" he called.

Toddling from the back room, the ten-months old baby girl wobbled, lost her balance and fell. She got to her feet again, took several more steps and managed to balance against the block of wood that served as a night stand by the bed. She grinned at Adam, then Bethea, but when she spotted Clifford, her little face screwed up.

Bethea swept the baby up into her arms, brushing her curly black hair from her face. "It's okay, little one, this is your...papa." The words sounded vile to her ears.

Clifford looked up from his meat and bread and studied the baby. "She don't look like the rest of my kids. Are you sure she's mine?"

"Pa, of course she's yours," Adam said. He went to Hallie and made a face and the baby giggled and slapped at him.

Clifford took another bite, his mouth opening with each chew. After he swallowed, he took a long swig from a flask he pulled from his vest pocket. "She looks mixed-blood to me," he said without looking at the child again.

Bethea prayed for someone to come knocking at the door. "She's yours, Clifford." *I wish she wasn't.* He finished his meal and wiped his mouth on his sleeve. She had never seen him in such an unkept condition. "Where have you been?"

He tipped his chair back on its back legs and smiled at her. "Well, let's see, in May I was sitting at a table in a chop shop in Eagle Rock reading about a honeymoon trip being taken by Mr. and

Mrs. Adler as if the bride had a right to sleeping with another man. The article didn't say where they'd gone, only that they'd high tailed it to Butte for the ceremony."

"We visited the geysers," she said, unable to resist taunting him.

He leered at her. "A few months later, I happened to pass through the county seat while a notorious murder trial was going on. Seems the very same Mr. and Mrs. Adler had plotted to kill her husband. Know anything about it?"

Adam's eyes began to narrow. "Pa, Mr. Adler went to prison for ten years for killing you, but if you're here, he couldn't of done it."

"He sure the hell shot me," Clifford said.

"He was honest enough to report it and it cost him his freedom," Bethea said. "I saw the body, Clifford. I told them it wasn't you, but he was about your size. Who was he?"

Clifford smiled, then bent to pull his boots off. "Son, give me a hand here," he called.

Reluctantly, Adam knelt at his father's feet and helped remove the worn boots. He turned away quickly and coughed as the room filled with the strong odor.

"Who was the dead man?" Bethea asked again.

"He was a no account tramp who crossed me," Clifford said.

"You shot him, Pa?" Adam asked. "Why?"

"He tried to steal some money," Clifford said. "He said he was hungry but when we stopped in Spring Hill, he didn't buy himself a meal. He said he was broke, but I knew he was lying. We hitched a ride in a boxcar with two other men. He jumped me while I was asleep and tried to steal my money, and I blew his face off." Clifford ran his finger around the rim of his plate, then licked it. "Good meat, even if it is Alice beef."

"But those two men insisted he was you. Why?" Bethea asked.

"A few coins can grease a lot of palms." Clifford looked at her as if he considered her an imbecile.

"I figured Adler was dead, too, until I read you'd married him," he said. "I couldn't believe Adler would be stupid enough to confess, but I went crazy thinking of you sleeping with a breed, you so righteous and proper. Meeting up with this guy from Illinois was a perfect way to get even. They both said he looked enough like me to pass for my brother, so I got this idea. If I was declared dead, I'd start over with a clean slate. Proud of your old husband?"

"You bastard!" She had to get out of his sight before she did something that might endanger the children. She headed toward the back room. As she busied herself with the beds, she tried to think of a way to escape. She looked up at the small window. It didn't open. If she broke out the glass, he would come to investigate. She would be trapped and her children in peril. No, she would have to think of another way to escape.

When Bethea returned to the outer room, Hallie stood at the corner of the bed, clinging to the brass bed post and staring at Clifford, her green eyes reflecting her uncertainty. Adam sat stiffly on a chair answering questions from his father in terse one-word replies.

Bethea smoothed the folds of her blue skirt and garnered her courage. "Clifford, you must go."

He looked surprised. "I'm sleeping right here in this brass bed. I bought it. It's mine. And you'll sleep in it with me. It's been a long time since I was with a white woman who didn't charge me for every fondle."

"Clifford, please don't talk that way in front of the children," she warned.

Clifford grinned. "Adam is a big boy. Why, he's almost a man himself. I'll bet he thinks about the girls he's seen flaunting themselves when he's in town."

Adam blushed. "I've only been to town a few times, Pa. I went with Grandpa Adler for supplies, and once with Grandma Adler for some clothes...and to court."

"Don't call them Grandpa and Grandma," Clifford shouted, his hand dropping to the revolver in the holster at his hip.

Bethea shook her head slightly and hoped Adam would understand.

"Those people are out of our lives now," Clifford said. "Tomorrow we'll hitch up the wagon and go get your sisters and brothers. I'm taking you all back to Missouri. I've got money now. It's stashed in Virginia City. I'm damned sick of this territory. Nothing good has happened to me here. We're going home. Now, get to bed!"

Adam flinched and glanced helplessly at Bethea.

"You're wrong, Clifford," she said, swinging Hallie up in her arm and taking Adam's shoulder. "My attorney closed the accounts. The money is now in my name in an account in Dillon. You can't touch it."

"Why the hell did he do that? That's my money!"

"You were presumed dead, thanks to your own doing," Bethea said, fighting to keep her voice even.

"Then we'll go into Dillon tomorrow and you can get it back out," Clifford insisted. "You're my wife and what you have is mine. The law says so." He settled back into his chair and smiled confidently across the room where she and the children stood pressed against the dry sink.

An idea came to her. "Clifford, the children must go to the necessary before they go to bed. We broke our chamber pot."

Clifford waved his hand. "Then sent them out."

"Hallie needs help," she said. "She's just learned to not be afraid. Sitting up on that seat can be frightening for a baby. We make a game of it."

"Adam can help her," Clifford said. "You've turned him into a damned woman anyway, doing dishes and caring for babies."

"I have to go with her so she won't cry," Bethea replied. "She can't go when she cries. Adam, get your warm coat and Hallie's, too. Please hurry."

"But it's not cold outside," Adam said, then stopped, staring at her.

"You have chores to do before you can go to bed," she reminded him. "Just because your father is home doesn't mean we can neglect our chores. Please get your warmest coats."

"Yes, ma'am," the boy said, disappearing into the back room. When he returned, she helped Hallie into a bulky coat she'd sized down from one of Faith's. "We'll be back when the chores are done," Bethea said, holding the door open for the children.

"Well, hurry up, woman, I'm not going to wait all night," Clifford called.

Outside, darkness had settled but a full moon was about to make its appearance. The eastern horizon glowed with promise.

"Ma, I'm sorry," Adam whispered. "I hated Mr. Adler for shooting Pa, but it's Pa who's the bad man. He framed Mr. Adler, didn't he?"

"Yes, Adam," she replied. "Now hurry along."

"Has he always been like that?" Adam asked. Before she could answer, he spoke again. "I reckon he has. He never said a good thing to Ben or me. He never did keep a single promise he made. Ma, I'm sorry."

She hugged him. "You were his son and you made excuses for him. We all did." She looked off into the darkness.

"What are we going to do now, Ma?"

"First you go inside and take care of your business. I'll think of something." She waited until he returned, then gripped his thin shoulders. "Adam, listen to me. Your father doesn't expect us for a while. Saddle your horse."

"But Ma, the chores..."

"Saddle your horse," she hissed. "I want you to take Hallie and ride as fast as you can to Monida. Tell Mr. and Mrs. Burns that Clifford is here." She glanced at the cabin. "Tell them to send for the sheriff."

"But what if he hurts you?" Adam asked. "He's mean, Ma."

"I know, darling, but I can take care of myself." She kissed his cheek. "Saddle the horse while I take Hallie inside. I'll meet you at the barn. The moon will give you some light, but you must ride carefully."

When she and Hallie met him in the barn, he was mounted and waiting. She handed the baby up to him and waited until Hallie was settled in front of him in the saddle. Taking the reins, she led the horse from the barn and away from the cabin, through the aspens for several hundred yards, then onto the road. She gazed up at her children, wondering if she would ever see them again.

"Your father was right, Adam. You *are* almost a man, and this is a man's job I'm asking you to do. If...if something happens to me, tell the children I loved them."

Adam's eyes glistened. "Ma, don't say that."

"Just ride as fast and as safely as you can and get help," she said. Hallie started to whimper.

"Go!" she cried and turned away.

As the darkness swallowed her children, she turned toward the cabin and Clifford Kingston.

THE RIDERS FROM MONIDA made their way over the rocky trail for two hours when the moon rose over the eastern mountains to light the night sky.

"We've got to make better time," Con said, kicking Hellion in his flanks.

"And break an animal's leg?" the sheriff warned. "We'll be there by sun up."

Con reined the stallion back to a reasonable pace. How could he be so close yet so far from Bethea? What if Kingston had taken a different route and was already at the cabin? If the man so much as touched Bethea, Con would kill him, no questions asked. It didn't matter if others witnessed the crime or not.

They reached the abandoned cabin that marked the halfway point and stopped to rest the horses, then rode again.

Hours later, Con saw movement on the trail ahead. "Someone's coming. Be alert."

Several minutes later the horse and rider reached them.

"This is Sheriff Jones," Jones called. "Who goes there? Speak up or risk getting a piece of lead in your gullet."

"It's me, Adam Kingston," the boy called. "I have Hallie."

Con slid from his saddle and grabbed the boy's leg. "Are you all right?" He swept Hallie into his arms and hugged her tightly. In spite of their time apart, she seemed to remember him, smiling as he kissed her cheek. He turned to the boy. "Where's your mother?"

"She's at the cabin."

"Alone?" Con clutched the boy's knee.

Adam began to sob. "My pa is there and he's got a gun." He wiped his cheeks. "She said to ride to Monida for help. You gotta help her. I'm scared he's gonna kill her or beat her again. I'm sorry for what my pa did to you. I was wrong to say what I did about you."

"It's okay now, Adam." Con turned to David Addison and handed him the baby. "David, take her and the boy to the hotel and wait for us there. The rest of us can be there before daybreak if we don't waste any more time."

David nodded. "Let's go, Adam."

Con knew the children were in good hands. He kicked Hellion into a cautious canter and headed east.

WHEN BETHEA returned to the cabin, Clifford had made himself another sandwich. Only his chewing broke the silence. She wondered how long before he noticed the children's absence.

"Where's the kid?" he asked before shoving the last bite into his mouth.

"She went with her brother," Bethea said. "She likes to pet the horses."

Another hour passed. Bethea sat stiffly on a chair at the table, pretending to study a mail order catalog and wondering what kind of progress her children had made on the trail.

"Those kids are dawdling," Clifford said.

"I sent them away."

"What the hell?" He jumped from his chair and grabbed the front of her dress, jerking her from her chair. "You did what?"

"They're gone. We're alone."

He grinned. "It's been a long time since we've fooled around alone."

She grasped for straws. "I'm having my monthly flow."

He frowned and shoved her back into the chair. "Just my luck." He stared at her and she shifted uncomfortably. " Aren't you curious about what happened?"

"When?"

"Hell, when I shot Adler." He rubbed his whiskers. "I shot him in the chest. He should have dropped dead on the spot, but he rode away. Those Injuns don't even die like white men."

She studied her hands. "We found him the next morning, near death, but I saved him."

"Well, someone saved me, too," he bragged. "Being gut shot isn't the easiest way to take a bullet, but it didn't hit any vital parts. A band of renegade Snakes found me and I traded them whiskey for some medical care. I stayed with the filthy bastards for two weeks, then promised them the rest of the barrel if they would take me to Eagle Rock. If they hadn't found me, I would have froze to death. The shot went clean through me."

"Con said he hit you twice," Bethea murmured.

"He nicked me and I played dead," he replied. "I knew I'd hit him in the chest and it was just a matter of time before he went to his happy hunting ground." He grinned across the table. "Tell me, Bethea, how long before you took him as your lover? I thought he'd already had you, but he said no. Did you let him into your bed right away?"

"I was eight months with child," she reminded him.

"Inconvenient, heah?"

He studied her for several minutes. "He probably can't read. Did you entertain him by reading your obscene stories out loud to him. Is that how you got him riled up?"

"He reads fluently," she retorted. "He's a graduate of Boston University. He's well educated."

"Then he must have been quite a novelty for those damned easterners. Is he a good lover? What does he do to you that I didn't?"

"He's gentle. He doesn't hurt me."

Clifford chuckled. "Women like to feel pain. It's gets them excited. Damn, just talking about this makes me hot. Too bad we can't do it tonight."

"Then you'll go?"

"I'll sleep on it," he said, getting to his feet. He dragged the table to the door, shoving it firmly against it to form a barricade. "Now lie down."

"I'm not sleepy," she said.

He lifted the revolver part way from its holster. "Get into the bed. I want a woman beside me even if I can't have any fun."

"I won't undress."

"Fine, but lie down."

Hating herself for giving in, she crawled onto the bed to lie along the far edge. He turned out the lamp and the bed creaked as he lay down beside her. In the darkness, she tried to concentrate on Con, recalling the memories this bed held for them. Having Clifford contaminate even the quilt top was a sacrilege.

His breathing softened and she hoped he had fallen asleep. She waited another hour before she eased up from her pillow. A hand grabbed her wrist and twisted. She dropped back to the bed, her breathing ragged with fear as she waited for daylight to come. Another hour passed.

Images swam before her; Con and herself beside a brook eating a picnic dinner of fried chicken. He offered her a bite and refused to give it to her until she kissed him, a price she gladly paid. A man's hand touched her breast.

"Con, is that you?" she murmured, drifting from her dream to reality. "Con, kiss me. Make love to me," she whispered. "I miss you so much."

The hand stroked her abdomen and the pulsating area below, then returned to her breast. A burst of pain shot through her and her eyes flew open.

"You're a lying bitch. You ain't wearing a rag or nothing else, and the minute I touched you, you began to squirm like a whore. Get that dress off."

"Clifford, don't do this," she pleaded, searching the room for her bearings. The room had turned gray with morning light.

"Get it off or I'll rip it off," he said, his breath brushing her cheek as he yanked the buttoned collar at her throat. A cool draft brushed her left shoulder as the fabric gave way.

"I...I'm pregnant again," she said, her heart exploding in her chest. "It's Con's child."

His expression made her want to laugh and she took advantage of his confusion. She spotted the gun and holster hanging on the brass bed post near his feet. Leaping to her feet, she scrambled around the bed, grabbed the holster, and pulled the gun free.

"Don't you ever touch me. Only Con has that right."

Clifford sat up. Ignoring her completely, he put on his boots and rearranged his trousers. His arousal made his body look deformed. The thought of him invading her nauseated her as she cocked the hammer and pointed the gun directly at him. "You touch me and I'll blow you to Kingdom Come," she threatened. She stepped away from the bed until she felt the wall behind her. Using her hip, she edged the table away from the door, then felt behind her until her hand touched the leather pull. "Stay there or I'll pull this trigger."

He stood up, grinning as he approached her. "Do you think I'd be foolish enough to leave a loaded gun for you to use?"

"You're lying," she said, easing the door opened, trying her best to keep her fear under control.

"You might as well give up, Bethea. You're lying about carrying his child. You figure that would make me change my mind, but it hasn't. I want to see what he finds so fascinating. We're going to spend this morning making love."

"You don't know how to make love," she cried. "You only know how to hurt and degrade a woman. You're scum, and I want to see you dead." She closed her eyes and pulled the trigger.

Nothing happened and her eyes flew open.

He smiled, working his way alongside the bed. She pulled the trigger again and a click sounded, then another. Chuckling, he started approach her. She yanked the leather thong and pulled the door open, then threw the gun. He flinched when it hit his cheek and she took advantage of his distraction to race from the cabin.

She flew down the path past the spring house, stumbling on a root and catching her balance. If she hid in the willows, surely he would give up and leave.

Near the edge of the lake, she crouched, listening for his footsteps. Minutes passed, then she heard a branch snap. She swallowed her panic and waited. Through the bushes, she saw his trouser legs move past her on the path. She waited until he returned. For the first time, she saw the rifle in his hand.

When he reached the spring, he stopped. "Bethea, give up. If I shoot the brush, I might hurt you."

Panic stricken, she stood up and ran. A shot zinged past her shoulder and she changed direction, running directly into the shallow lake. The dry fabric of her skirt billowed, then slowly sank as the water surged around her thighs. Her weight became her enemy and her feet sank into the bottom. She tried to pull her foot free but her boot clung to the bottom as if it were nailed down.

Clifford reached the shoreline and grinned at her as he waded into the water. When she stepped backward, she lost her balance and fell. The murky water filled her mouth and she gasped and choked. A hand pulled on her hair, helping her to balance, and she opened her eyes.

Clifford gathered her against him with his free arm, his other hand holding the rifle out of the water. "We'll go back now, Bethea," he groaned in her ear. "Behave yourself and I promise not to hurt you. If you'd told me before you didn't like the pain, I would have tried something different."

She struggled, her arms flailing against him. He bit the torn fabric at her shoulder and yanked on it, exposing most of her breast. His head dipped and his tongue touched her flesh.

"Leave me alone," she sobbed. "Leave me alone." She worked one foot free from the boot stuck in the muck and brought it up hard against his groin.

He grunted, but his hold on her waist never slackened. She kneed him again and he let her go. "Damned bitch," he shouted, swinging the rifle at her head and clipping her temple.

She reeled, her arms flailing the air as she tried to fought to keep her balance. He pulled her against him again.

Behind them, a voice thundered through the cool morning air. "Let her go, Kingston."

Clifford's hold slackened and Bethea pulled free.

She turned.

Con Adler dismounted from his prized stallion. He looked different, yet he was the same. He waded into the water, reaching out to her.

She strained to reach him but the tentacles of the undergrowth encircled her legs. When their fingers touched, Con clutched her hand and pulled her into his arms.

"Adler, you're a fool," Kingston shouted. "You're not even armed. You can die with her," he screamed, lifting the rifle to his shoulder and sighting down the barrel.

CHAPTER THIRTY

CON STARED AT THE RIFLE BARREL pointed directly between Bethea's shoulders. He hadn't come this far to let her die in his arms. He swung her around in the water, her skirts wrapping around his legs. The water rose up to his hips as they sank in the mire.

He turned his back to Kingston, clutching her in his arms. Gazing down at her terrified face, he kissed her lightly. "I love you," he murmured, then tightened his hold on her and waited for the searing pain of the bullet to tear into his body. He prayed that the bullet would stay within his chest and not wound Bethea as well. He wrapped his arms tighter around her, pressed his mouth against her hair, and began to count the seconds.

This is the end, he thought, regretting not having had time to tell her all his hopes and dreams for their future that had enabled him to endure the previous two months.

Two shots deafened his ears and he flinched, but no burning pain followed. Had he died so quickly he'd been spared the pain of the bullet ripping through his body? Bethea stirred in his arms and he gazed down at her.

"Are you hurt?" he murmured.

She tried to speak, but her voice failed her.

"Neither am I." He looked toward the shore.

On the shore T. W. Jones and Matthias Adler stood side by side, each with a smoking revolver in his hand.

He glanced over his shoulder. In the water, Kingston's lifeless body bobbed beneath the surface of the lake, his blood coloring the surface in a growing circle.

"Take her to the cabin," Matthias said as they waded past.

Without looking back, Con put his arm around Bethea's waist and supported her weight as he led her from the lake. At the cabin door, he paused. "Do you have dry clothing?" he asked.

She nodded.

Inside, he searched a trunk and found undergarments. In minutes he had her out of her wet clothes, her shivering body rubbed down with a clean towel, and into white cotton drawers and a petticoat. He knelt and slid on a pair of dry shoes on her feet, then started to get to rise.

Her hand touched his bare head, brushing the short hair that had just begun to lay down. When he got to his feet, her arms encircled his waist and she clung to him for several minutes.

"I can't believe you're here," she whispered. "Con, you saved my life, but you risked your own. I would prefer it be the other way around, my darling."

"Hush, sweetheart," he crooned. "You're safe and I'm free, and we have each other. What more could we ask for?" He brushed her wet hair away from her face, lifting it off her back before laying a kiss on the wing of one pale shoulder. "Let's get you dressed before you catch cold," he said.

He selected a purple calico with tiny white flowers and dropped it over her head, waiting for her to slip her arms through the sleeves. When the buttons were fastened, he turned her around and began toweling her hair, then brushed it dry to cascade around her shoulders.

He spun her around several times and her skirt billowed around their legs. "More beautiful than I remembered," he said, smiling. He cupped her cheeks in his palms. "Now tell me the truth. Are you carrying my child?"

"Yes. It happened that night before the trial, when we were careless." She lowered her gaze. "I'm sorry, Con, I know you didn't want this to happen."

"I was upset when I read your letter, but that was when I felt so hopeless," he said. "Now I can think of nothing that pleases me more." He gathered her in his arms and as his lips covered hers, she sank against him, sliding her arms up around his neck.

When he lifted his mouth and she caught her breath, she smiled. Her hand brushed the back of his head. "Your face is still as handsome as ever, but this hair cut is a bit short, don't you think?"

They laughed for the first time in months.

"It wasn't my choice," he replied.

A soft knock sounded at the cabin door.

"Come in," Con called, letting his hand settle on her waist as his father entered.

"We're leaving," Matthias said. "You can follow us later." He looked at Bethea. "Clifford Kingston is dead."

She pressed her face against Con's shirt.

"Who shot him?" Con asked.

"We don't know."

Bethea looked at Matthias. "How did he die?"

"A bullet between the eyes," Matthias replied. "We both have the same caliber guns and only one bullet hit its mark. He died instantly." He came across the room and touched Bethea's shoulder. "I'm sorry, Bethea, there was no other way. It was him or you two. I wasn't going to lose either of you, not after all we've been through."

"He was a terrible man," she said, "but his children need to know that I took care of him in the end. I'll see that he's given a decent burial in Dillon."

Matthias hugged them. "I've said some unpleasant words to you, Bethea, and I'm sorry. I've always wanted my son to find happiness and I know he has. Not every man gets a new daughter and seven ready-made grandchildren in the bargain." He nodded solemnly and walked to the door. "We'll meet you at the hotel in Monida and send a message to Victoria. She'll be very excited about having a new grandchild."

"Tendoi says it will be a son," Bethea said, glancing up at Con. "Can he really know?"

"Time will tell," Con said, kissing her lightly.

Matthias rode away with the sheriff, Kingston's body draped over Kingston's saddle horse.

A half hour later, Con lifted Bethea onto Hellion's back and mounted behind her. He picked up the reins. "Let's go home, boy, and give this lady an easy ride. She's carrying my son."

He held her loosely in the circle of his arms as they traveled the thirty miles to the hotel. On the way he told her of the events that had brought him to the lake shore.

She looked up at him. "A moment later and it wouldn't have mattered."

"Ah, but it would have mattered so very much," he assured her.

391

Sally Garrett

EPILOGUE

October 6, 1887
Alice, Montana Territory

"IT'S LATE, BETHEA, come to bed," Con called from across the room.

"Not yet," she called. "I have to complete today's entry in my journal."

"But it's our wedding night," he called.

"Be patient, darling. We've had wedding nights before. You know what to expect."

He groaned. "That's why I need you over here. If you don't hurry, I'm going to turn over and go to sleep."

She smiled, confident that sleep was the last thing on his mind tonight. She opened the journal and found the last entry she had made. Picking up her pen, she dipped it into the crystal ink well and began to write.

"To my Kingston children, my yet unborn Adler children, and to all our grandchildren to come. I've reached the end of the third book and until I can purchase more, my entries will cease. As you read these journals, please be kind and judge not, for these were unusual times. Many would be less honest in their entries, but if I changed the story, it would not be ours.

"Now that I am once again married to my beloved Con, I am more positive than ever that our destinies crossed at the right time, at the right place, for I have never known such happiness as I feel when I am with him."

She looked up and found Con watching her. The quilt and blanket lay draped across his chest. He turned and propped his dark head on the heel of one hand, beckoning with his finger. His smile sent a surge of desire through her and she smiled in return. "In a moment, darling."

She tried to concentrate on the journal page.

"When we reached Monida several days ago, we spent the night there. Mr. and Mrs. Burns offered to take Adam and Hallie to the

ranch at Alice and we accepted, for we had a more difficult task ahead of us.

"Clifford's body was placed in a pine box and buried in the local cemetery. Con and I, Matthias Adler, David Addison, and T. W. Jones witnessed the burial.

"Clifford Kingston was a troubled man who never found peace. Con Adler and I have been more fortunate for we found each other. If you decide we have sinned, remember that we are human beings and the flesh can be weak. Try to forgive us.

"We were married this morning here at the Alice ranch," she continued writing. "Tendoi and his band came. I can still hear their laughter and talking outside for they have camped in the rolling meadow between our house and the brook.

"I say our house, because during the reception, my father-in-law announced that he and Victoria will be moving to the county seat. Matthias has been appointed to fill the unexpired term as Beaverhead County assessor who died unexpectedly and Matthias is of the same political party affiliation. He seems pleased and had vowed to run for the office when this partial term expires.

"He had hinted that he plans to scrutinize the assessed valuations of all the land and property owned by Judge Cornwall, Mr. Mellon, and every member of the jury who were responsible to Con's conviction. Such temptation would corrupt a weaker man, but Matthias Adler is an honorable one and I'm sure he will be fair in his dealings with these scoundrels.

"Our child will be born in mid April, 1888. If it is a boy as Tendoi has predicted, his name shall be Ian which means 'God is Gracious.' God has truly been gracious to us all.

If per chance we have a daughter, her name shall be Iris, which means 'rainbow,' for I have heard that there are eight colors in a rainbow and this child will be our eighth as well as our first.

Perhaps she will be called Ingrid, which means 'hero's daughter.' Can anyone deny that her father is a hero?

"But all this fretting over the name of our unborn child is of no consequence tonight, for my beloved husband waits and he is a desperate man, I fear. He keeps beckoning to me in the most enticing way.

"So, dear children and grandchildren, I know not where or how you may come across these three books, but read them and learn, be gentle in their care, treasure them with love, and judge us with kindness and compassion."

"Now I must say good-by, because my husband is on the verge of leaving his bed and coming for me. Few husbands and wives get to experience three weddings nights and have each one be more wonderful than the last. May you all find happiness as fulfilling as that which lies ahead of us."

She closed the book and tied the red ribbon, then put it away in the lower drawer of the white desk on top of the other two books. As she slid the drawer closed, she stood up and looked across the room.

Her heart began to thud against her ribs as she kicked off her slippers and loosened the tie at her throat. Tonight she wouldn't wait for him to make the overtures. Tonight she was truly his wife and their wedding gifts to each other would be their love.

--The End--

Centennial Swan

Acknowledgments

All characters in this book, including their names, personalities and events, with the exception of the information given below, have no existence outside the imagination of the author and have no relation whatsoever to anyone bearing the same name or names.

B. F. White operated a bank in Montana Territory in the 1880s.

Preston Leslie was the governor of Montana Territory at the time of Con Adler's incarceration.

Tendoi was a highly respected chief of the Lemhi Shoshoni tribe. He and his people traveled extensively in the lands depicted in the story.

Sheriff Will Jones held office during this time and was famous for "always getting his man."

William Wheeler was the warden at the Montana Territorial prison and the **Auburn** penal plan was in vogue there at the time.

The social customs and bigotry of the times are well documented in the area newspapers.

The winter of 1886-1887 was one of the worst ever experienced. The livestock losses in the county were fifty-sixty percent compared to eighty-ninety percent in the eastern section of the territory. These losses had lasting impact on the livestock industry and attitudes of land use.

Con Adler and his family are strictly the products of my imagination and the events told within these pages are purely fiction.

Bethea Kingston's spirit walked beside the author since 1988 each time the author visited the springs at the Lakeview campground in Centennial Valley. I'm sure in another time, she lived there. Her character is purely fictional, but her inner strengths have been validated by several women whose lives the author had researched, including but not limited to the following:

1) **Lillian Hackett Hanson Culver**, born 1850, who went to live in the Centennial Valley in 1887 and whose journals and photographs validate the conditions first hand. She died at age 86 still living near her beloved Picnic Springs in the upper end of the valley;

2) **Sarah Ann Graham Huff**, a petite woman who was born in 1830 and died in Dillon in 1910. She gave birth to her first child at age fifteen and remained slim and trim after giving birth to fourteen children from 1845 to 1874.

3) **Alma May Seybold Drown Anderson**, born 1880 in Glendale, Montana Territory. She became a widow with eight children on a desert

homestead after her husband was shot and killed in a gunfight in 1917 at Denning & Clark Sheep Company west of Dubois, Idaho. She maintained her household alone for several years before remarrying and having two more children.

An editor from a New York City publishing house once described this heroine and her story as "Unconventional." The manuscript was rejected on that basis.

The editor was correct. Bethea's story is unconventional and that is the way it's presented. These were turbulent times and Bethea found herself caught up in them.

I hope readers enjoy this story as much as I did researching and writing it. Con and Bethea are very much alive to me and I hope they will be for you as well. For the curious, Michael Adler, whom you met in *BACHELOR FROM BANNACK* is a direct descendant of Con and Bethea Adler.

If you wish to contact me, please do. Your letters keep the loneliness of writing at bay. Send mail to P. O. Box 212, Dillon MT 59725-0212.

Author Bio

Sally Garrett was born 16 Aug 1936 in Phoenix AZ. She moved to Montana in 1982 when she remarried.

Her prior professional background centered in managerial accounting. Since turning to free-lance writing, she has researched extensively and written about local southwest Montana history and family history articles.

This is her 13th novel. Her stories have been enjoyed around the world in more than a dozen languages. Her next contemporary novel scheduled is LISA: LOST AND FOUND, a sequel to her 1993 novel, BACHELOR FROM BANNACK. She has received the reversion rights to her first nine novels and has plans for them as well as four unpublished manuscripts.

She conducts family history and writing workshops and speaks on the ups and down of a "Writing Life," reproduces and interprets old photographs, and does genealogical research. Her four adult sons and five grandchildren are scattered across the United States. Her husband, Montie Dingley of Dillon MT, died in 1994. His family history has inspired many launching points for her fictional writing.

Sally Garrett

LISA: Lost and Found
excerpt from upcoming release

LISA ADLER GLANCED at the sheet of paper lying on the bucket seat of her Bronco. Although it was mid April, the heavy overcast sky had brought darkness early as the snow continued to fall. The digital clock on the dash read 6 p.m. Her appointment at the Hackett residence had been for four, but she'd been an hour late leaving Bangor and the road conditions had cost her more time.

Maybe she should stop and give Dr. Hackett a phone call. No, if she could find her way around the mountains of Montana, she could follow a hand drawn map her friend in Bangor had sketched.

She'd left her home town in southwestern Montana more than two years earlier, giving up a stable career in order to find herself. She'd always considered the expression trite, but since leaving home, she'd changed her mind. Surely there was a difference between shirking one's responsibilities and seeking freedom to find inner peace...only she'd yet to find that peace.

Her father had valued respectability in business, in his family life, in the community. He hadn't achieved them either, and with his death, he'd given her freedom beyond her wildest dreams. Discovering that he wasn't really her father had cast his peculiar set of values in a new light. She wanted no part of him or the memories he evoked.

This prospective job sounded perfect. It would end within a year. She wanted nothing permanent. Her salary would be small because it came from a grant, and that suited her fine. She didn't need the money.

A directional sign caught her attention, but the wet snow had obliterated most of its markings. That must be her turnoff. She applied the brakes cautiously. As the vehicle's tires crunched the fresh snow, she squinted through the ground blizzard to see where the road jogged. When she spotted it and turned on her signal, a movement near the stop sign caught her attention and she braked to a stop. A person? Hitchhiking? In this weather? Crazy.

The figure appeared too small to be an adult. The flash of a red hat, the muted green of a jacket. "Oh, God," she gasped. "It's a child!"

"JEANNIE'S GONE, I TELL YOU," Drew Hackett shouted. "She's gone and I've looked everywhere for her, so I came back home to call you, Sim, so listen to me. She knows not to wander out in a snow storm at dusk and get herself lost. I tell you, she's been picked up by someone, kidnapped!"

He pressed the earpiece to his ear and tried to cut through his cousin's platitudes. "You're wrong, Sim. She's been kidnapped. Living in this place is no guarantee against child kidnapping. Now, get that deputy of yours out looking for her. She could freeze to death in this storm. What if she's already out of the area? Call the state police. Put up road blocks. Do something."

He hung up the receiver and dropped to the nearest chair, his mind vivid with images of his pretty eleven year old in danger. He'd kill any bastard who harmed his Jeannie.

His daughter had changed this past month. Sometimes she acted less mature than his three year old son and at other times she seemed to mimic a thirty-year-old. God help them all if this was a foreshadowing of the teen years.

He glanced at the wall clock again. She'd been gone almost three hours. If someone had picked her up in a car, she could be over the state line and passed into the claws of some slimy owner of a kiddy porn operation in Boston.

He shoved his coat on again, then bundled his sleeping son in a comforter and carried him to the car. Maybe if he offered a reward. He could call the radio stations in Augusta and Lewiston, maybe even Portland. They would help.

As he turned the key in the ignition, he scowled. How the hell could he offer a reward when his operating funds were so meager. Last month he'd had trouble paying the utility company. He'd try to find her himself.

He drove to the tiny town of Leeds, circled back to Turner and south to Auburn. He stopped in Auburn and called her two friends' houses but no one answered. They must be at that god-awful mall in Lewiston that had started all the trouble.

His son squirmed from the comforter. "We goin' to dah mall?"

Drew gritted his teeth. "No, we're trying to find your sister."

"Whes she?"

"I wish to hell I knew," Drew muttered.

In the swirling snow ahead of him, he could see the faint form of a parked vehicle, its hazard lights flashing and its passenger door wide open. What kind of fool would park like that? he wondered. Maybe the driver needed help. But he had no time to help some foolhardy traveler who didn't know enough to stay out of a potentially dangerous spring storm in Maine.

He braked and turned off the engine. "Wait here, Jimmy." He glanced at his son who was scrambling over the back of the front seat.

"Me go too!"

"No, stay here. Don't you move." Trying to ignore the glistening of his son's gray eyes, Drew left the vehicle and slammed the door shut. He always caved in when his son looked at him that way.

He could hear voices as he approached the open door of the tan vehicle. The license plate was obscured with snow, but the word "Bronco" was easily readable. "Ma'am, can I...Jeannie?" He stared at his daughter, taking in her damp dark hair, her tear filled eyes, her shaking fingers as she tossed a half eaten cookie into the snow.

"Daddy! You found me!" Jeannie scrambled from the car and threw herself at Drew. "Oh, Daddy, she said she'd take me home, but I remembered what you said and...I was so afraid...oh, Daddy, I wanna go home."

The driver's door opened and a woman got out. Her blond head was bare and quickly became covered with snow. She wore a blue sweater that seemed to cling to her torso. The rest of her body was blocked by the vehicle and the darkness. *So this is what a kidnapper looks like.*

"What the hell are you going to my daughter?" he shouted.

Her eyes narrowed. As the snow melted, her blond hair began to hang limp over her forehead and she shoved it away with a sweep of her fingers.

Drew grabbed Jeannie's arm and glared at the stranger. "What did you do to my daughter?" he demanded. "Did you hurt her? You should be put away." His voice rose with each syllable. His daughter tugged at his sleeve. "Get in the car, Jeannie. I'll handle this." He turned his wrath toward the stranger again. "What the hell were you going to do to her, anyway?" he shouted.

The woman stared back at him, the expression in her eyes unreadable. "Are you her father?"

"Of course, I am," he replied. "I'm the last person you wanted to see, right? How many young girls do you snatch a week, anyway?"

"Daddy?" Jeannie called from behind him.

"Get in the car, damn it, and keep Jimmie there," he called. "This woman can't hurt you now."

The stranger hissed an expletive. "You fool. It's your fault she left, and against my better judgment I was going to take her home. Maybe you don't deserve her."

"You? Telling me how to be a good parent? You tried to kidnap her."

"Daddy?" Jeannie called. "Daddy, I need to tell you..."

The stranger whirled around and climbed back into her Bronco, locking the doors immediately. Before Drew could reach the driver's side, she started the engine and shifted into gear, the tires spinning precariously before gripping the snow packed road.

"Damn it, I should have made a citizen's arrest," he muttered as the vehicle disappeared into the darkness.

At least his child was safe. If he hurried home, he could still call the local police and report the woman's whereabouts.

He settled into the driver's seat, torn between wanting to hug his daughter and scold her for running away. She'd put him through hell.

"I'm sorry, Daddy," Jeannie whispered, shivering in her quilted green jacket.

"I know, honey. Let's go home."

Neither spoke until they reached their front door. "Daddy, I didn't...quite..."

"It's okay, honey, it's okay now." He unlocked the door and motioned them inside the stone and clapboard house. "I've got to call Sim." He grabbed the phone. When the officer answered, he shouted, "Sim, I found Jeannie, and she had been kidnapped but I got there in time. I know who took her. If you move fast, you can set up a road block. I'll press charges."

400